PRETTY RED FLAGS

A DOMESTIC THRILLER

THE PRETTY RED FLAGS DUET
BOOK 1

HEIDI STARK

FOREWORD

"You tamed the Dragon," the Dragon said.
"Everybody else has tried and failed.
But you.
You're different.
You're special."

But in reality, the Dragon
was taming me.

JOIN ME!

Love exclusive content, early access, and all the behind-the-scenes chaos?
Then you belong in my world.

Hang out in my Reader Group – Where we obsess over morally gray men, scream about cliffhangers, and share the kind of bookish chaos you won't find anywhere else.

Get my Newsletter – Exclusive teasers, giveaways, bonus scenes, and secrets I don't share anywhere else, along with early opportunities to join my ARC team for upcoming releases. If you love surprises (and trust me, you do), you don't want to miss this.

Welcome to the dark side. You're going to love it here.

DEDICATION

To the survivors. The people who have escaped.
The people who are still going through it.
The people who are not quite ready to get out yet.
And for those who never made it out alive.
For those who never go through it, and to the people who say 'why
didn't you just leave?',
you are lucky as fuck.
(And please stop saying 'why didn't you just leave'.)

IMPORTANT NOTE

This is an intense, pitch-black domestic/psychological thriller with very triggering situations involving graphic descriptions of domestic violence and other violent situations. Please take this warning seriously.

Adoption
Alcoholism
Attempted murder
Attempted suicide
BDSM
Blackmail
Bullying
Captivity and confinement
Cheating
Child abuse (mention)
Coercive control
Daddy/praise kink
Death of a friend
Dissociation and dissociative episodes
Drink spiking

Drug and alcohol addiction and recovery
Drugging
Drug use
Dubcon
Emotional abuse
Financial abuse
Forced drug use
Gore
Grievous bodily harm
Homelessness
Infertility
Intrusive thoughts
Kidnapping
Mental health issues
Mention of past sexual assault
Murder
Narcissistic abuse
Non-consensual sex
Paranoia
Pedophilia allegations
Period sex
PTSD
Physical abuse causing serious injury
Poverty
Public sexual activity
Racism
References to pregnancy
Revenge pornography
Schizophrenia
Self-harm
Self-loathing
Sexism and misogyny
Sexual coercion
Sexual assault
Sexually explicit scenes

Sleep disorders
Slut shaming
Somnophilia
Squirting
Stalking
Suicidal ideation
Threats of violence
Torture
Toxic relationships

SUPPORT

If you or anyone you know is experiencing domestic violence and needs support, please call 1-800-799-7233, or if you are unable to speak safely, you can log onto thehotline.org or text LOVEIS to 1-866-331-9474.

PLAYLIST

Boulevard of Broken Dreams - Green Day
Love on the Brain - Rihanna
Sweet but Psycho - Ava Max
Bad Things - Camila Cabello and Machine Gun Kelly
Lovefool - The Cardigans
Bad Guy - Billie Eilish
Circus Psycho - Diggy Graves
Gangsta's Paradise - Coolio
GTFO - Doechii + KUNTFETISH
Waiting for Never - Post Malone
Breaking the Girl - Red Hot Chili Peppers
I'm His, He's Mine - Katy Perry, Doechii
Death of Piece of Mind - Bad Omens
Breaking Up The Girl - Garbage
Walk - Foo Fighters
Baby Don't Hurt Me. Extended - Anne-Marie, Coi Lerai, David Guetta
Toxic - Britney Spears
Bad Kind of Butterflies - Camilla Cabello
Hypochondriac - Sasha Alex Sloan

Illusion - Dua Lipa
Choke - The Warning
Stockholm Syndrome - One Direction
Hot & Cold - Katy Perry
Better Man - Pearl Jam
Anti-Hero - Taylor Swift
Kill - Trophy Eyes
Bed of Lies - Nicki Minaj
Ay! – Machine Gun Kelly

PROLOGUE

A Long Time Ago

I've had crushes on older guys before. But nothing like this.

I mean, sure, I've liked boys in my year before—guys a little older than me, by six to eighteen months. When you're younger, this age gap feels like a world of difference. But this... this is different. This isn't just some boy I see at school, or some cute guy on a TV show. This is Dex, my brother's best friend.

Dex is a whole *man*, not some boy still figuring out how to talk to girls. He's confident, funny, adventurous and accomplished in a way that makes my heart race every time he comes around. And he's engaged—happily engaged, apparently. But that doesn't stop me from thinking about him.

And to say I'm crushing hard is an understatement. At least, a crush is what my mother calls it.

At first, I didn't know what it was that I was feeling. I thought maybe he was just like a bonus big brother. The way he's always laughed with me since I was little, spinning me around, or throwing me over his shoulder and pretending to drop me—on the surface, it's all innocent fun. But, as I've grown older, it's morphed into something else, for me. There's nothing sisterly about the way my heart pounds when he touches me, or how I feel when he looks me in the eye with his own hazel- and gold-flecked aquamarine masterpieces. It's something deeper, something... exciting and forbidden.

I can't help it. When no one's looking, I write our initials inside the drawer of my desk, tiny little 'D+M' in swirly hearts, or on the corner of my notebooks, like I'm casting some secret spell that'll make him notice me in the way I want. But he's *too* good, too decent, to ever cross that line, even though his tattoo-covered body says total bad boy and screams otherwise. I'd never been close to a guy with tattoos before Dex, and I like them.

He's kind, but never creepy, like my mother warns me some guys can be. He treats me like his friend's kid sister. When my brother ditches attending my school plays or dance concerts at the last minute, Dex still shows up. In my senior year, he even brought me flowers at the school play. But they're not romantic, I know that. He just feels bad that my brother's a douche canoe who always lets me down.

And I know that should be enough. More than enough. But it's not.

I remember the first time I met his fiancée. She seemed... fine. Perfectly nice, even. Pretty. But the minute I saw her standing next to him, holding his hand, something inside me shriveled. I hated her. It wasn't fair, I knew that, but she was the obstacle in the way of my schoolgirl daydreams. I'd never admit it to anyone—especially not Dex or my brother—but part of me wanted her to disappear. Just vanish, like in some magical movie where the princess finally gets the guy.

It doesn't help that Dex is so different from any of the guys I know from school. He's got this whole life outside of our small world. He's not stuck in some boring job or routine. No, he's always coming and going, doing who-knows-what for his secretive, adventurous career. It's like he has all these layers I want to peel back and understand. While I'm stuck daydreaming in school, he's living life, free and unbothered. I wonder what it's like to be that grown-up, to have all those experiences.

Before Dex, I thought maybe I'd just marry my dad one day. Isn't that what all little girls want at some point? It's the only template for love I had—until he walked into my life. Now there's someone else filling my head.

But that doesn't stop me from being confused. One minute, I'm doodling 'Dex' in the margins of my notebook, and the next, I'm distracted by the cute guys at school. There's Matthew in my math class with the dimples when he smiles, Brian in science with his shaggy hair, and Dylan in English, who looks like one of my favorite actors on TV. I mean, how can a girl focus with all that around her?

Still, Dex stands apart. He's not just another teenage crush. He's the one I secretly imagine when I think about the future, even though I know it's impossible—he's off-limits, too old, too engaged, too everything. But that doesn't stop my feelings. It just adds to the thrill of it all, like some big, exciting secret I keep to myself. I dream of the impossible: that one day, someone like Dex—someone worldly and adventurous—will look at me the way I look at him.

Maybe it won't be him. Maybe it'll be someone else. But deep down, I'll always know where that feeling came from. I'll always remember the first guy who made my heart flutter in that impossible, forbidden way.

And one day I'll find my own version of Dex.

Or at least, I hope I will.

PROLOGUE

Several Years Ago

The Past

Mother: You're so lucky we adopted you.

Your birth mother could have chosen other options.

But she chose us to be your parents.

And we chose you to be our child.

Me: I'm lucky I exist? And am wanted?

Mother: Yes. Exactly.

If we didn't adopt you, you would have grown up
on a farm.

With seven brothers and sisters.

And your mother would have been your sister.

And your stepfather who would also be your grandfather would have been physically and emotionally abusive.

You're so lucky we chose you.

I love you so much.

Me: Thank you so much.

I am grateful.

And I love you so much, too.

~

SEVERAL YEARS Ago

I'm minding my business at my favorite place in town to grab a drink, the old Irish dive bar many people don't even know exists.

It's very... wood-forward, I guess you could say. A long, battle-scarred bar that runs the entire length of the front room, lined with nondescript bar stools.

The walls have ornate wooden detailing at the top, and the back of the bar has built-in wood shelves.

Whoever designed this place really loves wood.

They have all the typical booze you'd expect for an Irish bar—a bunch of beers on tap, a ton of Irish whiskey—and then some weird choices, like a big-ass bottle of blue curaçao. There has to be a story about it, but it's not one I've asked, even though I've talked to the people who work here for many, many hours on end.

And one of my favorite things is the noticeboard, where the staff members place notes for each other, and put up pictures of them doing silly things—face painting, bad karaoke, and so on. I love sitting down that end of the bar so I can be nosy and read it. Because the staff here have all become my friends.

They love to make silly check names for me, and it's become a bit of a competition. Puns on my name... Margaux with the Flow. Let the Good Times Margaux. Let it Margaux. Margaux your own Way.

Margauxna Be A Star. And my personal favorite, Margaux All Night Long.

I feel at home here. I can come and sit after a stressful day at work.

My phone lights up. *Please don't be a work email.* I can't take any more for the day. Probably some dickhead from Tinder, anyway.

DEX:

> Hey Marg! I'm in town… want to grab a… marg?

I roll my eyes, but I can't stop from smiling. Dex is just as punny as the team here.

"Oooh, who are you talking to?" Pamela, one of my favorite bartenders in the world, asks. "I see that look on your face. You're positively beaming."

"Ah, it's no one." I can feel myself blushing.

"Doesn't look like a no one," she winks. "And you're beet red by the way. Your face matches your hair."

I feel my face getting even hotter. "No no. It's my dickhead brother's best friend. It sounds like he's in town. He likes making puns out of my name, just like you guys."

She laughs. "Sounds like a real doll. Why don't you get him to come by?"

I grin. "Maybe I will."

I text him the address.

ME:

> It's not really a margarita kind of place. But I know you like whiskey, and they have plenty of that.

Half an hour later, I'm flicking through my phone and half-reading some random article about celebrities behaving badly, when I hear a familiar voice booming from the entrance.

"Well, if it isn't Margauxrita sitting at an Irish dive bar, in all her redheaded glory?! I'm shocked to find you in an establishment such as this!"

Everyone in the entire bar seems to stop what they're doing and turn to look at him.

And I mean, I can't blame them. I'm staring too. He's very easy on the eyes, and I swear he gets even more attractive every time I see him.

He has a deep tan—must have been working outside again—and he's tall as fuck. I'm thinking six-foot-four or so, but I've never asked.

He's absolutely covered in tattoos, and his long, light brown hair is pulled back in his signature man bun.

And then there's his smile that could make a nun question her life choices.

He's holding his motorcycle helmet under his arm.

Oh my god, I forgot he rides a motorcycle. Kill me now.

I blush and shake my head as he approaches me.

Hopping off my bar stool, I turn to face him, and he wraps me in a bear hug.

It's a long hug with a little bit of twisting, and I feel my bones crack in a good way. I never want to let him go.

Dex has always been an epic hugger, ever since I was little. I think he builds a little bit of chiropractor stuff into his squeezes, because I always come away from his crushing feeling a little more aligned and a lot warmer than I was before.

"Gosh, he says," looking me up and down. "You're looking great, Marg! How long's it been, like 6 years? And what's this flowery stuff you've got on, eh? I thought you hate flowers." He grins at me. "You look good in it, though."

I blush, suddenly self-conscious. I'm still dressed in my corporate work clothes, although I try to keep it as business casual as possible without breaching the dress code. But work slacks and a flowery top with cap sleeves are definitely not my preferred look.

"Oh thanks," I say, swiping a loose strand of hair from my face. I gesture at my outfit. "You've gotta do what you've gotta do in these corporate gigs." I glance at him again and feel a little shy when he catches me staring. "Um, you look good, too. Really good."

The words make me blush again. He's wearing a leather jacket over a collared plaid shirt, and gray jeans of the skinny kind which cling to his giant quads and highlight his... um.. package. "And yeah, I think it must have been six years. Have you talked to Danny recently?"

He laughs and shakes his head. "Nah, he's off doing his thing. I try not to bother him, and stay out of the drama. You know what he's like."

"Oh, I definitely do."

My brother Danny is the reason Dex and I know each other.

Danny's a lot older than me, and he and Dex grew up together in New Zealand in the same small neighborhood after Dex's dad got a work transfer from the US.

They were really close as kids, but I guess after a certain amount of time around my brother, Dex started to see his true colors. Which is fair enough, because I've distanced myself from him too, and only engage in polite exchanges around the holidays.

It helps being in a totally different country and in a different time zone.

Eventually, Dex moved back stateside, where I've found myself, too, and he occasionally reaches out to see what I'm doing. But he's right, time flies. It really must have been a full six years since I last saw him.

"Well, it's so good to see you, Margaux, truly," says Dex, and I find myself getting lost in his eyes.

The amount of times I thought about him when I was growing up, even though he was old enough to be... well, a lot older than me, but not old enough to be my dad, at least. Still, I know the only reason he showed an interest in me was because he was friends with my older brother, and he's someone who knows how to be polite.

I blush and inwardly cringe as I remember forcing him and my brother to sit through many awkward dance performances put on by me and my friends.

God, I'm lucky he gives me the time of day anymore now that he's not obligated.

Pamela walks past, and I catch her winking at me from behind the bar. She can feel it, too. There's always been a chemistry between us, some kind of connection.

But Dex would never cross that line.

Even though my brother Danny is far from perfect, Dex operates by a code of honor.

He wouldn't hit on his best friend's kid sister.

And besides, last I heard, he was still engaged. He might even be married now.

"So, uh... what's new? How's... what's her name, Stephanie?"

A strange look passes over Dex's face. I could swear he's blushing, too. "Oh, we, uh... things didn't work out between us."

"Oh wow, I'm sorry. I thought you were going to say you were married with like three kids."

He smiles, and I detect a hint of sadness. "Well, let's say I dodged a bullet."

I get the sense he doesn't want to talk about it, so I don't press any further.

"How about you, Marg?" He quirks a brow. "With your beauty and brains, and your deranged sense of humor, I'm sure you have a line of guys waiting for you around the block."

I groan. "Oh my god, the dating scene is so bad in this city. I have a million horror stories that I could share with you, but you'd have to have all night. I won't bore you."

He laughs and shakes his head. "Fair enough."

The rest of the evening goes well. We pay up at the Irish bar and head to another place with live music.

We dance, which feels really good. It's not something I normally do, but the live music and the few drinks we've had have got me feeling a little loose. The bass is heavy, and I'm enjoying the way it's vibrating through my body. It's a release after the hell week I've had at work.

At one point, Dex pulls me close, and I find myself melting into him.

The music slows and I glance up at him, and there's a spark between us, more intense than anything I've felt before.

I tilt my head up, and I think he's going to kiss me.

But right as our lips are about to touch, he pulls away. "I—I should get going," he says. "I'm still jet lagged, and I have a meeting first thing in the morning."

Oh god. I've read the signs completely wrong. "Dex, wait, I—"

"Sorry, Marg. I've got to go," he frowns. "Get yourself an Uber and get home safe, okay? It's late."

And the six-foot-four godlike man takes off into the crowd, weaving his way through the array of dancers and out the door. Vanished from my life just as quickly as he re-entered it.

Ugh. If only men like him existed around here.

And if only Dex wasn't my brother's best friend.

1

———

NOTHING TO STOP HER

he Past

Friend: I'm so glad you broke up with your boyfriend. He reminded me of the Cookie Monster.

Me: He did? Because he had blue hair?

Friend: That probably helped. But it was his entire personality. Just like the Cookie Monster.

Or maybe Beavis and Butthead, but I'm not sure which is which.

Me: You didn't say anything for the last 3 and a half years, but you're telling me this now?

This is important information.

Friend: Well, I knew you wouldn't have listened. None of us do when we're in it.

The Present

I'm on Zoom with my friend Stacey, sipping wine during our virtual happy hour. We live on opposite sides of the country, so it can be a little challenging to find times that work, but we make it happen when we can.

The glow from the screen feels warm and familiar, like we're sitting across from each other in a bar, but without the background hum of conversation.

"Listen," Stacey begins tentatively. "I didn't want to say anything, but your ex seemed nice... It's just—."

"Spit it out," I urge her. "I won't be offended, promise." Besides, I'm pretty sure I know where this is headed.

She inhales deeply. "Okay, it's just that you're so *outgoing*, and he... wasn't. It seemed like a weird pairing."

I laugh, shaking my head. "It seems like everyone has been waiting for me to break up with him to share their thoughts."

Ever since I broke up with John after a pretty stable six year relationship, everyone is coming out of the woodwork.

Wouldn't it be more helpful for people to share their thoughts like this while you were still *in* the relationship?

But I guess my friend was right back in the day, when I broke up with my first serious boyfriend. I wouldn't have listened.

When I divorced two of my three former husbands, they were the same way. Except for the second one—everyone loved him.

"True." Stacey's voice softens. "But I still think you did the right thing."

"That sums it up," I shrug. "He's a great guy. But there wasn't a romantic spark. We didn't have sex for five years."

She practically spits her drink out and starts coughing.

"Careful now, don't choke," I say, trying not to laugh.

She coughs some more. "*Five* years? Like half a decade?"

"Yes," I reply. "That's the one."

"Well shit," she says. "My sweet friend, I'm getting way more action than you, and I'm single!"

I shake my head and laugh, but it feels bittersweet. "Yeah. There were great things about the relationship, but it just wasn't romantic. He's a good person. Just not *my* person, if that makes sense."

"It totally does," she agrees. "You can love and care for someone without being in love with them. And you two did seem like great companions. I always enjoyed seeing your travel pics." She hums thoughtfully. "But you totally should get to feel desired. To feel adored without having to ask."

"I was definitely missing that piece," I nod, taking another sip of my wine. "We genuinely enjoyed each other's company. I could count on him to pay his share of the bills. He was a generous person. Fun to travel with. But I want to feel like my partner is attracted to me. I feel like that's important. It's not everything, but it's part of a healthy relationship for most people."

"Well, again, I think you did the right thing, even though I know it was hard," she says. "And I see big things for you. What a time to really think about what *you* want, without having to consider someone else."

She's so right. After years of planning everything with another person's preferences in mind, I get to think selfishly. There are so many places I want to go, and so many things I'd like to do.

Luckily, I can do my job from anywhere in the country, so that leaves a huge amount of possibilities.

I have some more big decisions to make.

THE NEXT DAY, I call my friend Rebecca.

"You've definitely made the right decision, and I'm super proud of you," she says. "Sometimes, when a relationship feels comfortable and safe, we don't stop and really ask ourselves 'is this my person?' And then suddenly years and years have gone by and we realize we've been trapped in an unfulfilling relationship. But you're taking the initiative to get out of it now, which will free you up to find your true person."

Her words are deep, and they hit me square in the chest. She's not just talking to me—she's speaking from her own life. Her relationship is a tangle of resentments and compromises, and I know she's projecting a little. But still, her words ring true.

I could have stayed in my comfort bubble for the rest of my life, and things would have been... okay. I would have paid my share of the bills and could trust him to do the same. I'd have a built-in travel buddy. We both like cats. We both like good food.

But the spark would always be missing.

"I just need to figure out where to go next," I say. "I don't want to stay here. Wherever I decide, I just need to get through the next few weeks of awkwardness until we can end the lease. Luckily, he's arranged to be away on a work project for most of that time. So it's just me and my cat and his cat."

"Ugh, breakups are so awkward when you're living together. I understand."

"Yes. So a few more weeks and then I guess the next chapter of Margaux can begin."

"Seriously, though, Marg. This is a defining time for you that you may never have again and that not many people ever get," she continues. "This is your time to be selfish. The gap will close, but right now? You're untethered. You can literally look to the universe and go *anywhere*, do *anything*. Without having to worry about a partner, or kids, or any of that other stuff that tends to keep people stuck in one place."

Her words send a thrill through me, like a jolt of electricity. I've been following other people's plans for so long—his job, his preferences—that I've barely considered what I actually want. But now, suddenly, the whole world feels open, full of possibilities.

An idea starts to form. It's something I've thought about for years but have never thought possible, at least not yet.

I've always wanted to live on a tropical beach. Specifically Sunset Cay, a tiny archipelago off the California coast. My parents used to take me there every summer, and those memories are some of the happiest of my life—lazy days on the sand, the smell of sunscreen and saltwater, beach walks, and nights filled with bonfires and laughter. Back when dad was still alive and my parents still cared for each other.

It was always a *someday* dream, one I shared with my mother. Something I thought I'd do when I was older, retired, maybe ten or so years from now. But now I'm thinking—what if someday could be now?

"I've been dreaming of moving to the beach for a long time now," I say aloud, excitement bubbling just beneath the surface. "What if I moved to Sunset Cay?"

Rebecca lets out a delighted squeal. "Yes! *Do it!* What's stopping you?"

And just like that, a switch flips in my mind. *Nothing is stopping me.* I can do my corporate job from anywhere in the country, and I've been writing more on the side—I can continue to build out my backlist. This could be the beginning of something incredible.

We chat some more and then I hang up, and there's a lot on my mind.

The more I think about it, the more I realize island life is what I want. Writing books on the beach, enjoying warm weather year-round. It's my idea of pure bliss.

My heart beats faster as the idea takes hold. I open my laptop and start researching—housing options, pet-friendly rentals, how to get my cat, Sabre, through quarantine. He's been across the world with me, and lived in multiple states, and he's definitely coming with me on this next chapter. Sunset Cay's unique ecosystem makes things a little more complicated—it's why they have so many beautiful tropical fish and birds. So there's an extra stepping stone to get him there. But that's fine. I'm used to quarantine because New Zealand has always been the same way. Nothing I can't handle.

Sabre, curled up beside me, lifts his head as I scratch behind his ears. "How do you feel about living at the beach, little buddy?" I ask with a grin.

He lets out a soft meow, brushing his ear forcefully against my hand, his purr rumbling like a tiny motor.

"Good boy," I smile at him. "Let's make this happen."

I feel lighter, like for the first time in years the weight of compromise and obligation has fallen away. It's not just about escaping a relationship that didn't fit. It's about stepping into the life I've always dreamed of, one where I wake up every morning to the sound of the ocean, write my stories under the sun, go for sunrise and sunset surfs, and feel the warmth of freedom on my skin.

My dream life is within reach.

This is my chance. My reset button.

The beginning of the next chapter.

And I'm ready to dive in.

2

———

DO IT SCARED

he Past

Friend: You really applied for an apartment sight unseen?

Me: Sure did!

Friend: Damn, you're brave!

Me: I've done it that way several times. I do my due diligence and research the hell out of every place online.

Friend: Wow. Well, that's very brave, like I said. I hope it works out the way you want it to.

~

THE PRESENT

I find the perfect apartment, right in the center of Sunset Cay's booming resort area.

It's in a brand new building, on a high floor, with a secure 24/7 concierge service and a bunch of amenities including a state-of-the-art gym, a gorgeous pool, and multiple outdoor courtyards.

They seem to host a range of events and place an emphasis on community as well, which should be good for making friends.

It's surrounded by a bunch of popular restaurants and bars and shops, and even has what looks like a really nice market on one of the lower floors.

This entire place is designed for convenience, and it's in an area I'm very familiar with. I have so many nice memories of this part of Sunset Cay specifically. Time on the beach, reading by the pool, teasing my dad about bodysurfing at the gay beach—he was adamant it had the best waves. Ice cream and McDonald's happy meals for dinner. It might not sound like much, but to me, these trips were everything. New Zealand didn't have a lot of the same things back then that America did. Even the happy meal toys were better.

And now, I get the opportunity to return as a grown-up and make this place of wonderful memories my home. I'm so freaking excited.

I double-check reviews, and people are highly complimentary of the amenities and the convenient location of the building. It's managed by a well-known, reputable property management company. It feels like this is a fairly low-risk decision from my perspective.

Because of the ownership by a larger company, I also feel good about Sabre and his paperwork. In my experience, companies like this are generally far more used to dealing with emotional support animals, and less likely than an individual landlord to give you a hard time about it.

So I contact the leasing agent, and she's friendly and professional, urging me to get my application in before prices go up in a few days. Anxiety pulls at me. Work has been really stressful, and I've had to conduct several rounds of layoffs in the preceding months. It's been depressing and extremely overwhelming, and I'm finding myself easily anxious at even the most straightforward things. But this is an exciting thing to be stressed about.

There are many apartments available, because it's a new building. I ask her about various floor plans and views from different parts of the building.

"You should definitely go for apartment 23C," she says, without hesitation.

"Oh, why's that?" Her answer is almost too quick. I glance at the floor plan, and don't see anything particularly special about that specific apartment.

"It's just the best of the remaining apartments," she explains. "The view is really nice. I think you'll just love that one. Not many of the apartments get that view of Strawberry Head and the ocean, as well as the mountain range. You should definitely pick that one."

"Oh okay. I was kind of interested in 24E. It looks like the view should be about the same?"

"Seriously, don't waste your time," she says. "23C is the one to get. The view's much better, and the layout just makes a lot more sense."

She's oddly persistent about this particular apartment, but without being there to see it for myself, I take her word for it. I can see by the floor plans that the points she's making about the layout are accurate, although they don't seem all that different from each other. What do I know? She's the one with boots on the ground.

I apply for 23C based on her recommendation, and wait with eager anticipation.

The next day, she notifies me that I've been approved.

I get Sabre added to the lease as my emotional support cat, providing the necessary paperwork for that.

Renter's insurance. Check.

Signing a bunch of waivers for the property. Check.

From a logistics point, I'm set.

At least from the Sunset Cay perspective.

New apartment, new life.

Now I just need to ride out the rest of my time in San Francisco, and pack up my life here to facilitate my move. More stress, but I see a very sweet, sunshine-filled light emerging on the other side.

I SPEND a little time thinking about how I want this new chapter of my life to be—who *I* want to be—what I want, and what I don't. It's time to be intentional.

After making a list, I realize that I definitely want more adventure, less unnecessary stress, and to feel like I can express myself more freely. And I can't stop thinking about how that plays out in terms of physical expression with my body—the ideas of getting my nipples pierced, as well as the sleeve tattoo I've always wanted, won't leave my mind. So, I give myself a day or two to think about it—whether I'm really sure these are things I want as part of my new life, do some research, and book myself in for both.

I'm a little apprehensive about the pain associated with the nipple piercings, but I've always had an okay pain tolerance, and I can't help but imagine what my breasts will look like with gorgeous little silver bars running through both nipples. I know, without a doubt, they'll look hot and sexy, and make me feel empowered, as well as being more sensitive as a result. They tingle at the thought of it. It's always seemed like something that badass women get done, and in this next phase of my life, I most definitely plan on being a badass.

And the sleeve tattoo is something I've contemplated for years—I think black and white tattoos are so gorgeous– and I find an artist in the Mission District to consult with. He's from Brazil, and loves the idea that I want to get a tropical-themed tattoo done in San Francisco that will link my move from there to Sunset Cay.

Over the next week, I get both done—my piercer is an exquisitely alternative woman who gives me total roller derby vibes and I imme-diately feel comfortable letting her shove sharp needles through my nipples. From her experience, nipple piercings are empowering, and I love it when she tells me they're an intimate piercing that I have control over, in terms of whether I choose to show them to the world or not, on any given day—"you could wear a thin bikini if you want the bars to show through, so people are very aware you have them, and on other days, you can choose to wear something with a bit more padding—you get to decide." She gives me solid advice on aftercare, and I leave the studio feeling like a million bucks.

And the tattoo goes well, too—it takes about six hours in total, my tattoo artist chatting the *entire* time on every topic you could think of.

I don't mind the pain at all, and in fact, I quite enjoy the sensation of the needles distributing ink all over my upper arm, creating wild patterns with plumeria, hibiscus, and gorgeous, detailed leaves. He's animated, funny, interested in dark romance, and possibly even more excited about my move to Sunset Cay than me.

Looking at myself in the mirror, I already feel like I'm stepping into my new life, and I couldn't be more eager to start the next phase.

3

———

A FORK IN THE ROAD

The Past

With Work Colleagues at Happy Hour, a few months before the move

Colleague 1: Who's your hall pass person?

Colleague 2: I really like Alexander Skaarsgard.

Colleague 1: Oooh, good choice. He's hot. Margaux, what about you?

Me: Me? I don't really have one.

Colleague 2: Come on, there must be a celebrity you find attractive.

Me: (thinking about it)

Hmm... maybe Steve Peacocke back in the day, when he was in Home & Away?

Colleague 1: Let me see a picture? Oh, you like tattooed surfers, Margaux! I see you!

THE PRESENT

The days drag on, the countdown to my move looming high in my mind.

I let my work know that I'm moving, and suddenly there's an unanticipated issue that threatens to derail my entire move.

"We're not set up in that part of the state," they say. "Anywhere except Sunset Cay would be fine, but you can't move there."

I'm gobsmacked. "But there are people who work from there now and that's okay? I was literally in a meeting with someone working from there the other day. They've been there like a year, and it hasn't been an issue."

"Well, that's not official. We weren't aware of it, because they clearly didn't follow the proper process. And we don't want you to operate from there. It's our prerogative as a company, Margaux. The decision is final. If you move there, you can't work for us anymore."

"Are you serious?" I plead. "I've signed a lease. The move is happening. This is so unfair!"

Meetings are held, and many very senior people advocate for me, but a couple of senior execs won't budge on their very arbitrary decision.

I'm shocked, and there's a part of me that feels defeated, like it might just be easier to figure things out and stay in the same city.

But I'm deeply unhappy with my work, and if I found another job here, I'd just be staying for that. The city's great, but I'm in desperate need of a fresh start. I only moved here because of my now ex's job limitations. Staying here is just not feasible for me.

So I crunch the numbers based on this new scenario, and I figure out that if I cash out my stock, I have enough to support myself getting set up on the island while pursuing writing full time. As scary as it is, I take it as a sign from the universe that I'm meant to make this jump. I was always planning on doing it at some stage. And after the year I've had, I'm ready to be out of the corporate world, and to do the work that sustains my soul.

Like it or not, ready or not, I'm about to become a full-time author much earlier than anticipated.

~

OVER THE FOLLOWING FEW WEEKS, my brain starts to get a little loopy.

My ex has to come back and stay at the apartment for a few days here and there. We're amicable and respectful of each other and our belongings, but it's awkward living in the same place as someone you've just broken up with.

No matter how much we avoid each other, there are little interactions that feel brutal after years of a close relationship. It's just facts.

And weird shit keeps happening. Like, while my ex is staying over —I let him stay in the bedroom while I sleep on the very comfy couch—some guy I haven't spoken to in literally over a decade starts blowing up my phone and calling me 'just to say hi'. I tell him to piss off, but I'm on edge the entire time, just trying to make things okay and get through us both being here post-breakup.

And work has become awful. It's that phase where everyone knows I'm leaving, so they've started excluding me from meetings. Leaving me out of conversations that might have longevity beyond my last day. So I spend a lot of time sitting here, drumming my fingers on my desk, thinking about my decision and mentally figuring out how I'm going to pack up this apartment for the move. I'm in absolute purgatory.

What I'd give to be doing something useful.

And I'd spend the time writing, but I'm in such emotional turmoil with the unexpected job loss, the move, and of course the breakup after six years, that there's no way I could write anything remotely coherent.

So instead, I pick up my barely used roller skates, and I skate around my apartment. I watch YouTube videos to help me with my basic skills, and before long, I'm working on T-stops and transitions. Round and around the kitchen island I go, gradually getting more confident on eight wheels.

And that's really all I do. Skate, occasionally remember to eat, feed the cats, and watch my shows. Anything to stop my mind from thinking, because right now, thinking brings only sadness and pain. And even though I have Sunset Cay to look forward to, time is dragging, and it feels like torture not being able to just move there and start the next chapter of my life.

4

THERE'S SOMETHING ABOUT TIMMY

I hop on a couple of dating apps—Tinder and Bumble. It's too soon to contemplate anything serious, but I want to see what the guys are like in Sunset Cay.

It'll help to deal with my brain that's racing to process my breakup. And what harm is there in a bit of window shopping, after all? Maybe flirt a bit, and have some connections before I arrive.

It's a nice distraction from this horrible moment in my life. I can swipe through cute guys and have conversations with some of them. It takes my mind off the general shitness of 'now', and makes me focused on what could be. And, when the time is right, I'm hopeful I can find someone who wants me, someone who loves me and shows me in the way I need.

And in terms of where my heart is at, my relationship has been platonic for so long that I feel no sense of intimate connection with my ex. It's almost like I broke up with him mentally and emotionally —and definitely physically—a long time ago, so I feel more ready than what might be considered normal after most breakups.

I chit-chat with a few guys, and it's fun. It's been so long since I've felt that someone has had any form of interest in me, that they might find me attractive. I'm very sure that most of the guys on here are fuckboys looking for hookups, but I found my long-term partner of six years this way, so there are some gems in there, too. Giving myself a head start in weeding some of them out before I get there will only help to save wasting time with a bunch of assholes.

There are a few guys that catch my attention early on. There's Nate, a guy who's ex-military and lives in town. He's a foodie too, and likes exploring the local restaurant and bar scene. He responds scarily quickly to everything I say, and then is apologetic and defensive on the rare occasion when he doesn't respond straight away. I get the impression he's had a past partner who maybe expected instant replies.

"Hey, I don't expect an instant response, by the way," I say. He then ghosts me for a few weeks.

Then there's Rex, a surfing instructor who promises to teach me. He seems like a straightforward, laid-back person who likes to spend his free time relaxing. Which honestly sounds like just what I need right now. I'm so tired of my work, laying people off and giving bad news, that the thought of someone who leads an uncomplicated life could be really nice.

Then there's Michael. He seems to be some kind of millionaire businessman, always off on some exciting travel adventure but with a home base on the island. He has an ex-wife and a few kids, which isn't something I'd considered before, but he has a similar passion for fitness and he's quite witty over chat. His age doesn't show up on the app, which seems weird as everyone else's does. And the more I think about his success career-wise and his intense approach to life, the more I start to feel slight serial killer vibes.

And then I notice a new match. Timmy, 39. The first thing I think when I see his pictures is that this guy looks like a character. His bio is disarming, very non-threatening, and suggests he's looking for friends and that he likes surprises. He sounds spontaneous and funny and low-pressure. His pictures are interesting, and he's got the cheekiest grin like he's up to mischief. He has a couple of photos that I find unusual–in one, he has what appears to be some kind of branch around his neck.

And I notice he's sent me a message.

TIMMY:

Omg hello Margaux. Your cute.

I resist the urge to write you're*, and instead I take the compliment.

ME:

Thank you!.

TIMMY:

Omg I was so hoping you would say hi.

Mmm hmm.

So, you do anything interesting lately?

I'm waiting for a new renovation job site to start.

Going bonkers. I haven't worked for two days!!

His words resonate with me. I'm working, but in a dead man walking kind of way. It's driving *me* bonkers. So I completely get the sentiment.

He messages again straight away:

TIMMY:

Ohhh we have the same eyes.

I look closer at one of his pictures, and he's right, we *do* have the same eyes! Blue, with a darker blue ring on the outsides. And flecks of hazel or green throughout our pupils, depending on the light.

But that's where the similarities in our appearances stop.

Because I'm a pale-ass ginger on the short side, with freckles and a dimple, and he is one extremely cute surfer boy, with long brown hair that flows wildly around his face, and smooth, deeply tanned skin.

He has the cutest smile–cheeky and confident, and his eyes are kind.

He has tattoos, too, all over his arms, chest and back—my weakness.

And he's muscular. Drool.

He looks like he's having fun in every photo, genuinely enjoying himself.

So much better than the photos where guys pose with fish, or where there are so many people in the photo you end up playing *Where's Waldo* to figure out which one is him.

I scan his profile. It says his interests are surfing, cooking, dancing, movies and beach bars. All things I like. Well, I don't really dance much anymore, but I'm still into the other things.

It says he's looking for new friends. Great, me too.

He's a Cancer. Hmm, so was my mom, and she's super problematic, but it's more about the person than the star sign. I like astrology, but I don't think it always tells you everything about a person, and can make it too easy to stereotype.

According to his profile, he has a Bachelor's degree, he's vaccinated, and his love style is 'thoughtful gestures'. I'm not seeing anything bad here so far.

Pets: pet-free. Hmm, that's okay. As long as he likes animals. And there's a picture of him with dogs, and another with birds, so I have a feeling he does.

Drinking: socially on weekends. Okay, that's good. Me too. Well, I also have a few drinks during the week while I relax. So it would be good to be around someone who keeps it to the weekends. He might even be a good influence on me!

Smoking: Non-smoker. Awesome, because that's a bit of a deal-breaker for me. I can't stand the smell of cigarette smoke, and it's just such a waste of money, in my opinion. Cancer sticks.

Cannabis: occasionally. Great, me too.

Workout: often. Amazing! I need a gym buddy when I move to the island.

This sounds like someone I'd like to meet. Someone I could be friends with, if nothing else.

TIMMY:

Where are you moving? Oh to Sunset Cay? You're not here yet?

ME:

Yeah, next month.

I'd move sooner, but have to wait for my cat to get his rabies test so he can come too.

TIMMY:

Yay, welcome! And good morning to you!

Later in the day, he messages again.

TIMMY:

How's your afternoon going?

ME:

Good. Getting my apartment sorted out so I can move.

Where'd you drive to?

TIMMY:

Running errands.

At home relaxing now.

What are you up to?

I don't see his message for a while, and he follows up with another.

TIMMY:

Can you surf?

ME:

I took a lesson a few months ago.

I really enjoyed it, but I'm not very good.

> When I had my lesson in December and they had me practice on the sand. I fell off.

> ON THE SAND!

I still think of my surfing lesson often, even though it was a few months ago. I felt invincible, soaring along the water, propelled by the sheer power of the ocean, and I can't wait to do it again. To live in a place where I can even make it part of my daily routine!

TIMMY:

> We can fix that!

My stomach does an excited flip.
The thought of this guy teaching me to surf makes me smile.
How fun!
I'm sure if I practice a few times a week, I'll get my confidence up fairly quickly. There's nothing quite like the feeling of zooming along a wave, and that's when I don't even really know what I'm doing! Imagine being good at it, being confident about making turns and riding bigger waves. Bliss! And practicing my roller skating can only help with surfing, with both being so good for your balance and core.

He bombards me with a series of funny GIFs of people surfing while sitting on deck chairs and playing electric guitar. I laugh.

TIMMY:

> I'll call you a little later. I've got to go see a friend.

ME:

> Lol, I'm not much of a phone call person.

I'm really not. I'm much better at texting than talking. Especially with people I've never met. Especially in my current anxious state.

TIMMY:

> I'll just have to wait to see you then... I'm really easy to talk to.

His simple response brings me comfort. Not pushy, just waiting until I'm ready for him.

I respect and appreciate his patience. I don't want to be with someone who pushes too hard. I want someone who accepts me for who I am and who is willing to accommodate my timeframes.

His patience is soothing.

A couple of days later, he messages again.

TIMMY:

Hurry up.

ME:

Working on it! My cat was officially approved for my apartment today.

He sends me several cat GIFs.

A man who sends cat GIFs? Be still, my heart.

TIMMY:

Check out my special hat and my crazy sunglasses!

When I put my special hat on, people look at me like I'm Miss America!

It's an interesting thing to say, and it makes me laugh. He sends me a picture of himself in said hat, and some very unconventional sunglasses. He looks like quite a character. This guy must be like five-foot-two, for sure, I think. One of those short, extra funny, flamboyant types of guy. There's no other explanation for it.

But he says he's looking for friends, and he seems like he would be fun to maintain a conversation with and go out for a drink or something with when I get there. He seems kind of like a low-threat, high-fun type of person. And that's definitely what I need in my life.

The days continue to creep by slowly, and I find myself getting more agitated. I've started to pack, and having suitcases splayed around the apartment that I used to share with my former partner is depressing and... well, weird.

All I can do is continue to skate around and force myself to eat from time to time.

Work has become almost unbearable by this point, and I've already said most of my goodbyes.

My anxiety is peaking, and I start having intrusive thoughts that keep me up at night.

I'm second-guessing myself on everything, and in constant panic mode.

On impulse, I reach out to the leasing agent at my apartment in Sunset Cay. "Is there a possibility of moving sooner?"

"Yep, we can get you in a few weeks earlier if that works for you. Just let us know the exact date."

That's one of the good things about a brand new apartment. You're not waiting for someone to move out.

I check things on the San Francisco end, too. "Any chance I can end my lease sooner than expected?"

"Well, you've technically started your notice period, so you need to wait that out or pay a fee."

I check my airfare, and I'm able to change flights at no extra cost.

I weigh things up. Staying here feels like torture. I'm a mess, and I'm starting to worry about my mental health.

The move is so close, yet so far.

Even though paying a lease break penalty fee for my current apartment seems like a gigantic waste of money, I decide to prioritize my mental health and I bring the move forward.

The one logistical thing I still have to figure out is my cat and the quarantine situation. His rabies test is stuck in the backlog somewhere in Texas or wherever. Worst-case scenario, he'll have to stay at the quarantine facility for a while, which gives me cause for concern, but is something I figure I'll work through.

LATER THAT DAY

TIMMY:

Wassup. You moving on the first?

ME:

Well, I did a thing today.

I was meant to be moving on the 23rd of this month.

But now I'm moving 2 weeks from today!

TIMMY:

Yay. That's awesome. You'll be surfing in no time!!

ME:

Hopefully!

He moves the conversation from the app to text pretty quickly, and I'm fine with that. Every time he texts me, I get butterflies.

He chats about his day, what he's doing. Running a lot of errands and working a lot on renovating condos around the coast. His work sounds interesting, and he gets all excited about it, which is cute.

Job? Check.

Excitement for life? Check.

Cute? Check.

Surfs? Check.

Funny? Check.

He's checking all the boxes.

He insists on a phone call, and by this point, I'm ready for it.

"Hey Margaux! I'm so glad you wanted to speak on the phone with me!"

His voice is deep, resonant. He sounds hot as hell. And the way he says my name... my god, I'm instantly wet.

And he has this quirky speech pattern that's ultra-American combined with ultra-surfer boy, ultra-outgoing.

His laugh makes me smile.

He has a quirky sense of humor, just like me.

He seems adventurous and carefree and fun.

Everything about this guy makes me smile from ear to ear.

I can't wait to meet him in person.

Of course, I'm not putting all my eggs in one basket, and I'm going to continue chatting with other people.

But there's something about Timmy that makes me smile a bit wider, makes my heart beat a little bit faster.

Timmy gives me butterflies that I haven't felt in years.

5

____

FOR HER OWN GOOD

Dex

I just saw Margaux's relationship status change from 'in a relationship' to single. I wasn't prying, it just showed up as a notification. I mean, I follow her, so I get updates when she changes things like this.

I hack into her dating apps and emails.

Not too difficult, given what I do for work. Something at the more simple end of my skill set, you could say.

Maybe if I identify any real losers, I can unmatch with them before she notices.

She needs help, because her picker is clearly off.

There was the emotionally unavailable guy who she was with for what seemed like an eternity, but at least he was safe. I guess she just broke up with him–they must have been together for five or six years. I never felt like they were a good pair, but I left them alone because he seemed to pull his weight and be a decent guy overall.

And before that, she saw a few chefs. Nothing serious, but I remember a few of them treating her like garbage, playing silly games, ghosting, that sort of thing.

The one creep who she found shooting up Adderall into his veins with a syringe in her bathroom. That guy was absolutely insane, and two of her friends had to help her get him kicked out.

There was the one small-time coke dealer and bartender who tried to invoke squatter's rights in her house when she broke up with him. The audacity.

Oh, and that waste of space bar manager with a secret habit of stealing from his workplaces. She stuck with him for far too long.

Yep, Margaux needs help in the dating department. I don't know why she's always settled for these types of guys, ones that clearly aren't good enough for her.

I know she's self-conscious about having been married multiple times, but her mother's been married four times, so I know it never carried quite the same weight it does for a lot of people. And there were extenuating circumstances for two of the three. There was the one she married in high school to get emancipated from her mother when her dad was dying. Then there was the cop—he was a good guy. Ugh, and the one she married last, the one who threatened to break her jaw and couldn't keep a job to save his life—he was helping her to escape from her rapist, even though he harmed her in other ways.

Hell, I can't blame people for proposing to her, and I'm not judging her. But just because people propose, doesn't mean she needs to say yes. For whatever reason, this last guy didn't ask her to marry him, which I was happy about. Less paperwork to deal with, and a cleaner break.

I'm worried, though, because she's in a vulnerable state again now, although I'll always probably see her a bit that way.

But she's fresh out of a long-term relationship, and about to embark on a new life in a new city. She doesn't know anyone there, even though I know she's moved alone to different cities before.

Based on the emails I've seen flying back and forth, she has to change jobs, so there's not the continuity there I imagine she was expecting.

Everything about her life is going to be new for her, except for her cat. And even then, her cat's going to be in quarantine for a while. So it will just be Margaux, out alone in the wild.

While I'm excited for her about making this move, I feel like she'll be easy prey.

I scan through her recent matches.

Colin, the actuary. Nope. Delete. She's not dating anyone named Colin, and *especially* not an actuary. I just don't see that for her. Unmatch.

Russell the trail-blazing entrepreneur with all the cannabis leaves after his name. Nothing against cannabis, even though it's not something I'm into. But I think she can do better. Unmatch.

Brad the personal trainer. I swipe through photo after photo where he's barely clothed and looking for 'short-term fun.' Oh hell no. Unmatch.

Three chefs. Nope. Nope. Nope.

I continue flicking through and unmatch a few more, and then I force myself to close out of the app even though I haven't gone through the hundreds of guys who have already liked her profile. I know I can't go too crazy, because she'll notice if suddenly her Tinder is empty. That would be a hard one to explain.

And this is probably a creepy thing to do. But I'm doing it for the right reasons.

To protect Margaux. Just like I always have.

6

GUNS, GUTS & GRINDR

The Past

Paulo: Stop dating chefs.
Me: No.
Paulo: Stop dating chefs with tattoos.
Me: No! Good luck finding any haha.
Paulo: Stop dating chefs with tattoos on their faces.
Me: No!
Paulo: Stop dating chefs with tattoos of food on their faces.
Me: (Sigh) Fine.

～

I text my good friend Paulo some pictures and he replies instantly. We're both fans of a good perv on the dating apps. He'll send me his

from Grindr and Hinge from time to time, and I'll send him Tinder
and Bumble.

> PAULO:
>
> Nathan is cute, he's my favorite.
>
> Dan looks okay. He's older. Need more info.
>
> Why is Timmy wearing a human spine, and
> what is he doing with that gun?
>
> And surfing instructor dude looks like he's on
> drugs or something.

I laugh.

His comments make me zoom in on Timmy's photos. Paulo has
always been way more observant than me, his inner artist noticing
the details that my own scattered brain glosses right over. I realize
that the things I thought were branches are actually some kind of
antlers, as well as something that looks like... I want to say, a spine
that he's wearing as a necklace? I guess that is kind of weird.

And then one where he's pointing a gun out a window into what
looks like a forest. I'm reminded that sometimes I can overlook things
like this. I thought in the one with the gun he was just sitting at a
window. I was distracted by the cute expression on his face, swiveled
around to face the camera. He looks happy and free.

> ME:
>
> Oh man, I didn't even notice the gun.

> PAULO:
>
> I figured. It didn't seem like your kind of guy.
> Pro-gun, hunter, man of the wild.

> ME:
>
> Lol. I mean, I'm not getting Tarzan from
> this guy.

> PAULO:
>
> I wouldn't be so sure. He's wearing antlers
> and what I hope are animal bones. Dude.

I laugh and shake my head. It is a bit weird, but we all have our quirks. I guess I'll just have a few questions for this guy.

ME:

> What have you been up to, anyway? Any hot dates?

PAULO:

> Oh, you know. Focusing on my art. Work. The odd fisting date.

Paulo always knows what to say to make me laugh. He has a warped sense of humor like me.

ME:

> Don't get your arm stuck up there!

> Oh, by the way, totally unrelated, but guess who showed up on my 'people you may know' on Facebook?

PAULO:

> Let me guess. Brian Smith?

ME:

> LOL no, although he has shown up before.

I simultaneously laugh and shudder at the reminder of the finance exec whose office I walked into one day while he was watching porn. Gross!

ME:

> Sarah Dinkle!

PAULO:

> UGGHHH! Don't even say her name.

I laugh again. Paulo and I met while we both worked at a hotel many years ago, and we ended up working together at another company a few years later. Our friendship is built on shared experiences and a lifetime of crazy work stories. I enjoy tormenting him by reminding him of psycho former bosses and weird situations.

We have the kind of friendship where once I helped him to catfish his ex after a traumatic breakup.

ME:

Oops! Sorry not sorry lol.

PAULO:

Bitch! Okay, I have to get back to work. Ttyl.

ME:

Byeee! Xo

7

―――――

NOBODY'S GOOD ENOUGH

Dex

It's a few days before I get to log into Margaux's accounts again. Work had me pulling a couple of all-nighters which needed all my attention.

As soon as I get back in, I freeze and feel a pit in my stomach. Fuck, little Margaux has been quite the little chatty Cathy while I've been gone.

She's struck up numerous conversations with new guys, and a few others I didn't have time to unmatch her with the last time I swiped through to see what she'd been up to.

And I feel a bit twisted up inside looking at some of their profiles. This batch looks even more questionable than before.

There's one guy in particular that seems to be sending more messages than most, and they seem to have migrated their conversation to text. Timmy. What kind of dumbass fucking name is that for a grown man, anyway?

He tried talking to her on the phone, but she put him off at first. Good for you, Margaux. Stand your ground. Although now it looks like they've had at least one phone conversation.

There are a few of his photos I find concerning. I'm definitely someone who has their fair share of weapons, but I wouldn't feel the need to put a gun on my dating app profile. Yet here he is, looking all proud of himself. I guess at least it looks like a hunting rifle rather than a handgun.

And another where he's wearing a pair of deer antlers. It gives me the shivers when I first look at it. Who wears animal bones?

He just gives me a weird vibe. I know I'm biased, but I can tell straight away he's not good enough for her. Then again, nobody is. But he has a fun, spontaneous vibe about him that I just know she's going to be attracted to, especially after everything she's been through recently.

And her dad's name is Timothy, so I feel like she's going to read into that. She's all about signs from the universe, and this is going to be a big fat blinking neon Vegas sign saying 'this way to a complete dickhead who will break your heart' and she'll say, 'yes please, I'll take three.'

Maybe I shouldn't be meddling in her life this way. She needs to have the space to make her own mistakes. And who am I to tell her who she can and can't date? I'm definitely crossing a line. But I feel this duty to protect her. Always have since she was a little girl, and will until the day I die.

She doesn't have it from elsewhere in her life, and I feel the obligation to take on that role.

It's not just because she's gorgeous, because she is.

It's not just because any thought of a relationship with her would feel extremely forbidden. Because it does.

I'm going to be there for her, no strings attached.

Because that's what she deserves.

And I don't know if the way I'm going about it is socially acceptable. Okay, I know people would consider it a breach of privacy. But how the fuck else will I be able to save her from herself?

And right now, I'm wondering if I've just made things a million times worse.

8

———

GONE, GIRL

My phone dings.

AND THEN HE JUST… disappears for a few days.

I reply to him, but he doesn't answer back.

It makes me feel flat.

I'd enjoyed his daily messages, and they suddenly dried up.

Maybe he's got sick of our conversation and just ghosted me?

But, I mean, if he's showing his friend around the island, I guess it's reasonable for him not to be constantly checking his phone. Then again, it only takes a moment to text someone, and his attention is noticeably absent.

He'd said 'she' when referring to his friend when he briefly mentioned the visit on the phone the other day. But I didn't think much of it, because I have a ton of male friends. All platonic. Mostly, but not all, gay. Of course Timmy can have female friends.

But his radio silence makes me feel uneasy.

I tell my friend David about it.

He messages me back straight away, no hesitation.

DAVID:

> Well you could file a missing person's report.

> But I think you just need to face it—that guy is totally banging his friend while she's visiting.

> I'm sure he'll be back. But that's what he's doing right now.

The thought of it makes me feel a little bit sick, but it's not like we're in a relationship or anything. I haven't even met Timmy in person yet.

Yet the thought that he's telling me he's just hanging out with a friend, when he's potentially really off banging them, feels a bit disingenuous.

Ugh.

I try to push all thoughts about it from my mind.

Instead, I focus on skating.

At one point, I decide to video myself. A few loops around the kitchen island, and then I tackle a transition, where I go from skating forward to backwards, and I nail it! Success! It always looks so cool when other people do it, and it's scary just leaning into it and hoping for the best.

I leap up to do another transition, and end up way too high in the air. I come crashing down, smacking my tailbone hard on the ground and my legs flip back behind me. I almost do a complete backward flip. After a moment of being stunned, I get back to my feet and giggle as I turn off the video. Ouch! My tailbone stings, but at least now I have a funny video from it.

I send it to a few friends and post it as a Facebook reel, and it has hundreds of views within an hour.

David texts again.

DAVID:

> But it's okay.

> When he does come back, because he will…

> send him that video of you roller skating and falling over.

> He'll never look at another woman again.

Who knew my first ever boyfriend would be my wise dating therapist twenty-something years later? I shake my head and laugh. Life. But David continues:

DAVID:

> But, I get the sense this guy is deeply insecure.

> He's going to hurt you by acting out and cheating on you or something, if you do get together with him.

I'm shocked by what he has to say.

ME:

> Woah. That's a big leap. Calm down.

DAVID:

> You'll see.

It's weird, because we haven't been talking for long, but I miss Timmy during his absence. I've gotten used to looking forward to hearing from him, and even though it's early days, I just have a feeling about him.

And the other guys I've been chatting to really aren't holding my attention in the same way.

I'm caught up on my TV shows, and other than skating around my apartment, I'm left with the daunting task of packing everything up.

It's quite miserable, frankly. I'm sad about my breakup, even though I know it's for the best, and I can't punish myself by sitting here dwelling on that pain.

A Few Days Later

TIMMY:

> Hey.

Sure enough, he appears again, acting like nothing happened.

ME:

> You disappeared.

TIMMY:

> Sorry, shit just got busy.

> I had to drive my friend around a lot and was working.

His excuse rings a bit hollow, but again, I'm not dating the guy, so I don't really have any type of claim on him or how he chooses to spend his time.

I have a ton of questions, but it doesn't feel like my place to ask.

I just know this doesn't feel good.

TIMMY:

> What were you up to while I was gone?

ME:

> Check this out.

I send him the video.

TIMMY:

> Oh my god, that is fucking awesome 😍. I keep watching it.

> Did that hurt? Are you okay? You ate shit
> pretty hard!

ME:

> I was stunned for a moment, and my tailbone
> still hurts a bit.

> But I think it bruised my ego more than
> anything.

He sends a laughing emoji, which makes me laugh out loud for real.

It reminds me that he's funny and sweet and charming.

This whole 'friend visiting' situation is all in my head.

I'm just on edge and anxious to move, and my mind wants to ruminate on anything, everything.

Right now, everything seems weird, and I'm reading into every word, every piece of body language. It's not just him, it's everyone. I have so little to do at work, and so much to do to prepare for the move. My life is upside down and sideways, and I'm generally just very out of sorts about lots of things.

I push all thoughts of anything sketchy between him and his friend out of my mind, and the conversation flows easily once again.

He's a nice distraction. Something to look forward to in a way, if we do end up meeting.

Because right now I feel like I'm in purgatory, in limbo. I'm running around trying to get rid of all my shit and pack my life into suitcases.

I still can't quite believe I'm moving to Sunset Cay—it seems like a dream. Work is becoming increasingly awful and uncomfortable. Beyond talking to Timmy and a few others, I just skate around my apartment. I feel like a fake shell of a person, completely useless.

So, having Timmy take an interest in me is nice, even if he disappeared for a few days. That was kind of weird and I still have a nagging feeling about it, but there's not much I can do about it from here. Or at all. Because he doesn't have to answer to me.

If this guy wants to invest time into me and whatever, I should be grateful, and I should enjoy it for what it is.

Whatever this is.

9

FOUR BAGS, NINE LIVES

Now that the move is happening sooner, I really need to get this apartment sorted.

My gut churns as I survey all the furniture and the work that still needs to be done.

I'm leaving the big pieces for my ex because I'm not a petty bitch, and it would be impractical to transport any of them to the Cay—so the mattress, dresser, nightstands, exercise bike, couch, TV, entertainment stand... all of that will stay.

But I have all this smaller stuff and I somehow have to ruthlessly prioritize what to take with me. I just can't afford to hire movers and take everything I own. I'm on a budget, with no vehicle. Everything I take has to come with me on a plane and fit into suitcases.

I sigh as I look at the hand weights I've treasured and used for the past several years. And my beautiful stand-up paddle board that I barely got to use. It'd be perfect where I'll be going, but I'm going to have to say goodbye.

Fuck, I hate this. Breakups are depressing. Leaving a life you thought was going to last forever hurts like hell, even though I know it's the right decision.

I feel lonely now, but I felt pretty lonely in the relationship, too.

Better to get out now rather than just keep things going because it feels comfortable and safe.

I turn on a podcast and get to work, organizing and sorting. I carry trash bag after trash bag of items that I won't be taking and drop them into the trash chute. It's sad to get rid of so many things, but hearing the bags thunking down the chute, pinging against the little metal panels, is oddly cathartic. I feel wasteful getting rid of some of it, and I'd inquired with a junk company, but they literally wanted to charge more than the cost of Sabre's and my plane ticket just to haul a couple of items away.

I need to be pragmatic and less hard on myself. Sure, in an ideal world, I'd donate more and sell more things, but I'm just not in a position to do that. If I delay this move any further, I'm going to be sacrificing my already declining mental health. I can't do that to myself, or I'll be no good to anyone. For once, I need to prioritize me. Sabre feeds off my energy so hard as well. He bites my ankles extra at the moment, and I can't blame him. I'm uprooting his life, too, after all. Hopefully it'll be an upgrade. I guess we'll see when we get there.

A FEW DAYS later

The stress of hauling four suitcases and a cat through the airport is intense.

The cart stand is broken, so I basically have to hoist Sabre onto my shoulder and then drag the suitcases one by one just a little bit further, until we're finally in queue with the check-in team. Because I have a cat, I can't just go to the machines to check in like I normally would. A few people look at me with amusement.

"Quite a few suitcases you have there," says one nosy old man, smirking as I walk past, my breath ragged.

No fucking shit, Sherlock, I think.

Nobody offers to help, not that I would expect them to, and comments like his make me want to stop what I'm doing and knock the smirk right off his face. But I'm naturally polite in these types of interactions, and although it's something I'm working on, I just give a tense smile and move on. Then I'm so fucking mad at myself for smiling at an idiotic comment. But I'll worry about that later.

Finally, we're all checked in and the bags are whisked away on a conveyor belt.

It's just me and Sabre now. Much easier to maneuver than hundreds of pounds of stuff. I really hope everything makes it there safely, but it's completely out of my hands, so I make peace with that. One less responsibility until I get to the other end of the trip.

10

60 DAYS IN: CAT VERSION

I get off the plane, and Sabre is immediately whisked away by a quarantine official.

"Bye, Sabre! I'll see you soon!" I say, helpless. I'm advised to go to the nearby quarantine station after I pick up my bags, to make sure they have all the necessary paperwork to process Sabre.

At baggage claim, I reconsider my decision to figure this all out by myself. It's overwhelming, these four giant suitcases containing my life's belongings. But, I manage, hoisting them onto a cart, and make my way toward quarantine.

Timmy and one other guy, Felipe, had offered to pick me up at the airport. Timmy even sent me a picture of the back of his truck to show me all my suitcases could fit. But it just seems really soon to be meeting someone and have them help me, and have them come to my living space that I haven't even seen for myself yet. So I'm stuck with figuring out how to get all these bags sorted and into a large enough Uber to transport everything.

As I make the trip along the bumpy sidewalk, my suitcases fly off the cart a couple of times. It's sweaty work loading and reloading them, and I glance around, embarrassed at my clumsiness.

I get to see Sabre again for one brief moment at the temporary quarantine station, handing the officials my paperwork before he's taken away again. They tell me he'll need to be in the facility for anything from a couple of weeks to a couple of months.

The lady behind the counter sees the helpless look on my face. "You can visit, you know," she says gently. "The people who operate the facility genuinely love animals. And the space for the cats is wonderful. He'll be partially indoors, partially outdoors, in his own private suite. There's lots of fresh air, and he'll get to see mongooses and deer and all sorts of other things."

I breathe a huge sigh of relief. Her words mirror the way it's described online.

Visions of Sabre in a dimly lit maximum security prison cell, being allowed to stretch for an hour a day, flee my mind. That's one thing I don't need to worry about.

I'd researched this already, but it's extra reassuring hearing it directly confirmed by someone working closely with the facility.

I'll miss him, of course, but it will be more stabilizing for him to have everything set up in the apartment by the time he moves in.

I'll get my bearings, too, so he won't feed off my own anxiety as I adjust to the new location.

And I feel a tiny bit free. After looking after Sabre for twelve years, which I've loved every minute of, I'm going to have a little bit of time to just settle in and get myself oriented to the new city. I won't have to worry about food or water or giving him attention, not that Sabre is high maintenance at all.

Right up until I left San Francisco, I was feeding John's diabetic cat, and giving it insulin twice a day at set times, so going from that to no cats for a couple of weeks feels like a huge amount of freedom from timetables and parental responsibility. I feel guilty and selfish for feeling this way, because Sabre asks very little of me and gives me so much affection and companionship in return.

I hope he enjoys his little getaway.

And I really hope the quarantine facility is as nice as I've heard it is.

11

HER MOVE, MY OBSESSION

Dex

I'm tracking her flight, and she's landed.

I'll get a notification when she orders her Uber and will track her from there.

I just have an uneasy pit in my stomach.

She has to give up her beloved cat for at least a few weeks, too. And I know he's a real source of stability for her. Literally an emotional support cat.

As soon as she lands, I see two incoming text notifications.

> MICHAEL:
>
> Welcome! How was your flight?
>
> TIMMY:
>
> Welcome to Hawaii!

Jesus, these guys are real predators. It's as if they're trying to be the first to message her on arrival so they can lock her down.

It's like they were tracking her flight.

David always tracks her flight, but he lives on the other side of the world and is obsessed with planes. But these guys?

Well, shit. I mean, I guess I'm doing it too.

But I'm doing it from a good place, not to take advantage of a lonely and vulnerable woman who's just arrived in a new city.

And sure, I'm now reading through her texts and her dating apps and following her Ubers around. God, I'm sounding like a real creep.

But I need to make sure she's okay. I just have a feeling she's very, very not.

I looked at flights to Sunset Cay last night, and almost booked one, but I decided not to at the last minute.

That's the last thing she needs in this new phase of her life, her brother's childhood best friend following her around and hiding behind trees while she tries to live her day-to-day life. She'd be so pissed if I did that.

She'd be so pissed at what I'm doing now.

But I can't stop seeing what she's doing, and checking in on her, because I care.

A secret protector, from a distance.

12

CHASED ON ARRIVAL

The apartment's view is even better than I expected. From my balcony, I can see the beach and a well-known mountain peak, Strawberry Head, on one side, and then a golf course and mountains on the other.

As I take it all in, the leasing agent says, "Oh, and you might hear a dog yapping from time to time, from the apartment to your right. Sorry about that in advance." She lets out a little laugh. "That's my dog. I'm actually your neighbor."

"Oh," I say, a little surprised. "I didn't realize that." Not sure what else to say, I awkwardly add, "Hi, neighbor!"

I feel a little confused as I remember back to her insistence that I move into this specific apartment. You'd think that, given she lived right next door, she would have mentioned that. But she's springing it on me now, as I'm moving in.

Why did she want me to move in next to her so badly? It just seems like an odd thing to do, especially as she waited to tell me this piece of information. Not that I'm expecting to host ragers or anything, but living next to someone who works in the building makes me feel a little bit like I'm under surveillance.

But I try to shrug it off. Maybe she wanted someone around her age, a single woman, to live near her. Thought I would be quiet and keep to myself, versus someone moving in with their partner and children. Maybe it was just selfish on her part. I'd say I'll be keeping an eye on her, but I have this weird feeling she'll be keeping an eye on me.

She leaves me to it, and I begin to bring the suitcases up one by one. It's easy to unpack, given I don't have much stuff. I load up the brand new washing machine with clothes—because they all have that ick plane smell—and take a moment to sit and just look out at the view. For the first time in a while, I exhale, and I'm still.

Although I'm glad to be here, I feel discombobulated, disoriented—my mind still hasn't quite processed that I live here yet—on this island. But I know the hardest parts are behind me. Packing up the San Francisco apartment, getting my cat and my belongings here, and moving my things into this gorgeous place. I'm here now, and my mind will catch up soon. Getting Sabre out of quarantine will be the last step in setting up this exciting new chapter.

My phone pings. It's Timmy again.

TIMMY:

Hey! Let's go feed the ducks at the park!

ME:

Oh man, that sounds fun but I'm exhausted.

Can we do it another day? I just got all my stuff moved in.

TIMMY:

No pressure. I'm just really excited to meet you in person!

ME:

I'm excited to meet you too!

Sweet. It's nice to have someone champing at the bit to see me the moment I arrive. I just don't think I have it in me today to make a good first impression. I'm just so very tired.

I sit for a while in the apartment, taking it all in. I hop in the shower, washing off all the plane 'stuff', and come out feeling refreshed, like I have a second wind.

I realize I don't have any food in the apartment except for the snacks I brought from the plane. And now that I live here, I'm only a short ten-minute walk away from one of my favorite restaurants in the city, Dock Bar. So I get dressed and walk down there.

The warm air caresses my skin, a gentle breeze carrying the scent of palm trees and sunscreen and sea salt. I smile as tourists walk past, chatting away about their plans for the evening and the remainder of their trips.

I really live here now. I don't have to jampack my schedule with stuff to get the most out of a finite period of vacation. I get to take my time, and do all the things when I want to, without rushing.

I get to my favorite restaurant and it's as gorgeous as always, with the most spectacular view of Strawberry Head as well as the beach. I sit at the bar, my favorite place. The bartenders recognize me, and I order one of their signature mai tais and a caesar salad. The mai tai comes out just as I remembered them, pale in color with a gorgeous purple flower garnish. I still can't believe they make these on draft, because they're seriously the best ones in Sunset Cay. I don't even particularly like mai tais, but these are amazing! The bartender and I make small talk while she works, and I munch on my salad.

Feeling emboldened by my drink, and feeling great about being here in general, I text Timmy.

ME:

Hey! I've got a burst of energy so I'm down at Dock Bar having some food and a drink.

TIMMY:

Oh my gosh! Want me to come and see you?

I'd really love to meet you! I've been waiting forever!

I laugh and feel my face flush a little. His persistence is flattering. It feels good that someone wants to make the effort to see me.

ME:

Sure!

TIMMY:

On my way. Be there in like 20 mins.

I grin, but I suddenly feel nervous. It's one thing to text someone I met on a dating app, but it's been a long time since I've met a guy for the first time in person.

But something tells me this is the right time.

And it's so sweet that he wanted to meet me as soon as I got here.

13

FEELING SEEN

T*he Past*

The Creep: You'd be just perfect, if only you were wearing a black bra.

And also, I want to paint your nails.

I glance self-consciously at the grey and white bra strap that's escaped the confines of my tank top. His words make me feel a bit strange, like I'm almost but not quite up to his standards, somehow, because of these fatal bra and nail flaws.

That he knows just the trick to make me into his perfect type of woman.

The Creep: I'm very good at painting nails, you know I have a very steady hand.

I can't wait to paint yours.

A little shiver runs through me. I can't quite put

my finger on it. His words remind me of a crime show I recently watched where the killer painted the fingernails and toenails of his victims each a different color. I shake it off. Clearly, I've been watching way too much trash TV if a minor comment about my own fingernails has me thinking of that.

I glance down at them. I don't bite them anymore, but I do have a tendency to pick at them when I'm nervous or stressed, and the move to a new city has definitely had me in that state. A few of them are jagged, and the pink nail polish I applied a couple of weeks ago has well and truly started to wear. There are spots where it's fully worn away. No wonder he noticed.

He's just trying to help me to be my best self.

But he's eyeing me in a way that seems.. I don't know… like I'm a doll that he wants to dress up or something.

It's not a look I've seen before.

Sure, I've had plenty of guys stare at me in that hungry way that means they want to fuck. Where they're barely containing their lust-filled drool.

And he's kind of doing that, but this is different somehow.

~

THE PRESENT

Based on his dating app pictures—angled selfies and slightly awkward poses, I figure there's a ninety-eight percent chance that Timmy's a few inches shorter than me. I generally do prefer taller guys, as superficial as it sounds. And I have a feeling that this guy will lean heavily on personality rather than height.

So when this six-foot-two guy appears at my side, I almost lose my shit. His profile was so detailed, and yet somehow he missed this important information.

And wow—he's adorable. That easy grin, the glimmer of humor in his sparkling eyes, and the way his messy, sun-bleached hair sits just right under his cap—he screams effortless surfer charm. There's an energy, a sense of ease about him, like someone who belongs to the ocean, radiating warmth and carefree vibes.

His voice is deep, smooth and surfery, with just the right touch of mischief that makes me want to hear everything he has to say. I have to stop myself from swooning.

I feel like I've been transported to one of those perfect tropical island sunset scenes where everything is mellow and golden, and life feels simple.

"You look even better than your photos," he says, flashing that cheeky grin again. I swear my knees wobble.

He's so attentive, making solid eye contact. As a high-functioning autistic person, my ex had real trouble making and maintaining eye contact, so Timmy's attention feels extra intense.

We chat easily as I enjoy my second cocktail, the sweet and tart pineapple notes mingling with the buzz of excitement that's starting to hum inside me. He nurses a dragon fruit cider, swirling the can lazily between his large hands.

"You know," he says, "I actually designed packaging for this cider company."

He pulls out his phone and shows me a vibrant design—a mix of swirling waves, oranges and teals, and bold typography. "They didn't end up using it, though. Creative differences."

"Oh wow! You're really talented!" I exclaim, genuinely impressed.

I knew he'd studied graphic design, but up until now, he'd mainly talked about his condo renovation work and vehicle detailing.

To me, being creative as an artist is one of the sexiest things.

There's something magnetic about the way he lights up when

talking about his art. He tells me about winning an art school contest, and how his professors believed he had endless potential.

We're two artists, two creators vibing over our shared passion—his art and my books—and it feels electric. The way he listens, really listens, makes me feel seen. His curiosity is genuine.

He asks about my writing process, plots, characters, what I'm working on now, my backlist, what I love about writing, my cover designs. I pull up a few of my covers and he looks at me like I'm his new favorite person. I get the rare thrill that my work actually matters to someone else.

"I think it's soooo cool that you're a writer," he says, his grin infectious. "And *dark romance*? That's sexy as hell."

Given my ex's total lack of interest in my writing, this kind of attention makes me feel like I'm winning the lottery. I've spent so long craving this kind of connection—someone who not only likes me but also finds my passion for my writing attractive.

When it's time to pay, the barback hands Timmy the bill with an exaggerated wink in my direction.

Timmy's smile falters as he sees the total. "Fifty-eight dollars for a cider?" he mutters.

"Oh, I put her caesar salad and two cocktails on there as well. Is that an issue?" She grins unapologetically.

Timmy shifts in his seat, clearly flustered. "Oh, uh… okay…"

I feel a twinge of guilt. "I can get it," I offer. "I wasn't expecting you to pay for my meal or the drinks I had before you got here."

"No, no," he says, taking a deep breath, collecting himself. "But you're getting the next one."

My stomach flutters at the idea of a second date. Despite the awkwardness, there's something endearing about his determination to push past it. He isn't trying to impress me with flashy spending—just genuine kindness.

I feel a tension, like this might be all the money he has in his account or something. But he's told me he's working, and he's even called me from his job. So I know he has one. Renovating condos can't pay too badly. And when he's not doing that, he's detailing vehicles. Says he gets several hundred dollars for a couple of hours of work. Maybe it's the day before payday. I don't want to come off as judgmental.

"So," he asks, leaning in. "What do you want to do now?"

"I mean, I'm getting kind of tired again," I admit, though the buzz from the cocktails has given me a third wind. "But we could go somewhere else for a bit."

I could stay up for another couple of hours if the conversation remains this good.

He smiles knowingly. "Let's go for a walk," he says. "Come. There's this place I know that has a killer view—and pool tables, if you're up for a game."

"Well, that sounds fun," I reply, smiling back.

He takes my hand, and I feel an unexpected rush of comfort. His hand is large, warm and strong. And it's not just the touch—it's the way he holds mine, like he's already decided he'll look out for me.

We step into the elevator, and we ride it down to street level, where the salty breeze wraps around us. He guides me down the street, the ocean breeze ruffling his T-shirt, and I feel like I've found my own sexy surfer tour guide—someone who knows Sunset Cay like the back of his hand. As we walk, he points out little nooks and hidden spots. Some of his stories are a little crazy, but hey, it's nice to be with someone so carefree. So in tune with nature and the island. I laugh, charmed by his buoyant story-telling.

We walk through a few of the larger resort hotels, and he shows me a place with pool tables and shuffleboard as well as a koi pond. On the way, he plucks a plumeria from a nearby tree, spinning it in his fingers, and tucks it behind my ear.

I smile at him. Nobody has ever put a flower behind my ear before, or at least not since I was a kid.

"Beautiful," he says, appreciating his work. "Just like you."

I beam, feeling warmth bloom in my chest. Nobody else has ever done something so sweet, so simple and genuine, for me, not like this.

"Oh shit," he says, a sheepish grin spreading across his face. "I made you a lei, too. As a welcome gift. But I left it in the fridge. But this looks really pretty with your gorgeous hair. And I'll bring the lei to you another time." He pulls out his phone and shows me a picture of the lei, fashioned out of twisted ti leaves. I've never seen one like this.

How cute and thoughtful! Nobody has ever made me anything like a lei before. In fact, I don't think a guy I've been seeing has ever made me... well, anything.

Maybe dinner, sure, but nothing creative or arty.

But Timmy seems different. Full of surprises. And he keeps making me laugh. There's something about his sense of humor that's cheeky and a little dark, which matches well with mine.

I laugh. "Okay, I'll imagine that you brought the lei. Thank you, it's beautiful. It's the thought that counts."

He grins at me. "You're so welcome. Next time, I promise."

We wander through more resort hotels, past koi ponds where fat, colorful fish glide lazily through the water, and over wooden bridges strung with soft, glowing lights. The night feels alive—full of possibilities.

He hands me his drink bottle. "Want some? It's tequila mixed with an energy drink."

My favorite–well, the tequila part, anyway. I smile and take a sip, wondering if I mentioned it to him before, or if it's just another uncanny thing we have in common.

The pool tables are occupied, so we head out and he takes me to a bar on the main strip. We order mojitos, and then he leads me outside where we can see people wandering around on the street below. I love people-watching, and I love this particular beach. This feels like heaven. We talk about nothing and everything, just relaxing in each other's company. I feel utterly content.

He leans in close, his sun-kissed arm pressed against mine. He grows quiet for a moment, and his fingers trace a slow, deliberate path along my forearm.

"Your freckles," he whispers, his voice low and genuine, "are the most fucking adorable thing I've ever seen. I mean it. They really are. I'm not blowing smoke up your ass. I really fucking love them."

I feel a spark, something I haven't felt in a long time. Like I'm not just seen, but cherished. I look up at him and smile. He grins back, and his eyes are kind and sparkling.

His gaze makes me feel beautiful in a way I didn't know I craved.

We've only just met, but it feels like I'm exactly where I'm meant to be—here, on this island with this unexpected, wonderful person who looks at me like I just might be his dream girl.

And it feels amazing.

14

THE WAY YOU MAKE ME FEEL

T*he Past:*

Nobody: ...

Work colleague's partner at a casual Friday work happy hour: You know what everyone's been thinking? That you're an ugly, crazy-looking bitch with your lazy eye. Everybody sees it. You look so stupid.

Me: (jaw drops)

Me: (runs from the room crying)

～

THE PRESENT

"Your eye is one of the first things I noticed about you. It's something that makes you unique and special. I love that you have a lazy eye."

I pause and stare at Timmy, not quite sure how to respond. He sounds like he's being genuine, but there's an automatic defense mechanism within me that makes me worry he's making fun of me, secretly laughing at me while pointing out one of my most sensitive flaws.

"Um, huh?" My eyebrow quirks above my non-lazy eye.

Timmy smiles warmly, leaning in closer, as if to reassure me. "Seriously. I appreciate unique features in people—they make them special, and that's one of yours. I find it interesting. I like it."

"Oh." I'm caught off guard. For pretty much my entire life, my lazy eye is something I've tried to hide, something that's made me shrink. And now Timmy is here telling me how much he *loves* it? It feels foreign, almost unreal. No one's ever said anything like this before—most people just ignore it or pretend not to notice it, even long-term partners. But Timmy? He's embracing it.

"I actually have monocular vision," I explain, feeling the need to fill the silence. "Which means I don't see out of both eyes at the same time. They're constantly swapping in and out. It affects my depth perception, which can make parking cars in tight spaces tricky for me. A doctor once even told me I was meant to be terrible at tennis, but I'm actually surprisingly okay at it."

"Really?" He looks at me like I've just told him the most interesting fact. "That's so interesting and awesome," he smiles. "We should totally play tennis some time. That sounds like a lot of fun!"

I haven't known him for long, but this man already never ceases to amaze me. I don't take compliments well, but there's something about his words that seems to see beyond the surface and into what's going on beneath. I'm not used to it—I'm used to feeling invisible.

With Timmy, I'm basking in the glow of his attention, intoxicated by his flattery. With my ex, I could walk in with the sexiest lingerie known to man, with my hair done and full makeup on, my body ripped as hell, and he probably wouldn't even notice. But Timmy notices every little thing about me, and he seems to love everything he sees.

"I love how soft your skin is," he says, running his massive hand along my arm. "And the little ginger curls at the nape of your neck. So cute." He grins, a playful glint in his eyes.

I laugh, shaking my head. "You're the only person who's ever said that."

"Well, they're cute as fuck," he insists, pulling me closer.

It's these little things, these tiny compliments that really catch me off-guard. The things I've been self-conscious about, like the curls I usually try to hide.

"I love your lips, too," he tells me. "That slightly fuller lower lip? So sexy."

The way he sees me. The way he notices me, like an artist painting me might. The way he loves all my quirks and makes me feel like they're charming rather than flaws.

And then there's the way he talks about manifesting me. Like I'm some dream come to life. "I was dreaming of a redhead with freckles and milky white skin," he says, his voice soft with a hint of wonder. "I feel like I manifested you. You can ask Matty. Back on St Patrick's Day, I told him I was going to find someone who looked just the way you do. I dreamed you into being."

My heart swells. I've never felt so wanted in my life.

When he tells me he loves my lazy eye, it's like something heals deep within me. It undoes all those painful moments, like at the work happy hour when someone cruelly mocked me for it in front of everyone. His words have a way of making the world's harshness disappear.

Being with Timmy feels like magic. He takes all the things I've been insecure about my entire life and turns them into treasures. He makes me feel beautiful and adored in a way that feels so real and genuine.

15

DID I FUCK IT ALL UP?

Dex

I'm second-guessing myself. I feel like a stalker.

Well, if I think about what I do in my day job, and what I'm doing here with Margaux, I guess that's a fair assessment.

But why her? What's compelling me?

I guess it's helpful to remind myself where it all started.

Her brother, Danny, and I were like two peas in a pod growing up. Always together, creating shenanigans around the neighborhood—riding our bicycles, throwing rocks at cars. Typical boy shit.

But when Danny got to about eighteen, something in him shifted.

Now, I'm no angel. But there are two ways you can ride into the darkness—with the intention of adding to it, or dealing with the worst kinds in the right way. That's where we veered down two different forks in the road.

At first, it was subtle, but I slowly saw Danny changing, his morals becoming nonexistent.

I guess you could say I live by some kind of code. One where I only fuck up bad people.

Whereas Danny seems to think it's fine to treat anyone any way he wants. To get the most out of them, manipulating them for his own gain. Even good people. Even his own baby sister, Margaux.

And that bugged me—family is family, you know?

So I guess that's where I stepped in.

She idolized him—really put him up on a pedestal. Not that he deserved it.

He'd do the shittiest things—like invite her to concerts and then right at the last minute either tell her she couldn't come, or that she had to pay for the ticket, because he owed someone else money for drugs or whatever.

Or he'd promise to come to her school plays and then he'd just be a no-show.

I could tell how every time he let her down, it crushed her.

Every time he'd make some tiny gesture, she'd take it as a sign he'd changed. That he was going to be the big brother she'd always dreamed of. The one that matched the vision in her mind.

But I knew that was never going to happen.

So I became that person for her instead.

Once she got to a certain age, though, I guess it felt kind of weird.

Because it's hard not to notice how gorgeous she is, how smart and funny and kind.

She'll always be vulnerable little Margaux, but now I've started seeing her in a new light.

It's not going to stop me from being protective.

And in fact, I think—if anything—it's made it worse.

16

JOYOUS TOMFOOLERY

T*he Past*

My Mother: Your eyes are glowing a very bright blue.

I've noticed they do this when you're really, really excited and happy.

~

THE PRESENT

We're in a Christmas store, of all things, and Timmy pulls a stuffed octopus toy from the shelf. It's one of the few non-Christmas items they sell, and he puts it over his head like a hat. He looks ridiculous, and I giggle at him.

Then he puts the octopus on my head and laughs.

And he tilts my chin up, and he leans down and kisses me.

It's like something out of a movie.

Time stands still as our lips meet, and everything fades away but us.

His tongue finds mine, and he's a wonderful kisser.

It's like our mouths are made for each other.

Thank god. Nothing worse than starting to dig a person and they turn out to have a lizard tongue or they kiss like a grandma.

But thankfully, this is far from that. It's the most special, most romantic first kiss I've ever experienced. This is how it's meant to be. Like literal magic. I almost want to pinch myself to make sure I'm not dreaming.

I love the way I have to tilt my neck, and the way my body feels against his.

His arms are wrapped around me and I feel safe and secure and comfortable, and very, very giddy. And turned on as hell.

"You know you're not staying over tonight, right?" I say, suddenly anxious that it's what he's expecting after this kiss.

But his smile is easy. "Oh, I know."

I glance at him, trying to read him.

"We need to build a friendship," he says, "and I'm not just going to try to slide straight into home base."

My body clenches at the thought of home base, and I'm glad he also understands it's not going to happen today. But oh, how I want it to happen and soon.

He holds my hand as we leave the store. And not in a possessive way that makes me feel like he's being a sleaze. But just like he wants to hold it, and because it feels good to him to be touching me. And, for me, it's the first time in so long I feel a bit protected by that type of action. He might be tipsy, but he's also obviously smart. And very, very cute.

As we're walking down the street, he suddenly pulls me to him. "Kiss me, now!" he says. And I do. "Keep kissing me, the cops are going by," he says. "You're my disguise."

I laugh, but I oblige. Again, the feeling of his lips on mine is exhilarating.

Finally, we pull away from each other. "Haha!" he says. "I tricked you into kissing me again. Yesss!"

I pull back and he winks and laughs, and I swat at him playfully.

"You're so silly," I grin.

Because he absolutely did not have to trick me. I will willingly kiss Timmy every day, every moment, no tricks required.

He gives me butterflies again.

Every kiss with this guy is electric. We've only had a few, but it's like we know each other's faces, each other's bodies, each other's souls.

Yes, it's woo-woo and whatever... but I've always *wanted* someone who makes me feel this way when I kiss them for the first and second and infinity times. And no matter how hard I wished for it in previous relationships, I never felt... *this* feeling. This isn't just our mouths touching, it's some other kind of connection. Our lips and our tongues and our chests and our hips and our entire beings, melded together. And yes, my pussy twinges *hard* throughout. But this is about so much more than that. I really think he's the person I've been searching for my whole life.

And he's so playful and cheeky. Full of mischief. He makes me feel free to adventure and explore. With someone like him, we can navigate our path together as we choose, convention be damned. I've never felt anything like this before.

I'm so lucky. This feels perfect. And the best part is, it's really happening. It's not a dream. I finally branched out from my former day-to-day. I've barely started just living for me, and following what brings me joy. And I've already found a person who seems like the one!

He drops me off outside my apartment and gives me another kiss. "This was really fun, Margaux. I'm so glad we got to meet today. I'll text you later." I watch as he walks off, smiling and still feeling the sensation of his lips on mine.

When I get home, I look in the mirror, and my eyes are glowing blue. And I feel it. My energy is up. I know I'm meant to be here. I can't wipe the smile off my face, and I don't want to. What joyous tomfoolery already.

17

THANK GOODNESS FOR SEX WEDGES

T he Past

Mother: When you grow up, you will be an actress or a dancer.

And you will marry a plastic surgeon who is very wealthy,

and he will give me facelifts and other cosmetic procedures for free.

Kids at school: You're such a snob. Richie Rich girl growing up.

~

The Present

When I get back to my apartment, I check my mail and pick up a couple of packages.

As a hobby, I do some micro-influencing, which means I don't have a ton of followers, but companies will send me their products and then I provide an honest review on my social media.

And, thankfully, one of the items they offered was a triangular pillow, otherwise known as a sex wedge. It made me giggle when I saw it, but the legitimate advertising around it is that it's good for posture, and you can almost use it as a desk, or to elevate your feet. I figured that, without any furniture to start with, it might come in useful, and that's what I picked for the month and had it delivered here, to my new apartment.

So I use that as a pillow, and I line up a small selection of my most sentimental stuffed toys—a whale, an octopus, Oscar the Grouch, and Sabre's banana bed, and they become my bed for the evening. It's not comfortable, but it'll do the trick. I didn't want to tell Timmy that this was going to be my bed, because I know he'd have invited me to stay over, and I'm not ready for that. We literally just met, and I want to spend my first night here by myself.

Truth be told, I'm also a little bit embarrassed about where I'm staying. It's far fancier than I imagined it would be, with a really bougie lobby that looks like something off the front page of an interior design magazine, with a 24/7 concierge.

I've always railed against money, and I've had a money block for as long as I can remember, believing it was evil. I know that about myself.

My mother was just always so... obsessed with it. It was a huge source of conflict with my dad. It was her sole focus. Money makes her world go around. That and aesthetic appearance and keeping up with the Joneses.

And if there's something I don't want to be, it's my mother. I want so badly not to be her that I've become hyper-independent. I find it hard to receive money from any man. 'Fuck off, I can do it myself,' is my automatic response. During my six-year relationship, I chilled on that for a while. I made more money than him, but he was generous and always paid his way and more. It was... nice! Even if it took a little bit of getting used to.

So I don't want to make myself seem flashy or ostentatious, to
Timmy or anybody else.

I really expected this place to be a little more low-key. Sure, it has
nice amenities, but this screams extravagant luxury and it's a little
intimidating, a little cringe.

Before I go to sleep, I sit for a while, just looking out the window
at the gorgeous city lights.

I don't know how I got this lucky.

~

I WAKE up to my phone dinging.

> TIMMY:
>
> Hey! Get up!
>
> I'm coming to pick you up!

> ME:
>
> You are?

> TIMMY:
>
> Yep! I've got a full day planned. We're getting
> your apartment set up.

> ME:
>
> We are?

> TIMMY:
>
> Yep! I'll be there in 20.

> ME:
>
> Give me 30.

> TIMMY:
>
> Fine! See you soon. Miss you! Xo

He pulls up and I hop into his truck, which I recognize from the
photos he's sent me. I'm still feeling a bit tired after the flight, and of
course, my makeshift bed wasn't the most comfortable.

"Hey! You look beautiful today," Timmy says as I lean in for a kiss.

I feel another spark as our lips make contact. There's definitely chemistry between us.

"Thank you! You look nice, too." I smile at him. He's wearing a black T-shirt and board shorts with a cap.

"Thank you," he grins. "I know I do."

"Haha, okay," I say, shaking my head and laughing at his confidence.

"How was your first night in the new apartment?"

"Good!" I say brightly.

"Good? Did you have anyone over?" He quirks a brow, a little seriousness in his tone.

I quirk my brow back. "No. Who would I have had over? You're the only person I know here! You're silly!"

He nods, seeming pleased. "Good, just making sure. How did you sleep?"

"Well, I made do with what I had. I figured I'd get a mattress today."

"You slept on the floor? Oh my goodness. I had no idea."

"Well, I wasn't going to tell you and have you think I was inviting myself to your place or anything."

He laughs. "Fair enough. But..." he pauses, "we just got done with a condo at work and I got two brand new mattresses. They've never even been slept on. I put them underneath my main big mattress and you're welcome to borrow them. Together they make like a queen size or whatever."

"Oh, thank you," I say, with hesitation. It's a very generous offer, but it seems a little forward. "I'd be happy to buy one today. I don't expect you to give me your furniture."

"Look, you just got here. You want to make sure you pick out the right one. I'm not giving you the mattress. I'm just loaning it to you. But you need to be comfortable. And plus, when I come to stay, I'm going to need a comfortable mattress."

I laugh. "*If* you come to stay."

He looks over and winks at me. "Okay, so I'm going to take you over to my place so we can grab the mattresses and a few other things. And then we'll go shopping for more stuff."

I'm thrilled. He feels comfortable taking me to his house, and it's going to be a huge help to borrow his mattress.

WE ARRIVE AT HIS PLACE, and I have no idea what to expect.

It's in an area of town that I've heard isn't great, but I don't really know much about it. And I've lived in up-and-coming areas in cities before.

It's a multifamily property. He leads me up some external stairs to a door at the end, and the smoke alarm is screeching inside. He unlocks the door to reveal smoke is pouring out of the oven in a small corner kitchen, with no cook to be seen.

"Oh, Matty," he says, rolling his eyes and laughing. "He always does this."

"Matty!" he calls out in the direction of a very short hallway with a door at the end. "If you're in there taking a shit, your pizza is about to be on fire! Don't you hear that?"

A brown-haired guy of medium height stumbles out of the bathroom, his hair all messed up and his eyes groggy from sleep.

"Oh, hi," he says, waving at me awkwardly while they both take care of the smoke alarm and a charred pizza.

"This is Matty!" Timmy says with excitement. "Matty, this is Margaux! She's from New Zealand. She just got here yesterday!"

"Oh yeah. You mentioned," he says, his voice monotone. Matty goes over to the couch, and flicks through some TV channels before landing on an action movie.

His behavior seems a little off, like he's being friendly but also entrapped in his own little world. Like he doesn't know how to make basic small talk. But that's okay. I feel awkward being here, too.

Timmy gives me a grand tour of the apartment, which doesn't take long, because it's a tiny one-bedroom unit. There's the main living room we entered into, with a small kitchen in the corner. Then there's a bathroom. And one bedroom.

The first thing I notice about the bedroom is the two beds.

There's a proper bed with a frame and everything on one side, presumably Matty's. And then a pile of mattresses on the floor.

Side by side.

In the same room.

It seems weird, but I don't want to be judgmental, so I stay quiet. Even though it looks like a setup right out of *Charlie and the Chocolate Factory*.

But what do I know? It's my nature to give the benefit of the doubt. Maybe this is totally normal here. The cost of living in this part of the city is super high, so maybe this is a common practice and everyone else lives like this, too.

18

UNCLAIMED BAGGAGE

I notice a small, black wheeled suitcase sitting on Timmy's bed, its presence oddly out of place in his and Matty's cramped, shared bedroom.

"Why is this suitcase here? Going somewhere?" I ask, half-joking, half-curious.

He pauses, frowns slightly, and then just shrugs. "Oh, it's my friend's from when she visited. She left it here. I keep asking her to pick it up, but she won't."

"So, some girl stayed with you and her suitcase is on your bed? That seems... a bit weird."

Timmy laughs it off, brushing away my concern with a flick of his hand. "Yeah, well, it's the only place to really put it. This apartment is too small, you can see that. It's no big deal."

He gestures around, and to be fair, the apartment is cluttered—almost comically full of random things.

I'm actually surprised and impressed by the constant variety of items Timmy keeps pulling out of his jam-packed closet to show me.. Hats, clothing, random home decor items. He's like one of those magicians that keeps pulling an endless string of brightly colored handkerchiefs out of his sleeve.

Still, something about the suitcase bothers me. Where did this friend of his sleep? How long did she stay? Why is her stuff still here? He shrugs it off, but I can't shake the weird feeling creeping over me. I press my lips together, but don't say anything more.

"She's like my evil twin," he says after a moment, grinning. "I call her 'The Worst', because if you turned me into a girl and magnified all my bad qualities, you'd get her."

I don't really know what to say, so I keep quiet.

"She's actually *super* annoying," he adds with a smirk. "But I kicked her out, so she's gone now. Thank god. I'm glad she's out of my hair. She's so annoying to be around after more than five minutes."

It's a weird way to talk about a friend, but I don't respond.

I try to laugh along instead, but the whole thing feels off. And I've noticed her nickname, 'Worst', popping up on his phone more than a few times. He doesn't answer, but she's the only person who really seems to call him other than his boss.

Before I can dwell on it too much, Timmy pulls me back into the moment.

"Here's the mattress—well, two technically—I'm going to lend you," he says. "These ones underneath the top one. It's brand new, like I said, from one of the condos we were renovating."

"Oh wow, thank you. Are you really sure?"

"Yeah," he nods. "I'm not giving it to you. Just lending it."

"Oh okay. Well, thank you so much!" It's really nice of him. I try to focus on his generosity, how kind it is of him to help me out.

As we load the mattress onto his truck, he expertly throws it on top and ratchets it down, securing it. Which is one of those really hot handyman types of things a guy can do.

But as we drive back to my apartment building, I can't help but think how large of a gesture this is for someone I've literally only started seeing a day ago. It's thoughtful, sure... but also I don't know —a little much. It's something I'd have real trouble moving by myself, and I can't help but feel it's another way he's becoming embedded in my life very quickly.

"It feels like you're moving in here or something!" I joke nervously as he unties the straps holding it to the vehicle and we load the mattress onto a cart at my apartment building.

"No, no, not yet," he laughs. "Although, I mean, I'd love to spend night after night with you. I figure you can buy a base to go under this, and then this can be the main bed we stay in when I'm over here with you."

My heart skips a beat. There's something flattering about how much he wants to be around me—but again, it's a lot.

"Oh, okay!" I say. "That makes sense. Thank you for helping me get all set up. I was a bit overwhelmed when I arrived. You've helped me a lot."

"No problem at all. It's fun helping you pick things out," he beams.

He wanders around the apartment, checking out some of my stuff. He points at my roller skates. "The famous skates from the video you sent!"

I nod. "Yep, those are the ones."

He picks up two dolls that look like me. "What are *these*?"

I laugh. "Long story. These are my creepy Margaux dolls. I helped bail someone out of jail, a mad scientist type. And afterward, he saw these at a Goodwill and thought they looked so much like me he bought like five and sent them all to me."

Timmy cracks up laughing. "That's hilarious, oh my god. I'm going to take one with me if that's okay with you. It can live in the truck."

I shrug. "Okay! Just don't do any voodoo on it."

"I promise I won't." His voice changes to a mock-serious tone. "But listen—no letting any other guys sleep on these mattresses, though, okay? Only me."

I laugh, trying to shake off the weird feeling that's creeping up again. "Okay, I guess I'm stuck with you then."

Timmy narrows his eyes at me, a playful but intense look in them.

I quickly add, "I'm happily stuck with you," to smooth over the moment.

He smirks back, clearly pleased. "Good. Just how I want it to be."

I smile, but the way he says it... something makes me feel like I've just made a deal, but I have no idea what the terms are.

19

DO DO DO YOU EVEN SURF, BRUH?

From the moment Timmy and I set foot in the lively marketplace near my apartment, it's like he's guiding me into a hidden slice of paradise. Not that I haven't been here before—I have, many times, it's a prime destination on the tourist strip—but it's the first time I'm seeing it through Timmy's eyes. He grabs my hand and leads me into a bustling local bakery, his eyes alight, and orders a series of pastries with tropical flavors that I've never tried—guava-filled donuts, passionfruit danishes, things I've only ever read about.

Of course, I pay, and I don't mind in the least. With Timmy, life feels like a celebration—he's taking me on a whirlwind tour of Sunset Cay, and I'm loving every second of it. He's already helped me out so much, from lending me mattresses to driving me around. Buying a few bougie pastries seems like the least I could do for him.

As we dig into the pastries, I find myself involuntarily moaning at the taste—totally out of character for me, and usually a bit of an ick when other people do it—but somehow, around him, I'm comfortable letting myself enjoy things so openly.

He notices and bursts out laughing, playfully mocking my reaction with a dramatic "Mmm!" and adding, with a wink, "Bet you didn't think I'd have you moaning so soon, did you?", drawing a blush to my cheeks and making me laugh. For someone so full of quirks, he's remarkably carefree, leaning into the absurdity of life in a way I feel myself oddly charmed by.

When we take his truck to the local secondhand store, I'm a little surprised. It's not a place where I'd usually think to shop. But he takes me by the hand, leading me in, and walks straight up to the shelves, pulling down the oddest-looking kitchen decor and holding it up with a delighted grin. He's a scavenger with a taste for the eccentric, and somehow, he has an eye for the best among the clutter, finding high-quality knives and practical cookware buried in bins I would have avoided. Before I know it, I'm laughing with him over some creepy ceramic teddy bear he's pretending is our future dinner companion.

He's showing me how fun it is to treasure-hunt in unexpected places, and I realize that I've been such a snob, in ways I hadn't even noticed.

As we get in line to pay for the items, Timmy tries on a few pairs of sunglasses from the display, posing in front of the mirror. "Don't I look cute in these?"

I laugh. "You sure do."

As we get back to the truck after paying for my items, I spot him still wearing the sunglasses he tried on for fun, on top of his head, and he's holding an extra Hydro Flask he'd picked out. "Um, Timmy," I raise an eyebrow. "Why do you have those?"

"Oh!" he says with a little jump, wide-eyed, as if he just realized. "Guess I forgot I was still wearing these, and totally forgot about the Hydro Flask." He lets out a little laugh, unbothered, and I can't help but see the harmless innocence in it, like the time I witnessed an elderly woman accidentally shoplift a bag of lettuce at the grocery store because it was wedged in her cart, unseen.

After the second-hand store, we go to Walmart, and my chest blooms with warmth as we walk, hand-in-hand, through the aisles. He bumps into someone he knows, a guy pushing his own cart along.

"Hey man!" he says as the guys fist-bump. "This is my girlfriend, Margaux."

"Nice to meet you," says his friend.

He seems to know people everywhere we go, like he's a well-known figure in the Cay, and it feels reassuring, like he must be a good guy who might help me to build my own community here, too.

Shopping with him is a whirl of laughter and silly poses as he pops out from behind shelves or pretends to spy on me, peering through the most random of objects. It reminds me of shopping trips with my dad when I was young, where he'd chase me down the aisles making animal noises and I'd run gleefully away—joyful and unexpected—and I realize I haven't laughed this much in ages.

We pick up bedding—a nice duvet set with matching pillowcases. He insists on getting the soft lilac print, his favorite color. And soft lilac towels and washcloths and a bath mat. It's not my top color choice, personally, but he's so persuasive and it brings him so much obvious joy, the more soft lilac items that are placed in the cart. He's so excited, so in love with every choice, that I can't imagine taking that away from him. I realize his style might not be what I'd naturally choose, but watching him light up with each item he picks out is something else.

At one point, he finds a large stuffed Baby Shark toy. "Baby shaaaaaaaaaark!" he says with the excitement of a two-year-old who's just enjoyed way too much sugar, his muscular, tattooed arms clinging to the oversized toy like his life depends on it.

I quirk a brow. "You really want this toy?"

"Yessss! Baby shaaaaaaaark!" He giggles.

"Fine, add it to the cart," I laugh, rolling my eyes.

"Really?" His eyes grow big. "Baby Shaaaaaaaaark for Timmy?!"

"Bruh, are you speaking about yourself in the third person?" I laugh and shake my head. This guy.

We find chopping boards, basic groceries and cleaning supplies, as well as a little table and chair set that can serve as a computer desk.

"We've done well! I think we're all set!" I say, surveying the contents of the overstuffed cart.

"Let's get a TV, too!" he suddenly says. "We—you're going to need one."

"Oh no," I say, shaking my head. "I wasn't planning on getting a TV here. I want to focus on writing, and can always watch things on my computer."

"Okay," he says, frowning, jutting his lower lip out just a little.

We're distracted from the conversation as we reach the checkout.

It's so helpful having him here to help hoist the heavy items into the truck, and having the truck that can fit all the items, too. He makes a task that would otherwise seem daunting feel effortless and even enjoyable.

We park right in front of my building. Having a strong man to help me load things onto a cart and then get them up to my apartment makes a big difference, and it's also pretty hot watching him lug things around with ease.

It would have taken me a lot of Ubers, and more expense, to get things ready by myself. And I would have been hesitant to get some of the items he assured me I'd need.

He's making it fun, and he seems to genuinely enjoy helping me.

He even brings over potted plants from Matty's place to give the balcony some personality.

"This was my best friend Darren's mom's plant originally," he explains as he carries a massive pot to the truck. "It's full of coconut and succulents and banana and ti leaves—one of the most beautiful leaves on the planet if you ask me. You're going to love it when things start growing bigger. It'll be like a real little jungle on your balcony."

Looking around the apartment at all the shopping bags and piles of items, I feel a little overwhelmed, but exhilarated. I have a rough idea of where things are going to go, but spatial planning isn't my forté.

In fact, when I move to a new place, I usually draw a diagram and send it to Paulo because he's much better at it than me. But this time, I don't need to consult with Paulo, because I have Timmy.

"I have plans for this place!" Timmy says excitedly. "Just wait until I have it all set up. Do you trust me?" He looks at me eagerly, expectantly.

"Yes, I trust you!" I laugh.

He beams and runs over to kiss me. "I love being around you so much."

"I love being around you, too," I grin, as he races back to the corner of the room.

It's not lost on me that strong language has been exchanged so soon, but it's exciting and feels so good and real that I love saying it to him, and love hearing him say it to me. It's not like we're actually saying 'I love you', after all.

"The desk is going to go here so you can see the ocean while you're typing, as well as the mountains," he says excitedly. "But I'll put that together tomorrow. And then the bed will go here," he gestures to the spot next to where he's planning on putting the desk, "so we'll still be able to see the ocean lying down."

"Okay!" I say, trying to visualize everything as he explains it. This is a much better layout than one I would have come up with myself.

He works away while I continue to unpack kitchen things and load up the dishwasher and washing machine, and within an hour or two, he says, "Ta da! What do you think?"

He shows me around, and it might be a small apartment, but he's done such a thoughtful, amazing job.

As promised, he's saved space so that, while sitting at my desk once it's assembled, I'll have the most gorgeous view of the beach and the famous mountain, as well as the hills off in the distance.

From the bed, we can see surfers way out at the break at one of his favorite surfing beaches.

"What do you think?" he asks again, watching my reaction closely as if I'm a competition judge about to give him a score for his efforts.

"Oh my gosh. It's just amazing. Seriously, Timmy," I say, hugging him tight and tilting my head up to kiss him. "Thank you so much. I feel a lot better seeing this starting to look like a real apartment, a real living space."

"I'm really good at stuff like this," he explains proudly. "And I'm so happy to help you. I figure we'll be spending a lot of time here, so we may as well have it set up as perfect as we can get it."

We get changed and head down to the pool area where he immediately launches himself in, full Superman-style, creating a splash big enough to draw the attention of a few onlookers. He stays under for a while, and then bursts from the water, laughing, unbothered by the stares and enjoying every bit of the fun he's making of himself—and for me. This free spirit of his is contagious, and I feel lighter than I have in years, as if the weight of my previous worries has drifted away with the ripples he's made in the pool.

Later, he takes me to a trendy but laid-back bar across the road with swinging chairs—a feature I'm particularly weak for. He snaps photos of me as I sway, and when he proudly shows them to me, teaching me how he adjusted the light and focus on his phone's camera, I notice he's captured some kind of radiance in me that I'd almost forgotten I had.

The bartender knows him, and we all chat away like old friends while I sip on a daiquiri made with local rum, and Timmy suggests we share a fresh smoked local marlin dip, and I realize this is the exact life I envisioned—only it's better because he's here. After a leisurely snack and cocktail session, we head back to the apartment.

With everything now unpacked, Timmy takes the Baby Shark toy and cuddles with it, beaming as he wraps it in his muscular, tattooed arms.

I snap a few pictures as he grins and rolls around on the bed, looking ridiculous, this giant 39-year-old man with a massive yellow-and-white stuffed toy.

"My baby shaaaaaaark!" He says, grinning, wrapping his arms around it. "Thank you so much for getting this for me. I love it so much!"

After a day full of laughter, adventure, and little discoveries, I hop onto the bed beside him and we lay side-by-side for a bit. My life here is chaotic, it's unexpected, it's full of soft lilac, and it's completely Timmy.

And, like a gentleman, he goes home, promising to pick me up again early the next day.

20

TRUST THE CHARM, IGNORE THE EDGE

I wake to the sound of the ocean, its breeze drifting in, carrying with it the scent of salt and plumeria, filling the small apartment with a sense of promise. I pull an oracle card from my deck. DREAM.

It feels like the universe is nodding in agreement. After years of stress, corporate drudgery, and making compromises that chipped away at my soul, I'm finally free—living the dream I've whispered about to myself on restless nights. No more firing tons of people over Zoom. No more forcing myself into places where I never really felt I belonged. Now, it will be just me and Sabre, the ocean, my writing, and, hopefully, someone to share it all with.

Whether or not that person turns out to be Timmy, I know one thing: I'm not settling any more. This is my new life, and I intend to live it fully.

Timmy picks me up bright and early again, and we wind our way along the coastal roads to a beach I've never been to before—secluded, and framed by man-made lagoons surrounded by jagged reefs.

The water is clear and sparkles in the sunlight. In the distance, the sleek high-rises of the resort district rise against the backdrop of the rugged, emerald-green mountains. The water stretches out in shimmering shades of turquoise, so clear I can see schools of tiny fish darting just below the surface.

For a fleeting second, my mind forces me to take a detour: *I don't know him that well. What if he's not who he seems? What if he's a serial killer?* But surely not. Nobody this fun and laid-back could be a serial killer.

He scrambles easily up the sides of the reef, his long limbs moving with the confidence of someone who's spent their whole life hopping across rocks and waves. His feet grip the uneven surface like they belong there. He turns, motioning for me to follow.

"Come on! What are you waiting for?" His grin is infectious.

"I don't exactly have your mountain goat-like agility," I laugh, eyeing the rocks skeptically.

I watch in awe as he runs along, leaping over little gaps and divots with ease.

He eventually convinces me to jump up, reaching down, taking my hand and effortlessly helping me onto the reef. "There you go," he says, pulling me up with surprising strength. "You're sure you're ready to surf? Because with balance like that..." he teases, flashing me a playful smirk.

I blush, and, laughing, I tell him the story of slipping my way through a waterfall hike with a friend in Puerto Rico. He laughs, his large hand brushing a stray strand of hair from my face. Then, without missing a beat, he leans in and kisses me—a kiss that tastes of salt and unspoken promises. "You're perfect just the way you are," he whispers, his lips lingering against mine. "And you're going to be an amazing surfer."

Later, we head to a tropical-themed bar nearby, one I discovered many years ago. The place is a hidden gem, tucked away in an industrial side street where tropical decor drips from every wall and ceiling beam.

Masks, old surfboards, glass floats and worn-out license plates tell stories of countless visitors who have stumbled upon this hidden-away slice of paradise in Sunset Cay. The bar smells like pineapple, rum, and nostalgia.

"Whoa," Timmy's eyes widen as he takes it all in. "This place is *wild*. How have I never been here?"

Timmy strikes up a conversation with the bartender, and soon they're swapping names of surfers and locals they both know. I watch, fascinated. Timmy fits into the world so naturally, moving through it like he belongs in any setting—a stark contrast to the cold detachment, the hesitancy in communicating with strangers, the sometimes outright rudeness that I'd encountered in my last relationship. His ease draws me in like a warm current, and for the first time in years, I feel like I'm floating rather than treading water.

As Timmy wanders around while our drinks are being prepared, exploring the decor, he snaps a few pictures. "I'll have to send this to a friend," he says, his tone casual. "She loves tiki shit."

"Oh yeah?" I arch a brow.

He grins but doesn't elaborate, just continues scrolling on his phone.

Then he pauses, his gaze catching on an old black-and-white photo on the wall. The photo shows a young woman in a vintage bikini, her smile wide and radiant. "She has a beautiful smile," he murmurs.

"Oh, I thought you said *I* had a beautiful smile," I nudge him playfully. I have no problem with him complimenting the woman—I'm definitely not threatened by an old photo, and she *does* have a beautiful smile—I'm just giving him a hard time.

His eyes flick to mine, and for a brief moment, there's something unreadable in them—something just a little too sharp to be playful. "More than one person can have a beautiful smile, Margaux," he replies, the edge in his voice unexpected.

I blink, caught off-guard by the swift change in his tone.

But, just as quickly, the moment passes, and he's back to grinning at me, light and easy.

I tell myself it's nothing.

Relax. Focus on the fun.

WE LEAVE the bar and head back to the main strip. We stroll down the boardwalk, the night air warm and tinged with the scent of sunscreen and barbecue. The stone path along the beach is bustling with life—street performers, tourists smiling and laughing, and couples hand in hand.

Timmy spots a familiar face in the crowd, a street performer with birds perched on his shoulder. Without hesitation, he plucks a banana from the guy's hand, grinning as one of the birds swoops down to perch on his outstretched arm.

The crowd gasps, and Timmy just laughs, unfazed by the bird flapping its wings inches from his face. "What? You've never seen a guy share a banana with a bird before?"

I laugh, the tension from earlier melting away. Timmy's got that kind of charisma that draws people in—a carefree recklessness that's both thrilling and disarming.

As we wander further along the boardwalk, he turns to me, his grin sly and full of promise. "So... are you gonna let me stay over tonight?"

The thought sends a flutter through my stomach. The apartment's still relatively sparse—just the mattresses on the floor and a quilt, thanks to Timmy's help—as well as the other items we picked up from the store, the desk still waiting to be set up. But the idea of spending the night wrapped up in him, of letting go of everything and diving into something spontaneous and wild, makes my pulse quicken.

"Yes," I say, my voice softer than I intended. "You can stay over."

He beams at me, his hand slipping easily into mine as we continue down the boardwalk. The night stretches ahead of us, full of possibility—like the ocean just before a storm, calm and inviting but with a thrilling undercurrent of something about to break.

I know, deep down, that there's more to Timmy than he's letting on—more than just charm and good vibes. And the fact that the photos from the bar went to *her*—a friend, maybe, but possibly more

—sits uncomfortably in the back of my mind. I'm not a jealous person by nature, but the way he said it just made me feel weird.

But for tonight, I don't care. We just met, we haven't by any means discussed exclusivity other than his cryptic comments about nobody else being able to stay over at my place, and of course he's allowed to have female friends. It's not like I don't have plenty of male friends.

Tonight, I'm not going to worry about it anymore. I'm ready to be swept away.

21

HE LIKES MY CAT

T*he Past:*

No one: (tumbleweeds roll by and crickets chirp)

~

THE PRESENT:

He assembles my desk and the matching chairs, and looks around the room.

As promised, he positions them so I can see the ocean while I'm writing. "For inspiration," he says. "Because I know you love being able to look at the ocean."

It's like he's listened to every word I've ever said, every story I've ever shared, and absorbed it all. And then he puts them into practice in the most subtle, thoughtful ways.

I've never felt cared about like this. Had someone put themselves into my shoes and think about what would work best for me. I feel almost... adored... I guess you could say. And it's a wonderful feeling.

As we're setting up my apartment, every look he gives me, every glance we share, feels charged with something more than just the ordinary thrill of moving into a new place. There's this sense of electricity coursing between us, a chemistry so potent it feels like a magnetic pull. We've already been struggling to keep our hands off each other, and when we finally let go, it's a rush of pent-up desire, and raw, undeniable need.

He slides my top over my head, and his eyes go wide as he notices the little silver bars that run through both of my nipples, as if he's seeing a gift just for him. An involuntary groan escapes his lips, and his expression is so feral, so primal, that I almost lose myself.

"Oh my fucking god, I didn't know your nipples were pierced," he growls, nearly breathless. "Holy fuck, that's hot." The intensity of his gaze has me feeling both powerful and completely vulnerable.

"They're new," I say, a sly smile playing on my lips. "I just got them done a few weeks ago, so please be gentle. They're still pretty tender." I can tell by the way he's looking at them he wants to either yank on them or put them in his mouth—maybe both—his expression turning reverent, as if he's unwrapping something secret and sacred.

"They're so fucking hot," he says. "Oh my god, you're amazing. Every fucking day I find out at least one new amazing thing about you, usually way more than just one."

I don't need to worry about him being too rough with them, though. He leans down and places a soft kiss on each, sending a shock that zips through my whole body. His touch is electric, and as his lips brush over my skin, any fears I had about remembering how to be intimate melt away.

When he lowers his board shorts and his cock springs free, my breath catches. Girthy and thick, with a slight upward curve that makes my stomach clench with excitement. And it's rock hard.

"Jesus, you have a huge cock," I blurt out, my face flushing, feeling myself grow even wetter, and he smirks.

"I know," he growls, confidence radiating off him.

After five years, it felt like that whole part of my body had closed up shop. You know, insert jokes about cobwebs and the like.

But he makes me feel beautiful, desirable and worshipped in a way I never have before. My body responds to him as though it's been waiting for exactly this.

I'm so horny right now, and as I see the lustful look in his eyes, my concern dissipates in an instant. He looks at me like he wants to eat me. And then he does, yanking my thighs apart and diving between them headfirst.

I moan as Timmy's hot, wet tongue teases its way up the inside of my thigh. I can feel his cocky grin even though my eyes are closed, his fingers gently exploring my lips.

"Your pussy is so pink," he says. "And oh my god, you taste so good. Mmm, you're soaking wet for me, babe," he purrs, making a trail of kisses across my pussy. "Bet you've been aching for this, haven't you?"

"Oh, fuck, Timmy," I gasp, arching my back as he slips a finger inside me, curling it in a way that drives me wild. "Yes, yes, don't stop."

He laughs softly, his voice low and husky, sending shivers down my spine. His free hand caresses my stomach, his thumb tracing patterns over my navel as he works a second finger into me, stretching me just right.

"That's it, baby. Let me know how much you want this," he growls.

"Fuck, Timmy, I've been wanting this—you—so much," I moan, pulling at the sheets beneath me, my body quivering with desire.

He laughs, the vibrations of his chuckle heating my core even more. "I've been wanting you so badly, too, sexy," he whispers, before he closes his lips around my clit, sending electric shocks coursing through me.

"Oh my God, Timmy!" I gasp, my toes curling as he laps at me with an eagerness that I don't know I've ever experienced. He expertly flicks his tongue over my clit, making me squirm and buck against him.

"That's it, baby," he mumbles, his voice vibrating against my pussy.

"I've been wanting to taste this sweet pussy of yours. Fuck, you taste so good."

"Fuck, Timmy, don't stop," I beg, one hand in his sun-bleached hair, the other gripping the edge of the mattress as pleasure courses through my veins. His soft laughter hums against my clit, the vibrations making me moan even louder.

He groans before he adds a third large finger inside me, stretching me, curling them into that special spot that sends me close to the edge.

"Oh my fucking God, Timmy, yes," I moan, my hips bucking against his face as he sucks my clit into his mouth, teasing it with his skilled tongue.

"You like that, baby?" he asks, then bites down lightly on my swollen clit, making me see stars.

"Oh, fuck, yes, don't stop," I pant, my mind lost in a sea of pleasure. He echoes my moans with a growl, his cock hard and throbbing against me.

"You taste so fucking good," he groans, and I can feel him leaking pre-cum onto my leg.

I pant, grinding my hips against his face, seeking more of his skilled tongue.

His breath is hot against my sensitive skin, sending tingles all over my body. And just when I think I can't take it anymore, with one final, hard lick, I fly over the edge, crying out his name as the world explodes around me.

My body arches off the bed as the most powerful climax of my life washes over me. Timmy doesn't stop, lapping up every drop of my essence, until I'm spent, panting and shaking, my nails embedded in the sheets.

He works me through quivering aftershocks, licking and sucking until I'm a trembling, spent mess on the bed, my body singing with pleasure.

"Damn, you're good at eating pussy," I manage to gasp, my chest heaving.

"Oh, I know," he replies, grinning up at me with a smug look on his face, a cocky confidence that makes me go feral.

Finally, when I can't take any more, I pull him up, my hands shaking as I reach for him. He stands up, his hard cock inches from my face.

"It's my turn now," I pant, a wicked smile playing on my lips.

Timmy grins, his eyes dark with lust as he obligingly lays back on the bed, his massive cock hard and throbbing, just for me.

"Oh, my," I breathe, my eyes widening as I take in the sight of him up close. "You really do have a massive cock."

He chuckles, a cocky grin on his face. "What can I say, baby? Eating your pussy makes my cock grow harder."

I roll my eyes, but I can't help the smirk that tugs at my lips. "Well, then, let's see how it feels in my mouth."

I lower myself to my knees, my eyes locked on his, my heart pounding in anticipation. I run my tongue along his length, savoring the taste of him, salty and musky, a heady aphrodisiac that sends shivers down my spine.

"Fuck, Margaux," he groans, his hands fisting in my hair as I take him deeper into my mouth. "You really know how to suck my big, fat cock."

I moan around his length, the vibrations sending shivers through his body. I love the way he responds to me, like I'm the only thing that matters in this moment.

I increase my pace, bobbing my head up and down his shaft, my tongue swirling around his tip. My other hand wraps around his base, stroking him in time with my mouth. I can feel him throb and twitch in my mouth, and it makes me moan, knowing I'm having this effect on him.

He pulls me up with his strong arms and I straddle him, our naked bodies touching in this way for the first time. He grabs a condom from a box to the side of the bed and expertly rolls it onto his cock.

I feel the heat emanating from Timmy's body as he shifts beneath me, his muscles tense with pent-up desire. His deep blue eyes, usually so full of mischief, are now hooded with lust, and I can't help but shiver in anticipation. Desire courses through me as I line him up with my entrance.

Timmy's hands grip my hips, guiding me downward. His massive cock, rock hard and throbbing, teases my entrance. I take a deep breath, inhaling his familiar scent of sun and sea, and even though this is our first time together, it's as if my body has missed him all along.

With a moan of surrender, I lower myself onto him, my walls stretching to accommodate his insane girth. He fills me so completely, every nerve ending in my body is on fire, and all I can think about is how right this feels.

As I sink down onto his hardness, everything comes rushing back. It really is like riding a bike. You never forget. The sensation is overwhelming, a mixture of lust and exhilaration that blurs the line between pleasure and something deeper, something addictive. We're caught in this perfect rhythm, a seamless blend of bodies and energy, something transformative.

"Oh, fuck, Margaux," he groans, his jaw clenched in ecstasy. I meet his gaze, our eyes locked as our bodies finally meld together.

I begin to move, rocking my hips in slow, sensual circles, relishing the feeling of him inside me. Timmy's hands slide up my back, leaving a trail of goosebumps in their wake, as he guides me into a rhythm that has us both gasping for air. His generous cock hits all the right spots, and I can feel the intensity building deep inside me.

"Faster," he growls, his voice raspy with need, and I oblige, grinding my hips against his as the heat between us builds to a fever pitch.

"Oh, Timmy," I pant out, my nails digging into his chest. "You feel so good."

"God, baby, you feel so good too," he groans, his eyes glazed over with desire. "Your tight little pussy, your sexy moans."

His dirty talk sends a shiver down my spine, and I moan louder, spurring him on. His hips buck upwards, meeting my every thrust, his massive cock hitting depths I didn't know existed. The tension coils tighter and tighter within me.

He flips me over onto my back, and I lay on the bed with Timmy above me, our bodies intertwined in a passionate embrace.

His tattooed biceps flex and the sound of our heavy breathing fills the room as he thrusts into me, once again filling me up completely. Time seems to stand still as our hips grind in an erotic symphony, his girthy cock stretching me in ways I'd nearly forgotten. It's been years since I last fucked anyone, but it feels like no time has passed at all.

His hands grip my hips firmly, guiding me to meet his every thrust, ensuring we both feel every single inch of each other. Sparks fly inside me, and my body is alive with pleasure like I've never experienced before with any other man.

His cock hits that spot deep inside me, and I throw my head back, moaning in ecstasy. Despite it being our first time together, it's as if he knows my body better than anyone else, and he uses that knowledge to drive me wild.

"Margaux," he growls, his voice low and guttural as he plunges deeper and deeper, inch by delicious inch. "I've been dreaming about this. Your tight pussy wrapped around my cock, squeezing me like a vise."

His dirty talk sends shivers down my spine, and I can feel pleasure continuing to build inside me like an unstoppable wave. I dig my nails into his back and he groans.

"Yes, fuck me harder," I beg, my voice a desperate whimper.

He grunts in response, picking up the pace even more, slamming into me with an intensity I've never felt before. It's like he's claiming me as his, marking me as his own, and a part of me thrills at the thought.

"Fuck, Timmy," I scream, my toes curling, chills running through me, tearing me apart and stitching me back together again. "Oh my God, yes!"

He buries his face in the crook of my neck, his hot breath sending shivers down my spine. "Oh fuck, Margaux," he murmurs into my hair. "I'm coming."

His grip on my hips tightens, and he groans my name again as he unloads himself deep inside me, his body shuddering beneath mine.

As our breathing eases, we collapse onto the bed, our hearts pounding in tandem. I wrap my arms around his tattooed chest, inhaling his intoxicating scent. We remain entwined, our bodies joined together. I've never felt more connected to anyone than I do in this moment, as if nothing could ever break this bond we now share.

"You're amazing," I whisper, my voice hoarse from the intensity of our lovemaking.

He pulls back, his eyes shining with emotion, "You're amazing, Margaux."

He kisses me, his lips soft and tender, a far cry from the passionate frenzy of moments ago. My heart swells for this man.

Slowly, Timmy pulls out of me, and I can't help but whimper at the loss of him.

We lay here, sated, tangled in each other. He pulls me close, his hand tracing soft patterns on my back that make my skin tingle.

"Wow, I meant what I said before. You really *are* good at eating pussy," I moan.

"Oh, I know," he says. "Fucking hell, that was good. That's the best blowjob I've ever had in my life. And that's definitely the best sex I've ever had."

"Seriously?" His words, so raw and genuine, make me blush. I can't help but giggle at his unabashed confidence. It feels easy with him—natural.

"Yes. Most definitely," he nods, and sighs contentedly. "Your pussy feels different, you know?"

"Oh," I say, my face flushing. "Well, nobody has ever said that before, but I have a tilted cervix, so that could be it." I've had sex with a decent number of people, and nobody has ever mentioned it. But Timmy has this sexual confidence that exudes from him. He definitely has the BDE to go with his actual big dick.

"Well, I have a curve in my dick," he explains. "And it seems to be at just the right angle. We're perfect together."

I laugh. Such a random thing to say, but again, he has this way of noticing details that nobody else ever has, or at least not that they've mentioned. He makes me feel special. Like as a couple we're magical, made for each other.

And it doesn't stop there. The way he jokes about keeping other guys off the mattress he's hauled up to my apartment. His possessiveness is cheeky, but it sends a thrill through me, as if he's claiming me. Every moment with Timmy is like a jolt of something intoxicating—this blend of adrenaline, lust, and happiness that I've never felt before. He's so thoughtful, so genuinely invested in everything that makes me unique, and I feel so utterly seen in a way I didn't even know was possible.

We lay here, entwined in each other's arms, the room silent save for our panting breaths and the distant sound of waves crashing against the shore. I've never felt more at home, more content, than I do right now with Timmy.

The outside world fades away, and it's just the two of us, enjoying each other, like nothing—no one—else exists. It's as if our connection transcends time and distance—just Timmy and me.

"That really was so good," I whisper, my eyes drifting closed as sleep begins to claim me.

"Mmhmm," he smirks, kissing my forehead gently. "Sleep now, baby. I'll be here when you wake up."

And with those words echoing in my ears, I slip into a deep, contented sleep, my heart lighter than it's been in years.

THE FOLLOWING MORNING, I wake up and he's sprawled across the mattresses. He's taken one of my creepy Margaux dolls that looks just like me, and he's wearing it on its dick like it's sucking his cock. I laugh and snap a picture. He's seriously the funniest person I've ever met.

He takes me out to a famous local spot that plays live music at brunch. We sit at the bar and, once again, he chats away with the bartender and other bar patrons. A kind woman offers to snap a photo of us together at the bar. It's an awful photo, but he's clinging to me and I look happy. The feeling I have inside is so much more than what can be conveyed by any picture, though. I have constant butterflies. Every moment with Timmy is filled with possibilities and adventure, and I've never felt more excited about what my life is going to bring.

He's so cute and snuggly. His back is smooth. And it's big and strong.

I love wrapping my arms around him.

I love the feeling of his skin. I love the way my arms feel when they're entangled with him.

The way he looks at me.

So kind, so caring. Full of humor. Mischievous!

He makes me feel alive.

And his sense of humor is warped, like mine. I can say the darkest shit and he'll take it one step further. I've never been with someone who makes me laugh so hard. Deep belly laughs that result in tears running down my face multiple times a day.

I'd long ago given up on the idea of soulmates, but now I feel like I've found mine.

When I tell him things, he usually pays attention. Like the way I like my onions raw or at least still a little bit crunchy. The way I put hot sauce on basically everything. Sometimes I have to repeat myself, but who in a relationship doesn't? And it's taken us a little moment to understand each other's accents, so that adds to it.

I'm swept up in wave after wave of his admiration. None of it seems disingenuous or over-the-top. He makes comments when it makes sense to do so, not like he's coming up with a list and saying it just because he wants to win me over. It's thoughtful and thought out, and I feel so seen.

He's always up for an adventure. For once, I feel like the least crazy one in the relationship. He's spontaneous and, well... fun!

And he takes the lead with sex and makes me feel beautiful and sensual. He notices parts of me that nobody else ever has.

Everything is just going so well.

Here's this very cute, tall, athletic man who has taken time off work to drive me around and help me set up my apartment. Lifting heavy things, grabbing things from high places. Being thoughtful and considerate about what I might need in order to be comfortable.

And also being able to enjoy mind-blowing sex with him?

Moving here really was the best decision.

It feels like things are finally coming together for me.

22

KNIVES & BONES

There's something morbidly fascinating about Timmy's attachment to all his bones and blades. In addition to the knife he always carries—a switchblade, he's got a full pair of deer antlers, and the deer spine necklace I recognize from his Tinder profile. The antlers are huge and pointy, and the necklace is pretty sharp too, actually. It's like a lei, but made of animal bones. And he also has a deer skull with antlers attached. Definitely weird.

He wears the antlers and the vertebrae necklace around a lot. It's like he's reenacting some primeval rite.

The odd part isn't just that he wears them out in public or at all—it's the pride he takes in them, a glow that crosses his face whenever he describes how he hunted the deer and stripped its bones.

Okay, I guess I kind of get it. He's proud of it, his first time hunting.

I'm not opposed to hunting, per se, especially when the meat is utilized, and clearly these items bring him joy.

But it's definitely unusual to wear antlers and a spine around.

He also has a different necklace with beads and deer... claws? Hooves? Something like that.

And then one day he randomly gifts the claw necklace to me. He puts it around my neck. "This is for you," he says. "I want you to have it."

"Thanks?" I say. I'm not really a big… wearer of dead animals. But I don't judge people who wear leather or fur super harshly, I suppose, although I prefer the faux versions for myself.

Just a Timmy quirk.

He brings the antlers and spine necklace over and stores them in my apartment so he can wear them on a regular basis. I don't love them being there, but they're not hurting anyone.

"I always carry a knife," Timmy says casually, indicating the sharp blade hanging from the top of his board shorts. "You never know when you might need it around here."

The knife itself, sinister and sharp with its dark handle and silver detailing, seems more suited for a survival show than the busy streets of Sunset Cay lined with restaurants and beach shops.

I glance around the tourist district, where the biggest threat is usually an overpriced meal or sunburn.

"Okay? Why exactly?" I give him side-eye. "Like for construction work or something else?"

"Things happen around here," he explains, his voice low, glancing around as if he's used to spotting trouble before anyone else does. "You'd be surprised. I like to be prepared to intervene if I have to."

It sounds a bit over-the-top, but, then again, I know people carry self-defense items all the time. Hell, isn't this the country where people carry guns around just in case? I know I've carried pepper spray and cat-ear keychains that could poke someone if needed. So a knife seems… reasonable? And useful, I suppose? He's always cutting leaves off things to make leis and whatnot, too.

"Intervene?" I laugh nervously, wondering if he's exaggerating or if there's some hidden world in these streets that I just haven't seen yet. "You mean, like, defend yourself or something?"

He shrugs, smirking a little. "I mean, yeah, like I'd be able to defend you if some weird people started following us or starting a fight. It happens, you know. And it's better to be prepared." There's a flash of something in his eyes, like he's playing out a scene in his mind, and it's oddly both unsettling and oddly reassuring.

"It does? Around here?" While there are definitely people up to no good here, just like anywhere else, they tend to stick to themselves. There's a heavy police presence to protect tourists, and I haven't really felt in danger except when I've accidentally wandered down a dark alley trying to find a restaurant or something.

"Yeah, once I actually saved a girl," he says earnestly, his eyes lighting up. "Her boyfriend was strangling her. I jumped over a bush and punched him in the face, and then distracted him with my knife while she ran away to safety."

I gasp. "Oh wow. That was heroic of you."

"Yeah, he tried to fight me, but I pulled out my knife to show him I wasn't playing around," he explains. "So I always think it's important to carry it and have it readily available."

"That sounds intense," I say. Because it really does. I've lived in several big cities around the country, where crime rates are known for being high, and I don't remember anyone I know ever having carried a knife around. Pepper spray, maybe. But never a weapon. But maybe lots of people I've known have carried knives and they've just kept them concealed. Harder for Timmy whose signature uniform is board shorts, no shirt, no shoes.

Besides, he knows this island way better than me. And I've mainly stuck to the tourist spots. Maybe things get a little rowdier, a little less heavily policed, where the locals hang out.

He continues. "You wouldn't believe some of the things I've had to do. Some of the things I've seen."

His words come out of nowhere, and there's a darkness about him that I haven't really seen before.

"I've spent so many nights in game rooms and other shady places. I've sold drugs and festival balls and all sorts of things I needed to."

He's making himself sound like a tough guy out of an action movie.

"Um.. wow. Okay, what's a festival ball?"

"It's a big firework. Very loud, beautiful when it goes off."

"And what's a game room? Like an arcade?"

"Kind of. It's where all the gang members and drug dealers go to launder money. There's gambling and all sorts of stuff going on. And you can hire people to... take care of certain things."

"Oh, I see," I frown. "Well, I'm glad you're not doing that anymore."

He looks almost wistful. "When someone really fucks up on this island, they sometimes get dealt with. There's a wood chipper..."

"A wood chipper?" I flinch at the thought, immediately understanding he's not talking about using it to process wood..

He nods, a dark gleam in his eye, as if he's proud to know the gritty details most people don't. "Can you imagine what a human body looks like, being processed through a woodchipper? What that *sounds* like?"

My mind flashes back to a movie where that happened. I can't remember which one, but I remember what it looked like, and I shiver.

"I—I guess I can, but I don't really want to? I guess like a meat grinder, but for humans?"

"It's very loud, and very disturbing to watch," he nods, his mouth pressed together in a grim line, his eyes gleaming. "But it's also very quick. Efficient. And there's little to no chance of anyone ever identifying the body. Because it's in tiny little pieces. And it gets scattered around and buried in mulch, like regular fertilizer. That's how we take care of things around here." He looks wistful again.

I'm pretty sure he's full of shit, so I change the subject.

He's a storyteller, and I imagine that kind of talk impresses some of his male buddies. But I just think it's him being a weirdo, and it's making me feel uncomfortable.

If anything, I might be able to use it in a book, I suppose.

I try to laugh it off, but there's an unease that lingers. I'm assuming he's just pulling my leg, but the glint of pride, or something like satisfaction in his expression, makes me wonder just how close he's really been to things like that.

23

HE LIKES MY OTHER CAT, TOO

"Let me take you to see your cat," Timmy says, smiling at me. "Would you mind?" I feel my eyes grow large at the prospect of seeing my baby.

He kisses me on my forehead. "I'd seriously love to."

We hop into his truck, and it's so fun driving with Timmy, different from what I'm used to. He cranks the stereo and plays all sorts of songs I've never heard before, exposing me to new music, as well as some songs I do know. It feels so free.

One of my joys has always been driving around listening to music —I love music in general—and it's with a bit of shock that, when I think about it, I realize I didn't really listen to music for the past six years or so. My ex only liked to listen to music he made himself, and he'd seem offended when I'd listen to anything else.

He was also adamant about not listening to music while driving— again, unless it was his own—so I gave up that joy, and I'd really not given it much thought until now.

But Timmy is like my own personal DJ, playing everything from classic rap to the latest EDM and house, pop, R&B, even reggae and local Sunset Cay jams. I feel like my mind is being re-expanded.

As we drive, Timmy leans back casually, one hand on the steering wheel, the other gesturing as he talks and occasionally landing on my thigh, bouncing from topic to topic as the songs change. He has a way of describing things that almost feels like he's pulling them out of a dream, mixing memories with imagination, past with present. The way he talks, it's like everything is happening now, and I keep having to mentally rewind and sort through what he means.

"You know the kids, they get me to do this all the time," he laughs, gesturing at the radio. "'Turn it up, louder, louder!' they'll demand. And they're all in the back, screaming like it's some kind of dance club."

"Oh, right... the kids?" I reply, trying to follow along. "Which kids are you talking about, again..?"

"Oh, back at Darren's place. I live in the room next door to him. And my ex's kids. They're always listening to music, skateboarding around the yard. I swear my daughter's going to be like that."

I frown slightly, sorting through his mix of words. Does he mean... kids he might have one day? Or actual kids that exist now? "Wait, your daughter? You mean... *if* you have a daughter?"

"Yes, exactly." He glances over and winks. "I just know she'd be skateboarding, a tomboy."

I nod, catching up slowly. "Got it, a hypothetical future daughter." A little puzzle piece falls into place, although not quite snugly.

He smiles. "Yep!"

"Oh," I say. "So you don't have kids?"

"No, no," he says quickly.

I get it now, and I breathe a sigh of relief.

"And you live with Matty. You don't still live with Darren. That was a while ago, right?"

"Exactly!" He flashes a grin, like I've solved some sort of mystery. "It was Darren's ex's house. We all lived there. And then I lived at *my* ex's place, and her kid lived there and his friends would be over all the time. And then I moved out to Matty's a couple of months before you got here."

It's starting to feel like a language all his own, a peculiar mix of nostalgia and daydreams.

Timmy's stories flow around us like a stream, and I'm content to wade in it, letting his disjointed words wash over me. When he talks, there's no need for anything to be clear or linear. It's all part of the ride, part of the way he experiences life—a little chaotic, a little random, with memories and dreams just blending in together.

"Ever been swimming with the dolphins?" he asks, changing subjects entirely.

"No, but I've always wanted to," I reply.

"Ah, that's too bad. We'll fix that," he says, his own train of thought seemingly back in some ocean memory. "I've been a few times. What about surfing with a dog on the surfboard?"

I laugh. "No, I can't say that I have."

"Darren's a champ at that. You'll have to see it one day."

I grin, picturing it in my head. "Sounds like a good time," I reply, and he just beams, his eyes on the road but his mind clearly back in that memory.

Timmy's words weave a world that doesn't necessarily make sense or line up neatly, but it's carefree, just like him. I won't overanalyze it, although I'll clearly need to seek clarity from time to time. It's Timmy's unique version of reality, one that's endlessly colorful and unpredictable, even if a little confusing.

"I'm so glad that you're not from like... the middle of America," he says randomly. "That you have some knowledge of beach culture. That you can like... pronounce things here, native words. That you understand the meaning of how things work over here. I couldn't bear to start from scratch with some basic Becky from Utah," he laughs.

And I smile back. It really does seem serendipitous. He's so patient with me when it comes to new words, taking the time to explain them and give examples of how things work in practice. But I do feel like I'm starting with a higher baseline than most, solely because of my own upbringing on an island with a similar culture to Sunset Cay. I never expected to find this in a partner, and it's uniquely refreshing.

We pull up to the quarantine facility and I'm nervous. The whole paperwork situation is a bit confusing. I have money orders, but I don't know if they're for the right amount. And I'm just worried there's going to be some technicality where I can't see my sweet baby Sabre. I miss him, his cuddles and his purrs.

At least I know the quarantine facility is nice—it's just how the lady at the airport described, a little indoor-outdoor type situation where he can see mongoose run past, and of course he has other cats as neighbors, although they're partitioned off so they can't actually see each other.

We laugh when we get to Sabre's 'unit', I guess you could call it.

Because right there, on the sign, it says:

*Sabre. *Caution*.*

"I WONDER where he gets that from," Timmy laughs, poking me on the arm.

"That's my cat," I laugh, proudly. He's always been feisty with authority figures. And with me. "Sabre! You have visitors!" I call out, and he lets out a little meow in response and runs to the door.

"I'm going to make him feel comfortable around me super quick," Timmy says. "Watch."

He lies flat on his back, arms by his side, and I sit on the floor next to him.

Sabre circles him, sniffing and inspecting him from every angle.

"This is how we train dogs," Timmy explains. "I'm doing this on his terms, making it clear I'm no threat."

"Wow," I say, impressed. "I've never seen this before. That's so cool!"

Sabre hops up on his little bench and tucks his paws under himself. He watches Timmy, casually observing him. But he's comfortable enough to be resting around him.

"See? He's already starting to get comfortable with me," says Timmy.

I smile. It's important to me that Sabre feels comfortable around Timmy. After making him go on yet another flight and relocate once again, I feel like making sure he's secure in his own place is the least I can do.

After a moment, Timmy gets up and sits on the bench near me so that he's positioned slightly above me.

"Suck my cock. Quick!" urges Timmy.

"What?" My eyes grow wide. "Right now? Are there cameras?"

We both crane our necks, but don't see anything.

"Nope!" he says. "Go! Go!"

I shrug and laugh. "Okay then." I feel reckless and excited. Sure, I've had sex outside before, but I've sure as hell never sucked a dick in an animal quarantine facility.

He whips down his pants and flops out his cock. It's semi-hard, and I quickly put it in my mouth and begin to lick and suck. He moans in pleasure.

I feel like we're getting away with something delicious and naughty. It's exhilarating.

After a while, I remove his cock from my mouth and I giggle.

"Okay," he says and puts it back in his pants, grinning. "I can't believe you just did that," he laughs.

"Me neither," I grin. "But it was fun."

"God, I love you," he says, mussing my hair from where he's sitting above me.

I smile at him. "I love you, too."

~

Five minutes later

Timmy is regaling me with a random story. "When I was naked, running around the doctor's backyard."

"Which doctor's backyard were you running around naked?"

He looks like he's been caught with his hand in the cookie jar. "Uh, nobody."

Suddenly, it clicks. "Wait, you're telling me about running around naked in the backyard of the doctor you were *dating*? Why would I want to hear about that?" It's an unnecessary story, not particularly interesting, and I don't understand why he needed to share this with me. Is that how they were when they were together, running around naked all the time like a bunch of naturists? Fucking all the time? I feel a knot forming in my stomach.

"Fuck you," he growls, his eyes growing dark.

"Wait, I was just trying to understand—"

But he doesn't stop. He storms out of the quarantine cage, and I close the door quickly before Sabre can follow him.

I sit with Sabre and give him cuddles and treats, trying not to cry, not really understanding what just happened.

When he returns about fifteen minutes later, he's on the phone.

"Yeah," he mutters, his voice low. "I know." He hangs up.

"Who was that?" I ask.

"Darren, not that it's any of your business," he growls.

Then his voice softens.

"Look, I'm sorry I got upset," he says. "Can we just go?"

"I'm sorry I did, too," I say. "I know you've dated people before me. I just didn't understand why you didn't tell me that's who you were talking about. And why you were telling me this naked story. And yes, let's just go." I sigh.

I give Sabre one last cuddle before we leave. "I'll be back to visit you soon," I say. "I promise."

When we leave and hop into the truck, Timmy brings out the creepy Margaux doll that he's started carrying around everywhere. He hangs it from a fishing lure that dangles from the rear-view mirror.

"That's a bit creepy!" I say. "It looks like it's literally hanging from a noose."

"That's why it's funny," Timmy laughs. "And it looks like you."

He cranks the stereo on the way back, directing me to play this or that on Spotify.

"Damn, you're a bit of a shit DJ," he teases me, as I fumble to find the right songs a couple of times. His phone is set up quite differently from mine, and he has a different version of Spotify, so it's just easier to find things on my own phone.

"Stop," I laugh, but it's shallow, and I feel heat rising to my face. "I'm doing my best." I know he's only teasing me, but his comment makes me feel just a little bit embarrassed.

I think he can tell, because he takes my hand and glances over at me. "It's okay, Margaux. Your DJ skills aren't why I think you're so amazing. Everything about you is amazing, except for how long it takes you to find songs."

We drive back to town, and Timmy takes the creepy Margaux doll from its makeshift noose, and he shoves it upside down in his board shorts. I laugh as he walks down the boardwalk with a tiny doll replica of me sticking out of his pants. You can just see a bit of the bright red hair, along with its legs and boots on full display.

It's ridiculous.

He's ridiculous.

And I'm having so much fun.

24

SHARING IS CARING

We talk about everything.

I've never had this before, a partner who's genuinely interested in the intricate workings of my mind, my soul. He's interested in my deepest fears and regrets, as well as my hopes and dreams.

And Timmy listens, he really listens. He leans in, his gorgeous blue eyes locked on mine, as if nothing else in the world exists except our conversation. It feels intoxicating, like a drug I didn't know I needed.

My exes have never really been into deep conversations, especially my most recent one, who would shove away any type of conversation about existentialism or anything else that would make him focus on human emotion. Any emotion, or anything painful, would make him shut down and retreat into his own little world, brushing it all off as if it didn't matter. That was his actual saying: *nothing matters.*

And Timmy is such an opposite swing of the pendulum. It's as though I've been walking around half-asleep for years, and suddenly, Timmy's awakened this dormant part of me, encouraging me to unravel parts of myself that I never thought I'd share with anyone.

Sure, some people know the basics, but I take him to depths I thought were buried deep inside.

"Tell me more about him, and what he meant to you," Timmy says softly, after I mention my uncle—who was such a special part of my life, who died too young, too unexpectedly. The weight of the memory presses on my chest, but Timmy's gaze is so full of warmth and understanding that I find myself opening up with him more than I have with anyone before.

"He was my hero," I start, my voice trembling as I recount memories of a man who always believed in me, who was always proud of me, and was one of my biggest champions. Who helped me through one of the darkest times of my life. "When he passed, I just... I don't know if I ever really recovered. It feels like I lost part of myself, you know? Like this big chunk of care and security that I'll never get back." Tears prick my eyes, and I feel my throat tighten, but I press on, trusting Timmy with a part of me that's raw and vulnerable. "Sometimes, I still wake after a dream that makes me feel like he's still alive. But then everything comes rushing back, and I remember that he's gone."

Timmy reaches out and grabs my hand, squeezing it tight. His eyes are wet, too. "I get it," he murmurs, his voice thick with emotion. "Loss like that... it leaves a mark. I've had several friends die in the past few years. And their deaths still hurt like it was yesterday."

The moment feels profound. For the first time, I'm with someone who seems to be able to understand. Someone who can *feel* things the way I do. Someone who doesn't shy away from difficult emotions, or retreat when the conversation gets too heavy. Timmy leans in, brushing a tear from my cheek with his thumb, and my heart swells. His emotional sensitivity—it's like a form of intelligence I've never encountered before in an intimate partner. It feels like he's seeing *all* of me, and accepting every damaged piece of me without hesitation. And his unconditional support feels like an emotional balm, healing me in places I didn't know I needed.

I take a deep breath, encouraged by his tenderness. I've alluded to my sexual assault with him before, but never gone into explicit detail.

"There's more," I whisper, my heart pounding as I prepare to expose more of one of my greatest wounds that I generally keep buried. Like, people are aware it happened, but not the extent to which the events of that incident have affected me. How depraved my attacker was, and the indelible imprints he's left on me. The emotional scars. "It left me broken in ways that I'm not sure I'll ever be able to fix, despite all the therapy." My voice falters, but I push through the tremble. "I have PTSD. Certain sounds, certain places... they take me back to it, and it's like I'm there all over again. I'm sensitive to loud noises, and I can snap back into hypervigilance even though it happened so many years ago."

Timmy's eyes flood with tears. His hand tightens around mine, and he shakes his head as if my story is almost too much to bear. "That's so horrible," he whispers, his voice cracking. "I'm so sorry you went through that. No one should ever have to feel that kind of fear."

He looks down for a moment, his own breath hitching, as if he's absorbing the weight of my pain. Then, without prompting, he shares his own story. "My family... I love my parents, but they were never really there for me once I became a teenager. After a fight with my sister's boyfriend that turned physical, they kind of cut me off. They moved away, leaving me here on the Cay. My dad, especially. He couldn't handle me. I guess I was always 'too much', you know?" He smiles, but it's a sad, broken thing, filled with unspoken wounds. In that instant, while Timmy is certainly 'a lot' at times, I vow to never exacerbate his wound by telling him he's too much. I feel protective of him, defensive of anyone who would make him relive how those relationships made him feel. "That's why I haven't been speaking with them lately," he explains. "Well, that, and because my mother refuses to stop speaking to my ex."

The connection between us deepens in this moment, a shared understanding of hurt and loss. It feels like we're two broken people who have finally found the other person who can help to make us whole again. I feel free, open to be vulnerable. There's no judgment, no impatience—just tenderness and empathy.

I wipe my eyes and look at him, grateful for his presence. "Thank you for listening, for caring. And for sharing with me, too. It means so much."

He smiles at me softly and leans forward to kiss my forehead, although his eyes are still clouded with emotion. "I care about every-thing that makes you you," he says, his voice gentle but sure. "Every little thing. Just like I care about every one of your freckles."

I smile, feeling a little lighter. God, this man is everything.

"I've never been able to talk like this with a partner before, to speak in a way that's raw, and have someone really understand and reciprocate."

Timmy's expression hardens for a moment, almost imperceptibly, before it softens again.

He leans in closer, swiping a stray lock of hair off my face. "Well, those people were all idiots. You're so kind and sweet and you've been through so much," he says, his voice deep and reassuring. "I can't imagine not knowing everything about you. I'm here, Margaux, and I want to hear it all. You never have to hold back with me."

It's like a weight lifts off my shoulders. For the first time, I feel truly safe. I tell him more—about the nights when I wake up from nightmares screaming, drenched in sweat, the memories of the assault clawing at me, leaving me breathless. I tell him about how scared I am sometimes, how fragile I feel when those moments hit me. How I know I've made so much progress, but those setbacks have me reeling and it feels like I'm backsliding every now and then. And Timmy listens intently, nodding, squeezing my hand, his face a picture of compassion.

He starts sharing again, too, but his stories are different. Vague. "I've lost people, too," he says. "And been hurt by others." He glances away, as if the memory is too painful to hold eye contact over. "The ones who have passed... friends, family, people close to me. I keep little things to remember them by, like this quilt." He gestures to an old, threadbare stitched blanket on the chair. "It's falling apart and covered in stains that I can't get out, but it means the world to me. It's all I have left."

I reach out to touch the quilt, feeling the worn fabric beneath my fingers, taking care not to knock one of the patchwork triangles that's hanging by a thread next to an unknown mark that looks a bit like ketchup. "That's beautiful," I say softly, but something nags at the back of my mind. He's mentioning friends and family, but not by name. "Who gave it to you?"

He hesitates, his eyes distant. "A friend. Someone you don't know. It's not important." He smiles, but this time, for some reason, it feels more like a mask. "What matters is that I have it."

The conversation shifts, and he talks about other trinkets he's kept that he holds dear. A couple of rings another unnamed friend gave him when he helped her to move, a small foil baby shark balloon that he claims holds sentimental value as it starts to sag as the helium deflates out of it. He's emotional about these objects, tears welling in his eyes as he talks about how important they are to him. But he leaves it at that, seemingly preferring not to go deeper.

Still, I don't press. It's enough that he's sharing. He's being vulnerable in his own way. He doesn't need to tell me everything, and if he wants to, he will in his own time. We're a safe space for each other now.

It's so freeing, like I can finally truly breathe. That I have a partner to share in my joy, my pain, and my mess—our mess, now. I drown in the sweetness of his attention, in the idea that I've finally found someone who gets me. Someone who cares.

He makes me feel so safe.

He makes me feel so seen.

It's the two things I've craved all my life.

When I've been abandoned by nearly everyone, he's just what I need. Kind, attentive, a protector who also makes me laugh—and he's cute. Every insecurity I have is something he *loves* about me.

Every fucking thing.

When I was younger, I felt like I had a true love, a soulmate waiting in the wings, somewhere, somehow. I believed it was in my cards. That hope had faded over the years, like it was just a silly thing, a nice concept that doesn't actually exist. But now I have Timmy.

And I have never ever felt such pure joy.

25

STARFISH... BUT NOT THE COOL KIND

Over the next few days, Timmy is always here—everywhere I go, every waking second, and then next to me when I sleep. He wants to be part of everything I do, every little errand or mundane task.

"I'll come with you," he says every time I suggest running out to the grocery store.

He insists on driving me to the post office rather than having me walk all that way, even though I love the exercise. I've never had someone want to accompany me on *every* errand before. With others, they were always happy to let me go off by myself to tackle whatever tasks they felt were boring—now, it's the exact opposite. And while it's a little smothering at times, there's something about it that makes me feel special—like I'm the center of Timmy's universe.

Consciously, I know that it's not *normal* to have someone want to spend 24/7 with you. People need space, right? At least, that's always what I've been told. But at the same time, it feels... really nice. Knowing I mean so much to someone that they want to be with me every second of the day. It's flattering... almost intoxicating.

But sometimes, when I do manage to slip out on a solo errand, I feel this tiny spark of relief. I get onto the sidewalk, and crank my music on my headphones as loud as I can, and for a brief moment, I'm just *me* again, alone with my thoughts. Part of me wants to keep walking for hours... to run... the wind whipping through my hair, belting out the lyrics to songs he doesn't like, or listening to one of my podcasts that he'd probably find boring. I let myself imagine it—just me, lost in my own world, free.

But then, that feeling fades. Because as soon as I picture him, waiting for me with that cheeky grin, I feel an odd sense of guilt for even wanting a sliver of time apart. I think of how cozy it is to sit beside him all day, curled up on the bed, his hand brushing against mine as he turns to me and whispers sweet things.

I've never been with someone who wanted this level of closeness, this much intimacy, day in and day out. Timmy talks about our future with such passion, weaving dreams of what our life will look like. "We'll get a little house, just the two of us, and I'll design everything. You can write all day in peace. We'll have a beautiful garden with exotic plants, and we'll grow our own vegetables. We'll have a state-of-the-art grill, and even a little pizza oven beside our fire pit. Doesn't that sound perfect?" His voice is soothing, painting a picture so vivid that I can almost see it—this future we're building together.

He talks about his graphic design work with such enthusiasm, creativity pouring out of him, and he loves listening to me talk about my writing, encouraging me at every step. It's like he's always right there beside me, helping me envision this life we're working towards.

It's what I've always wanted. Someone who's just as invested in our future as I am. Someone who's as affectionate and loyal as I've always craved. So how could I say no?

But sometimes, it's a little... much. Like when I go to the bathroom, and he just walks in. No knocking, no asking, he's just there. "What?! I missed you!" he'll say, as if it's no big deal. I'll be peeing or showering, and he'll just wander in, like my personal space doesn't exist. He'll watch me shower, a cheeky gleam in his eyes, and it's not uncommon for him to bundle me up in one of the fluffy lilac towels and hoist me over his shoulder, carrying me to the bed for more earth-shattering sex which will no doubt result in me needing yet another shower.

And when I pee, he yells 'Starfish!' And pretends he wants to pee while I am as well, aiming just in front of me into the bowl. One time I even let him do it, and he cackles as his pee sloshes from the bowl and splashes me on my leg. Gross!

At first, his constant attentiveness and random bathroom appearances make me laugh. "Timmy!" I'd say, playfully pushing him away. But now it's just part of our routine. He's *always* there, whether I want him to be or not. And while part of me feels a little suffocated by it, another part of me finds it... sweet? Endearing, even.

Because when he holds me, it's like I'm wrapped in something warm and fluffy—like a cloud, or maybe a delicious croissant. Something soft, comforting, and buttery.

His arms around me feel safe, like a cocoon I never want to leave. And when he looks into my eyes, I see a tenderness there, a kind soul who truly wants to spend every moment with me. It's flattering, honestly. I feel cherished in a way I never have before, like I'm the most important person in the world to him.

I've never been good at balancing closeness and space. As a stubborn Taurus with a streak of codependency and an anxious attachment style, I'm all in when it comes to relationships. So maybe this is what love is supposed to feel like. Maybe this constant closeness, this 24/7 connection, is just part of being with someone who truly cares. It's not like he's doing anything wrong. I guess it could seem like he's keeping tabs on me, but I get the feeling he just... wants to be with me. And isn't that a good thing?

Still, there's a small voice in the back of my mind, whispering that I might need more space. That it's okay to want to do things on my own sometimes. But when I think of him, how much he loves me, how much he wants to be around me, I brush the thought away.

Because who am I to say no to someone who loves me this much —who makes me feel this special, this needed?

26

STEVE THE HORSE COP

he Next Day
"Let's go for a drive around the coast! There's so much I want to show you."

Timmy's voice is bubbling with excitement, and I can't help but smile. This trip feels like a redemption arc for me too. Last time I visited Sunset Cay, it was with my ex, and the memory is less about the coastline's beauty and more about his relentless complaining. I'd planned a scenic drive just like this, eager to explore hidden beaches and charming roadside cafes. To show him places where I had fond memories with my parents, back in happier times. But my ex ruined the day, saying it was a waste of time to sit in a car when we could be drinking by a pool. That day trip ended in a fight that tainted every stop we made.

Now, though, Timmy's excitement is infectious. The way he talks about the beaches and surf spots, it's clear he loves this place with every ounce of his chaotic heart. I watch him gear up for the day, throwing on a Superman cape, a bold USA flag cap, and his deer claw necklace. He looks ridiculous—and perfect, in his own way. That's Timmy. Always a spectacle, always unapologetically himself.

As we hit the road, I feel like I'm reclaiming the experience I wanted on my last vacation here. The palm trees sway over the road as we drive past packed beaches and quaint coastal neighborhoods, the kind of scenery I've always dreamed of living in. And now, somehow, I do. I pull out my phone to record short videos and take pictures, thinking how surreal it all feels.

"This place is so gorgeous," I say, glancing at Timmy. "You know what we should do? We should make a TikTok account. Share our adventures."

He grins, his eyes lighting up. "Like a podcast?"

I laugh. "More like short videos. Reels and stuff. We could capture the fun, you know? I bet people would love it."

"Hell yeah!" He bounces in his seat. "I've got a few ideas for pranks that would make people laugh."

It feels good, this shared excitement—this sense that we're building something fun together, moment by moment.

We make several stops along the coast, and at one point, Timmy pulls into a small farm surrounded by swaying fields and distant mountains. "I just need a minute," he says, hopping out of the truck. "A friend of mine's in the hospital, and his neighbors are watching the farm. I want to check in and see if they need help."

While he talks to a woman near the fence, I watch him from the car, marveling at how well-connected he is. Timmy seems to know everyone, and not just in a casual way—he genuinely cares about these people. It's one of the things that draws me to him, even if his eccentricity can be overwhelming at times. He's like a patchwork quilt of wild, messy kindness.

When he slides back into the driver's seat, he's still animated. "I really want you to meet Steve," he says as we pull back onto the road. "He's one of my best friends, and has been since we were kids. Always got my back."

"What does he do?"

"He's a park ranger on another island. Pretty cool job—he works on horseback. Steve the Horse Cop, we call him. His family's over there, but when he's off, he stays with his parents here."

I like the sound of Steve. From the way Timmy describes him, he seems grounded, a stabilizing presence in Timmy's otherwise unpredictable world. It's reassuring. Maybe Timmy has his wild streak, but if a guy like Steve is still in his life after all these years, it suggests Timmy knows how to keep some things steady when it matters.

But as we get closer to Steve's place, Timmy's mood shifts. He stops to grab a bottle of Fireball and downs some of it on the road, his energy morphing into something more volatile.

"You're a shit DJ," he snaps at one point, swiping the phone from my hand when I can't find a song he requested quick enough for his liking. "Just give it to me. You fucking suck at this."

His words hit like a slap. "I'm really sorry," I mutter, feeling the sting rise in my throat.

He scoffs. "Don't quit your day job."

Tears well up, and I fight to keep them at bay. "Are you crying?" he asks, his voice sharp.

"No," I whisper, biting my lip.

By the time we reach the estuary where Steve is waiting, I feel like I've been emotionally whipped around. I wipe at my face, trying to salvage what I can of my makeup before we step out of the truck. Steve greets me with a polite smile, and we exchange a hug.

Timmy, barefoot and buzzing with energy, immediately runs off to feed the ducks, leaving me with Steve. I can't help but ask, "Is he always like this?"

Steve shrugs. "He's a lot. I've known him since we were kids, and I can only take him in small doses." His eyes lock onto mine, serious now. "Maybe you should do the same."

His words linger, a subtle warning I can't ignore. Coming from anyone else, I'd dismiss it. But Steve's got that quiet, measured way about him. He's a cop—or close enough, as a ranger—and there's a gravity to his words that makes me listen.

"Well, I'm an all-or-nothing person," I say, putting on a bright smile. "So I guess I'm fucked."

I can't shake what Steve said, even as I rationalize it away, settling in my mind like a splinter. But Timmy told me himself—he has moody days driven by his mood disorder. Maybe this is just one of them.

And what we have is special. Timmy isn't perfect, but he's mine. He's everything I've been missing: affectionate, funny, protective, creative, and intensely loving. Our sex life is incredible, and the way he makes me feel seen—really seen—is unlike anything I've ever experienced.

Steve might think he knows Timmy, but I see a different side of him. Steve isn't living in the moments when Timmy holds me close, kisses my forehead, and makes me laugh until I can't breathe. Steve doesn't see the guy who curls up next to me at night, all snuggly warmth and whispered promises.

Timmy's rough around the edges, sure, but that's part of his charm. And the parts that aren't charming? We'll work on those. He cares enough to try, and that's all I need.

BACK AT MY APARTMENT, the tension melts away. I slip into something comfortable and set up my influencer post with the sex wedge, feeling more at ease now that we're home.

Then I see the email—and my heart leaps.

Sabre's rabies results are in. The quarantine station has approved his release, three months early.

"Oh my god!" I whisper, a wave of relief crashing over me. My baby is coming home. Soon, I'll have Sabre with me, and everything will finally feel right. The quarantine facility is really nice, but I still feel guilty thinking about my affectionate little boy sitting there day after day, all by himself.

Timmy notices my excitement. "What's up?"

"Sabre's coming home early!" I beam at him, and he grins back, the day's tension already forgotten.

We stop by Matty's later, where Timmy poses with his fingers like devil horns above his head for a few goofy photos. As I snap the shots, I feel that familiar warmth return. Timmy is chaotic and unpredictable—but he's also mine.

But in the corner of my heart, a small knot of unease tightens. And I know that something in this picture—this strange, chaotic love—might be bigger than me.

27

BAD GUY

The night buzzes with energy, the kind that makes your skin prickle with anticipation. There's some type of event on the main street that runs down the length of the beach, transforming the vibrant tourist hub into a carnival of sound and color. Food trucks line the sidewalks, filling the air with the mouthwatering scent of grilled meats, sweet fried dough, and spicy sauces. Live music spills from every corner—a blend of reggae, surf rock, and acoustic ballads. Crowds ebb and flow, clusters of friends laughing, even some couples dancing, and strangers embracing the freedom of a warm, coastal night in Sunset Cay.

"I know you love people watching," Timmy says, smiling as he watches me take it all in. "Come on," he says, playfully grabbing my hand. "Let's grab some little bottles of Fireball, and then I have the perfect place for us to sit."

As usual, his spontaneity thrills me. I never know what's coming next with him, but it always feels exciting—like a never-ending adventure. We duck into a nearby convenience store and grab a few flight bottles of Fireball.

He grabs my hand and tugs me back toward the main street, toward a large utility box, its dark green surface weathered by the salt air. "Come on," he says, crouching to give me a boost, hoisting me up onto it before jumping up himself. We're higher up than most people, and can see everything going on in both directions. It feels like we're perched on top of the world.

From here, the street unfurls in both directions—waves of people, the glow of string lights, and the music drifting on the breeze. The view is exhilarating, like we're part of the crowd but above it at the same time. Timmy cracks open one of the little bottles of Fireball and hands it to me. The cinnamon whiskey burns down my throat, filling me with a giddy warmth that makes everything shimmer a little brighter.

He drapes his arm around me, pulling me close, and kisses me on the side of my head. "Isn't this amazing? I love you so much," he murmurs against my ear, his voice low and sincere.

It's moments like this—when he's spontaneous, adventurous and affectionate—that make me feel like I've found *my person*. He brings out a side of me that I didn't know existed—one that craves fun and freedom, that feels carefree and uninhibited. With him, it's like anything is possible.

I feel a bit like a naughty school kid sitting up here. But what's the worst that can happen? Someone asks us to hop back down from the utility box? No big deal at all. This is just silly, innocent fun. And I want to hold on to this feeling for as long as I can.

We sit quietly for a while, content, just enjoying the buzz around us.

Then his voice drops to a growl. "We're going to go home and fuck now."

The bluntness of his words sends a thrill through me.

I love the way he's so direct about sex, so matter-of-fact and sex-positive. His confidence is intoxicating, a far cry from my ex who could barely say the words 'sex' or 'fuck' without blushing. In any case, Timmy's openness makes me feel alive, as if I'm gradually shedding my inhibitions. I wonder if old me—before I started reading and writing dark romance—would have been able to handle someone like him. Now, though, I find myself grinning.

"Well, that sounds good," I reply, biting my lip. "But we need to go to the store first. We've run out of condoms." The way we've been fucking, we're single-handedly boosting the condom economy.

Timmy groans, rolling his eyes with playful exasperation. "Do we really need to get more? Can't we do it without?"

A flicker of unease creeps in, but I push it aside. "No, we need to get some more," I insist, keeping my voice light but firm.

He lets out a theatrical sigh. "Fine then, let's go." He helps me down from the utility box, and I laugh as I stumble slightly as I make my landing. Then he leads me to a convenience store where I buy an overpriced pack of condoms. Timmy's fun and spontaneous, but he wouldn't push me to do something I'm not comfortable with.

THE MOMENT we step back into my apartment, Timmy undresses with the urgency of someone starving for touch. His clothes hit the floor in a heap, and he's already pulling me close, his hands everywhere all at once.

"We should do it without a condom," he murmurs against my neck, his voice rough and persuasive.

The unease returns, stronger this time. "I don't feel comfortable doing that yet," I say, trying to keep my tone light.

"Come on," he pleads, sliding his massive hands over my hips. "We need to. I told you I got tested recently. We'll be fine."

I hesitate, caught between wanting to please him and wanting to honor my own comfort. "I don't know," I say. "I'd rather not yet."

"Oh, come on," he pleads. "It'll feel so much better and I'll feel so much closer to you. It'll be great for both of us."

"No, I don't feel comfortable doing that yet," I say. I always feel awkward having this conversation, but it's important and I stick to my guns.

His face tightens with frustration. "Come on, it'll be fine," he says, and before I can react, he shoves his cock into me.

The shock of it knocks the air from my lungs, and for a moment, I don't know how to respond.

But he does feel really good inside me.

Letting him slam his massive cock into me, every thrust feels like a badge of honor, a war between pleasure and discomfort, pain and desire. My body aches under the force of him, but there's something exhilarating about how much he wants me, about the way he's looking at me like I'm the answer to every need he has.

"Jesus, Margaux," he groans, his hands gripping my hips like a lifeline, as if he's putting his full two hundred pounds into every thrust as he slams into me with full force. "You're letting me fuck you so fucking hard."

The praise sends a wave of warmth through me, my body responding even as my mind wrestles with the unease. His words sink deep into the parts of me that crave validation, and I feel myself clench around him.

After a while, it starts to feel uncomfortable, like my cervix is about to be dislodged, but it's that line between pleasure and pain, and I feel like I'm making him incredibly happy. "You're so fucking amazing, Margaux, taking my massive cock like this."

I feel a swell of pride, my praise kink continuing to kick in.

He groans, "good fucking girl," and I almost come around his cock.

His balls slam against me, and I feel little shivers radiating throughout my body. It's not an orgasm, but it feels so fucking good, and I lose myself in the moment. My limbs feel numb as he holds my hips so tightly I know it's going to leave bruises.

No one has ever fucked me so passionately, so violently, before.

"You're my good little fucking slut, you know that?" he growls, and his words hit me like a drug. I never knew I liked being talked to like this, but here I am, melting beneath his filthy praise.

My pussy clenches harder around his cock. "Yes, Timmy," I whisper. "I'm your dirty fucking slut."

He thrusts harder, his breath ragged. "And you're all mine, my little whore."

"Yes," I pant. "I'm your little whore."

The words unlock something within me—something wild and free, something I didn't know was buried deep inside. With each thrust, I feel myself letting go, surrendering to the moment as if I'm just a vessel here to serve his pleasure.

"Jesus, Margaux. You're so incredible," he says afterwards, as we lay entangled in each other's arms, still panting from the exertion. "Nobody's ever let me fuck them that hard," he murmurs, a note of awe in his voice. "You took that so well. My cock is huge, and I was really slamming into you."

"Yes, baby," I smile up at him, basking in the glow of his words. "That felt so good. You're amazing."

He leans down to kiss me on the forehead.

Later, he's still buzzing. "Margaux, I still can't believe how fucking insane that sex was. You're incredible. Your pussy is incredible. It's definitely the best sex I've ever had. And your blowjobs? Oh my god, also definitely the best."

I beam with pride and agreement, my pussy still tingling from earlier. "Yeah. Your cock is the best, too. That was some amazing sex."

Despite the praise, the knot in my stomach lingers. I try to ignore it, to focus on the pleasure humming through my body. But something about the way he pushed past my boundary gnaws at me, an uncomfortable truth I don't want to face.

"We'd better be careful, though," he says earnestly. "At this rate, I'm worried my dick's going to fall off from how much we're fucking."

"Well, neither of us wants that to happen." I laugh, but it feels hollow.

I want to believe what just happened is okay because we're in love, and he would never hurt me. But part of me knows something isn't right. I told him no, and he didn't listen.

I wish he would have been a bit more respectful and taken no for an answer. And it's not like I was denying him completely, even though that would have been my prerogative to do so. I was just asking him to wear a condom. It feels like he's putting his own pleasure or enjoyment over what I've expressed is important to me.

"See, didn't that feel way better? Your pussy was great before, but it's so much better this way."

I give a quick smile. "Yeah, it did feel really good."

He's not wrong. I push the thought away. *It's fine. Everything's fine.*

The sex was incredible. I just would have preferred he respected my boundaries a little more, that's all.

But even as I tell myself this, the uneasy knot refuses to untangle, sitting heavy in my chest like a truth I'm not ready to confront.

28

TALOFA

ater that evening

We get ready and head to Timmy's friend's club. It's been years since I've set foot in a nightclub, let alone an EDM one. Back on the East Coast, I'd only gone to a couple, and even then, the relentless bass, the swirling lights, and the pulsating crowd felt overwhelming. But I'm in Timmy's world now, and I'm willing to give it a go.

On the way over, Timmy brags about the club owner, Romeo—a supposed childhood friend turned prominent drug dealer and nightlife kingpin of Sunset Cay. The whole story feels off. From what I've gathered, Romeo is at least ten or fifteen years older than Timmy, making it hard to imagine them as schoolmates. I brush it off for now, though—the way Timmy talks, half of what he says sounds like it's been exaggerated or warped into legend.

He tells me, with unsettling pride, how he has access to an endless supply of drugs through Romeo. "Everyone in the club knows me," he says, puffing his chest out. "I've even danced so long that once I dragged a couch onto the dancefloor and slept right there. People just danced around me—and when I woke up, a bunch of people were stroking my body."

I laugh awkwardly, not knowing whether to be amused or disturbed. He takes it further, though.

"And I've always got to jerk off, like, three times before I go to the club. Otherwise, I'll, like, come in my pants on the dance floor. It's so stimulating. All the girls in their rave outfits."

That part makes me squirm, and I can't even hide it. "That's... a lot, Timmy. Why would you say that to me?"

He just shrugs, like over-sharing is second nature to him. "Girls there all want me, but I've never taken any of them home. It's just dancing. It's a vibe. They're all going to be so jealous of you." I guess I feel relieved that he's not known for taking all the girls home.

By the time we pull up to the club—an unmarked building hidden down a nondescript side street—I'm not sure what I've gotten myself into. The place looks nothing like a nightclub from the outside, designed to look more like a storage facility or some kind of office. A group of bouncers loiter near the entrance, adjusting their earpieces and sharing low conversations as they prepare for the night.

Without missing a beat, Timmy marches straight toward them, radiating the confidence of someone who thinks he's royalty. "Let's go," he says, tugging my hand.

The lead bouncer, a broad guy with tattooed arms, steps in front of him. "Whoa, slow down. We're not open yet, man. You can't come in."

Timmy puffs up, his posture almost comically self-important. "I know Romeo. I'm good."

The bouncers exchange glances, one of them visibly rolling his eyes. "Okay, buddy. Still not open."

Timmy scowls and pulls out his phone, shooting me an annoyed look, as if this minor inconvenience is a personal attack. "I'll call Romeo."

I stand there awkwardly while Timmy dials, feeling the heavy weight of the bouncers' judgment. I'm starting to wonder if Timmy even knows Romeo that well—or if this whole thing is just another one of his exaggerated tales. But to my surprise, after a brief phone exchange, Timmy hands the phone over to one of the security guys.

After a few terse words with Romeo, the bouncer hands the phone back, muttering, "Alright, you're in."

Timmy shoots me a triumphant grin, but it's clear the bouncers are not impressed. The tension between them and Timmy lingers in the air like a bad smell.

I notice one of the bouncers is wearing a cap from a Samoan clothing brand I recognize. The bad vibes between Timmy and the bouncers need defusing, so I step forward.

"Are you Samoan?" I ask, nodding toward his cap.

He gives me a curious glance, taking in my accent. "Yep."

"Oh nice! Talofa! I'm from New Zealand."

His face brightens, and just like that, the energy shifts. We chat for a moment, exchanging friendly words about home, and the heaviness between us dissolves. The other bouncers relax a little, more smiles now, and we slip inside, finally past the awkwardness.

The interior of the club is surprisingly cool. It's a cavernous, industrial space, with murals painted across the walls—giant, surreal figures outlined with neon, their features glowing under the black lights. It feels otherworldly, like stepping into a different dimension.

Timmy, still basking in his self-appointed VIP status, leads me by the hand through the dimly lit room. The DJ is setting up, testing some beats that pulse through the space like an electric heartbeat.

"This is my spot," Timmy says with a grin, looking around like he owns the place. "I'm, like, a legend here."

He breaks away from me to start dancing, slipping easily into a shuffle dance that's surprisingly good. I drop onto one of the couches along the wall and watch him. He's fully in his element, spinning, gliding, and twisting with a grin plastered across his face, the whole dance floor to himself. And even though I want to roll my eyes at how self-important he's been all night, I can't help but smile. There's something charming about how much fun he's having.

As people start to trickle in, the space slowly fills with energy. The music grows louder, the bass deeper, and the lights flash in hypnotic patterns.

I relax a little, reassured by the fact that Timmy's not seeking out drugs, or even alcohol, just enjoying his dancing and the ability to share this part of his life with me. The vibe is fun and light, and I start to think maybe I've been too judgmental. Maybe Timmy's world isn't as sketchy as it seemed.

~

WHEN WE FINALLY GET BACK TO my apartment, Timmy grabs his giant stuffed caterpillar—one of the many items he's moved over to my place from Matty's—and starts wiggling it from one end, making it ripple like a battle rope at the gym. I burst out laughing, the sight so absurd that I can't help myself.

My laugh echoes through the room, loud and unfiltered, but not *that* loud. Or at least, I didn't think so. But just a few minutes later, there's a knock at the door.

I open it to find the concierge standing there, an apologetic look on his face. "I'm sorry, but we got a noise complaint."

It's the third noise complaint we've had this week. I've never had noise complaints anywhere I've lived, and I honestly don't think we've been very loud at all.

I stare at him, stunned. "For *laughing*? We're not even listening to music."

He shrugs helplessly. "Apparently so."

I feel so deflated, like a schoolgirl being told off for something trivial. This building is starting to suck, with all these petty complaints—and they always seem to come from the leasing agent next door. She's had it out for me from day one, and it's starting to feel personal. So weird, considering she insisted I take the apartment beside her, not that I knew it at the time.

Timmy, now draped over the bed with the caterpillar on his chest, gives me a lazy grin. "Damn, babe. Your laugh is so powerful it causes complaints. That's kinda hot."

I roll my eyes but can't help smiling. It's ridiculous. All of it. But at least the night was fun—well, mostly.

As I sit back down, though, a flicker of unease returns. Timmy's world—this club scene, these strange connections—it feels exciting, sure, but there's also an edge to it. Like I'm brushing up against something dark, and I don't quite belong.

He behaved himself tonight, but his stories, his connections, his reckless confidence—it all hints at a life I'm not sure I can keep up with. It's fun, but it feels dangerous, too. Like I'm teetering on the edge of something I don't fully understand.

Maybe I'm overthinking it. Maybe I just need to relax, go with the flow.

But as I look at Timmy sprawled across my bed, grinning like the world is his playground, that nagging sense of being out of my depth lingers like a shadow I can't quite shake.

29

IF YOU THINK YOU LOOK GOOD TODAY, YOU SHOULD SEE ME

The Past

Mother: I have a fan club, you know.

Me: A... fan club?

Mother: Yes... so many men in this town would love to date me.

Me: But you're married... to dad?

Mother: Well, it's a nice confidence boost.

It's why you should always go out looking your best.

By the way, you need to get your eyelashes and eyebrows tinted.

Me: Why's that?

Mother: Well, yours are very pale. So you should get yours enhanced.

Or any man you're with will look at a woman who does.

~

THE PRESENT

The way Timmy looks at me makes me feel like the most beautiful woman in the world. When he says things like, "I love how your pale eyelashes make your eyes look soft, and then when you add makeup, they just pop—you're so naturally beautiful," it's not just generic flattery—it's specific to me. It's the kind of compliment that sinks deep into my bones. He notices me in ways that feel personal, like he's seeing me through a lens that nobody else has ever looked through.

I catch myself basking in it, craving his approval the way a plant craves sunlight. His praise is intoxicating. It pulls me closer into his orbit.

When I'm done getting ready, my hair neatly styled, my makeup subtle but enhancing, I emerge from the bathroom feeling confident. His eyes light up the moment he sees me.

"Damn, Marg. You're glowing." He lets out a low whistle, stepping closer. "Look at you, babe. That lip gloss is next level. By the way, whenever my exes used to wear that shit, I refused to kiss them." He plants a soft kiss on my lips, the sticky gloss gluing us together for a moment. "But with you, I love it. I still can't believe you're mine."

The warmth of his words fills me, melting away the edges of any lingering self-doubt, making me see myself through his lens, like a natural beauty.

But then his own reflection catches his eye, and just like that, his attention shifts. His grin turns playful as he straightens his posture and checks himself out in the mirror, adjusting his T-shirt.

"I look so cute, right? You see it, right? Look at my outfit. Everything matches perfectly." He turns to the side, tilting his chin up. "Come on, tell me. I look fucking great, don't I?"

I laugh, shaking my head. He's ridiculous. But part of me is a little startled by how much he needs to hear it, how he craves the same validation he gives me.

"You do look cute," I say, indulging him. "Very coordinated."

He grins. "Yeah, I know." Then his gaze sharpens, excitement bubbling to the surface. "Oh my gosh, babe—can you braid my hair? Please? Just two braids using the purple hair ties." He grabs two small sections of his hair, holding them where he wants the braids to go. "Forward, over my ears. Like this."

I laugh again, shaking my head. "You're a dork," I say, but there's a fondness in my voice.

"This is gonna look so good," he says with childlike enthusiasm. His eyes sparkle with joy, as if the simple act of braiding his hair will somehow complete his entire persona.

I fetch the soft lilac hair ties from the drawer and begin braiding his hair as requested. He sits, fidgeting slightly with excitement, while I weave the strands together.

"There we go," I say, securing the second braid.

He checks himself in the mirror, tugging on the ends of the braids to position them just right. Then he grabs a cap and places it on his head, angling it backward. "Perfect," he declares, grinning at his reflection.

It's fun. A part of me feels like I'm back in elementary school, sitting cross-legged on the playground, braiding a friend's hair. Timmy's playfulness is infectious. Being with him feels like an adventure, like we're two kids lost in our own world.

And maybe that's what this is—a secret world, just for us. A love bubble where nothing else matters but the way we make each other feel. A world where his quirky demands and strange antics are endearing instead of suffocating.

The way he makes me laugh, the way he feeds me little bites of food and tells me to blow on them so I don't burn my mouth—it's all so charming. Sweet, even. And when he holds me close, when he says, "You're everything I've ever wanted," it's hard to imagine a reality without him.

But there's a nagging feeling in the back of my mind, a knot of unease that tightens ever so slightly each time I think too hard about the ways he needs me. The way his validation seems to hinge on my constant attention. The way his excitement for us feels so all-consuming that it leaves no room for anyone else.

It's subtle, but I notice it more and more. How he seems happiest when it's just the two of us. How my world has quietly shrunk to fit inside the boundaries of his. Friends feel distant—whether by geography or by design, I'm not sure.

But Timmy fills the void so completely that I tell myself it doesn't matter.

This is what I wanted, right? Someone who sees me. Someone who loves me without hesitation. Someone who notices all the little things about me, the way I always wished someone would.

Maybe this is what real love feels like. Maybe the trade-off is worth it. Maybe a little isolation isn't such a bad thing, if it means I get to keep feeling this way. As long as I stay on his good side, as long as I keep things light and fun, everything will be okay.

Because when Timmy's happy, it's like the whole world is brighter. And when he looks at me like I'm the most beautiful thing he's ever seen, it's easy to forget everything else.

And so I smile back. I laugh at his jokes, braid his hair, and tell him how cute he looks in his cap and braids.

And for now, that's enough. It has to be.

30

OUT OF THE FRYING PAN

The next day, I take him for brunch at one of my favorite spots that I've visited before. It's owned by a celebrity chef who has appeared on a reality TV show.

We share a gorgeous plate of jidori chicken, as well as their famed hash browns, and a couple of brunch cocktails.

Timmy banters with the server, an alternative-looking guy with piercings and tattoos. He's friendly, and the conversation is funny. Then things get a little weird.

"I'm going to take this cast-iron frying pan when we leave," Timmy announces, indicating the dish on the table in front of us.

"Okay, do what you gotta do, man," says the server, his eyes widening as if Timmy just ordered a spaceship off the menu.

I think Timmy's joking, but as we pay up, he puts the frying pan down on his chair beside him. And when we go to leave, he picks it up and walks out with it.

"Timmy, what are you doing?" I whisper loudly. "You can't take that!"

"Shh," he says. "You should be grateful. I got this for your apartment."

"But it belongs to the restaurant!"

"They won't miss it," he rolls his eyes. "Besides, the server said we could keep it. He gave me permission to take it."

I think back to my time working in restaurants. "That's not really his decision to make, Timmy. And besides, I think he thought you were joking. I know I did."

He sighs as if I'm the most annoying drag ever. "Just be grateful, Margaux. I got you a frying pan for your apartment, for god's sake. Lighten up. You're always so uptight."

I shake off my apprehension as we drive to the beach, helped by it being a gorgeous day. The sky is turquoise, the ocean is teal, and the sand is a warm and toasty golden brown.

I watch as Timmy runs into the water and floats for a while.

The swimming time seems to lift his spirits again, and when he gets out of the water he's super affectionate. I feel relieved, and I'm over the whole frying pan scenario. I just want to have a nice day with Timmy.

~

I FEEL my cheeks blushing as I bend over in front of him, my heart pounding in anticipation. Timmy's voice is rough, commanding, and I can't help but comply as he growls at me to raise my ass high in the air and get down low on my forearms. I try to steady my breathing as I follow his instructions, my breasts hanging down, my pussy already slick with arousal and anticipation.

"Oh, look at you," he purrs, his voice low and dangerous. "You're all wet for me, aren't you?" he asks, his fingers trailing lightly up my inner thighs, sending shivers down my spine. "You must be thirsty for it, huh?"

I can't help but moan in response, my body betraying my need for him. His fingertips graze my swollen lips and I gasp, my hips bucking towards him involuntarily. "Such a naughty girl," he chuckles, his breath hot against my ear as he leans in close.

I feel his warm lips on my neck, trailing feather-light kisses down my spine, and I arch my back, my body begging for more. His tongue grazes my shoulder blade, and I moan again, my pussy clenching in anticipation of what's to come.

Then, without warning, his tongue is on me, licking broad, wet strokes from my wettest parts all the way up to my back entrance. I gasp, my hips bucking against him involuntarily as he laps at my ass, his tongue painting delicious, dirty circles around the sensitive opening.

"Let me in, baby," he groans, his voice muffled by my ass. "I know how much you love it."

"Yes," I whimper, my voice barely above a whisper. "I love it, Timmy. I want it so bad."

He chuckles and I feel him position himself, his fingers probing at my entrance, loosening me up for what's to come. "You're so tight, Margaux," he groans, his breaths coming in pants as he works me open. "God, I need to taste you."

And then, his tongue is inside me, invading my most private of places, licking and worshipping every last inch of me. My moans fill the room, my fingers digging into the sheets as I elevate onto my tiptoes, giving him better access. His tongue is relentless, probing my forbidden entrance while his fingers work magic on my aching clit.

"Oh fuck, Timmy!" I moan, my hips bucking against him as my orgasm builds. "I'm so close, baby. Don't stop."

But he does stop, withdrawing his fingers and tongue with a wet, loud sound, leaving me aching and wanting more. I whine in protest, my body convulsing with need.

"I know what you want, baby," he says, his voice a low growl in my ear. "But first, I want to see you come apart on my cock."

Slowly, he pulls me up until I'm straddling him, my back to his chest. His cock, hard and throbbing, presses against my entrance. "Ride it, Margaux," he growls in my ear, running his hands over my breasts, squeezing them roughly. "Show me how much you want it."

I don't need any more encouragement. With a moan, I lower myself onto him, inch by agonizing inch. His girth stretches me, sending blissful pain coursing through my body. I bite my lip, both to muffle my moans and to focus on the pleasure and pain that engulf me. When he's all the way inside, our bodies flush against each other, I throw my head back and moan in ecstasy.

"Oh fuck, Margaux," Timmy groans, his hands gripping my hips. "You feel so good, so fucking tight."

In response, I start moving my hips, grinding against him, taking him deep within me and then pulling away, only to repeat the motion again and again. He moans, his breathing ragged in my ear, spurring me on to go faster, harder.

"That's it, baby," he pants, his grip on my hips tightening. "Ride me, Margaux. Fuck, you feel so good."

His dirty talk sends me over the edge, and my orgasm builds in my core, tightening my muscles around him. "Timmy," I moan, my voice breathless. "I'm... I'm..."

"That's right, baby," he growls, his thrusts matching my rhythm. "Come for me, Margaux. Let go."

At his command, I do just that, my body shuddering and convulsing around him as I climax, my juices soaking his cock.

Timmy groans, his body tensing, and then with a final thrust, he spills his seed within me, our moans intermingling in the dark, air-conditioned room.

Afterward, panting and spent, I collapse against his chest, my back pressed against his sweaty torso. His arms wrap around me, holding me close. "That was...," I start to say, but I can't find the words to describe the intensity of the moment we just shared.

"I know," he whispers, kissing my hair. "It's just the beginning, Margaux. There's so much more where that came from."

And as we lie here, tangled in each other's arms, I believe him.

Timmy's words echo in my head as I catch my breath, my body still tingling with the aftermath of my orgasm. I can't believe how much I enjoyed reverse cowgirl. The way he'd filled me up, stretching me to my limits, had been both thrilling and overwhelming in the best possible way.

He must sense my thoughts because he gently nudges me. "Ready for more, Margaux?" he asks, his voice a low growl in my ear.

I turn around to face him, my hair cascading over my shoulder as

I straddle him. He's already hard again, his cock jutting out from his body, thick and throbbing. I run my fingertips along his length, teasingly, making him moan.

"I want you to fuck me doggy style," I purr, my confidence soaring. "I want to feel you deep inside me from behind, Timmy."

His eyes darken, his pupils dilating with desire. "Oh, baby, I've been waiting for you to say that."

He places one of the sex wedges on the corner of the bed, then rolls me over onto my stomach, my belly pressed against the cool, soft pillow. My heart pounds in anticipation as he spreads my legs apart, positioning himself at my entrance.

I arch my back, offering myself up to him, and, with one swift thrust, he enters me. Then he moves my legs back together so that my pussy squeezes even more tightly around his incredible cock.

"God, Margaux," he groans, his hips working me in a rhythm that borders on punishing yet oh so delicious. "You feel so good, so tight."

I grip the sheets, my moans muffled by the pillow as he pounds into me relentlessly. It doesn't take long before the familiar sensation of ecstasy begins to build again, coiling low in my belly, threatening to break free.

"I'm...I'm..." I pant, my body tense with pleasure.

"That's it, baby," he encourages, his grip on my hips bruising, but in the best way possible. "Come for me, Margaux."

And with those final words, I shatter into a million pieces, my orgasm ripping through me, taking Timmy with me as he groans his own release, collapsing on top of me, both of us panting and spent.

We lay there, entangled in each other's arms, for what feels like hours. And in this moment, all I can think about is how glad I am to have trusted my instincts and given in to this electric connection between us.

As we catch our breath, Timmy kisses my neck, his breath hot against my skin. "I can't wait to see what other boundaries we can push together."

I turn my head to look at him, a sultry smile playing on my lips, "Trust me, Timmy, this is only the beginning..."

And as our gazes interlock, I know we're both thinking the same thing: this is just the start of something intense, passionate, and utterly consuming.

The rest of the day is really chill and fun. We spend most of it naked, cuddling each other.

At one point, we put clothing on and walk down to the boardwalk and check out some surf shops. I laugh as Timmy picks up an ornamental conch shell in one of the stores, and blows it. People gasp and look over in delight. Just another quirky thing that Timmy knows how to do.

Later, we return to my apartment, and I drift off to sleep, safe and content in Timmy's strong arms, our bodies entwined, our hearts beating as one.

I'm glad I just shut up about the frying pan and let the rest of the day move along happily. Still, I really don't like that he took it.

But for now, I'll enjoy the sensations of my body and the memories we made, and I'll worry about the rest another day.

31

KIND OR CALCULATED

The next day, Timmy has more fun plans for us.

I can't believe this is only day four or five of my time in Sunset Cay. We've already done so much together. What a whirlwind start to my time here!

He has a few work errands to do, so we stop by the hardware store and I pick up some things for my apartment.

He takes me to a couple of tourist destinations and we walk around a big clock tower and look at a pirate ship from a distance. I snap photos as we chat and laugh, and his company is a pleasant distraction from a couple of work emails that threaten to ruin my day. I still can't believe I'm not going to be working for anyone else in just a few days. Technically, I'm on the clock now, but they don't expect me to do more than check a few emails here and there.

"They were lucky to have you, and the people who made that decision sound stupid." Timmy smiles at me, tenderly stroking the hair from in front of my face. "They're going to feel it when you're gone, for sure. But that's okay, because now you'll have a ton more time to spend with me!"

"I will be writing, though," I frown. "Like, it has to be something I treat as a real, full-time job."

"And I'll support you every step of the way," he smiles, placing his hand on my lower back. He makes me feel safe and secure, reassured, with even the most simple of gestures. How lucky I am to have met this incredible human.

Later in the day, he has a few hours of work to do. So while he tends to a condo renovation, I go to one of my favorite local bars for a martini while I get some writing done.

The bartender makes me the wrong one, thinking I want some sickly sweet concoction instead of their signature olive brine-infused dry option, and I end up with two martinis. I decide to take one for the team and enjoy them both.

The setting is inspiring, a cute little bar tucked inside a trendy hotel with a pool right in the middle of their lobby. It's art deco and vibey, and sitting there people-watching inspires me through a few chapters.

I feel warm and fuzzy by the end of the second martini, and as I take my last sip, Timmy texts me to let me know he's done with work. I settle my check and wander back to my apartment, feeling light and free and like everything is exactly how it's meant to be.

Later that evening

"Don't look!" he says. "Just keep watching the show!"

"Okay," I grin. I'm tempted to sneak a peek as I hear him rustling around behind me, but I resist the urge and keep my gaze on the screen.

"Surprise!" he says, grinning from ear to ear as he stands in front of me, his hands spread wide like he's just unveiled a masterpiece. "I know moving and getting things set up can be stressful, so I wanted to make this feel even more like home for you!" His tone is warm and gentle. I blink, taking it all in.

Everything is perfectly arranged—while the apartment isn't exactly inspiring based on its layout—a narrow rectangle—he's managed to make it look like something out of a design magazine.

I thought the initial setup he'd done had been pretty amazing, but there were still a lot of items to find homes for, and he's done it so I don't need to worry.

The bed is still positioned just right to catch the soft light of sunrise through the window, now with a cozy throw draped elegantly over the end. The pillows are positioned to create a fluffy backrest so that the bed can serve as a couch, and the stuffed animals have been positioned across them thoughtfully, as if they're acting out a scene. Even my books have been meticulously organized on a side table, almost like an artful display of who I am.

"Oh wow, this is amazing!" I say, my heart swelling with gratitude. I can't believe how thoughtful he's been. Every detail, from the throw pillows to the neatly organized kitchen counters and drawers, seems to have been planned with me in mind. It feels like he's gone out of his way to make the space perfect. "I don't even know what to say... thank you!" I turn to him, beaming, and he leans down for a kiss.

"You can show me," he growls, grinning, and my pussy clenches.

There's a momentary flicker of something in his eyes—something so subtle I figure I'm imagining it. "I just want to make sure every-thing's just right for you here. I know it's much more calming to have things uncluttered and less chaotic. You've mentioned having your friends help you set up apartments before, and I know you're far away from everyone you know, except me. This way, you don't have to worry about it. I really enjoyed doing this for you." His words are kind and reassuring, but there's a subtle weight behind them, as if he's done me a favor I now owe him for.

I'm too busy marveling at how perfect everything looks, how at home I feel in this space, to think too much of it. But over the next few days, little comments begin to slip into our conversations. "I spent hours organizing your apartment, you know," he says casually, a hint of pride in his voice. "It's probably better if we keep things how they are. I thought about putting it there, but the way I set it up is better..." And whenever I reach to rearrange something, even the tiniest amount, he'll appear out of nowhere, gently placing his large hand on mine, saying, "Don't you like it the way I have it set up? The way I arranged things is better. I put a lot of thought into it."

At first, I brush it off, still basking in how kind it was of him to have done all this for me. Lending me his mattress, taking me shopping, arranging everything so I didn't have to worry about it. But slowly, it's becoming clear that this isn't just about helping me. The apartment, this space that was supposed to be mine, has somehow become a reflection of him—his tastes, his control, his influence. The entire bathroom is covered in soft lilac towels and bathmats and poufs, because that's Timmy's favorite color. The kitchen is covered in odd trinkets I never would have picked out for myself. And the bed, the center of it all, is festooned in the ugly quilt that holds sentimental value to him, covering up the much brighter, more fun, more *me* duvet cover that we'd picked out at the store.

What I had thought was an incredibly thoughtful gesture has strings attached, invisible at first, but now tightening around me. And yet, part of me still feels guilty for even thinking that way, as if I'm being ungrateful for all that he's done.

I realize I've mistaken his grandiose gestures of kindness for generosity and altruism, not seeing that it was always about Timmy —his need to control, to claim the space as his own while making it seem like he was doing it all for me.

It's not my home, it's his stage, and I'm just the audience, dazzled by yet another of his performances.

32

DERELICT MANCHILD

he Next Day

We walk over to Timmy's truck, which is parked on the bustling street that lines Sandspit Passage, a busy canal that cuts right through the heart of the resort strip. He grabs his giant coconut hat from the back, plopping it on his head with a grin as he spins around to face me.

"Film me!" he demands, standing outside beside the truck as cars whiz by, his voice charged with sudden excitement.

I have no idea what he's up to this time, and with Timmy, guessing is futile. But I comply, pulling out my phone, holding it steady as I hit the record button. And then, right on the sidewalk, as cars rush by, he yanks his board shorts down, revealing stripy under-wear as he shakes his hips, grinning like a kid getting away with a prank. A few pedestrians glance over, looking both amused and bewildered, and a couple of drivers honk their car horns as they go by.

"Oh my god, Timmy! You're ridiculous." I say through my laugh-ter, shaking my head as he wiggles his butt, the oversized coconut hat flopping with every exaggerated shake.

He straightens up and snaps a few pictures of me sitting in the truck with my feet up on the dash. That's when I notice a big bruise forming on the underside of my thigh, a slightly painful but undeniable souvenir of the night before. It's weirdly hot, if I'm honest. Timmy's uninhibited personality carries over into the bedroom in the best possible way.

Back at home a little later, he makes me ramen. The aroma is incredible—the rich umami scent filling the room as I take long, soothing sips. He's gone all out, adding lots of extras like fish balls with the squiggly pink patterns that remind me of the movie Saw, as well as fresh cilantro and a ton of garlic, which he knows I love. I can't help but feel charmed by all the little touches.

We settle on the bed after eating, laughing at some silly movie, and out of nowhere, Timmy turns to me with a strange kind of pride in his eyes. "I am a manchild!" he announces, beaming.

"Huh?" I quirk a brow at him.

"Yep! I am!" He's grinning like he's just won an award.

"I heard what you said, but that's not... a good thing? Are you trying to say you're young at heart or something? Because that's not what that means."

"Yeah, something like that," he says, with the tiniest hint of doubt.

A moment later, he continues. "I am also a *derelict!*" He says it with gusto, as if being a derelict is something to aspire to.

"Um... that's a weird thing to announce." I squint at him, my head tilting like he's some rare species at the zoo. "Pretty sure that's not a compliment. You know what derelict actually means, right?"

"Yeah, yeah, sure I do," he explains, as if he holds a little-known secret. "People take it as a negative word, but it means someone who rejects society's norms. Like, the ultimate free spirit. Not tied down."

"I don't think that's what it means."

"Yeah it does." He's not budging, but I know he's wrong, and his insistence on his own personal meaning is bugging me.

"Um—okay, let's google this." I pull it up on my phone. "Here you go: *derelict. In a very poor condition as a result of disuse and neglect. As in, the cities were derelict and dying. Dilapidated, ramshackle, rundown, broken down, worn-out. A person without a home, job, or property. Tramp, vagrant, vagabond, down and out, drifter—.*"

"Okay, okay. I get the fucking point, Margaux," he snaps, rolling his eyes. "You don't need to keep going. You think you're so smart quoting the dictionary at me."

"I just don't know why you're putting positive spins on words that mean neglected, broken down, or without a purpose?"

"It's like a counterculture thing," he shrugs. "Going against the masses. Everyone's working in offices, hating their lives. I get a job here and there, just enough to live. I hang out outside, enjoy life, no rules. That's real freedom."

And, oddly, there is a bit of truth to what he's saying. After all, I did just leave the corporate world to pursue my dream of becoming a writer. But I put in years of hard work to get to this point. I saved, I budgeted, I planned. With Timmy, it's like he just falls into whatever comes along—helping this person move, detailing that person's car. There's no strategy, no end goal. Just existing, barely getting by.

"Went to the nude beach with two of my female friends," he says casually, leaning back with a self-satisfied grin, conversation changing course entirely. "The wind gave me a partial boner. So everyone saw my *massive dick.*"

"Um, gross, Timmy. TMI. That's not something I need to know. Why would you tell me that?" The man is full of stories, and I'm not quite sure why he picked this one to share with his partner. But I'm starting to question more than a few things coming out of his mouth.

He shrugs. "It's just a funny story!"

"That you have your dick out around your female friends? No. I don't want to hear about your nude beach boner that you have out around other women."

He scoffs. "You need to lighten up. It's not a big deal."

I sigh.

He shifts gears almost immediately, pulling a face and adopting a high-pitched sing-song voice. "I kill you!" He says, eyes widening maniacally as he leans in closer. "I kill you!"

Damn. Timmy is on a real roll today. I'm not sure if he's trying to test me, or if he really just doesn't have a filter. A lot of what he says is funny and has me crying with laughter, but today nearly everything he's saying is pushing my buttons in a bad way.

I blink at him, more shocked than amused. "Timmy, that's a really fucking weird thing to yell. I don't think you should go around saying that."

"Oh, chill out! It's just a joke." He shrugs. "You're right, though. I probably shouldn't. I did get arrested for saying it at the beach one time. Made a 'terroristic threat', they called it. Cops were just mad because someone didn't get my sense of humor."

"You were arrested for making a terroristic threat?" I ask, a little unnerved now. "For saying that?"

"Yeah, they said I was legit threatening to kill people." He laughs, not noticing my lack of amusement.

"Were you?"

"No! Of course not. It was just a joke," he laughs again. "Everyone needs to lighten up."

I sigh, feeling exhausted by the seemingly endless train of questionable anecdotes and misguided brags. "Timmy, I'm serious. Just stop saying it. It's only a matter of time before someone else takes it seriously, and then what? It's not worth it."

"Fine, fine," he says, putting his hands up in mock surrender. Then he grins. "I kill you—kidding, kidding!" he laughs. "I'll stop saying it. But y'all need to chill out."

Maybe it's my inner optimist, but I can't help but hope he'll grow out of this weird phase of say-anything, no-filter mentality. But every story, every bizarre moment, has me questioning a little more.

33

STICKY FINGERS

T *he Past*

Grandmother: Here, have a grape.
Me: Don't we have to pay for it first?
Grandmother: Shh, don't worry about it. Everybody does it.
Here's a piece of candy as well.
Me: Oh, um, okay. I guess. Thank you.

~

The Present

The fluorescent lights hum softly overhead as we weave through the grocery store's wide aisles, tossing groceries into the cart—snacks, pasta, heat-and-eat pizza, fresh fruit and vegetables, cottage cheese, cheddar cheese, and ice cream—always ice cream.

Our playful banter fills the space between the shelves, me teasing

Timmy about his love of canned soup while he makes exaggerated faces at my love of ridiculously spicy hot sauce.

Everything feels light and easy—the kind of fun that makes grocery shopping, of all things, feel like an adventure. We sneak in kisses by the produce section, bumping into each other playfully. I laugh as Timmy ties a helium balloon to the grocery cart, letting it serve as some kind of directional beacon if we lose each other in the store. We playfully argue over what bread to buy as if the fate of all further carb intake depends on it–Timmy wanting basic white bread, me wanting Ezekiel bread packed with seeds and grains.

As we stroll past the refrigerated section, Timmy grabs a cold smoothie from the shelf—one of those overpriced ones with high-quality ingredients—and twists the cap off without missing a beat.

"Thirsty," he explains, smiling before taking a long swig, as if it's the most natural thing in the world. He takes a couple more long sips and then drops the half-empty bottle into the shopping cart.

I raise an eyebrow, a small laugh escaping me. "You're supposed to pay for that *before* drinking it, you know."

He shrugs, and a couple of minutes later, he finishes the smoothie with a satisfying sigh. "It's no big deal," he says casually. "I do this all the time. I'll just leave it somewhere." Before I can respond, he sets the empty bottle behind a stack of soup cans, tucking it away like it's a secret.

My smile falters. "Wait... you're not actually going to pay for that?"

He smirks, apparently a little amused by my confusion. "Why would I? They charge way too much for those things, anyway. Corporate greed." He winks, as if that justifies everything, and then pushes the jam-packed shopping cart toward the checkout.

I trail behind, a knot tightening in my stomach.

He glances at me over his shoulder, noticing my concerned expression.

"You're overthinking it, babe," he says. "Everybody does stuff like this. It's really not a big deal."

The way he says it—so offhandedly, like it's an inside joke—

makes me suddenly feel small, like I'm missing out on a secret rule everyone else knows.

My mind flashes back to the time my mother and I were in the grocery store when the power went out. Standing in the darkened produce department, I remember my mom urging me to eat as many grapes as I could. I still feel guilt at what we did, even though I know it likely didn't matter in the scheme of things. And the way my grandmother had this self-entitled habit of helping herself to pick-n-mix candies and grapes every time we went grocery shopping. Maybe he's right. Maybe I'm just too uptight.

We reach the checkout, and I watch as Timmy unloads our groceries with an easy smile, chatting with the cashier like nothing's amiss. My skin prickles with discomfort, but I'm not sure whether it's because of what he did, or how normal he's making it seem.

As we leave the store, groceries in hand, the moment clings to me like a fog I can't shake. My gut tells me something's off—there's a dishonesty in it, a selfishness and sense of entitlement that leaves me unsettled.

But then, once the groceries are loaded into the truck and we both hop in, Timmy leans over and wraps an arm around my shoulders. He pulls me to him, kissing me gently on my forehead. "Come on," he says, grinning. "Don't tell me you've never bent the rules a little. You're so uptight sometimes."

His words, light and teasing, poke at something inside of me. I feel a flicker of embarrassment—maybe he is right, maybe I'm way too rigid, making a big deal out of something so trivial. And he's accurate, nobody even noticed, and it's not as if the grocery store is going to go bankrupt over one smoothie.

Still, the knot in my stomach doesn't loosen. Even as I laugh along with him, my nagging discomfort lingers, an unsettling ick I can't quite brush off. And, for a moment, I wonder if I'm starting to see Timmy in a different light—one I'm not sure I like.

34

BOARD SHORTS OFF, WALLS DOWN

he Next Day

It's officially been two weeks since I got my tattoo, and today is the day I've been waiting for—I can finally dive into the ocean. I've walked along the shore countless times, watching people splash in the turquoise waves, wishing I could join them. And now, I can. But what makes it even better is that this first swim will be with Timmy, my surfer boy.

The water sparkles under the sun, and as soon as it washes over my skin, it feels like pure heaven. Timmy is right beside me, grinning as I wrap my arms around his neck. The waves lift and cradle us, and he floats me around with ease, his body warm and solid under the water.

We kiss, laugh, and nuzzle each other as if we're the only two people in the world. It's impossible not to get lost in the love bubble surrounding us. Floating on our backs, we hold hands and let the ocean rock us gently. The sky stretches endlessly above, and the water below is as clear as glass. I've never felt so light, so free, or so perfectly content.

"Lift your lower back," Timmy murmurs, his hand grazing my waist. "Stick your chest out a bit more."

With a few tweaks, I feel myself relax even deeper, floating effortlessly.

"Once, I floated so long I fell asleep, and I was quite far out in the ocean," Timmy says, his grin mischievous. "Some guy thought I was dead and ran into the water to save me. I woke up with him carrying me to shore like I was a giant damsel in distress. He was even trying to do CPR." He pauses for effect, then adds, "It felt like Jason Momoa was rescuing me from the ocean."

I burst out laughing at the ridiculous image. He's always in the center of each outrageous story, usually involving him as the star of some absurd or mischievous adventure.

"I can't wait to take you surfing," he says, his voice full of promise as we watch surfers catch waves in the distance. "We'll have you riding the Juggernaut in no time."

I laugh again, knowing the Juggernaut is the stuff of legends— one of the island's most notorious surf spots. In winter, the waves swell into monsters for world-class competitions.

He grins, all charm and confidence. "For real, I have it all planned out, how I'm going to teach you. We'll go out together on one board at first. I'll float while you catch the wave. Then you'll paddle back out and get me, and we'll set you up for the next one."

I beam at him, my excitement growing. "I can't wait! Thank you so much!"

When we eventually wade back to shore, a woman sitting in the sand waves us over, her phone in hand. "This might sound strange," she says with a sheepish smile, "but I filmed you two in the water. Can I AirDrop you the videos?"

Timmy and I exchange glances, slightly bewildered, but we shrug. "Sure," I say.

Within moments, my phone pings, and I receive several videos and a few candid photos of us laughing and swimming. One video captures me with my arms wrapped around Timmy's neck, both of us laughing so hard we're doubled over in the water.

It's strange that she recorded us, but it's also kind of nice. Seeing us from someone else's perspective—a happy couple lost in our own little world—feels surreal. On camera, we look like two people completely in sync, perfectly content to just be with each other. Like a scene from a romance movie, or two loved-up celebrities being snapped by paparazzi.

"This is kind of sweet," I admit, showing Timmy the videos.

"Yeah," he agrees, pulling me closer. "That's us. We look so good."

After rinsing off at the beach showers, Timmy fusses over me like always. "You missed your heel," he says, gesturing at my sand-covered foot. I roll my eyes playfully, but secretly, I love how attentive he is.

As we dry off, we hear the faint strum of live music from a nearby restaurant.

"Come," Timmy says, tugging my hand with that mischievous grin I can never resist. "It's some of the best music on the island."

We slip into the restaurant's outdoor area unnoticed, the soft hum of native songs filling the air. Timmy leads me to a sun lounger and places me there with a playful flourish. "Sit here."

He disappears for a moment, returning with a freshly plucked plumeria blossom. He tucks it behind my ear, just like he did the first time we met, his gaze warm and adoring. "So beautiful."

"But don't we need to be guests to sit here?" I whisper, glancing around nervously.

"Nah," Timmy says with a carefree grin. "Don't worry about it."

We sit, listening to the music, lost in the moment—until a man in a resort uniform approaches, apologetically asking us to move.

Timmy doesn't miss a beat. "No worries," he says, taking my hand. "Let's find somewhere else."

And just like that, we're off again, hand in hand, drifting through the night like leaves on a stream.

THE NEXT DAY, I have my final work call, just to wrap things up. I've been dreading it—my boss is always condescending, and I know she'll try to guilt-trip me. Sure enough, she delivers her usual spiel: "You made the choice to move to Sunset Cay. Nobody forced you, and now you have to deal with the consequences."

Her words grate on me, but I bite my tongue, knowing she's just scared because she knows I'm more competent and better liked than she'll ever be. When she asks if I have feedback for her, I offer a sweet smile and say, "No, nothing I haven't already shared."

The second I hang up, I let out a loud sigh. "Thank fucking god that's over."

Timmy, sprawled across the bed, props himself up on one elbow, his grin turning wicked. "You never have to worry about those assholes again. You've got me now."

His voice drops into a growl. "Speaking of which... after I'm done with you, let's go visit Sabre again." He yanks off his board shorts, his cock springing free, hard and ready.

I gasp, already aching for him. I take him into my mouth, savoring the taste of him as he groans with pleasure. His hands tangle in my hair, and my core throbs in anticipation.

"Come here," he murmurs, pulling me up and spinning me around. He peels down my pants, positioning me so my pussy rubs against him, teasing us both. Then, with a smooth thrust, he slides inside me, stretching me open with that perfect pressure.

I cry out, clutching the edge of the bed as he slams into me, each thrust sending waves of pleasure rippling through my body. "Fuck, Timmy! Don't stop!"

The view from the window spreads out before us—the ocean, the mountains, the city lights. It feels like we're on top of the world, this place ours to conquer together.

"God, Margaux," he groans, his voice thick with pleasure. "You have the most amazing pussy."

His body tenses as he shudders, filling me with warmth. We collapse together, breathless and sated.

Afterward, we slip into the shower, the water cascading over us as Timmy gently soaps me with his soft lilac shower pouf. His tender touch makes my heart swell with affection.

When we step out, he towels me off and kisses the top of my head. "Now let's go see our fuzzy boy."

I look at him, feeling a rush of gratitude and joy. Timmy might be a little wild, a little chaotic, but he's mine. And in this moment, I know I've found the perfect man for me.

35

MOVING PARTY

The Next Day

The day starts with a light breeze and the soft chime of bells as we step into the electronics store. I'm on a mission to pick out a laptop. As soon as my eyes fall on the gorgeous rose gold MacBook, I know it's the one. There's something about it that feels like an investment—not just in my writing, but in the version of myself that I want to become in Sunset Cay. I picture mornings at the beach, my fingers tapping away as the sun rises over the water, the laptop complementing the dusky rose and purple tones of the sunrise. Heaven.

I cradle the laptop in my arms, excitement bubbling up inside me, and turn to Timmy, who's already smiling like he's enjoying watching me fall in love with a piece of technology. "You like it?" he asks, already knowing the answer.

"I love it!" I grin.

"Good. Now come to work with me," he says, casually, as if it's a normal part of our day.

I blink, caught a little off guard. "Are you sure I'm allowed to come with you?" I've never accompanied a partner to work, except for the one awkward situation where I dated a coworker—do not recommend, no go, do not do, will end badly, did end badly.

"Yeah. It's like 'take your girlfriend to work' day." He says it with his trademark smirk, the one where it's tricky to decipher whether he's being serious or trying to charm me into saying yes.

I laugh, but feel a twinge of concern. "Seriously, though? You won't get in trouble?" I don't want his boss to think I'm a stage five clinger who expects to follow him around and distract him from getting shit done. But at the same time, I can sit in a corner and work on my stuff while he fixes up the condo.

Timmy waves it off like it's nothing. "Nah, it'll be fine. I'll even introduce you to my boss. Come." His tone is so carefree that I feel silly for worrying.

I follow him, feeling the smooth rectangular laptop box in my hands. Apple does such a great job of making you feel special when you buy their brand-new products, like you're treating yourself to something that you know will do exactly what's promised. And now Timmy wants to spend the rest of the day with me.

It's flattering he still wants to spend every waking moment with me, and it still makes me feel special. But, at the same time, a small part of me wonders if this is sustainable. I mean, how many times can I follow him to work without it becoming a problem?

He gestures for me to follow him, and we head into the admin offices in a hotel building.

His boss is nice, an attractive blonde woman with bright pink lipstick and smoky eyes. He introduces us, and she makes me feel welcome, although there's a hint of something in her expression that I can't quite put my finger on. She seems more amused than anything else by Timmy's antics, watching him with a smirk as he launches into his usual no-filter commentary.

He jokes around like they're old friends, and she tolerates it— maybe even likes it. Still, I can't shake the feeling that bringing me to work every day might wear on her patience eventually. I don't want to be the reason he gets in trouble.

After a while, she's clearly done listening to his stories, and tells him to get to work.

After stopping by a convenience store, where Timmy picks up some hard seltzers—"In case we get thirsty," he says with a wink—we head to the condo he's fixing up.

I set up my new laptop while he tinkers away, tightening light fixtures, adjusting light switches, hanging prints.

I watch him as I type, noticing how much pride he seems to take in even the small tasks. I can't lie—I find it super hot when a guy does even the most simple of handy tasks. He's had three seltzers by the time I'm done with my first, but he's not tipsy—just a bit more animated, cracking jokes and moving around the room with more energy than usual.

By the time he's finished for the day, I'm feeling good, happy. Timmy's work day has flown by, and we've had fun together. I feel included, like he really wanted me to be there. And it's cute the way he showed off in front of me, showing me the tasks he was working on and how he focused on making sure he did everything just right. It's the kind of day that makes everything feel easy, like we're in sync.

THE NEXT DAY

I wake up to Timmy nudging me. "I want you to come to work with me again," he says.

I hesitate. "Are you sure? I know it was okay with your boss yesterday, and she seems really nice. But she might get tired of you bringing me along every day. It's kind of weird."

Timmy frowns, looking genuinely hurt. "Don't you want to spend time with me?"

"Of course I do!" I say quickly, sitting up. "I just don't want to get you in trouble because you feel like you need to keep me entertained or anything."

"Well, today I'm going to have you help me work!" He shrugs.

"We're going to be moving boxes for one of her clients. You'll get paid and everything."

That makes me feel a little better. At least I won't be standing around just lurking, and the idea of earning some extra cash is appealing. As will be getting some much-needed exercise.

So I agree, and soon we're loading up the truck with heavy boxes, Timmy in his element, directing me where to put everything.

On the way, we stop at another convenience store, where Timmy grabs water and some flight-sized bottles of Fireball. I raise an eyebrow, but don't say anything—this is just how Timmy is, a little extra, adding a little 'fun' into everything he does.

We make our way to a retro hotel right on the beach, and that's where the real work begins. His manager's client is setting up a condo here as an Airbnb, and our goal for the day is to get all the boxes into her unit. It's hot and sweaty work, the kind of physical labor that feels both exhausting and rewarding. We haul boxes into the service elevator, and up long hallways and into the client's condo, stopping every now and then to catch our breath. I'm grateful for the exercise, and for the fact I'm not just sitting around like yesterday.

At one point, we take a break. I notice that Timmy's energy hasn't waned a bit, despite the physical labor and the Fireball he's been sipping. "Come," he says, taking my hand and grinning, leading me to a secret elevator that opens up to a hidden floor with a panoramic view of the beach and the city behind it.

To the right of the elevator is a chapel, and I can't help but laugh as he gets down on one knee, wearing my big floppy hat, a wifebeater, and a pair of my sunglasses. He looks ridiculous, like a knock off Kid Rock, but there's something about the gesture—playful and sweet— that makes me feel lighter. He's always finding ways to make me laugh.

Afterwards, he takes me into the adjacent bar, ordering drinks while chatting with the bartender and enjoying the view. The bartender is friendly, and Timmy is in his element, chatting away with her about his friend's cacao farm, and I'm learning more than I ever thought I would about chocolate-making. There's a part of me that loves how comfortable Timmy is in literally any setting, how he turns every opportunity to show off or make connections. But there's still that nagging feeling, like this can't go on forever.

When our drinks are done and I've paid our check, Timmy's boss calls to check in. He reassures her that we're almost done and that we just have a few more boxes to move. The remaining boxes are quite heavy, and there's no cart, so we haul them one by one, sweat dripping down my back as I shove the last of them down the long hallway to the condo. By the time we're done, I'm exhausted but satisfied.

Once we're finished, the client pays us in cash, and Timmy immediately hands me a little more than half of the money. I blink at the bills in my hand. A couple of hundred dollars. Not bad for a few hours of enjoyable work.

"Are you sure?" I ask.

He smiles and nods. "I really appreciate you helping me today. It would have taken way longer and been way less fun without you."

"I had a good time, too." I smile at him, although my muscles ache from the effort, and he leans over to kiss me.

I know this can't last forever—going to work with him every day. His boss might tolerate it now, but what happens when she doesn't? And what happens when Timmy can't handle spending a day apart, even when it's necessary?

For now, though, I push those thoughts aside and let myself enjoy the moment, feeling the weight of the cash in my hand and the warmth of his kiss on my lips.

36

WELL THAT ESCALATED QUICKLY

"I want to take you to the botanical gardens," Timmy announces. "You're going to love it! It's very Jurassic Park-like, with the mountains in the background. And there's this beautiful lake."

"That sounds amazing!" I enjoy how excited Timmy gets around plants.

"Yeah, I love it there. I think you'll enjoy it, too. It's filled with all of my favorite native plants, and there are birds and stuff as well. I can show you all the wild ginger and palm trees I've been talking about. Succulents and so on. I can't wait to take you! We can have a picnic!"

When we show up, it's stunning, just like he promised. Lush vegetation sprinkled with vibrant, tropical flowers. The unique mountainscape looms in the background. I really do feel like I'm in a scene from Jurassic Park. There are more common plants like giant monsteras and plumeria, and other exotic ones I've never seen before.

"I'm going to call my dad," he suddenly says. "I want you two to meet. He's really important to me."

His dad, being a retired, decorated general in the army, is somehow a comfort to me, a bit like his friendship with Steve.

Someone who got to where he did in his military career, and his impressive corporate career following his military service as a VP for a pharmaceutical company, indicates there's something genetic in his makeup that makes Timmy also capable of being a productive human.

Sure, he has one sister and one brother, both with significant drug and anger management issues, but he also has a brother who has his shit together, too. So it's a theoretical possibility that he could 'turn out well,' I guess you could say.

Wow, this is feeling serious. An introduction to the parents already.

"Hello son," says an older man's voice on speakerphone.

"Hey dad," Timmy smiles. "I want you to meet someone. Margaux, this is my dad. Dad, this is my girlfriend, Margaux."

"Hi, Timmy's dad," I say, feeling nervous. "Nice to meet you."

"Nice to meet you too," says the voice. "Now son, girlfriend, you say?"

"Yes! We just met recently and we've fallen in love. Margaux is from New Zealand, and we have so much in common. And she takes care of me." He's bubbling with excitement, and I feel myself blushing.

"Well, son, you certainly need that," his father replies. "Someone to take care of you." There's no humor in his voice.

The comment unsettles me a little. Timmy's about to turn forty, and I'm his girlfriend, not his babysitter.

"And guess what? She writes, dad! She's a professional writer, and she writes dark romance, but I tease her and call it pornography. I'm in love with a pornographer!"

"Oh my god—" I feel my face burn beet red.

"Oh, haha, that's nice, son. What are the books called?"

"Oh my god," I say again, putting a hand over my face. This is just what I need, unexpectedly meeting my boyfriend's father over the phone, and him telling him all about my smutty dark romance books. Oy!

We hang up after a few more minutes of chatting, and find a cute spot down by the water, a little bench in front of the lake.

Timmy suddenly gets super excited, even more than normal. He's just about bouncing on his toes. "I'm going to propose to you to create a scene, okay? Everyone will be looking!"

"Huh? What do you mean?" I'm beyond confused.

"Just trust me. I'm going to get down on one knee and ask you to marry me. And everyone around us is going to be like 'ooooh aaaah' and it's going to be so fun. They might even take pictures of us and put them online."

I quirk a brow at him.

"Just for fun," he says casually. "Nothing serious."

I crack up laughing. "You're quite ridiculous, but okay."

He does as he promised. Drops to one knee and asks me to marry him. "The thing is, Margaux," he adds, "I'm not joking. I've never met anybody I love more. I want to be with you for the rest of my life. I really do believe you're my soulmate, and I've thought so from the moment I first saw you, and even from the moment we first spoke. I've never met anyone like you. It's like you were made for me. So please do me the honor of marrying me. Please say yes. I'll protect you and keep you safe, and we'll build our dream life together. You're an incredible human being. I've never felt this way about anyone before. I've never proposed to anyone before. But you're so special—you're beautiful, you're funny, you're creative, you're sexy, you're extremely smart. You write pornography! And I want to be with you forever. Nobody else. Just you and me, together. You make me into a better person, the best version of myself I've ever been. I'm a changed man, and you've tamed the dragon that nobody else has ever been able to do. I want to travel the world with you. I want to take the world by storm with our companies. I want to eat your pussy every day for the rest of my life. I promise you I'll do it every single day." He glances over at the two mongooses who are watching us and nibbling on the sausage he threw to them just before. "And with these mongooses as my witness, I am asking you, the love of my life, will you please do me the honor of marrying me?"

"Um... wow," I say, a tear falling down my cheek. I'm crying and laughing at the same time. "Are you serious, or is this part of the act? Because that was quite the speech." I'm so thrown. I don't know what is happening.

"Oh, I'm very serious," he says, his face reflecting his earnestness. "Deadly. I really want us to be together. Why do you think I called my dad just a little bit ago? I wanted him to hear your voice before I asked you. Kind of like getting his blessing to make it official. That's how important you are to me. I never want to hurt you, Marg. I want us—you and me—forever."

"Wow," I whisper, touched and also shocked. This is all happening very fast, but sometimes you just know when things feel right. And I'm feeling all the butterflies, and I'm a little lightheaded and tingly.

I take a deep breath, and he looks at me expectantly. "Well, in that case... my time with you has been amazing so far. So... yes."

I'm swept away by the emotions. I still can't even tell if he's joking. But I feel like it would be rude to say no. I can go along with it now, and we'll figure things out later.

We both glance at each other, and it's as if he's trying to decide if I'm joking or for real, too.

"You mean it?" he asks. "You really want to marry me?"

"Did you mean to *ask* me for real?" I ask. "Or was it a joke, a stunt, like you originally said it would be?"

"Yes," he laughs, tears in his eyes. "Margaux, I know it hasn't been long, but I love you so much. We're connected at a soul level, and there's nobody else I want to spend the rest of my time on this earth with. You're it for me. I'll never find anyone like you again."

"Okay, then I'm serious, too. I love you," I smile at him.

He leans down to kiss me. "I love you so much, too, my soulmate. My fiancée."

He turns around. There are a couple of people sitting nearby on a bench, and he waves at them. "She said yes!" They wave back, smiling.

A park ranger happens by and he tells them the same thing. "Congratulations," he nods and smiles.

He turns to the mongooses. "We did it! She said yes."

I laugh, so confused by what just happened, although I think... we just got engaged.

After about a week of knowing each other.

It's very quick, but everything has been going so well, so quickly. How could I possibly say anything but yes?

37

YOU WHAT THE WHAT, NOW?!

The car hums along the road as the botanical gardens fade into the distance behind us, my heart still fluttering from the proposal. Timmy's hand rests on my thigh as he steers, and he keeps looking over and smiling at me, his eyes bright and kind. The air between us feels light and giddy—like a dream I don't want to wake from.

I send my good friend, Paulo, the picture I snapped of a beautiful monstera earlier. He's a plant zaddy, and I know monsteras are one of his faves.

I follow up with a cheeky text:

ME:

By the way, I just got engaged!

My phone rings within 10 seconds. *Paulo calling.*

I smirk, knowing what's coming. I put him on speaker. "Hiiiii!"

"You *what* the *what* now?" Paulo's voice blasts through the car speakers, incredulous and tinged with disbelief and perhaps a hint of amusement.

Timmy's grin widens as he squeezes my thigh.

I bite my lip to suppress a laugh, but it tumbles out, still high on the rush of it all.

"He proposed," I say, my voice lilting with happiness. "And I said yes!"

There's a pause, just long enough for me to hear the gears turning in Paulo's head.

"Oh... well... congratulations! That was quick, guys! But I'm happy for you!" The warmth in his voice is genuine, but there's no missing the hesitation lurking just beneath it, the slight judgment coming through the speaker.

I know Paulo too well to be fooled. He's happy for me—he really is—but he's also wary, and his concern clings to the edges of his words.

But I'm delirious on the high of being engaged to this wonderful human, so I choose to disregard the hesitation and embrace the words, refusing to let anything negative kill the vibe.

Timmy perks up beside me. "I'm in love with your friend!" he calls toward the phone, loud and excited. "Tell him about the mongooses!" He glances at me with a playful grin, as if the mongoose brigade had been in on the proposal.

Before I can, Timmy speaks up again.

"They were totally watching," says Timmy. "It was like the universe sent them to bless us."

Paulo snorts on the other end, and I can tell he's trying not to laugh. "Mongooses, huh? Sounds... magical."

"And we fed sushi to koi at the lake," I add, giggling at the memory.

Timmy leans closer, nuzzling my hair. "I've never asked anyone to marry me before," he says softly, just loud enough for Paulo to hear. "You're really, really special, Margaux, and I couldn't ever hope to find someone like you again. So it would've been silly of me not to ask."

I grin, feeling like his proposal was ridiculous, and I was kind of joking when I said yes, but wondering if this was meant to happen.

"I'm going to be Timmy Benson O'Malley. Like your dad's name combined with mine."

My chest leaps. It feels like it's meant to be that he and my dad would share the same name. Like a sign that my dad approves of this whole crazy situation. That he's sent him for me.

It feels nice to be wanted. To be told I'm the missing piece for someone. Because I've always felt discarded, or not really seen. And here is this man who sees me. Who knows my past, sees all my flaws and doesn't just accept them... he embraces them. Loves me *because* of them.

His words are sweet, but they stir a memory I'd buried—the moment my third husband asked me to marry him, just hours after meeting in person. His exact words echo in my mind: "Well you're clearly way out of my league, so I needed to lock it down." I should have listened... like, really listened, to his words. And ran.

I try to push the thought away, focusing on Timmy and the warmth of his hand on my thigh. *This is different. Timmy is different,* I remind myself. He's nothing like my former husband. Besides, I can't help it if everyone wants to propose to me quickly. Maybe I'm just adorable like that.

Still, Paulo's silence on the end of the line feels weighted, as if he can sense the small flicker of doubt blooming in my chest.

"So," Paulo says, clearing his throat. "You're happy?"

"Of course I'm happy," I reply quickly, my voice bright. "I've never felt more seen or loved in my life. He makes me feel like the most special person in the world."

Timmy leans over and kisses my temple, his lips lingering as he whispers, "You are."

The warmth of his affection washes over me, making the flicker of doubt dim, at least for the moment. "He's like wearing rose-tinted glasses," I tell Paulo. "But they're for me. Everything I do makes him happy. Every story I tell, every fact I share... he loves it all."

There's a long pause on the other end of the line. "Well, as long as you're happy..." his voice trails off, the care in his voice unmistakable. "This is just... quite fast, isn't it?"

I roll my eyes fondly. "Yes, Paulo. It's very fast. I know it's quick, but it's not about the timeline... sometimes when you know, you just know. It's about how you feel in these situations, and I feel amazing!"

"Alright," he says, but there's a cautious edge to his tone. "I just don't want to see you get hurt again, that's all."

"I know," I reply, the weight of his words sinking in. Paulo has always been there, through every breakup and misstep, not piecing me back together so much as quietly observing. He's not trying to ruin my happiness—he's just trying to protect me, like he always does.

Timmy squeezes my thigh, reassuring me.

"Thank you, Paulo," I say, my voice gentle. "I love you."

"I love you too, Margaux... just be careful, okay?" His words carry a quiet warning, one I choose not to dwell on.

"I will." I promise, meaning it.

"I promise I'll take really good care of her," Timmy calls out.

I hang up, tucking my phone back into my bag. The car is quiet for a moment, the hum of the road beneath us filling the silence. I exhale, willing myself to stay present, to stay in the warmth of this moment with Timmy.

"You okay?" Timmy asks, his thumb brushing small circles on my leg.

"Yeah," I say, smiling at him. "I'm more than okay."

He grins, his joy radiating around us as he gives my leg a playful squeeze. "Good. Because I can't wait to start the rest of our life together."

And just like that, the flicker of doubt extinguishes—for now, I let myself sink deeper into the love bubble, savoring the feeling of being seen, cherished, and so intensely loved. Sabre is still at the quarantine station for a little while longer, so it's just quality time with the two of us. No worries in the world. Well, except for paying this exorbitant rent without a corporate job. But I'll worry about that later. Now is my time to just... feel. And be in love. And be loved.

Because for the first time in a long time, I feel like I belong somewhere. And that somewhere is here, with Timmy.

38

———

THE THIN SHROOM LINE

The day continues so innocently—a mix of Timmy's childlike excitement, and a hurried announcement to his boss.

"We're engaged!" he exclaims.

She quirks a perfectly manicured eyebrow. "Engaged? How long have you two been dating? Like 24 hours?" She glances at me and says "Congratulations!" But there's a question mark in her voice, almost a look of sympathy.

"Ten days, but when you're in love, you're in love! Plus," babbles Timmy, "she gives me twenty blowjobs a day."

"Twenty!" smirks his boss. "That's quite a lot of daily blowjobs."

I feel myself turn red, in disbelief he's discussing BJs with his boss. Definitely a no-no from an HR perspective, but I guess that's not for me to worry about. "He's exaggerating," I add, awkwardly.

"Am I, though?" He winks at me. "I think yesterday it might have actually been twenty." He turns to his boss. "Oh my god, and she's a really, really good cook."

Once we leave the office, Timmy gets even more excited. "Ooh, let's have an engagement celebration!" He starts texting friends, and even invites his manager and her husband.

He kisses me, a long one with tongue that takes me by surprise. "We'll go to Dock Bar where we first met in person! It'll be romantic!"

I'd hoped for a quiet, intimate evening, but he keeps texting more and more people, clearly hoping some will join to share our excitement.

"Okay," I laugh. "I don't have anyone to invite, though."

"That doesn't matter!" he says. "It'll just be a small, low-key thing."

We dress up and get to Dock Bar.

"Who else is coming?" I ask.

"Nobody seems to be able to make it," he frowns, barely concealing his frustration.

"That's okay," I say. "It's very short notice. You're literally inviting people same-day on a weeknight."

Timmy nods, but then frowns. "Shit, I meant to ask my boss if she'd mind paying me a few days early."

He taps at his phone and keeps checking it every few minutes.

"Ugh, she's not replying. I bet she's going to say no."

He seems agitated until his phone finally dings. He frowns again. "She fucking said no. I don't know why she's being like this. It's not a big deal. She can afford to pay me early. I just wanted her to give me a little bit of an advance. The truth is, I'm not going to have enough to cover our drinks, let alone food. I don't want you to pay for our engagement party, especially when it was my idea. It doesn't seem right."

Then his eyes grow wide, as if a lightbulb is going off in his brain. "Wait here, I'll be right back."

"Timmy, where are you—."

"Be right back, I said. Trust me." He kisses me on the top of my head and zooms out of the restaurant, leaving me alone at the bar.

About fifteen minutes later, he returns with an average-looking guy, friendly enough, but with an energy that makes me slightly uneasy. "This is my old boss, Parker," he introduces us. "He lives right around the corner, and he's a good friend of mine."

Parker grins and shakes my hand. "Nice to meet you."

"Nice to meet you too," I smile.

While Parker orders himself a drink, Timmy leans in and explains Parker is going to pick up the tab for our 'engagement celebration.' He also mentions that Parker has just taken shrooms.

I feel wary. Nobody else has agreed to meet us for this engagement party.

The bartending team is really nice, and they comp Timmy and I saucers of champagne, congratulating us, but I can't help but notice the weird looks a couple of them shoot my way.

I'm a little confused as to why Parker was randomly invited to our celebration—Timmy has only had negative things to say when he's mentioned him previously—but I figure he lives close by.

I'm also suspecting it's because Timmy's boss said she couldn't pay him today, and, as it's beginning to become clear, Timmy has absolutely no more money than what he earns from day to day. So, Parker must be willing to pick up the tab.

After settling our tab, we all walk to my apartment and take a seat on the floor. "Oh, I have some furniture you could have that would fit nicely in here," says Parker.

"Oh really? That would be awesome! Thank you so much," I smile. "People are so generous here helping with apartment setups."

"You should take my number, too," he says, giving me his details. "Just in case you need to talk to someone other than Timmy. Because you probably will."

It's kind of weird, the way he worded things, but he's right in pointing out I don't really have any friends here yet other than Timmy. Having a backup emergency number seems sensible. It doesn't seem like he's being creepy, although the way he winks to emphasize the point makes my skin prickle. I smile politely, hoping it's just his sense of humor.

We chat for a while, and then all of a sudden the tone changes. There's a weird energy between Timmy and Parker. They suddenly start getting snippy with each other over basically nothing—something about whether Parker got fired or whether he voluntarily left, and whether they were peers or if Parker was Timmy's supervisor, and then it turns into a full-blown, heated argument.

Parker storms out of the apartment, and about twenty minutes later, Timmy and I glance over and see Parker's keys looped around one of the kitchen cupboard handles. He calls Parker and puts him on speaker, and Parker starts screaming and swearing at Timmy. "You're such a fucking loser asshole, stealing my keys. Bring them here, you fucking thief!"

We walk back toward Parker's house, and Parker calls me. "Where are you guys?"

"Almost to your place. Can you walk and meet us halfway?"

"Maybe. Put Timmy on the phone," he demands.

I say "okay," and then give the phone to Timmy.

All of a sudden, Parker starts screaming at Timmy, calling Timmy a 'loser thief' and hurling insults that are just cruel. Timmy screams back, which seems justified. I'm defensive of Timmy, and Parker's shrieking is throwing me off. I'm not sure what provoked it—their argument seemed relatively benign and kind of out of nowhere.

We walk all the way back to Parker's apartment, but he's not there. So Timmy finds a place on the hood of Parker's car where he can discreetly tuck in the keys. It's not a long walk, but by the time we get there, I feel emotionally drained. It's not feeling like much of a celebration.

I think the situation is over, until my phone buzzes. I start receiving a series of messages from Parker on my phone.

His texts are full of rage, his words twisting into threats. Photos appear, and to my shock, they're selfies of Parker. I realize with horror that he's still hanging out in my building's lobby.

FUCK.

PARKER:

I'm going to mess this place up big time.

You'll be very sorry for fucking with me.

ME:

I didn't fuck with you though?

> I don't understand. Please don't do this, whatever this is.

PARKER:

> You stole my keys, you fuckers.

ME:

> Parker, you left the keys at my apartment and we just took them to you.

> But you're saying you've been at my apartment building all this time?

> Why didn't you just tell us you were still there?

PARKER:

> Nah, fuck you guys. You're going to pay.

I feel a cold sweat prickle in my neck as I read the texts, my hands trembling.

We rush back, and Parker is still in the apartment lobby, refusing to leave.

Oh my fucking god, why did Timmy invite this crazy man into my apartment? This is insane.

I call the police, and Timmy looks more than a little panicked as the sirens approach. "See you in a bit," he yells. "I'll explain later."

He runs off, leaving me standing here wondering what the hell is going on, even more than before, alone as the police arrive.

What the actual fuck?

I explain everything, mortified and apologizing profusely. "I'm really sorry—I feel ridiculous calling you out here. It's just... I don't know what's going on with Parker. I don't know him. My fiancé brought him here and then he just started acting crazy." My cheeks are burning. My uncle, a career officer, would be rolling in his grave if he knew what was happening right now.

"No, no," a female officer says, her face kind. "This is what we're here for."

Parker comes running past, chased by two officers. "Timmy

O'Malley has a warrant out for his arrest!" he yells. "He's the one you should be looking for!"

"What's that about?" the officer asks, glancing at me. "Who's Timmy O'Malley?"

"My fiancé," I explain.

"He has an outstanding warrant?" She quirks a brow.

I shrug. "Not that I'm aware of. I don't know anything about that."

A while later, the cops leave, promising to file a report and confirming that Parker is banned from the premises for the next seventy-two hours.

I dial Timmy's number, my hands shaking. I'm so upset that he ran away and I just don't understand.

A girl's voice answers the phone. "Hello?"

Again, what the actual fuck?

"He's a really nice guy, and he's getting blamed for things that aren't his fault," she says, before abruptly hanging up.

I text him:

ME:

You're hanging out with some random girl?

You left me when I called the cops?

You told me to let someone into my apartment who then tried to ruin it?

Timmy! I just moved in! This is so embarrassing and I'm so confused.

TIMMY:

I'm so so sorry. I'll be back soon.

I'll explain everything, I promise.

I don't know who the girl is, a bunch of teenagers just saw I was upset and she grabbed my phone.

I was so mad when she did that.

Can you meet me down a side street so we walk back in together?

ME:

Of course.

A knot of anger tightens in my chest. I've just had to call the police on my first full week in this new neighborhood. The only impression I've managed to make so far is of someone who can't handle my own friends—or my fiancé's, at least.

He sends me a pin with his location, and I walk to meet him. He's a couple of blocks away, and I meet him down a side street.

"I'm so sorry," he hugs me to him, kissing the top of my head.

I feel numb.

"I freaked out," he explains. "There's a warrant, and it's for a traffic thing, and I really didn't want them to look me up and arrest me."

"But you left me with the cops by myself," I frown. "That's awful. It's *your* friend that came and threatened to damage my home. And you abandoned me."

I had an ex with a warrant once. Some concealed weapons charge. That guy got really twitchy about that, too, whenever he was around cops. But still, it feels wrong that Timmy ran away and left me to deal with this by myself.

"Yeah, I know," he sighs. "I feel so bad about that. I've seen Parker be a bit weird from time to time, but he's never threatened to break someone's stuff or get violent like that. I don't know what was up with him. Maybe he was doing a bunch of drugs before we met up or something, because that's not how he normally acts. I'd never have invited him around if it was. I know he'd been taking shrooms. "

"Well, I feel like I'm at risk of getting kicked out of my apartment. I've been here less than two weeks and I've already had the cops come to the property. They're going to think I'm a problem tenant."

"No, no," he says quickly. "It was a one-off, I promise you. There's no way we'll invite Parker over again. I won't invite anyone over again except for myself."

"Who was the girl who answered your phone?"

"There were some teenagers on the beach. They saw me crying, and they just sat with me once I told them what happened."

"She seemed to know you."

"I know. I was so upset when she grabbed my phone. I don't know her, or why she acted like she knew who I was. They were just all hanging out and were trying to help me to not be upset. They felt sorry for me."

I sigh, feeling incredibly deflated. "Okay. I'm so embarrassed about all of this."

"I know. I'm really, really sorry. Can we just go inside quickly and have a nice night? I don't want to think about this anymore. I just want to get up to the room and cuddle with you and forget this all ever happened. I'm really sorry about Parker. I can't believe he did that. I just want to not think about it anymore."

"Okay. Yeah, let's just go inside."

We slink past the concierge, and they give us a look that says everything. The sort of judgment that makes me shrivel into a tiny ball—like I've brought chaos into a place that would otherwise have been calm.

"Ugh, did you see that look he just gave us?" I ask Timmy, as we ride up in the elevator, his hand clenched tight around mine.

He frowns. "Yeah, I did. What a dick. And I'm very sorry." He pulls me to him and kisses me on the head. "Everything's going to be okay."

Later in the night, as I lay next to Timmy, trying to forget everything that happened earlier, my phone dings again. Parker has left a voicemail.

"Call me if you fucking need help," he slurs. "I know you do."

Another message comes through shortly after.

> PARKER:
>
> I hope you're alive. Still, I really hope you're alive.

I don't reply. He texts again, still nonsensical.

> PARKER:
>
> Yeah, one moment. Well I'm still here. Should I make some noise?

> Wanna fuck around? So where are my keys?
> Or should I just call the cops?

I sigh and text him back.

ME:

> Parker. We were by your house and your keys
> are at your car now.

> Not sure what you'd need to call them for.

> You left your keys at my house and we
> brought them to you.

PARKER:

> I've got no fucking problem. Timmy's the one
> who's got a few cases.

> There are government keys on that chain.
> This isn't going to end well.

> It's funny, you were the only one with a
> problem.

A few more minutes go by.

PARKER:

> Funny I know the property manager.

> Someone couldn't show up to voice his
> opinions.

> Oh you got a warrant. Come fuck with this
> castle.

> Glad I bought drinks. Good night everyone.

With a sigh, I turn my phone off, which I rarely do, wanting nothing more than to sink into sleep and pretend this entire nightmare didn't happen. But I can't shake the feeling that, no matter how much Timmy promises otherwise, we've somehow brought chaos to Sunset Cay, and it's not going to let go of us anytime soon.

39

BIRD MAN

The Past

Grandfather: I never trust a person who doesn't like animals.

It suggests they have no empathy.

~

"I really want to take you to feed the ducks," Timmy grins. "It's really fun."

"Okay! I used to love doing it when I was little. It's been a while." I think back to my mother dressing me up in way too many layers, a puffy coat and a woolen hat, and taking leftover white bread down to the creek. We'd throw chunks of it into the water while the ducks quacked, and eventually I'd get a bit overwhelmed as they swarmed around me. It was a fun, innocent memory I hadn't thought of in years.

But apparently it's something Timmy hasn't outgrown, and it's just another cute and interesting thing about him. He grabs some bread from the convenience store and takes me to a little pond with a fountain over near the beach. As he throws out chunks of white bread, the pigeons come and land all over him. He laughs with delight as they perch on his arms and his head. I laugh, too. I've never seen anything like it. I even take a video because the man is literally covered in birds.

The ducks quack and honk from the pond and as they waddle up to his legs.

He's like this weird bird man, and he laughs with joy as he becomes surrounded by—and covered in—feathered friends.

And I love that he loves animals. He seems to live for them. His joy is palpable when he points out parrots that live in the palm trees, mongooses zooming across the grass, seagulls chilling on the shore-line, koi in the ponds. It's a beautiful quality, loving animals this way.

And I associate it with trust and empathy. Animals seem to have a sixth sense about people, and every animal I've seen has gravitated toward him. Dogs at the beach, these birds. I can't wait to see what Sabre truly thinks of him when he gets home. I bet they're going to love each other.

I watch Timmy longboard along the pathway for a bit, and then we return to the truck.

"Wait here," he says.

"Why? What are you going to do?"

"It's better if you don't know."

"Timmy, I'm not just going to sit in the truck and wait while you go do some mystery thing. Tell me what's happening. Please."

He rolls his eyes. "Calm down, Margaux. I'm just going to steal someone else's registration tags so I can put them on the truck."

"You're what now?"

"See? I knew you'd have that reaction." He rolls his eyes and frowns. "That's why I didn't want to tell you. But it's what I'm going to do, and you can't stop me."

I feel sick. I sit in the truck, and I'm shaking. Is he joking? It seems like a very specific thing he's doing, not a joke. Jesus.

His behavior is starting to make me feel more and more uneasy.

I don't want to be around someone who does stuff like this.

After about ten minutes, he runs back and does something to the back of the truck, presumably putting a stolen tag on it.

"There. Done." He's out of breath, and seems exhilarated by the whole thing.

He speeds us away. "We have to run. If the cops find me, they'll lock me up for this. It's a crime, you know. Stealing someone else's registration."

"Well yes, Timmy. Theft is a crime." My heart is racing. I feel like I've been sitting in a getaway car waiting for someone to rob a bank. "I can't believe you just did that."

"Neither can I!" says Timmy, grinning from ear to ear, his eyes sparkling. "It was amazing!"

"Not the word I would use, but okay." Reckless, unnecessary, stealing. Those are the words I would use. "Why didn't you just go and pay for your registration like everyone else, rather than stealing someone else's?"

"Too expensive," he shakes his head. Then he grins again. "And nowhere near as fun."

"You can't just steal other people's shit, Timmy. That person's going to be fucked if the cops notice they don't have tags. And they did what people are meant to do. Paid for their own registration."

He grins. "I know. Suckers!"

"No, Timmy. That's called adulting. You have to pay for this stuff. You can't just take it from someone else."

"Not me! Derelict for life!"

My stomach churns. I think this is my first *real* ick moment with Timmy, although there have been a few other incidents that have left me feeling less than comfortable. I know everything a partner does isn't going to be pleasing, but I have an ethical problem with theft. And, just the general premise that he thinks it's okay to take something that someone else worked hard for, just to make his own life easier. Nobody wants to pay for car registration. Literally nobody. And everybody else has other things they'd prefer to spend their money on. But Timmy thinks, for some reason, he gets to take the thing someone else paid for, just because he wants it.

But I push my thoughts back down. I'm making a big deal out of nothing. I'm way too uptight, and I've always been considered a goody two-shoes. People probably do this stuff all the time. I wouldn't, personally, but I'm sure he's not the only person who's done it. Right?

Ugh. I don't fucking know.

There are so many good things about Timmy. If the odd questionable action is all I have to worry about, I just need to calm down. We can work on his ethics over time. It's going to be fine.

He drives us to the top of a hill where roosters are roaming around in a pack. And the view is incredible, a sprawling panorama looking out over large, fancy houses to the beach. The ocean seems to go on forever, the coast peppered with palm trees and golden sand.

Timmy jumps over the cobbled wall lining the sidewalk and hoses himself off. He pours water into his mouth and blows it at me in a thick spout that falls near my feet, and then he does a ridiculous dance with the hose, a massive grin plastered across his face. I laugh and laugh, feeling lighter, as he puts on his little show just for me.

"Okay, now let's go over to where I grew up. I want to show you some more of that area." His eyes are sparkling and he seems excited, and I'm totally fine having my very own cute surfer tour guide.

The moment we crest the hill and the other side of the coast comes into view, I feel a little knot forming in my stomach. The energy has shifted again. It's only the second time we've been over this way, but I can feel the same sort of agitation emanating from Timmy that I experienced the first time when we came to meet up with Steve.

It's not any one thing that tips me off to how he's feeling. His words pour out a little faster, his movements get a little more rapid and less intentional. He drives a little faster. And the stories start to flow from him. Things he's shared before about when he lived with his ex-girlfriend's family on the beachfront. The time he went up to another friend's rooftop. Moments he spent at the dirt bike track and driving trucks around in the mud. It's almost as if these stories are some type of playlist that play on a loop whenever he crests this hill.

He drives us to a lookout with a pretty view of the ocean.

He starts talking to a random guy, and hands him our shared drink. The man is unkempt, clearly on some kind of drug, and his mouth is lined with little drops of spittle.

I'm annoyed. I don't share drinks with other people, other than my significant other or maybe a close friend. And here Timmy is, handing the can I just bought to some random nasty guy in a parking lot by the beach.

While he continues talking to the strange man, I wander around and notice a bunch of stray cats hanging out at the other end of the parking lot. Preferring their company, I walk over to them and they observe me with a cat's typical lazy, casual arrogance. I snap a few pictures and eventually make my way back to the vehicle.

Timmy finally returns, and hands me the can. "No thanks," I say, pushing it away.

"What's wrong?" he asks.

"You let that random guy sip out of our can. That's gross."

He looks shocked, a scornful smirk playing across his face. "Are you fucking serious?"

"Yes. I don't share drinks with strangers. It's disgusting."

"Jesus, Margaux. You're so fucking uptight. And rude. I share things with people. It's who I am as a person."

His words are like a slap. He does seem very generous, always offering to help people. And he's been so generous with me, helping me get my apartment set up, cooking for me. But I'm not going to flick a switch and suddenly get over my fear of germs from strangers.

"Well, I haven't had Covid yet and there's a reason for that. It's who I am as a person. I'm very picky about what I put in my mouth."

He smirks.

"I know. That's what she said." I laugh, and so does he.

But then his expression shifts again.

"There's nothing wrong with sharing, Margaux. You need to stop being so selfish. The alcohol kills the germs anyway."

I quirk a brow. "Does it, though?"

He nods, his eyes narrowing. "Yes. And fuck you for complaining. Because I was just talking to him about spray painting his car up like this truck. He might be paying me three hundred and fifty dollars, all because I was nice enough to chat with him for a bit and give him a sip of our drink. But all you want to do is complain about it. So if you'd like me to go back over there and say that sorry, my fiancée doesn't want me to have anything to do with you and thinks you're gross, so you can keep your three hundred and fifty dollars, I will. Is that what you want me to do?"

His words make me feel a bit foolish, and I look down. It's great if he's able to get some work out of the guy. Maybe I was a bit quick to judge him, even if he was sitting out at a beach park drinking by himself in the middle of the day. And it would be helpful if Timmy could get more jobs like this.

It's just different from how I would approach a situation, that's all. He's right. I'm just too uptight.

We drive a bit further, and stop at his hometown beach. He hops in the water and floats around for a bit while I watch.

Being in the ocean seems to calm him, and when he gets back, I can tell he's more settled and chilled out. He pulls up to the side of the road on a random side street, and I take another funny video of him dancing with a hose and pretending to threaten to splash me with a huge grin on his face.

He drives up to a parking area behind a nondescript strip mall. There's a door covered in bright graffiti.

"I'm banned from that bar," he says, a hint of pride in his voice.

I quirk a brow. "For what?"

"Oh, it was just a misunderstanding. Not a big deal."

A guy walks past on his way to the graffitied door, and he glances over at the truck, and then at Timmy. He does a double-take. "O'Malley!" He calls out, grinning from ear to ear.

Timmy's eyes grow wide and he beams. "Hey man! It's been forever. How are things!"

He comes up to the car and nods at me and smiles. He's got long, thick dreadlocks and is missing a few of his front teeth. But he seems friendly enough.

Timmy gestures at me. "This is my missus, Margaux," he grins. "We just got engaged. Margaux, this is Dogfucker!"

His friends have weird nicknames. I have no intention of asking how this guy acquired his.

"Wow, that's awesome, you guys! Congratulations." He shakes my hand through the window. "You coming inside?" He gestures his head toward the door.

"Nah, can't." Timmy shakes his head. "Still banned."

"Oh man, that sucks," the guy lets out a low whistle. "Well, if you want to do a bump, I can bring some out."

"Thanks man. I'll let you know," says Timmy.

"Okay, sweet," the guy says, and then heads inside.

Timmy looks at me, his eyes sparkling. "Well, should we go get a bump?"

"Can we just go?" I ask, frowning. A knot is wedging itself within my insides. I just have a really icky feeling. No, I don't want to go and do drugs outside a bar Timmy's banned from with a random near-toothless man named Dogfucker. I'm starting to get a bad feeling about Timmy and the people he chooses to acquaint himself with. He seems sketchy, not someone I'd ordinarily hang around with. Not trying to be judgmental, but this isn't how he presented himself to me up until now. Maybe I was missing some signs, and ignoring others, but I feel really out of my element.

Timmy lets out a massive sigh and rolls his eyes, his frustration exaggerated. "Fine, yes. We'll fucking go because you want to, Margaux."

40

———————

FALAFEL-ING FOR YOU

We drive through the rain, tropical sun showers drizzling down in bursts. The drops glisten on palm fronds and puddles, catching little moments of sunshine between the clouds. It's beautiful—the way the Cay breathes through these fleeting storms, a quick soak before the sun returns. I can already picture how perfect this is going to look on a TikTok reel.

At the grocery store, Timmy bounces with excitement. "Film me, film me!" I giggle as he grabs an eggplant from a produce stand, twirling it like a baton. He's totally shameless, dancing and making exaggerated faces, not caring for a moment that people are watching.

It's something I've never encountered before—a guy who's not just unbothered by looking ridiculous, but seems to thrive on it. He's not performing for anyone's approval, he's performing for attention—good or bad. He's having fun, and it's infectious, the kind of light-heartedness I didn't realize I needed in my life.

Back at the apartment, Timmy reaches for his tool bag. "Film this," he says, pulling out random objects one by one. "Here's a tiny skateboard," he shows the camera. "It's for tiny people to skate on."

I laugh, shaking my head at his random antics. "Where do you even find this stuff?"

"Usually on the beach," he shrugs. "Anyway, our TikToks are going to be epic!" he declares. When I'd floated the idea of having an account where we share our outings across the Cay, he'd been totally on board. That's one of the really fun things about Timmy. He's usually up for anything. His eyes sparkle with excitement, as he practically bounces on the balls of his feet. "Is this going to be like a podcast?" he asks, just like last time we discussed it.

I try to suppress a smile. "Well, not exactly. TikToks are different from podcasts," I explain. "TikToks are more like short-form videos—fun, quick snippets. Podcasts are usually audio, with maybe a video recording on the side."

He looks momentarily crestfallen. "And we're doing the podcast?"

I laugh, shaking my head. "No, Timmy. We're doing TikToks."

He rallies immediately. "Okay, so that means we need videos, right? I want to do the video one where people can see me—us." He's so excited, his eyes wide. "We're going to go to a bar and I'm going to make a scene. Like, a huge scene."

I feel a bit wary. "You don't need to do that. We don't need to make a scene or stage anything crazy. People will just really enjoy watching videos of our adventures around Sunset Cay. The place is interesting enough on its own, and we don't need to upset anyone who's just trying to relax."

His face falls for real this time. "So like... we don't need to come up with entire events where we make weird stuff happen? Like pranks and stuff? No huge scenes where we just mess with people?"

I laugh. "No, no. Other people do that. But where we live, and how we live our lives, is interesting enough on its own. We don't need to concoct scenarios. We can just be, and film some of it. That's all. Just us being us. I promise, it's enough."

He pauses for a moment, processing this new plan. "Okay, okay, I guess I was thinking of something different. But what you said is cool, too." There's a flicker of disappointment, like he's a kid and I've just told him he can't eat all his Halloween candy in one sitting.

But then he beams, his enthusiasm rebounding. "Our TikToks are going to be amazing. You'll see."

~

LATER, back in the kitchen, Timmy watches me set out the ingredients for dinner. "Wait, wait!" he says, quickly arranging them on and around the cutting board before snapping a picture. "Perfect," he announces, holding up his phone to show me.

I laugh, delighted. "Woah, that's so random! I do that all the time, too!"

I pull up my Instagram to show him similar photos I've taken—wooden chopping boards covered in colorful produce and neat piles of herbs.

He looks at my pictures, his grin widening. "See? We're totally on the same wavelength."

It feels like another little sign. Such a random coincidence, a confirmation that this whirlwind connection is really meant to be.

As I chop and sauté, Timmy stays close, asking questions about the methods I'm using. He's fascinated by how the chickpeas turn into these spicy, fragrant patties. "Wait, so you mash them first?" he asks, wide-eyed, as if I'm revealing some great culinary secret.

"Yep, it helps to bind everything together," I explain, as I add more garlic and spices to the mix.

He even helps with some of the prep, happily mashing chickpeas and chopping tomatoes, sneaking bites here and there, and pretty soon the wraps are ready—filled with spicy falafel, crunchy romaine, juicy tomatoes, a ton of garlic yogurt and hot sauce. Oh, and red onions, of course. I'm obsessed with raw onions. And cilantro too!

Timmy dives in without hesitation. "Oh my god," he moans around the first bite. "I'd only tried this one time, at a food truck, but this blows everything out of the water!"

"Oh, thank you!" I laugh, taking a bite. "I think I overdid the baking soda. But it's decent. Definitely full of flavor."

"No, no, no," he shakes his head emphatically. "This is perfect the way it is. Better than perfect. I think it might be one of the best things I've ever tasted, honestly." He pulls me into a tight hug, burying his face in my hair with crumb-covered lips, and kisses my forehead tenderly. "I can't believe you can cook this well, too. You really are like... the perfect woman for me."

I feel a warm glow in my chest, tilting my face up so our lips meet. It's not just the compliment—it's the way he says it, like he's genuinely in awe of me. I know it's just falafel, but his enthusiasm makes me feel like I just cooked him a Michelin-star meal.

"You're amazing," he murmurs, his lips brushing mine again. "How'd I ever get this lucky?"

I can't stop smiling. He really *is* this excited about me—about *us*. And the way he seems to genuinely love spicy food—with raw onions—makes my heart flutter, because that's hard to find. It feels good to be appreciated, to have someone so openly thrilled about the little things.

Not that my exes haven't enjoyed the food I've made for them. But he seems like a simple guy who knows what he likes. And apparently, he really likes falafel. And me.

"I've only had one girlfriend cook for me before," he says between bites. "And that was years ago, back in my twenties. You make me feel so special, doing this for me."

His words feel like another gift, wrapping me in warmth and validation. "Wow, really? I love cooking for people," I say. "Not a lot of guys I've dated could cook. But everything you've made so far has been so good—seasoned perfectly. You really know what you're doing. I've never met anyone like you."

He grins, leaning down to kiss me again. "I'm so in love with you, Margaux."

"I love you, too, Timmy."

After we finish eating, Timmy pulls out his phone and posts the photo of our ingredients to his Instagram. The caption reads: *"When she makes you falafel, you propose."*

I burst out laughing. "Are you serious?"

He beams. "Completely serious. You're *incredible*. I want everyone to know it, and to know that you're mine."

He's announcing this to the world. Announcing *us* to the world.

Any thoughts of him being embarrassed of me, any lingering doubts about him hiding our relationship, float away.

He's not worried about other girls seeing this. He's telling everyone who knows him that I am his person.

He's proud that we're together, and he's making that obvious.

In this moment, I feel truly special—truly, deeply special. There's no hesitation, no game-playing—just Timmy, loud and proud, telling the world how much he loves me.

And it turns out he's passionate about cooking, too.

We talk for hours about our favorite dishes, sharing ideas and swapping stories. He's so creative, mentioning healthy broths bursting with umami, venison burritos using meat from the deer he hunted when he visited Steve a few months back, and fried rice packed with veggies.

"I can't wait for you to try everything I make," he says eagerly. "I'm going to cook for you all the time."

I feel something I didn't expect—excitement over someone else cooking for me. I've grown so particular over the years, careful about what I eat to stay fit and healthy. But with Timmy, I look forward to his next culinary experiment.

His passion matches mine, and it feels like our cooking styles will complement each other perfectly. It's just one more way he fits into my life—like we were meant to find each other. And as I imagine the meals we'll make together, the laughter we'll share, and the adventures still ahead, I know I've found something special.

With Timmy, life feels exciting again.

"I love the way you speak with me," he says. "You're so affectionate, it makes me feel so special. You make me feel big and strong."

"You *are* big and strong. You're my protector."

He beams.

I'm so googly-eyed, my heart is about to burst out of my chest. He gives me the biggest butterflies I've ever felt. Because he wants me, and he adores me. And I've been so honest about who I was. And who I am. And he devours every word of it. Like everything I tell him makes him love me more.

I feel trust. Pure trust. It's freeing. It's wonderful. And I can't get enough of this.

Like every little thing—cooking dinner, filming TikToks, grocery shopping and dancing with eggplants—can be an adventure. Hell, he even makes showering fun.

And I can't wait to see where this adventure takes us.

41

BFFS

The Past

Mother: Who is your best friend?

Me: Felicity from school.

Mother: She might be your best school friend, but I'm your overall best friend.

Aren't I?

Me: Um, yes. You're my best friend, mum.

Mother: Good. Felicity is a fair weather friend, anyway.

She's not loyal like me.

For example, if you ever kill someone, I'll help you to hide the body, okay?

Felicity would never help you bury a body. You remember that.

Timmy and I are hanging out at my apartment, watching movies like usual. He's insisted we do a movie marathon tonight, just us. So the plan is to cook and hang out and snuggle and have sex. Cute couple stuff. I'm excited about it.

The vibe is cozy, and the scent of garlic and herbs fills the air. We move playfully around the kitchen, me chopping vegetables while Timmy sneaks a bite of red pepper off the cutting board, earning him a playful swat and a laugh. We steal kisses between tasks, my shoulder bumping into his torso as we navigate around each other in the kitchen.

After food, we stack blankets and pillows across the bed, reminiscent of the sheet forts I made as a kid. As the opening credits roll, we curl up together. I lay against his chest, our legs intertwined, cozy against the blanket behind us, but warm enough not to need one on top of us.

Partway through the second movie, his phone dings and he checks the message. He seems distracted. "Um, I have to go and meet some people."

"What? I thought we were hanging out here tonight." I'm so confused. The night has been going so well and now he just wants to dip out to meet whoever?

"Well, I thought we were." He shrugs. "But they need me to take them to get something."

I quirk a brow and frown. "Who are these people?"

"Rebecca and Jetson. They work on movie sets. They're some of the coolest people I know."

"And you don't want me to meet them? And you're going to ditch me to hang out with them because you think they're cool?"

He smirks, and it's cruel. "No. I don't want you to meet them." His tone drops lower, and his eyes narrow slightly, as if he knows something I don't—or worse, something that will hurt me soon. There's no softness in his expression. Instead, it's cold, calculated, like he's delighting in the torment his sudden unexpected change of plans is causing me.

I feel crushed. "So you're going to ditch me on a Friday night to go hang out with friends you don't want me to meet?"

He frowns. "Well you can fucking meet them, I suppose. Jesus Christ." His response makes me feel desperate, needy. It's not a rejection, but it's not exactly an invitation, either.

My stomach knots, and heat rises to my face. I hate coming across as thirsty for company or attention, and I know I probably just did. "I just don't understand what the issue is."

"You don't have to do everything with me," he says, his voice unusually clipped. "You always want to be together."

I feel dismissed, rejected. For someone so excited to spend the evening with me, he's sure ready to leave me the second someone else shows interest.

And he's right. I do enjoy spending every waking and sleeping moment with him. But it's definitely something that's driven by him. I'm not letting him off the hook that easily.

"You're the one over at my apartment. You're the one who keeps planning things to do together every day and every night. You're the one who takes me to work with you. You're the one who texts me constantly on the rare occasion we aren't together."

"Whatever," he says, rolling his eyes, a scowl etched into his face. "Way to twist things around."

My voice raises, even though I don't mean for it to. "I just don't understand why you're suddenly changing the plans and not inviting me. I feel excluded. It's weird." I feel like I'm whining. Maybe I am. But I'm just so thrown by his sudden demeanor switch and the way he's making it feel like it's my fault.

He lets out an exaggerated sigh, his own voice rising. "They want me to take them to go get drugs, okay? I thought you would judge me for that. Are you happy now?"

"Oh, I see." I frown, trying to understand why he didn't just tell me. Why he made it feel so secretive, and planned to leave me alone because of it. "Well, I wish you'd just been honest from the outset. It sounded like you were embarrassed by me and didn't want to introduce me to your 'cool' friends. Or that you felt like you'd found a more exciting way to spend your Friday night than hanging out with me."

He sighs again. "Jesus, Margaux. What the fuck is your problem? Stop assuming things. Neither of those are true. But I can go hang out with them without you if I want."

My eyes narrow. He's really pissing me off. "Great. And I can go hang out with whoever the fuck I like without you, as well."

His eyes are flinty slits. "No way. You're coming with me. I'll introduce you, it's fine."

Now I feel like I'm being a brat, forcing myself on his friends. But he's an asshole for trying to ditch me, or keep the truth from me, whichever is true.

My guilt settles in, heavy and unavoidable. I suddenly feel like a jerk for even asking. Was it selfish for me to ask? Should I have just let him go? I'm a big girl. I could have sat here and watched movies. I could have walked down the street and hung out somewhere. I could have just smiled and wished him a good time, played it cool, acted like I didn't care.

At the same time, fuck it. He came up with the plans for our night, and then he switched them up because he received an unexpected text. I feel valid for calling him out on it, empowered by making sure he included me. But now the air feels tense and awkward, and I created that.

He grabs a T-shirt and slips it on while I sit on the bed, awkward, going back and forth in my mind about whether I've done the right thing. He gives me a quick but distant smile. "Do I look cute?"

"Yes," I smile back. He does. The gray and pink T-shirt looks really cute with his long brown, sun-bleached hair and gorgeous blue eyes.

"We'll head out in a few minutes," he says, already staring at his phone again, already somewhere else in his mind.

I'm glad he invited me, eventually, but the guilt is gnawing at me.

Like I've done something wrong, inserting myself somewhere where I don't quite belong.

THE MOMENT I get into Rebecca and Jetson's car, all worries I had melt away.

They're friendly, a fun couple, I can tell from the get-go.

Rebecca is gorgeous, a vibrant blonde Floridian who likes to have a good time and doesn't take shit from anyone.

Jetson is tall and lanky, also a Floridian, and I can tell he's pissed off at Rebecca for something. I don't know what. Sometimes you can just tell when a couple has been bickering moments before you enter their orbit.

But they're both friendly and outgoing and funny, and they offer me a hard seltzer and we all drive off together in search of whatever they're looking for.

As we banter, I notice Timmy glowering at me, like he's mad I'm getting along with his friends. I immediately feel self-conscious. Am I being too loud? Too annoying? But Rebecca and Jetson don't seem to mind.

The gnawing guilt is just following me from our earlier conversation, and I realize that Timmy is probably annoyed he doesn't get to be the center of attention, the guy who they call when they need something only he knows how to find. So I make myself quiet, I shrink myself, and I let him take center stage. These are his friends, so it gets to be the Timmy show.

Still, they seem interested in me and both of them ask me questions. Each time I answer with something that makes them laugh or continue the conversation, Timmy seems to physically pull away from me, as if he's punishing me. The more they seem interested in what I have to say, the more he physically recoils from me.

After we get back from acquiring whatever it was they wanted, the guys go to get some drinks, leaving Rebecca and I together in my apartment.

The conversation flows. She's really funny, and it turns out she's a talented artist and her specialty is dark romance art. What are the fucking chances?!

She shows me through her work and I'm incredibly impressed. Each piece is exquisite, conveying the optimal mix of angst and sexiness and trauma and beauty... I'm fan-girling hard. We talk about the potential to collaborate together on some work, because her art would definitely complement my books and vice-versa. I've never even met someone who does dark romance art before. It's so fucking cool! I'm suddenly guilt-free about inserting myself into their little outing, and very glad I got to meet this wonderful and talented human!

After a while, Timmy walks back in with Jetson and just stops, eyeing us.

I walk over and give Timmy a hug and a kiss. "Welcome back! We missed you guys!" I smile.

Timmy kisses me back, and drapes an arm around me, but there's a tension in the way he holds me.

"Oh my gosh! Rebecca is an artist!" I tell him, wide-eyed with excitement. "We have so much in common! We're thinking of combining our talents and working on a project together." I'm gushing, so excited to share that the person he just introduced me to has something so specific in common with me.

It also feels really good to have made my first real friend here. She's funny and smart and interesting, and it's enriching to meet someone in this place where all I really know is Timmy.

"Well, isn't that just great." His smile is forced, weak, a flicker of irritation in his eyes.

We all chat for a while, enjoying our drinks and talking about life on the coast. Rebecca and Jetson head out and we agree to meet up with them at a nearby Irish bar later on.

After they leave, he's sullen.

"What's going on?" I ask, touching his shoulder.

He flinches away, his foot bouncing. "Well, I'm fine with you being friends with her. But just as long as she doesn't take up my place as your best friend. I'm your number one friend."

My mind flashes back to childhood, my mother saying the same thing: "Felicity might be your best *school* friend, but I'm your best overall friend. Felicity is a fair weather friend anyway. She's not loyal, like me."

Maybe this is just an emotional Cancer thing, seeing as my mother and Timmy share the same star sign.

But it sounds like he's truly worried. Like, because I got along with someone I just met, I'm suddenly going to deprioritize him and throw him away like a piece of trash.

The irony is that, while that's definitely not going to happen, he made me feel like that earlier in the night. Like he was going to discard me and our plans that *he* suggested because he wanted to help these people go in search of party drugs.

I don't like that he tried to ditch me, and part of me wonders if the reason he didn't want to introduce us is because he could tell we would get along well, and he was threatened by the idea of me making a solid female friend connection.

Either way, I have no intention of ditching Timmy, I got to meet new people including someone who really could be a great friend.

So all in all, I consider this day a win.

42

NOT TIMMY

He's getting drunker in the Irish bar, and I'm not even sure how—he doesn't have any money. I only bought him one drink. He must have sweet-talked someone in line to buy him a shot, or maybe he's found a way to scavenge drinks from patrons distracted by the live music or overhead TVs. I've seen him drunk before, of course, but this is the first time we've been in a bar and he's behaving this way. In any case, he's a mess.

The pub isn't one of those trendy, modern bars. It's old-school Irish, tucked away on a quiet street, filled with heavy wooden tables, low ceilings, and dim light that casts a perpetual amber glow. The air smells of stale beer, damp wood, and the faintest hint of cigarette smoke crossed with BO and aftershave. Football highlights flicker on the TVs mounted above the bar, while a group of regulars sing along to live music with raspy voices. The bar is essentially packed, and it's not the place for Timmy's antics.

Yet, here he is, in the middle of it all, doing his version of a shuffle dance, arms flailing, legs writhing like they're trying to escape from underneath him. But we're not at some EDM rave or a club where they're playing house music. The speakers are blasting the band's old Irish rock songs, and Timmy's out there trying to shuffle like he's in another world entirely. He weaves and sways, narrowly avoiding toppling over, and every few seconds he knocks into someone, their drinks sloshing up the sides and over the edges of their glasses as they glare at him. But Timmy is blissfully unaware, enjoying himself in the moment, the king of his own chaos.

The bartenders are too busy to notice, three deep with people calling for drinks the whole way around the bar. The bouncer, a hulking guy with tattoos running down his neck, doesn't seem inclined to intervene, even as Timmy's dance threatens to spill over into someone's pint. Instead, he just laughs. Timmy has bragged about knowing him, although I can't tell if the bouncer actually knows him or just finds his stupidity entertaining.

A woman sitting at the bar with her husband beckons me over, a vision of expensive surgeries and high-maintenance glamor. Her soft pink lipstick and perfectly sculpted cheekbones belong in a different setting—maybe a yacht club or a high-end casino—but here she is, slumming it in a dive bar with the rest of us. She winks at me.

"How do you know Timmy?"

"He's my fiancé."

Her eyes widen in disbelief, her heavily mascaraed eyelashes fluttering as she processes my words. "Your *fiancé*?" Her tone is incredulous. She glances at him, then back at me, like she's trying to solve a puzzle that doesn't make sense. "What's your name?"

"Margaux."

"Margaux," she repeats it like she's trying to convince herself. "He can't be your fiancé. Not Timmy. He can't." She looks at me and then at him. "No, for real. You can't be serious. He's not, right?"

I nod, unsure how else to respond. "He is."

"Margaux, sweetie," she shakes her head and trails off as he almost topples into a group of regulars who are clearly not amused. "Him? Really? Really, Margaux?"

I want to melt into the floor. But instead, I just offer a tight smile and a nod, pretending none of this is happening. Inside I'm screaming, how did I get there? How is this my life?

He's making a fool of himself and being a problem, a

menace, but I don't know how to stop him. I'm sure if anybody else acted half the fool Timmy is right now, they'd have been kicked out half an hour ago. He's seriously destroying the fun of all the patrons around him who are simply trying to move around on the dance floor and enjoy their drinks. But here Timmy is, creating problems, and the staff seem to be just fine about it.

Suddenly, Timmy makes a wild dash for the door, nearly colliding with a barback carrying a tray of empty glasses. Without a word, he's gone.

I blink at the spot he disappeared from. I look for him, but can't see him on the street. A few minutes later, I turn to the nearest group. "Has anyone seen my fiancé?" I ask the crowd around me.

Three guys immediately raise their hands. "I'll be your fiancé!" one yells, as the others laugh and join in. "Forget that guy, I volunteer to replace him."

I can't help but laugh, even as part of me wants to cry. Timmy's chaos is exhausting, but here I am with strangers, still holding onto the hope he'll somehow get his act together and we'll go home quietly.

Eventually, he comes back, just as drunk if not worse. His shirt is untucked, and there's a fresh stain on his pants that I don't want to think too hard about. He swaggers up to me, his eyes glassy.

"Let's go to the strip club!" Timmy announces loudly, like it's the best idea in the world.

Rebecca and Jetson and I exchange glances. We shrug and follow him out into the humid night air. The streets are damp, the occasional flicker of a streetlamp catching on the wet sidewalk. Palm trees sway in the warm breeze, the smell of saltwater mingling with the sound of waves crashing in the distance. Sunset Cay never sleeps, but this isn't the vibrant nightlife scene advertised in glossy brochures—this is gritty and real.

Timmy leads us down a nondescript alley and up some stairs to a poky little strip club—a small, dingy little spot with neon lights flickering over the door.

"That'll be a forty dollar cover per person," the cashier says, barely looking up from her phone. Timmy looks at us expectantly.

"Did any of us actually want to come here?" Jetson asks, deadpan.

Rebecca and I look at each other and shake our heads. Just another of Timmy's terrible ideas that he expects others to fund.

"Me neither," says Jetson. "It seems like Timmy is the only one who did, and he can't afford the cover for one, let alone four."

Timmy frowns as we traipse back down the stairs. "Well, I thought that would have been fun," he says, sulking. His disappointment is palpable, his shoulders slouched, his slightly wobbly pace slowing.

"Yeah, if everyone else was paying for you." I roll my eyes, shaking my head. "And you were the only one who wanted to go."

As if on cue, a nondescript woman in a sheer shirt walks past, her lace bra on full display. Timmy spins around like a compass drawn to magnetic north, his eyes wide as he watches her pass. He just about drools on the sidewalk.

"What?" he says, catching my irritated expression. "I get to look at girls, and say 'yeah you!' if I want! I won't touch any of them, just look."

"Can you at least pick an attractive person to drool over then?" I snap, my patience wearing thin.

He's pouting because he didn't get to see some half-assed strippers, and trying to start an argument by being disrespectful.

I'm putting this sloppy behavior down to his level of intoxication, which seems to be getting steadily higher even though I haven't seen him drink anything in quite a while. Maybe he's in stealth mode. At this point, I wouldn't be surprised to learn he'd been going around taking sips out of random people's drinks. There's no other real explanation for it.

At one point, we need to share the sidewalk with a family headed in the other direction. "Watch it!" Timmy shrieks at them for no apparent reason.

"What the fuck, dude?" Jetson says under his breath, and the three of us exchange glances as Timmy charges on ahead.

His behavior is more than over the top, but I try to shake it off. I'm enjoying spending time with Rebecca and excited to have a new friend here on the island. It'll be nice to plan girl outings and do fitness classes and restaurant stuff together. And she and Jetson seem like a solid couple, so we can do double dates. I glance at them and they offer me a sympathetic look. This isn't what I had in mind when I thought of a night out.

But I shake it off. I'm not going to ruin what could still be an enjoyable night out with friends because Timmy decided to have three too many drinks, or whatever this is.

This has to be a one-off, him stumbling around this way.

Nobody behaves like this all the time.

43

___

COCK-BLOCKER

few days later

A The sun is warm and bright as we wander down the main shopping strip lined with colorful stores. Timmy was apologetic the morning after his Irish bar antics, blaming his behavior on drinking too much, and he's been relatively calm ever since.

"Come," says Timmy, grabbing my hand in his and leading me into an indoor arcade.

We go into a surf shop that smells like sunscreen, saltwater and soft cotton, the kind of place that feels sun-kissed and easygoing. Boards are stacked along the perimeter, and racks of T-shirts, board shorts and caps also line the walls. As we wander in, a low indie song drifts from the speakers, adding to the laid-back vibe.

I have so much fun exploring surf shops with Timmy. He gets so excited discovering the latest designs, although he's always confident he could design something much more interesting himself. And, based on what he's shown me so far, I'm also confident he can.

I trail behind Timmy, my fingers brushing against soft hoodies and linen beach pants. The store feels alive with colors that represent the ocean and our tropical location—bright blues, pastel pinks, sandy neutrals—the lighting causing everything to glow with a sunny, golden hue.

Timmy, as usual, gravitates toward the hats. He scans the shelves thoughtfully, his fingers tapping on the bills of a few before he picks up two. He holds them against me, selecting one. "This is the one," he grins, holding it out to me. "Try this on," and then he turns me so I can see myself in the mirror.

It's pretty, from a popular surf brand, a black hat with brightly colored plumeria and a map of Sunset Cay on the bottom of the bill.

I hesitate for a second, surprised by how deliberate he's being, then I take the cap and slip it onto my head. The fabric feels cool against my skin, and the color underneath the bill automatically warms my complexion.

He steps back, tilting his head slightly as he studies me, a small, satisfied smile tugging at the corners of his mouth. "That's my beautiful girl," he says, gazing at me in adoration and kissing me. "You should definitely get this one. It looks perfect on you."

I glance at myself in the mirror, adjusting the hat slightly. I'm struck by how good it looks—how it seems to brighten my whole face. It's not a pattern I would likely have chosen for myself, but somehow it works—like it was made just for me.

I look back at Timmy, my heart swelling with a combination of pride and gratitude.

"How did you know?" I ask softly, running my fingers beneath the bill.

He shrugs, but there's a cocky confidence in the way he smiles at me. "I just know what looks good on you. It matches your beautiful skin tone. I'm a pretty amazing designer, you know. I know all about color profiles and what suits you." His gaze lingers, warm and appreciative, like he's proud of the way the cap brings out something unique about me—something only he could notice.

I feel a flush rise in my cheeks, not from embarrassment, but at how he's made me feel in this moment. It's not just about the cap. It's the way he pays attention—real attention—noticing things about me that nobody else has.

I've never had a man really help me pick out clothing before. He pays attention to my complexion and knows why certain colors go together. Whenever I've shopped with other guys, I've had to drag them kicking and screaming to the store. And then they've waited while I've tried things on. And occasionally, begrudgingly, helped me decide between two items that I'd selected by myself. But with Timmy, it's like having my own very cute personal stylist who loves the shit out of me.

For a moment, standing there under the soft glow of the store's lights, the world feels a little bit smaller and sweeter. Timmy, confident and carefree, in his element, and me, standing beside him, feeling beautiful in a way I never expected.

I pull the cap off and hold it in my hands, a small smile playing across my lips. "Okay," I say quietly, touched by the simple, thoughtful gesture. "I'm getting it."

Timmy leans forward and his lips meet mine, and then his grin widens. "Yay," he says, "I told you it would look good."

Then we move to the streetwear store that specializes in shoes and hats, drawn in by the trendy, vibrant displays, and I see some sneakers I really like. They're black and white with gold accents, and I love them. Because I had to shrink my life into a few suitcases and a cat carrier, I'm doing a bit of replenishment of my wardrobe. It's a treat. And it's a little retail therapy to distract myself from Sabre not being here. "These are perfect," I murmur, slipping them off the shelf to inspect the size.

"Oh yeah," nods Timmy. "Those are super cute. They'd look great on you."

I try on the shoes, and while I find the right size with the help of a sales assistant, Timmy wanders around the store looking at hats. He tries on a couple of caps in front of a mirror, grinning at his reflection as he turns his head this way and that. He's particularly enamored with one that says 'Cock' on it, alongside a picture of a rooster. I laugh and shake my head. Of course he would like that one the best.

I find the perfect size for the sneakers, and head toward the counter with the shoe box in hand. "These are a steal," I say with a playful smile, feeling content as I tap my card on the reader.

The cashier hands me the bag with a friendly nod, and I glance over at Timmy, still playing with the hats. He pulls one low over his brow, smirking at himself in the mirror one last time before we stroll out of the store together.

We're halfway across the indoor mall when something nags at the edge of my awareness. I glance at Timmy—and there it is, still perched on his head. The cock hat, bold and new, the price tag hanging off the back.

I stop in my tracks, my heart sinking. "Timmy...you didn't pay for the hat."

"Oh, oops!" he says, casually touching the bill as if he just noticed it, grinning lazily. "I had absolutely no idea I was wearing this. It's meant to be, I guess. I'm meant to have this hat."

My stomach twists. "You *forgot?*"

I think back to the smoothie at the grocery store, the sunglasses and water bottle at the thrift store, the registration tags, and even the frying pan at the restaurant. This seems practiced, habitual, and I don't like it at all.

He shrugs at me, giving that familiar, breezy smile that once felt genuine and charming, but is starting to feel more like a shield. "Yeah, it just slipped my mind."

But I'm starting to know better. Knowing that behind Timmy's seemingly casual actions is a calculated slyness, whether he'll acknowledge it to himself or not.

"Timmy, come on," I say softly, trying not to let too much frustration creep into my voice. "Please stop doing this. It's not right."

His expression shifts, his grin transforming into something much sharper. "What's the big deal?" he asks, a hint of annoyance slipping into his tone. "It's just a hat. Nobody even noticed. *I* didn't even notice."

I bite my lip, trying to keep calm. "It's not about that. I just don't want you to get in trouble. Or for *us* to get in trouble. And if you accidentally take something from a store, you need to take it back when you realize."

His eyes narrow slightly, his easy charm dissolving into something colder. "Jesus, Margaux. You really think I did this on purpose?" he asks, a defensive edge creeping into his voice. "I *said* I forgot. Why do you always have to make a thing out of nothing?"

I feel the familiar sting of guilt rise in my chest. The way he says it —like I'm being unreasonable, like *I'm* the one who's the problem— makes me doubt myself for a moment. He has a way of making me feel like his actions are normal and I'm the outlier.

The knot in my stomach tightens.

"I'm sorry," I mumble, not because I think I'm wrong or that he deserves an apology from me, but because I don't want this to spiral into another argument. I'm tired of the tension, tired of feeling like every objection I raise pulls us further apart. "I just... forget I said anything. But please, be careful that you don't take anything else. It just makes me feel really uncomfortable, even if it was completely accidental. How silly would you feel if you got arrested and ended up in jail because you took a hat without paying for it?"

Timmy lets out a short breath, rolling his eyes. "Whatever," he says, adjusting the hat on his head like it was always his to wear.

We keep walking, but the easy fun of the afternoon is gone, replaced with something much heavier, an uncomfortable silence stretching between us like a chasm.

I grip the bags with my sneakers and my hat—that I paid for— tightly, trying to convince myself that maybe I am really being uptight.

But deep down the unease remains, gnawing at me, whispering that something is off. And as Timmy continues to chat away lightly, discussing our next stop, as if nothing happened, I wonder how many more times I'll have to bite my tongue just to keep the peace.

44

N IS FOR NO

My friend Natasja messages me out of the blue.

NATASJA:

> Hey Margaux! I'm going to be in Sunset Cay
> for work in a few days.

ME:

> Oh my gosh, you are?!

NATASJA:

> Yeah, there's a conference I'm attending.

She sends me the address of the conference as well as where she'll be staying.

ME:

> Oh wow! You're going to be staying so close.

> If you have time, I'd LOVE to see you!

NATASJA:

> My schedule is pretty packed, but I'll see if I
> can get away.

> It would be nice to catch up.

It feels like an opportunity for a bit of a redo on our engagement party. Needless to say, Parker won't be invited.

And having Natasja meet Timmy is important. She'll be my first friend to meet him in person.

Natasja is a very smart, entrepreneurial businesswoman who travels the world for work, attending conferences and working groups.

The night begins with excitement and anticipation.

We choose a bar below my apartment, in the same building. It's an open air space, warm and inviting, with dim lighting and an eclectic mix of international flavors on the menu.

I see Natasja approaching the bar and run out to give her a big, warm hug. She's one of those huggers that squeezes you properly, and you can feel the energy transfer between you. Quality hugs, that one.

She's joined by two of her friends from the conference, making our group a lively five.

We start with a round of exotic cocktails—tart, vibrant drinks that take advantage of the local tropical fruits the area is known for, and a few tapas plates to share—their signature bao buns with applewood smoked bacon, tempura calamari, crispy pork spring rolls with pineapple relish, and grilled chicken satay with deliciously tangy pickled daikon and carrot.

Our group laughs and chats as we savor the bold, rich flavors. I beam at Natasja and her friends, happy to be able to share this moment with them.

Timmy is attentive, keeping his hand on the small of my back, leaning down to kiss me and smile at me regularly. It feels really good to be able to introduce him to one of my closest friends.

None of Timmy's friends were able to make it tonight, but that's okay. I really don't think too much of it. Because, after all, most of his friends live on the opposite side of the Cay, and this has all been planned same-day, short notice, just like our other 'engagement party'. Although I'm very relieved Parker isn't attending this one. What an unhinged dickhead.

Natasja's work friends are friendly, and the conversation flows effortlessly. The group quickly bonds over tales from the conference, and memories about Natasja's and my life and friendship back on the east coast where we used to live nearby. Timmy makes the group laugh with tales of growing up on Sunset Cay, and he's keeping his stories amusing, but also not over-the-top.

It feels weird to think about it this way, but I'm almost proud of the way he's behaving. Like he realizes Natasja is an important person in my life, and so he's dressed up nicely and he's still being himself, but perhaps a more dialed-in version. It's the kind of night that feels effortlessly fun, and like nothing can go wrong.

After finishing our drinks and tapas, we're all still enjoying ourselves and not ready to end the night so early. Someone suggests heading upstairs to the market to get a second round of snacks to enjoy in my apartment complex's gorgeous courtyard. The market is an explosion of sights and sounds—freshly prepared meals on display which are way different from what Natasja could find back in her hometown. The group wanders around in awe, and collects a few different options as we wander from stall to stall wowed by what's on offer. We end up with an eclectic mix of wood-fired pizza and artisanal salads. We grab poke bowls and sushi, and before long our arms are full of small, delicious plates.

With our bounty in hand, we make our way to the upstairs courtyard, and find a cozy, intimate space inside our own little private enclosed cabana with string lights overhead.

There, we spread our food out on the table, sharing our various finds as we enjoy more drinks. The mood is relaxed, and one of Natasja's acquaintances plays harmonica music on the phone, providing the perfect background as we all chat and laugh.

Timmy regales the group with more tales about growing up in Sunset Cay—his stories are so full of eccentric characters and increasingly off-the-wall scenarios, they feel like something out of a novel. His anecdotes are getting more outrageous as the night wears on, and the group is in stitches, caught up in the joy of the evening.

As the evening continues, we decide to hit a nearby karaoke spot to cap off the celebrations. Everyone is having a good time, and still, nobody's quite ready for the evening to end. It's the first time I've done karaoke in years, and while I don't relish the idea of singing aloud in a room full of strangers, I figure it'll be fun with this group. And especially with Timmy.

The bar is vibrant and buzzing with energy, dimly lit and packed with people who cheer and sing along with each song, the atmosphere alive with fun. Natasja and her friends take turns picking out cheesy pop songs and laugh as they sing off-key, the crowd clapping along.

Timmy and I sing Gangsta's Paradise together, and the song goes well. It's one I know all the lyrics to, and have for years. We laugh as we rap and the crowd sings along with us. Timmy beams and pulls me into his arms afterwards. "Oh my god, I can't believe you know all the lyrics to that song. We really are meant to be together. The crowd loves us!"

Then Timmy gets up to sing a second song, almost straight away.

At first, it's just another song—something everyone recognizes. But halfway through, Timmy's energy shifts. He's not just performing anymore—he's really *performing*. He climbs onto the edge of the small stage, gripping the mic like he's the headliner of some rock concert, then suddenly rips his shirt open with a dramatic flourish.

The crowd reacts with a mix of amusement and surprise—laughter and gasps echo around the room. But then he takes it a step further.

He unbuckles his jeans.

A nervous ripple moves through the room. Some people laugh awkwardly, assuming he's joking. But then, to my horror, he yanks his pants down to his thighs, thrusting his hips wildly to the beat of the song. The mood shifts instantly.

People stop singing. Several members of the crowd exchange uneasy glances. A bartender mutters something to another staff member. The DJ lowers the music slightly, clearly waiting to see if Timmy will get a grip.

But Timmy only doubles down. He starts hollering at the audience, encouraging them to join in, gyrating like he's lost his mind. Someone in the crowd boos. Another person yells, *"Put your pants back on, dude!"*

Timmy laughs, clearly reveling in the attention, and makes some crude joke about giving everyone a *real* show, motioning toward his underwear as if he's about to lower it. That's when security steps in.

"Alright, man, that's enough." A bouncer appears at the side of the stage, arms crossed.

Timmy glares at him. "What? I'm just having fun! Lighten up!"

But the bouncer isn't having it. "Pull your pants up, or you're out."

Timmy throws his hands up dramatically, playing the victim. "Ohhh, so you're going to pick on me for *entertaining your audience*?" He rolls his eyes, still making no move to fix his clothes.

What had been lighthearted and fun is turning tense and ugly.

When the music finally cuts out completely, Timmy explodes.

"Are you all fucking serious right now?" Timmy yells, his face contorted in rage. His words turn vile, spewing hateful words at anyone who will listen. He stomps around the bar, hurling insults with growing fury. The crowd recoils, and the once-lively atmosphere is now thick with discomfort and anger. All because of Timmy. He changed the entire vibe of the place from something so lighthearted to something ugly. People begin calling for him to be removed, and the staff quickly move to intervene.

I stand in shock with the rest of our group, our minds all a little fuzzy from our drinks, unable to process how the night has taken such a dark turn. The embarrassment is palpable, our laughter and joy from earlier completely evaporated.

Natasja puts a hand on my shoulder, signaling it's time to leave. Timmy's behavior has cast a long, disturbing shadow over the evening.

We slip out of the bar in silence, avoiding the angry glances being thrown in our direction.

Timmy stomps along behind us, his voice echoing, filled with anger and self-righteous indignation.

Nobody says much as we leave the area and Natasja and her acquaintances call an Uber to get back to their hotel, the celebratory energy of the night completely gone. The weight of what just happened hangs in the air, leaving us all feeling uncomfortable and drained.

Everyone except Timmy, who still seems to think he was somehow wronged by the whole situation as he mutters to himself. He stomps along behind us, his voice echoing, filled with self-righteous indignation. "Can you *believe* those guys? Acting like I was stripping or something! It was just a joke!"

I whisper to Natasja, "Oh my god, I don't know what happened. I'm so sorry."

She shrugs. "It's okay. Some guys just don't know when to stop."

I shake my head. "But it's not just that. He just... keeps pushing things too far."

She just presses her lips together and nods, then gives me another one of her amazing hugs.

When we finally part ways, the joy of Timmy's and my engagement feels distant—overshadowed by the disturbing and unnecessary storm Timmy unleashed.

Timmy and I walk back to the apartment in near silence.

"What?" Timmy asks me at one point when I look at him with concern.

I sigh. "Let's talk about it tomorrow."

EVERY TIME I think about Timmy's antics at the karaoke bar, I feel my stomach twist. He yanked his pants down so naturally, I sense it's not the first time he's done it. He glances at me, noticing my reaction, and moves on like it's nothing. For a moment, I think maybe he'll realize his behavior is completely outrageous and stop himself. But over the next few days, he starts to do it more frequently, as though he's been holding it back and has now reached some bizarre tipping point where he just *can't* keep his clothes on in public.

At first, it's just little things—an exaggerated hip thrust as a joke, yanking his waistband down slightly for a laugh, acting like he's going to moon someone but stopping just short. But then it escalates.

One afternoon at the beach, he wades into the water, fully clothed, and then dramatically peels off his shorts, tossing them onto the sand like it's some grand reveal. People glance over, startled, unsure if they should laugh or be horrified. Later, at a casual back-yard gathering, he does it again—this time hopping onto a lounge chair and lowering his board shorts to expose half of his butt crack while making a spectacle of himself, laughing like he's the funniest guy in the world.

It's bewildering. I tell myself maybe it's something specific to Sunset Cay, some weird island mentality because everyone's just so used to exposing skin. The locals certainly have their quirks, a few mannerisms that feel frozen in time, but Timmy's blasé attitude takes it a step too far.

It's unsettling. I find myself dreading the next time, unsure if he's just going to flash someone as a "joke" or outright get us kicked out of a place. He acts like it's a harmless bit, something everyone should just accept, but the more he does it, the less funny it becomes. It's almost like he gets a thrill from it, like he enjoys the shocked reactions.

One night, I've had enough. We're sitting on the bed, a quiet evening in, when he starts reminiscing about the karaoke night, laughing about how "people just can't handle a little fun."

"Timmy," I say, my tone sharp. "You really need to stop pulling your pants down in public. You're going to embarrass the wrong person one day, and they're going to punch you in the face, and I won't stop them."

He pauses and laughs, like I've just told him a joke. "Aw, come on, it's not a big deal. People in the Cay don't care about that stuff." He shrugs, almost dismissively.

Over the next few days, I realize I can't let this slide. Every time he does it, it's like a slap to everything I stand for. I can't keep making excuses for him.

"You know, Timmy," I tell him one evening, trying to keep my voice calm, "it's not just inappropriate. It's embarrassing. I can't understand why you *want* to do it in the first place."

I try to reason with him, appeal to his desire to be well-liked, to fit in with everyone he meets. "Maybe you think it's just a joke, but it's not. People don't take it lightly, and honestly, I can't be around someone who thinks that's okay. Surely, you saw how uncomfortable you made people at the karaoke bar. It wasn't funny—it was *awkward*. Even the locals didn't think it was okay. You could be arrested for lewd conduct."

He sighs and mutters, "Fine, I'll stop." And for a little while, he does.

But I notice that whenever he's had a few too many drinks, it creeps back in—the shirt comes off first, then the waistband tugs, then the exaggerated gestures like he's *dying* for an audience. It's like he *needs* the attention, good or bad.

One night, I finally call him out. "Timmy," I say, exasperated. "What is it with you and getting half-naked in public?"

"Oh, it's an in-joke between me and my ex's son," he replies, looking pleased with himself. "We think it's hilarious."

I raise a brow, not quite believing him. *Also, way to make it even weirder.*

He shrugs, unfazed, like I'm overreacting. "It's just how I am. I do it all the time."

I shake my head, disappointment gnawing at me. "Well, then, you're going to have to stop doing it around me. I can't make you understand why it's weird, but if you keep it up, I'll just stop being around you."

It hits me, watching his reaction, that he either doesn't care or doesn't get it. Maybe both. He nods, as if to humor me, and I wonder if I'm fighting a losing battle.

45

IT'S 5 O'CLOCK SOMEWHERE

few days later

The rain has stopped by the time we pull into the beach parking lot, finding the perfect parking space right by the particular strip where Timmy wants to take me. The sky is still cloudy, and the scent of wet pavement and salt air lingers in the breeze, creating that delicious post-rain calm that feels like the earth is catching its breath.

We wander towards a convenience store on the way to the sand. Timmy grips my hand, and there's an urgency to the way he tugs me along. "Come," he says, like he's on a mission. Inside, he picks up a half-pint of whiskey, and I get some water and energy drinks.

It's early to start drinking, but I don't want to be judgmental. I tell myself it's harmless—just a little fun, and I don't want to be the one who ruins the vibe. After all, it's only a small bottle, and just the two of us, not bothering anyone.

We reach the beach and he opens the bottle with a grin. "Just don't be obvious about it," he says as he hands it to me. I take a sip, the amber liquid warming my throat.

Timmy takes the bottle back, and this time he drinks deeply, draining nearly a third of it in one go before sprinting into the water. I watch as he swims out into the ocean, his body cutting through the waves with ease, and he floats around for a while. There's something magnetic about him—like he belongs out there in the water, where everything is fluid and wild.

I sit on a bench, enjoying the gentle salty breeze rippling through my hair, rustling the palm trees overhead. It feels peaceful in many ways, but there's a strange edge to the day—like a tune slightly out of key. Something about the way he's acting, a bit manic and erratic, makes me feel unsteady, like I'm riding a wave but I'm not quite sure where it'll crash.

He runs back from the water, grinning like a kid who just won a race, and rinses himself off under the outdoor shower. Without missing a beat, he grabs the bottle from me again, takes a few more gulps, and looks at me with that same wild grin.

"Let's go feed the ducks!" he announces, his energy surging. I'm not surprised he wants to feed the ducks. I mean, it seems like one of his favorite things to do. And it's really surreal watching the birds interacting with him. But I hesitate, that strange feeling stirring again in the pit of my stomach. Feeding the ducks is innocent enough, but there's something about the way Timmy hurls himself into everything that feels... off. Too fast. Too much.

Still, I follow him to the pond, determined to push away my unease and just enjoy the day. He's teaching me that life should be fun, and the way he interacts with the birds is unique, like he's somehow on their wavelength. They flutter around him once again, landing on his shoulders and arms, squawking as he feeds them hunks of bread.

This time, I join in. I've always been a bit fearful of birds, but it looks like so much fun. I hold out pieces of bread, just like he showed me, and they land on my arms and my head. Their claws are a little scratchy, and probably not very clean, but I can't even describe the feeling of having several birds landing on you and pecking bread out of your hands, using you as a perch, their feathers tickling your face. I'm not scared like I thought I might be. I have sunglasses on so I'm not worried about any of them pecking out my eyes. I never thought

I'd enjoy something like this, but here I am, covered in birds, laughing with reckless abandon.

BACK AT THE APARTMENT, the shift in Timmy's mood catches me off guard again. It's hot outside, as usual—sticky, oppressive heat— and yet he's pulling on jeans. I raise an eyebrow, but he's already admiring himself in the mirror.

"Don't I look cute in these jeans?" he asks, striking a pose. "Mmhmm? I know they look great on me," he brags. "They make my ass look fantastic."

I laugh despite myself, wishing I had even half his confidence. That I didn't judge and criticize every inch of my body. That I accepted my imperfections and even embraced them the way he seems to do.

He carries himself with such certainty, such ease. I wonder what it would feel like to look in the mirror and love everything I see, to move through the world with no reservations. To never doubt that I belonged in any setting.

Timmy makes me feel like I could maybe learn to do that—like I can stop second-guessing myself, stop being so self-critical, stop feeling like I almost have to justify my presence everywhere I go, to just *be*.

And I appreciate it. I lean into it. I've never had it like this before.

Then he adds his Superman cape to his outfit, and I laugh. This man is literally running around in nothing but jeans and a Superman cape and a hat. No shoes, no undies, no shirt. Just the essentials from his perspective, I suppose. And a grin that says he knows how absurd he looks—and he loves it.

He braids some ti leaves into a gorgeous bracelet, and ties it around my wrist with a flourish. "For my love, the love of my life," he says, leaning down to kiss me. "You are everything I've ever asked for and more, Margaux. I'm so lucky to have you."

His words make my heart flutter, and I kiss him back, sinking into the moment. It's passionate, our tongues exploring each other, and my pussy clenches hard. What a gorgeous man, treating me this way. Making me feel so special, so adored.

There's something intoxicating about the way he treats me—like I'm the only person in the world who matters to him.

～

WE GO TO THE ZOO, Superman cape and all.

Before we go in, we frolic. *Frolic*, of all things. Because that's what life with Timmy involves. A lot of frolicking. He chases me around a giant banyan tree, and I laugh as he darts through the tangled roots, his Superman cape trailing behind him. He catches me, pulling me into a kiss, and I get butterflies. It's like we're in a scene from a romantic movie. Nobody has ever chased me into a tree and kissed me before, but it's totally something that Timmy would do.

Things feel light and perfect. But at the same time, there's still that same nagging feeling in the back of my mind. The way he throws himself into everything—whether it's feeding birds, wearing ridiculous outfits, or sprinting through the zoo. He's having fun, and making me laugh, but it almost seems a little... unhinged.

I tell myself that it's just spontaneity, that I should enjoy it, but it doesn't sit quite right. His energy feels almost too frantic, like a balloon over-inflated and ready to burst.

We grin as we snap a few selfies, leaning in to hold each other. I look at the photos, and we seem so happy—our eyes sparkling, our smiles wide. *This is fun*, I tell myself. *This is good*.

～

BACK AT THE APARTMENT BUILDING, Timmy's antics continue. I gasp as he dives into the pool, belly first, the sound echoing off the water. I gasp as he stays under for what starts to feel like way too long, and then he pops back up, water spraying wildly around him as he emerges, a huge grin plastered on his face.

He films himself underwater. "I got a good video! Check it out!" he says, holding out his phone.

"Wait, are you sure your phone is meant to be in there?" I ask, frowning.

"Yeah! It'll be fine!" he assures me. "iPhones are all water-resistant."

"Oh okay," I say. "I was today years old when I learned that." If that really is the case, I wish I knew ages ago. I've bought so many waterproof phone cases over the years. But he seems to know more about this stuff than me.

After his swim, we go back upstairs where he discovers his phone did not, in fact, agree with the chlorinated water. It starts glitching, and then turns off completely. He paces back and forth, his mood swinging wildly from irritation to indifference and back within minutes. "Fuck it, I'm so angry. It's meant to be water-resistant," he complains.

When I ask if he'd like me to take him out for a nice dinner, he perks up immediately, like a switch has flipped. He puts on my floppy hat and a bone necklace, and we head to one of my favorite spots for pizza and martinis. His outfit is quite ridiculous at this point, and he seems to bask in the amused glances of other pedestrians as we walk there and back, as if it fuels him. I laugh, but that feeling—the one I keep pushing down—lurks beneath the surface.

The day is fun, but I just don't quite feel like myself. I'm swept up in a wave, a riptide, of Timmy, swept along by his energy. He's impulsive and spontaneous and fun, and I like those attributes, but he seems to be getting into some type of manic episode. His mannerisms are becoming more erratic, his stories are getting wilder. He's wearing more and more eccentric outfits.

But it's been a fun day, overall, and I don't want to ruin the moment. And I certainly want to distract Timmy from being angry over his waterlogged phone. So I push the uneasy thoughts away. *Just enjoy the day,* I tell myself. *Ride the wave.*

But deep down, I know that waves like this always crash. And when they do, they leave you gasping for air.

46

———

FUCK OFF, K THANKS BYE

His phone buzzes again. And again.

The word, 'Worst'", keeps flashing across the screen like a taunt, each ping grating on my nerves.

Worst.

Worst.

Worst.

Then a new message lights up the display:

It's impossible not to see it—I mean, maybe I am craning my neck a little, but can you blame me?

My gut twists into a knot, the sinking feeling dragging me deeper with each buzz.

The casual way he lets her messages pile up, completely unconcerned, makes it worse. It's as if her texts don't even register as a problem to him, but they're glaring at me like a neon warning sign. Every time his phone buzzes the image of her suitcase on Timmy's bed creeps into my mind.

"Why the fuck is this girl blowing up your phone?" I ask, trying but semi-failing to keep my voice calm. My heart beats fast against my ribs. "I thought you said you didn't want anything to do with her." I raise a brow, the unease racing through me.

Timmy shrugs, his face annoyingly neutral, like this is a minor inconvenience. "I don't."

I narrow my eyes. "Well, she doesn't seem to have gotten the hint."

He shrugs again, his indifference only fueling my irritation. "I'll tell her to piss off. She's annoying. She must just want something."

Annoying. That's all she is to him, he says. But my gut keeps whispering otherwise, and I can't shake David's words from earlier. *"He's banging her. That's why he went radio silent for a few days. He's insecure, and people like that cheat—especially when they know you're out of their league."*

David's words swirl in my mind, needling at my insecurity, making it impossible to ignore the nagging doubt. *He has an agenda, too,* I remind myself. But no matter how hard I try to dismiss it, the suspicion sticks, sharp and persistent.

I need to know the truth.

I take a deep breath, steeling myself. "When she visited," I ask slowly, "did you sleep with her?"

The question hangs between us, heavy and loaded. Timmy blinks, clearly taken aback by my directness. "What kind of question is that?" he snaps, his tone defensive.

I watch his face closely, searching for any flicker of truth. And there it is—something fleeting, a flicker of guilt or frustration, maybe both, gone almost as soon as it appeared.

"Well, did you?" I ask again.

His expression darkens. "No," he scowls. "And it's none of your business. We weren't together then, Margaux. We hadn't even met in person. Stop asking me if I slept with her."

The sharpness in his voice feels like a slap, leaving me embarrassed and stung. My cheeks burn with shame. *He's right,* I tell myself. *It's not my business.* If something did happen between them, it happened before *us,* before Timmy and I existed as a couple, so why does it matter? And he's saying nothing happened, so I should trust him.

"Um okay," I mutter, feeling like I've been put in my place.

We drive in silence for a few minutes, the weight of the conversation hanging heavy, the hum of the car engine the only sound between us.

Just as I think the conversation is over, Timmy speaks again, his voice quieter but no less jarring. "Well...okay. I did have sex with her."

I feel like the ground just dropped out from beneath me. My stomach twists violently, bile rising in my throat. "Excuse me?"

"It didn't mean anything," he says with a shrug, like he's explaining away something very minor. "She's just this annoying girl I've hooked up with a few times. I didn't even know for sure you were coming to the island, and she was just... there." His tone is flat, unbothered, as if this explanation should just somehow make everything okay. "She's just a friend, though. We don't like each other as anything more than that. Never have, never will. I'd certainly never date her. She's a mess."

The words hit me like a punch to the chest, and I try to breathe through the sting. "Right..." I frown. My fears have been realized.

It's not that he slept with her—it's the *lie*. I asked him point-blank, and he lied about it.

And now, here she is, still texting him, still blowing up his phone, still trying to insert herself into his life, into *our* life.

"It's not the sex that bothers me," I say, my voice tight. "Because you're right, we weren't together. We hadn't met yet. It's the fact you lied about it. I know you've been with other people before you met me—of course you have. But you specifically lied to me about *her*. And now she's still reaching out to you, still trying to get your attention. That's what makes this gross."

Timmy sighs, rubbing his face as if I'm the one being difficult. "She probably just needs a ride somewhere," he mutters. "She uses people like that." He looks at me with an almost childlike expression, almost as if he expects me to take his side. "We're not interested in each other like that. You have nothing to worry about."

I want to believe him. I really do. I try to tell myself that we weren't together when it happened, that it was in the past, and that it doesn't matter. But the fact she's still texting him—trying to get him to go and pick her up from somewhere—makes it very much my business *now*.

I swallow hard, trying to push the knot of discomfort deeper down. Maybe he's right, she's just someone from the past who won't take a hint. Maybe I'm overreacting. But the truth still gnaws at me— if everything is as simple as he says it is, why did he lie in the first place?

He speaks up again. "And I usually had to initiate conversations with you, and I'm used to being pursued. And she wanted to meet up with me. And so I did."

Weird. So it's now... at least partially my fault he went and slept with his friend that he told me he was going to meet up with? When I was hours away and hadn't even met him? And what is this nonsense about him being pursued? Are there more like her, trying to get in his pants even though he's in a serious relationship?

We drive on, the silence between us heavy and uneasy. I stare out the window, watching the palm trees blur past, trying to make sense of everything.

I want to trust him. I want to push these doubts away and just enjoy being with him. But the lie sits between us like a stone, impossible to ignore. Just like the missed messages and calls on his phone.

No matter how hard I try to convince myself otherwise, I know something isn't right.

And she needs to leave us the fuck alone.

47

BRUISES FADE BUT THE STORIES THEY TELL LINGER

The Past

Lawyer: So, you're accusing my client of raping you. And part of that evidence is the bruises on your body. Is that correct?

Me: Yes.

Lawyer: And you moved a week before, right?

Me: That's correct.

Lawyer: But, as a redhead with pale skin, would you say you bruise easily?

Me: Not really... I haven't noticed that before.

Lawyer: It's well known that people with your complexion bruise easily.

Me: ...

Lawyer: So, given that, isn't it more likely that the

bruises were caused by the fact you moved heavy boxes, rather than the allegations you've made against my client?

Me: I didn't rip my vagina and my anus when I moved boxes, no.

~

THE PRESENT

A day or two go by, relatively uneventful. Timmy's phone stays quiet. Good, finally she maybe got the hint and will stop intruding on us.

But now, here I am, staring at my left arm, covered in splotches of gray and purple. My entire upper arm looks like I just got out of a paintball fight I never signed up for. I trace my fingers along the tender skin, wincing. It looks like someone grabbed me and squeezed hard—like the bruises on my legs from all those years ago.

Timmy, lounging on the bed, laughs. "Haha, I've been poking you so much to get your attention I've left bruises on you."

I force a smile, though my stomach twists uncomfortably. *It's fine,* I tell myself. I know I bruise easily. It's nothing.

But the sight of the bruises tugs at something deep inside, like a loose thread unraveling a tightly woven fabric. The memories I've worked so hard to suppress start clawing their way to the surface. My mind drifts back to those awful photos—evidence taken after the assault. I remember the ugly purple and gray marks on my legs, the ones the lawyer tried to explain away with his slick words about moving boxes and pale skin. *These bruises don't look so different,* I realize, my pulse quickening.

But this *is* completely different. *Right?*

My PTSD is just making me correlate two completely separate things. Timmy didn't hurt me. He was just being playful—excited, even. He was showing me the Cay, poking me to get my attention, sharing his joy. That's not abuse. It's... affection. *Isn't it?* It was *just* poking.

Timmy catches me staring at the marks on my arm. "Aw, babe," he says, his grin widening. "I really didn't mean to bruise you up so bad. I forget how strong I am sometimes. I'll try to be gentler."

He reaches out and strokes my arm lightly, as if that erases the purples and blues blooming under my skin. "I would never hurt you on purpose," he says softly, brushing my hair behind my ear. His eyes, wide and sincere, make me want to believe him. *This is just how he shows love and enthusiasm.*

I laugh, though it feels brittle in my throat. "Just maybe don't do it so hard next time, okay?"

"Deal," he says, still smiling. "I mean, I wanted a redhead with creamy, milky white skin and freckles. I didn't know you'd bruise like a banana," he teases, and before I can stop him, he pokes the exact same spot again.

It's playful—it's *supposed* to be playful. But the poke lands heavier this time, like a little jab to my soul.

The room feels different now, like the air has thickened with something I can't quite name.

My laughter dies in my throat, and I shift uncomfortably. The playful moment has turned into something else entirely, though I can't quite explain why.

He grins, as if he doesn't notice the shift—or worse, as if he *does* notice, and finds it amusing.

I try to laugh it off again, but my voice sounds strange to my own ears. The discomfort lingers, curling deep inside my chest like a coiled spring ready to snap. I tell myself it's nothing. He's not hurting me. He's just playing around.

But the flashbacks won't stop. I see the lawyer's smug face in my mind, the disbelief in his eyes as he tried to make my pain seem insignificant. I remember how easily the truth was twisted back then, how I was made to feel like I had overreacted.

And now, standing here, staring at my bruised arm, I can't help but wonder—*am I doing it again?*

I brush the thought away, force a smile back onto my face. Timmy means well. He loves me. He's not like the others.

But the atmosphere in the room stays heavy, and the little knot in my stomach twists tighter. Because deep down, a quiet voice whispers: *This isn't okay. This doesn't feel right. And it's a precursor to something that's going to be much worse.*

48

IN THE SAME PLACE

Timmy and I are hanging out at Matty's when we have another fight, and we fight hard—words flying like daggers, sharp and relentless. He starts another argument over what feels like nothing, and his cruel words sting in a way I don't expect. Needing air, I leave the apartment without another word and head down to the beach. I need space to think, to untangle the mess in my mind, and to breathe without feeling suffocated by him.

The sand is cool under my feet as I sit near the water, listening to the waves slap the shore. The sun is dipping low, the sky streaked in oranges and purples. The sound of the surf is usually enough to calm me, but not today. My emotions are too tangled—hope, frustration and confusion swirling together like a storm cloud.

I open my phone and pull up a playlist I've been building. It's called Timmy—with a broken heart emoji tacked onto the end. I scroll through the songs, playing a few, letting the lyrics hit hard. Every word feels like it was written for me, for this exact moment. The knot in my chest tightens, my emotions too close to the surface.

My phone buzzes. It's him. Of course it's him. I ignore the call. Moments later, a flood of texts lights up my screen. Apologies—

rushed and messy—pour in, and I can almost hear the desperation in his voice through the words on the screen.

TIMMY:

> I'm so sorry.

> Please, Margaux.

> I don't even remember what we were fighting about.

> Just give me a chance to talk to you.

I exhale sharply, my resolve crumbling faster than I'd like. I shouldn't answer him. But the void inside me—the strange, aching emptiness—grows bigger without him around. He's become like gravity, pulling me in, bending me toward him even when my better judgment tells me to resist.

So I reply.

ME:

> Okay. If you promise you'll stop treating me this way.

TIMMY:

> I promise, Margaux. Please, just let me see you.

ME:

> Fine.

TIMMY:

> Can you get me an Uber?

I roll my eyes and let out an audible groan, feeling a mix of frustration and shame as I pull up the Uber app on my phone.

Why am I doing this? He could easily walk—it's a twenty-minute stroll, maybe thirty. But here I am, once again enabling him, throwing money at the problem to bring him back to me. It feels ridiculous. He's a grown man, for god's sake. But that void gnaws at me, and before I know it, I've ordered the Uber.

I stay sitting on the sand, the waves lapping at the shore as guilt settles over me like a heavy fog.

Not long after, I see his familiar shape approaching the beach. He's clutching a large tote bag, and the moment his feet hit the sand, he runs toward me with open arms. He scoops me up, holding me tight, like he's afraid I'll disappear if he lets go.

"Oh my gosh, Margaux," he whispers into my hair, his voice a mix of relief and something almost frantic. "I've missed you so much. I love you. I thought I'd never see you again. I was so scared."

The intensity of his words makes my heart ache. He feels so big, his love so all-consuming, and I can't help but get swept up in it.

Then comes the bag.

He pulls it open with a flourish, grinning wildly. It's like a magic show—only instead of a rabbit, out comes the oddest assortment of trinkets: his tiny zebra figurine, his miniature skateboard, random shells he's collected from the beach. Each one is presented to me like a treasure, with a backstory about how it reminded him of me.

"These shells? They're beautiful, just like you. This one's a speckled ginger one, see?"

"This skateboard? It's tiny, like you. And because you like to roller-skate."

"This zebra? It's quirky—just like the way you laugh. And because you like to wear black-and-white stripes sometimes."

He beams with pride as he hands me each item, his grin stretching wider with every new offering. His enthusiasm is infectious, but there's also something unsettling about it—a manic energy that I can't quite place. This man has literally brought me a bag of junk. Things he found on the beach, things someone else might have thrown away. But he's offering them like they're treasures, and he has weirdly customized each of them to me.

"Um, thank you?" I say, holding a shell in my hand, turning it over to study it. It's chipped along one side.

"Well, it's all I could do right now," he says, his voice softening. "But I really wanted you to know how much I've been thinking of you. It's the only way I could think of to show you how sorry I am."

~

LATER AT MY apartment

Timmy sprawls out on the bed while I sit at my desk, participating in a video call with an investigator from my old job. While I no longer work there, they reached out for my help. As I speak, rattling off names, dates, and critical moments with ease, I feel something I haven't felt in a while—confidence. It's like stepping back into a version of myself that I thought had faded away. I know my stuff. I've lived and breathed this work for years, and it feels good to own it.

When the call ends, I close my laptop and lean back with a sigh of relief.

Timmy's eyes are wide with awe, and I can see a bulge in his pants.

"Oh my fucking god," he says, voice thick with admiration. "That was the sexiest thing I've ever heard. You're so capable and confident. Talk about a giant boner. That's what you've given me, just listening to you know your shit."

I laugh, feeling a warmth bloom in my chest. It's flattering—especially coming from him. I hadn't realized how starved I was for recognition. For someone to see me, to really see me, and appreciate me for all the hard work I've done—especially given I wasn't receiving the same kudos at work.

It's nice to have someone compliment me for my work. And he's right. Twenty years of really hard work has got me to the point where I indeed know what I'm talking about. It's a shame the company I worked for didn't think the same. Well, actually, most of them did—I did my job reliably with rave reviews by my client groups. But the bitch in charge of my division hated me for some inexplicable reason. It wasn't my fault she was a frumpy, jealous cunt. Seriously, the way she's photoshopped her LinkedIn profile is a tragedy. No Marsha, we see you.

I often find that people who define themselves as strategic automatically are dismissive of me. They're often narrow-minded glorified admin personnel who weasel their way into the C-suite, all the while I'm actually carrying out multi-year plans. But go off, Marsha.

I'm salty. I don't apologize.

And Timmy sees my skills. He's probably never heard anything like this before. He dated a doctor once. Or maybe she was a dentist. But anyhow, he obviously couldn't watch her work, and he likely hasn't been exposed to what real career professionals do on a day-to-day basis. And it turns him on. And the fact it turns him on turns me on. I'm finally feeling recognized as a badass bitch. And I love that he sees that in me.

Sure, my ex would compliment my grace in the most difficult meetings that he couldn't help but overhear, acknowledge my competence in passing. But nothing like this. Nothing so... electric. This intense appreciation is new. And it's flattering.

And the fact that Timmy finds it such a literal turn-on? That's also new. And intoxicating.

"Seriously," he grins, coming over to kiss me deeply. "You're amazing. I loved hearing you talk like that."

The words fill me up, bolstering me in ways I didn't know I needed.

But even as I bask in his praise, a part of me knows I'm standing on a dangerous edge. Timmy's love feels so big, so all-consuming, that it's hard to separate myself from it. His compliments are addicting, pulling me deeper into his orbit.

It's like being caught in a vortex—one moment spinning with joy, the next disoriented and unsure of which way is up. Time bends around him. My judgment slows, and I find myself making choices I wouldn't have made before him. Like ordering him an Uber when he could have walked. Like laughing off bruises left by playful jabs. Like ignoring the red flags that keep unfurling around me.

He sees me in a way no one else ever has. He makes me feel beautiful, cherished, adored and understood. But at what cost?

Even as I relish the way he admires me, a voice in the back of my mind whispers: *Be careful. You're giving away too much of yourself. He's holding you too tight.*

And yet, I don't pull away.

Because right now, the pull of him is too strong.

And I can't seem to find my way out.

49

DENTACLE PORN

It's starting to get heavy—this strange, chaotic dynamic with Timmy. Every time I buy something for myself, I feel the tugging obligation to buy for two. At first, it seemed like a sweet gesture. It's not that he demands it, because Timmy rarely asks for anything outright.

It's the way he looks at me when I have something and he doesn't —a flash of need, followed by that wide grin when I give in. He's always so appreciative. His eyes light up like a child at Christmas, and he'll wrap me in his big arms, pressing kisses to my forehead. "You're the best, my love," he murmurs. And in those moments, my doubts float away, carried off by the tide of affection he pours over me.

But each little expense is chipping away at my savings, and I can feel it—subtle, but insistent. I didn't budget for this. When I moved here, I imagined my expenses would be manageable—just me, living on my own terms, maintaining my corporate job. I never planned to be thrust into unemployment, let alone also financially responsible for another grown adult, all while trying to build my fledgling author business. But Timmy has a way of turning everything into an adventure, convincing me that it's fine to split a plate of fries or share a beer. It feels romantic, like we're a team, and it's not like he's pushing it, trying to order the most expensive items on the menu or anything like that.

Except, I can't help but feel twitchy. There's something in the back of my mind—an old memory stirring. Years ago, I had a friend who played this same game. They'd accompany me to restaurants and bars, insisting they didn't need anything, only to end up sharing half of mine, because of course I'd inevitably offer them some, rather than have them sit there watching me eat and drink. Or worse, I'd cave and buy them their own, just to avoid the awkwardness. And here I am again—buying for two, convincing myself it's not a big deal.

It's not just the money. It's the slow erosion of a boundary I swore I'd never cross again. I told myself I wouldn't let someone mooch off me, not like before. And yet, here I am, tangled in the same web.

The difference this time? Timmy isn't just some friend crashing on my couch. He's the man I love, the one who says all the right things and makes me feel special in ways I've never experienced. And that scares me.

AFTER THE WORK call is over, Timmy busies himself decorating my kitchen with the random trinkets he revealed on the beach. It's all stuff he brought over from Matty's—things that are either bizarre or useless. A spice organizer that looks like it belongs in the 1970s, tiny plastic animals, random shells, and of course, the miniature skateboard.

"I cleaned everything really well," he says proudly, as if he's just performed some grand act of service.

I smile, but internally I'm cringing. The last thing I need is more clutter. Still, it's a sweet gesture, in its own strange way. He's trying to make this place ours, filling it with things that make him smile. And I love him for that, even if I plan to discreetly disinfect everything later.

For lunch, I whip up my famous potato salad—my go-to recipe for barbecues and gatherings. The smell of garlic, capers, and freshly boiled potatoes fills the apartment. As I mix everything together, Timmy sneaks over, dips a finger into the bowl, and takes a taste.

"Fuck, that's delicious!" he says, grinning at me like a kid who's just stolen a cookie from the jar. "I'm so glad I'm with someone who cooks."

"Same," I reply, smiling back. In these moments, I feel the warmth of our connection. It's not all bad. We share these little joys—me through food, him through spontaneous affection.

He likes to share food plates with me and feed me, so we have our potato salad from a shared plate.

"Blow on it first. It's hot," he'll say when he puts the spoon near my mouth for me to take a sip of one of his soothing broths. "I don't want you to burn your mouth."

They're such simple gestures, and they're touching. A little weird, I suppose. I know it gives some people a major ick, but when he feeds me, it makes me feel like he really cares about me. There's a gentle tenderness about the way he does it as well.

But then, mid-dishes, something shifts.

He grabs my brand-new chef's knife and, with no warning, stabs it through a lemon and into my new wooden cutting board, splintering it down the middle.

"Timmy!" I exclaim, heart racing. "You just ruined the cutting board and probably damaged the blade! Why did you do that?"

He shrugs, a smug grin on his face. "Because it looks cool."

I stare at the ruined cutting board, stunned. He pulls out his phone and snaps a picture, uploading it to Instagram without a second thought.

"Can you please be more careful with my things?" I say, trying to keep my voice steady. "Just... don't go around stabbing stuff, okay? It's unnecessary."

He freezes, the grin slipping from his face. His expression shifts, darkening. His jaw tightens, and his nostrils flare. For a moment, I think he's going to laugh it off, but his eyes narrow, locking onto mine with an intensity that sends a chill down my spine.

"It's just a stupid fucking cutting board," he growls, his voice low and sharp.

He yanks the knife out of the board with a jerk, the blade clattering into the sink, making me wince. I know, without looking, that one of my new dishes is now chipped as well.

"You care more about that dumb piece of wood than you do about me," he mutters, his tone bitter.

I stand here, frozen, trying to make sense of the situation. All I asked was for him to be careful with my things, and now it feels like I've insulted him in some irreparable way. The shift in his mood is sudden, unpredictable—like the sky before a storm. I feel trapped, boxed in by his anger and the physical presence of him standing between me and the door.

I put it down to a joke. Nobody would react like that to such a small thing. He was just playing a part, acting in a role, and I'm the one misinterpreting it. Because nobody sane would ever act like that.

"Fuck it," he snaps, and for a moment, the room feels like it might explode. But then, just as quickly, the tension dissipates. He picks up the remote, plops down on the bed, and acts like nothing happened.

"So, what should we watch?" he asks, smiling again, as if the last few minutes didn't just unravel me.

Later, he finds Sabre's banana bed and plops it on my head, laughing at how ridiculous I look. He snaps a photo, and shows it to me. I'm laughing, a goofy grin on my face. I hate people touching my head, putting things on my head. But with Timmy, I don't seem to mind as much. He's giving me cute attention, and it reminds me of the day he put the octopus toy on my head, and leaned in for our first electric kiss. It's absurd, but it makes me smile. He's back to being silly again, pulling me into his whirlwind of nonsense.

He stands across from me, a goofy grin plastered across his face, one hand holding a baby pacifier while the other clutches an oversized baby shark toy. His body is a strange contradiction—a large, fully-grown, shirtless man, with childlike enthusiasm.

He places the pacifier between his lips, and he lets out a high-pitched chuckle, totally lost in the moment, completely aware of how ridiculous he looks. I snap a picture and he cocks his head to the side, eyes growing large in mock surprise, as if he's the star of a show that's both hilarious and completely baffling.

And then he yanks off his pants and wraps his giant caterpillar around himself, like a diaper. "Take another picture!" he says, muffled by the pacifier.

In this moment, he seems to relish the attention, a combination of childlike wonder and unabashed silliness. He's enveloped in being the center of attention, even though it's only us, embracing his inner manchild to a degree I've never seen.

Then he takes it a step further. He removes the caterpillar and places the baby shark toy down on the bed, and picks up his deer skull with antlers attached. And then he places the skull on his semi-erect cock, the white bone stark against his skin.

My mind races at the absurdity of this. He has a way of challenging the bounds of comfort and normalcy, all while maintaining a carefree smile that invokes both laughter and disbelief.

"Take a picture!" he says, his voice playful yet daring, as if he's presenting some kind of avant-garde art piece.

So I do.

He runs around naked and keeps getting me to snap pictures of him placing his hands above his head in the shape of devil horns. He's excitable and definitely experiencing some kind of mania again. So I just let him do his thing and laugh, because some of his antics are quite funny.

"I'm obsessed with cuddles and sex and ice cream." He says it with such joyful abandon.

"You definitely are obsessed with those three things," I smile. "You speak the truth." And none of those are bad things. In fact, they're all wonderful things. He loves to make us special ice cream sundaes every night, and we sit in bed and he spoon-feeds me while we watch movies.

"Dentacle porn!" he yells at one point.

"Excuse me?" I quirk a brow at him, thinking I misheard him. "You mean... tentacle porn?" It randomly came up in conversation the other day. He hadn't heard of it before, and so I'd explained what it was. He seemed fascinated, instantly googling it and bringing some up on his favorite porn site.

"Nope!" He exclaims proudly. "Deep throat dentacle porn. It's like tentacle porn, but with dentists. Or vehicular dentacle porn, which is all of that, but it happens in a car."

I laugh and shake my head. He's on one of his rolls where he just says weird shit. And that's fine. He's making me laugh. It's one of his quirks.

"Be careful having that on the bed," he says, pointing at my laptop at one point. "The computer will heat up. It'll get brain damage, just like a brain."

"There are 48 hours in a day," he announces a while later, cracking up at his own comment when he realizes his math is off.

His antics are funny, and he has the funniest way with words. I can't deny that. But beneath the laughter, a knot tightens in my stomach. He's unpredictable, swinging wildly between moods—playful one moment, angry the next.

I have butterflies—but not the good kind. Frantic, heavy wings beat against my ribs, signaling that something isn't right. My heart races, a persistent gnawing dread creeping through my veins. I can't shake the feeling that something is wrong—I don't know what, but I can feel it in my bones.

It's like I'm living on a knife's edge, never sure which version of Timmy I'll get. And the more I laugh with him, the more I feel like I'm losing tiny pieces of myself along the way.

He curls up beside me in bed later, spooning me, and whispers into my ear, "I really care about you, Margaux. I just want to be close to you all the time."

His words are sweet, but they also feel heavy, like an anchor sinking into my chest.

I'm tangled in him now, deeper than I ever intended to be.

And I'm not sure if I'll be able to pull myself free.

50

___

SHARKS EVERYWHERE

The Next Day

I have my period, and I'm feeling slightly uncomfortable, but pain relief is finally starting to kick in. Timmy's being super attentive, cracking less silly jokes, and seems genuinely concerned about making sure I feel comfortable.

When I told him about my endometriosis diagnosis, he was tender and caring, and seems to have taken it to heart, making sure I'm equipped with drinks and snacks at all times including a warm and comforting aromatic broth, and rubbing my lower back to soothe my pain. He even suggests I pick a show that will make me feel better.

I'm assuming he's not going to want to do anything intimate—so many guys don't when it's that time of the month—so I'm surprised when he gets a mischievous gleam in his eye and turns toward me. "So... you wanna fuck or what?"

"Hell yes, I wanna fuck you," I grin back, my pussy clenching in anticipation.

He goes to the bathroom and returns with soft lilac in hand, the plush towel Timmy spreads across the bed looking absurdly domestic, given the tension that hums between us, thick as the humid night air beyond the windows.

I watch him, mesmerized by the deliberate way he smooths it out, as if he's giving the act reverence, preparing for something sacred. The moonlight streams in through the floor-to-ceiling windows, wrapping us both in a soft, silver glow. The moment is intimate, electric—our very own universe where only we exist.

When Timmy finally turns to me, the mischief in his eyes sends my pulse skittering. It's the look of a man who knows exactly what he's doing to me—but with no trace of regret. That grin, cocky yet charming, pulls me toward him like gravity.

"You sure about this, Red?" he murmurs, his voice low and rough, the way a wave sounds just before it crashes onto shore.

"Yes," I breathe, my heart pounding. "I've never been more certain."

That's all the permission he needs. In one fluid motion, Timmy closes the space between us, his hands framing my face as his lips crash into mine. The kiss is deep, insistent, and scorching—an explosion that leaves me dizzy and breathless. His body presses into mine, firm and hot, as if he's trying to fuse us together. His hands move over me with purpose, like he's mapping every curve, every dip, committing me to memory all over again.

I run my fingers down his abs, feeling the way they flex beneath my touch. Each ridge, every muscle, is a testament to how effortlessly powerful he is. My hands tremble as they find the drawstring of his pants, loosening the knot with eager fingers.

When his cock springs free, thick, hard, and perfect, my breath catches. The sight of him—completely uninhibited, every inch of him demanding my attention—makes heat pool low in my belly.

Timmy groans as I reach for him, his accent thick as molasses. "Fuck, Margaux. I can't wait to be inside you again."

"Me too," I whisper, my cheeks warming under his intense gaze.

He slides a hand beneath the strap of my bikini top, dragging it slowly over my shoulder. The friction of fabric against skin sends shivers racing down my spine. His lips trail down my neck, teasing the sensitive curve where my shoulder meets my throat, and I tilt my head to give him better access. His breath is hot, his tongue wet as he tastes me, his stubble grazing my skin just enough to leave me breathless.

"You've got the most perfect tits," Timmy murmurs as his hands cup my breasts. His fingers play with the metal bars piercing my nipples, a touch both teasing and reverent. I arch toward him, biting my lip to contain the moan that rises in my throat.

"Careful," I gasp. "They're still a bit tender."

He chuckles, the sound vibrating through my chest. "I'll be gentle," he promises, but the wicked grin that follows says otherwise.

Even the slightest brush of his fingers over the piercings makes me moan, the sensation electric and deeply satisfying. Pleasure spirals from my breasts to the molten heat between my legs, leaving me aching for more.

"What do you want, Red?" Timmy's voice is low and dangerous, like the calm before a storm. His eyes are dark with desire, and his grin holds the promise of something wild.

"I want you," I whisper, my voice trembling. "I want you inside me, Timmy. Now."

There's no hesitation in his movements. I slide off my bikini bottoms, and with a quick, practiced motion, I pull my tampon free, setting it aside. For a moment, a flicker of embarrassment tightens my chest, but it vanishes the second Timmy's eyes meet mine. His expression doesn't change—if anything, the desire in his gaze deepens.

"I don't care," he murmurs, brushing a strand of hair from my face. "All I want is you."

Relief washes over me, and the intimacy of the moment feels even more potent. With a groan, Timmy lowers me onto the towel and spreads my thighs wide, positioning himself between them.

He runs his cock along my lips, teasing me with slow, deliberate strokes. The slickness of my arousal mixed with my blood adds a delicious friction that sends sparks of pleasure shooting through me.

"You're so fucking wet for me," he growls, his voice a low purr in my ear.

"Yes," I gasp, my hips lifting to meet him, desperate for more.

Timmy positions himself at my entrance, his body tense with restraint. "Fuck, Margaux," he groans. "I love this pussy."

With one deep, powerful thrust, he buries himself inside me, stretching me in the most exquisite way. I cry out at the overwhelming sensation, my nails digging into his shoulders as he begins to move.

At first, his thrusts are slow, deliberate—teasing me, coaxing me closer to the edge. But soon, the rhythm shifts, and he drives into me harder, faster, each movement staking his claim. The bed creaks beneath us, rocking against the wall with the force of our passion.

"Tell me how much you love it," he demands, his voice a rough growl in my ear.

"I love it," I gasp, unable to form any other words as pleasure floods my senses. "I love it so fucking much."

Timmy grips my hips, his fingers digging into my skin hard enough to bruise, but I don't care. All I can think about is the way he feels inside me—the perfect stretch, the intoxicating rhythm of his thrusts. I tilt my hips, meeting him stroke for stroke, lost in the primal rhythm of our bodies moving together.

"Fuck, you're so tight," he groans, his voice thick with need.

I arch my back, moaning as his cock drags along every sensitive nerve inside me. The pleasure builds, coiling tighter and tighter until it's almost too much to bear. My nails rake down his back, leaving red trails in their wake.

"Timmy," I cry out, the intensity of my climax rushing toward me like a tidal wave.

He grunts, his rhythm becoming erratic as he chases his own release. "I'm gonna come, Red," he rasps, his breath hot against my neck.

"Do it," I gasp. "Come inside me."

With a shuddering groan, Timmy drives into me one last time, his body tensing as he spills deep inside me. The feeling triggers my own orgasm, and I scream his name as pleasure crashes over me in powerful waves.

Timmy collapses on top of me, his chest heaving as we both catch our breath. I wrap my arms around him, savoring the warmth of his body pressed against mine.

"That was incredible," I whisper, my voice hoarse from moaning.

Timmy rolls onto his side, pulling me close. His fingers trail lazily through my hair, his touch gentle and soothing. "You're fucking amazing, Margaux," he murmurs, his grin crooked and satisfied.

We lie there for a while, tangled together, the moonlight casting soft shadows across our skin. The air is thick with the scent of sex and sweat, but I've never felt more content.

"We should go again," Timmy teases, his voice laced with playful mischief.

I laugh, pressing a kiss to his chest. "Maybe after we clean up."

He groans in mock annoyance but helps me to my feet. Together, we stumble toward the bathroom, hand in hand, our bodies still humming with the afterglow of passion.

Under the hot spray of the shower, I lean into him, the water washing away the evidence of our lovemaking. "I really enjoy our time together," I murmur, my voice muffled against his chest.

Timmy tilts my chin up, his gaze soft and sincere. "I care about you, Margaux," he says. "I really feel like we're meant for each other."

His words sink deep, filling me with warmth. And in this moment, under the cascading water, I believe him.

As we step out of the shower, Timmy picks up the towel from the bed, scrunching it up and tossing it into the laundry basket. He pauses for a moment, as if considering something.

"You know," he says, his voice thoughtful, "I've never really been into... that."

"Into what?" I ask, curious.

"Having sex when someone's on their period." His expression softens. "But with you, it's different. I don't mind at all. I just want to be close to you. I just want to be inside you."

His words wrap around me like a warm blanket, making me feel cherished in a way I've never felt before. It's as if every experience with me is new for him, something profound and meaningful.

Then, with a grin that's equal parts playful and wicked, he

murmurs, "I'll put a baby in you, by the way." It comes from nowhere, totally unexpected. The intensity in his gaze sends a shiver down my spine, and to my surprise, the idea stirs something deep within me— something unexpected but undeniably real. I don't know if he's being serious, or just playful, but either way, he's just activated a part of me I thought was long buried.

This man really is full of surprises.

51

GIRL RUNNING

Dex

I can't stop thinking about Margaux. Worrying about her.

She moves around from place to place what feels like every couple of years, and I can't help but sense she's running away each time.

It looks glamorous and nomadic, but her life hasn't exactly been stable.

But there is a certain freedom in that. She's doing something not a lot of people do.

She keeps getting involved with these dickheads, though.

I don't think she purposely goes out there trying to find losers.

But I do think she's easy prey.

Because she's a genuinely kind individual. An empath.

And I get the sense that she overanalyzes her perceived flaws.

When she started dating the special agent, I felt a sense of relief. I always imagined her being with some kind of law enforcement guy. The good kind, though, because there are plenty of assholes there, too.

But I might be biased because of my own line of work. Not that I'm on that side of the law.

I'm more comfortable with the idea of her being with someone a bit nerdy. Maybe a software engineer or an architect, something like that.

But I know she wants and needs to feel protected.

I would protect her with everything in my being.

I'm trying to do what I can from afar, but it's never going to be enough.

52

THE NUMBERS GAME

Timmy keeps slipping out to smoke cigarettes, leaving the apartment to head down to the sidewalk. Each time, it pulls at me in small, uncomfortable ways, like a stone in my shoe. There's something unsettling about the fact he needs to leave the building entirely, pacing back and forth under the palm trees and streetlights at odd hours. I don't want to be that person—the one who makes smoking a dealbreaker, *or* someone who doesn't trust their partner whenever they're not in the same room as them—but it bugs me, especially in the middle of the night.

When I'm done with some emails, I decide to head down to join him, hoping it will make these smoke breaks seem less... distant. But as I step onto the street, I see him standing with a blonde girl. She's leaning toward him, the way people do when they're locked into good conversation, her face tipping up with laughter that I can't quite hear.

Then, just as she leaves, something strange happens—they both make a gesture, like they're miming sending a text. It's subtle, but synchronized, like an unspoken agreement. My heart drops. The scene feels oddly intimate, like the kind of exchange that shouldn't be happening between strangers that aren't wanting something more.

The thought slithers into my mind before I can stop it. Did he just get her number? I try to shake it off, but the way it makes my stomach churn makes it impossible.

"Did you get that girl's number?" I ask when he sees me, my voice sounding more accusatory than I intended, but I can't help it.

"No! Why would you say that?" Timmy says, his face twisting in offense.

I cross my arms, the knot in my chest tightening. "Why were you talking to her?"

He exhales, the cloud of smoke curling away into the night. "It makes me feel better about myself to talk to strangers," he says, rubbing the back of his neck. "When I walk past people, I feel like they're judging me, assuming the worst. So I go out of my way to chat, and when I get a good reaction, it makes me feel okay again."

The vulnerability in his words catches me off guard, tugging at my heart. I feel bad for him, and want to comfort him. It must suck to feel that way.

After being with a huge introvert for more than half a decade, I'm not used to someone striking up conversations with strangers, regardless of gender. With someone as outgoing as Timmy, I'm going to have to get used to it and trust him. Still, something's still not sitting quite right, and the image of him and the girl lingers in the back of my mind like an itch I can't scratch.

I sigh. "That's rough, Timmy. I'm sorry you feel that way. But why did you both gesture like that? It looked like you were pretending to exchange numbers or text each other."

He shakes his head, frustration flickering in his expression. "I don't know. I didn't get anyone's number. Why would I? I've got *you*. We have so much sex I couldn't possibly be looking for any more. My dick is about to fall off, for real." He shoots me a grin, but there's a flicker of something beneath it—impatience, maybe, or the hint of a performance. "And besides, I really like you. Why would I fuck that up?"

His answers reassure me, at least on the surface, but that tiny gesture between them keeps playing on repeat in my head. I guess she might just be one of those people that gesticulates freely when she talks. *I do that too*, I tell myself. But it was so oddly specific. *Maybe I'm reading into it.*

LATER IN THE EVENING, the thought still gnaws at me, small and persistent, like a splinter.

"You're sure you didn't get her number?" I have to ask, hoping I'll feel better if he reassures me one more time.

His smile drops, his features darkening. "Oh my god, you're still going on about that?" His voice sharpens. "Can you please just move the fuck on?"

His reaction stings. "I'm sorry," I frown back, my cheeks heating with shame. "I just can't stop thinking about it, and I'm trying to be open and honest with you rather than me being upset and you not knowing why."

He sighs deeply, rubbing his hands down his face like I'm exhausting him. "Well, you need to get over it," he says flatly. "I didn't get anyone's number. I wouldn't."

I nod, trying to believe him. "Promise?"

"Yes. Jesus Christ, Margaux. Please, just stop. If I knew you were going to be this jealous and insecure, I never would have pursued anything with you."

"Okay, sorry," I say, his words landing like a slap, sharp and stinging. I sink back onto the bed, disappointment hanging heavy in my chest. I hate that I let this spiral out of control. I *should* trust him. He's right—this kind of paranoia isn't me.

"I just thought I saw something, but I guess I was mistaken," I mumble, my voice small. "Let's just watch a movie."

Timmy softens, at least a little. "Yeah, let's do that." He pulls me closer, his arms draping over my shoulders as if to seal the moment shut. He's attentive for the rest of the evening, skipping the rest of his smoke breaks for the night. I don't bring it up again, and I try to let it go.

As we sit there, though, the gnawing feeling in my stomach won't entirely fade. I already feel like I nagged him about it. I'm disappointed in myself, and hate that I mentioned it more than once. He told me he didn't get her number, and I need to trust him.

Besides, he makes sure I'm always with him. He takes me to work. He calls me during breaks on the rare occasion he goes without me. He texts me whenever I'm out of his sight. Hell, he never even leaves me alone in the apartment for more than a few minutes, barging in when I shower or use the bathroom.

There's logically no time for him to cheat. And he's always saying how much he loves me, how great things are between us. He asked me to marry him because his feelings are so strong. His logic makes sense—why would he fuck this up when we're having so much fun?

I need to calm down, swallow my doubts. There's no way he got that girl's number. I'm just being jealous and insecure and weird, and I'm sure it's wildly unattractive. I need to nip it in the bud now, because that's not the type of person I am.

Maybe I'm just acting this way because I care so much about him. Maybe it's just fear—fear of losing something so special.

But deep down, a small voice whispers: *That hand gesture wasn't nothing. You saw what you saw.*

I push it down, forcing myself to breathe through the anxiety.

Enjoy this, enjoy us, I remind myself.

Because most of the time, *us* is pretty fucking awesome. He makes me laugh. He makes me feel adored. He's different from anyone I've been with before, and I need to focus on that. I can't let my mind ruin something that could be beautiful.

I snuggle closer to Timmy, burying my doubts deep. Tomorrow I'll be better, I'll be calmer. This isn't who I am.

Everything is fine. It has to be.

53

21

Dex

It was only when she turned 21 that I began to see her in a slightly different light.

She was suddenly mature, beautiful. Not that she hadn't always been beautiful, but I guess I'd just never looked at her like anything more than Danny's kid sister.

But something about the night of her 21st... maybe it was the way she looked in her gold gown that set off her red hair. I'm sure that had something to do with it. But she was just so happy, full of joy, really coming into her own. And it stirred feelings inside of me that I didn't expect.

But out of a healthy respect for her and her brother, I stayed away.

I didn't want to come off as some old creep. And if there's one thing about me, I'm loyal as fuck. Sure, her brother and I have had our issues.

It's funny looking back, because I was always the 'bad' one in our duo. The one voted most likely to end up with a mugshot. Danny was always more flashy, a real salesman, who presented himself as this squeaky clean family man.

But we ended up falling out.

He wasn't who he pretended to be on the outside. He's a serial cheater, among other things, and seeing it devastate his family really rubbed me the wrong way.

But even though we don't really talk anymore other than shooting each other a Facebook message or a quick text to say happy birthday each year, I still respect the guy in a few ways.

Even though she's beautiful, intelligent, funny… there are so many women out there who aren't his little sister. And so out of respect, I'll stay away.

But it doesn't mean I'll ever stop thinking about her.

54

BUTT STUFF

Timmy's words catch me off guard. "I don't think you'd like me if I didn't have a massive cock," he says, out of nowhere, frowning. "Sometimes I think you just want me for the sex."

I blink, startled by the sudden insecurity woven through his voice. "That's not true," I say, though his words linger in the back of my mind.

I wonder, just for a second, what things might look like if the sex weren't so good—if he didn't make me feel so desired, so close, so alive in those moments of intimacy. It's undeniably a core part of our connection. When his hands are on me, I feel worshiped, like a goddess in a temple of lust.

Would we still have that spark without it? I like to think so. There's more to Timmy than just the way he touches me—there's no way this is a simple case of being dickmatized. There's his sense of humor, his unpredictable creativity, the way he draws attention to the little joys of life. He makes me laugh until I can't breathe every single day. And sometimes, when he's kind—really kind—it feels like I'm the only person in the world who truly matters to him.

And yet, there's a nagging part of me that wonders, if the sex weren't as electric, would I still feel the same pull toward him?

Maybe, I think. Probably? But I don't have to answer that question, because right now, the sex *is* incredible. It's everything I never thought I could have. It makes all the complications feel distant, at least for a little while.

"You're so silly," I say, playfully poking him in the ribs. "There are a million things I love about you. You make me laugh every day. I love the way we explore the world together. You're my best friend, Timmy."

His expression shifts, softening as his eyes glisten with satisfaction. He tilts his head slightly, wearing that same goofy, contented look that cats get when you scratch them just right. It's adorable. The way he leans into praise, basking in it like sunlight, melts something inside me every time. I've never met anyone who thrives so fully on admiration and validation.

I know that's part of why he wears the ridiculous costumes—the Superman cape, the bone necklace, the oversized sunglasses. It's all designed to catch attention, to draw compliments from strangers. I understand the game, and part of me even admires it—he knows what he needs, and he seeks it out unapologetically.

But I wish he could see that he doesn't need any of that with me. He's enough just as he is. Without the gimmicks. Without the theatrics. He doesn't need the validation of the world when he has me. And yet, maybe we all seek affirmation in our own ways. I can't fault him for being human.

LATER IN THE EVENING, he pulls me close, his voice low and full of mischief. "I want to put it in your butt," he murmurs, trailing kisses along my neck.

"Oh, you do?" I tease, feeling both amused and curious.

"Yeah, big time," he grins. "I love your ass—it's so perfect and curvy. I just want to bury myself in it."

I laugh, a little surprised by how blunt he is, but not opposed. I've only done it once before, back when I was a teenager, but Timmy has this way of making me feel open to new things. His enthusiasm is contagious, and he makes me feel sexy in ways I never imagined.

And so I let him.

He's gentle at first, applying lube to both himself and me, taking his time. "This is just the tip," he announces with a proud grin as he eases himself inside.

Fucking hell, it stings. But not in a bad way. It's a strange mix of pain and pleasure, and I can feel myself adjusting to him, to the fullness. He moves slowly, gauging my reactions, making sure I'm okay.

"Damn, Margaux," he growls, his voice thick with arousal. "You're such a good girl. Not many could take this, but you? You're a fucking beast."

I laugh, feeling proud, the sound pushing him out slightly, and he thrusts back in with a grin.

"That's my girl," he whispers, his tone filled with reverence. "You're taking it so well."

And I am. I feel powerful in a way I can't explain—like I'm doing this not just for him, but for us. His pleasure becomes mine, and the intensity of it is almost overwhelming. I know I won't come this way, but it doesn't matter. What matters is the way he looks at me, like I'm the most incredible woman he's ever known.

When he finally comes, his body trembling, he pulls out and kisses me tenderly. "Jesus fucking Christ," he murmurs against my lips. "You are the woman of my dreams, Margaux. That was fucking amazing."

I smile, flushed and breathless. "I'm glad you enjoyed it." And I mean it. The way he makes me feel afterward—cherished, adored— makes everything worth it.

In the shower, he soaps me up with care, his hands gentle as they glide over my skin. He kisses my forehead, wrapping me in a fluffy towel when we're done. I feel cocooned in warmth, in love, in something that feels like safety.

～

THE NEXT MORNING, he's practically glowing. He makes breakfast, grinning from ear to ear. "Last night was incredible," he gushes, his excitement infectious. "I can't believe you took my entire cock in your ass. Fuck, Margaux, you're so amazing."

His words fill me with a kind of pride I haven't felt in years. It's the same sensation I used to get when I won an award or aced a test—like I'm being recognized for something extraordinary. And the fact it's coming from Timmy, the man I love, makes it even sweeter.

"You're so talented," he continues, setting a plate in front of me. "Smart, sexy, funny—everything I could ever want. I'm the luckiest guy in the world."

I smile, feeling like I'm floating. His adoration is like a drug, and I'm completely hooked.

For now, everything is perfect. Timmy's love feels all-encompassing, like a wave that carries me away from all my doubts and fears. As long as I have him, I can believe in this version of us—the one where we're happy, where we're enough for each other, where nothing else matters.

But somewhere, deep down, I feel a flicker of unease. Like the tide could shift at any moment.

For now, I push that thought aside. For now, I bask in the warmth of his love.

55
____

FAKE FUTURES

Timmy's excitement is contagious as we drive toward Darren's apartment. The car hugs the curves of the mountain road, the scenery shifting from dense jungle to sweeping views of the ocean below. The breeze flows through the open windows, warm and salty, carrying the scent of frangipani and wet earth.

I'm excited to meet the friend he's mentioned at least a thousand times, the one he used to live with. They seem really close, so of course I want to meet him, to learn more about Timmy from him.

During the drive, Timmy excitedly talks about our future together, and how we're going to meld our creative enterprises—my books and his clothing lines.

"We're going to be so amazing," he says, gripping the wheel, his voice brimming with optimism. "Just picture it: a huge office in a trendy warehouse. Open floor plans, big windows with views of the ocean. Your office is right next to mine with a sliding door—so I can shut it if you start annoying me."

I laugh, imagining it with him. It's hard not to get swept up in the way he describes it: the effortless success, the creativity pouring out of us, the life we'll build side-by-side. His voice is like a soothing rhythm, painting a future I never dared to believe I could have.

"We'll have an amazing team," he continues. "And we'll treat them so well—no bullshit like those corporate jobs. We'll design, create, live, you know? And we'll be really, really happy."

He paints a compelling picture, describing the finest details of our office space. It sounds really cool. And then he goes into more detail about his plans for his clothing brands. The way he's talking is visionary. He has a main umbrella brand mapped out, along with smaller brands that fall within it. He wants to sell off some of the smaller brands as they become more popular, and keep the main one, as well as any that become more like passion projects. His babies.

It sounds idyllic, and his enthusiasm and creativity are contagious. I picture myself surrounded by books, with assistants handling my marketing, my social media, book signings—everything I never have time for. And Timmy's energy feels unstoppable, as though his clothing brands are already a hit, as if the world is just waiting for us to seize it. It's easy to fall into his dream, to imagine us thriving, building something meaningful while the world unfolds around us like an adventure waiting to be had.

I've never been in a relationship with someone who can visualize the future with such passion and excitement—who wants to plan a future where both of us can live out our dreams. And where we're so successful we're able to turn our efforts to helping others, to building community.

As we reach the peak of the mountain range, the road levels out, and Timmy points out landmarks from his past. His stories are as colorful as ever. "See that hill over there? That's where we ran away from the cops on our dirt bikes—there's a fence now, probably because of us."

I grin, shaking my head.

"And that street over there?" He points at a dusty trail. "That's where I drove my truck down, covered in mud, and a whole row of guys came out to cheer me on from their balcony. They thought it was the coolest thing they'd ever seen."

I notice how every story seems to cast him in the starring role. He's always the hero, the one being celebrated or admired. It's endearing, even if it feels a bit self-indulgent. But that's just Timmy. He loves attention, and I don't mind giving it to him.

When we finally pull up outside Darren's place, Darren is already waiting for us, standing by his front door, ready to go. He's a big guy, heavily tattooed, with a round belly that stretches his faded T-shirt. There's a gleam in his eyes that makes me wary, but his grin is wide and warm.

"Hey, sweetheart," Darren greets me, wrapping me in a big bear hug and planting a kiss on my cheek. "Been hearing a lot about you."

I force a smile, a flicker of unease stirring in my chest. I remember what Timmy told me about Darren—the volatile temper, the history of physical abuse with his previous partner, the drug use. But Timmy insists Darren is a loyal friend, a 'teddy bear' most of the time. I decide to give him the benefit of the doubt—for now.

We drive Darren to a friend's place, where Timmy helps them chop down trees that threaten the house's foundation using the two chainsaws he brought with him from Matty's place. The air smells of sawdust and green wood, mingling with the delicious aroma of pork roasting on a spit. In the courtyard, the atmosphere is laid-back and jovial. Timmy stays close to me, making introductions, his hand resting protectively on my lower back.

I start to relax a little, letting the warmth of the evening and the camaraderie around us sink in.

Darren, surprisingly, abstains from drinking or drugs, saying he's 'taking a break.' I try to take his presence at face value, but I can't quite shake the feeling that there's more to him than the friendly facade he's presenting. He seems to be observing me from a distance, silently scrutinizing me as if he's trying to get a read on me. But I guess that's normal, trying to figure out what would make one of your best friends propose to someone in such a short time.

When the night begins to wind down, I glance at Timmy. "Are you sure you're okay to drive?" I ask, eyeing the empty shot glasses scattered on the table.

"Yeah, yeah, I'll be fine," Timmy waves off my concern. "Darren gave me a bump, so I'm good."

My stomach tightens. I'm out of my depth with drugs—sure, I've tried a few things before, but Timmy moves through this world like a seasoned pro. Still, his driving seems steady as we wind back down the mountain, and I let myself relax a little, lulled by the night air and the sound of the engine humming beneath us.

Timmy pulls a clear plastic bag with white powder from his pocket and shakes it at me. "Want some?" he asks with a mischievous grin.

I hesitate, but the unease that's been lurking all evening bubbles to the surface, and I find myself curious about how it would affect me. Maybe this will take the edge off. Maybe it'll help me feel more in tune with this wild, carefree life Timmy seems to navigate so effortlessly.

"Sure," I say, forcing a smile. I tap a little onto my hand and snort it, the powder burning slightly as it goes up my nose.

Almost instantly, my nerves melt away, replaced by a buzzing sense of euphoria. I feel light and invincible, as though the world has cracked open just for me, revealing endless possibilities.

Timmy glances at me, his grin widening. "Oh, we're going to have some amazing sex tonight," he whispers, and I believe him.

And he's right. When we get back to the apartment, the sex is wild, passionate, and overwhelming. Timmy explores every inch of my body, worshiping me like a goddess. We lose ourselves in each other, in the heat and intensity of it all.

It feels like nothing else matters. Like this is what life is supposed to be—messy, chaotic, exhilarating. Timmy's unpredictability makes everything feel more alive. He's a storm, and I'm riding the waves with him, unsure where they'll take me, but exhilarated all the same.

As we lie tangled in the sheets afterward, Timmy kisses my shoulder. "You're incredible, Margaux," he murmurs, his voice soft with affection. "I'm so lucky to have you."

I smile, basking in the warmth of his words. In these moments, it's easy to believe in the dream he's selling. Easy to imagine a future where it's just us against the world, building something extraordinary together.

But somewhere deep inside, a small voice whispers that maybe I've drifted too far from shore. Maybe I'm in deeper waters than I realize.

I push the thought aside, determined to let Timmy lead the way. This is his world, after all. His Sunset Cay. And I've chosen to follow him into it.

56

UNINTENTIONAL BONER PARTY

The Past

Me: My grandmother emailed me to tell me that my father made sexual advances on me when I was younger.

Therapist: Do you have any memory of that?

Me: No. He would never have done that.

Therapist: Well then, don't let your grandmother skew your memory. The thing with memories is that they're very malleable. And if someone gets something like that into your head, you could start to believe it, even if it's not at all true. In that sense, memories are very easily manipulated.

The Present

The ridiculous noise complaints from my neighbor keep coming.

The concierge knocks for the second time this week. I open the door, plastering on a polite smile.

"Sorry to bother you again," he says, glancing nervously at the apartment behind me, noticing Timmy in the back corner. "But we've received another complaint. This time about... the TV volume."

"We were just watching a TV show on my computer," I explain, truly surprised by his visit. "The volume wasn't even loud."

"I understand," the concierge says, lowering his voice as if trying not to set off a bomb. "But the building has quiet hours, and sound carries easily with the balcony doors open."

I'm so frazzled by these complaints that by now, every time we watch TV, I'm on edge. The computer's volume doesn't even go up that high.

I nod, feeling weary but compliant. "Okay, sorry. We'll turn it down."

But before I can close the door, Timmy appears behind me. His eyes are dark with fury. He's already bristling, ready to fight.

"This is fucking insane," he snaps at the concierge. "She pays how much for this place? And now we can't even watch TV without being harassed?"

I press my hand lightly against his chest, trying to steer him away from escalating the situation. "It's fine, Timmy," I say. "We'll just turn it down."

I don't mind watching things at a lower volume, because we can still hear it if we try. But really, it is a bit ridiculous. Even though this apartment is new, they don't seem to have done a great job with the soundproofing. And if the balcony door is open, noise travels. While it's a bit over-the-top, I tend to be compliant and laid-back, and so I just figure we'll turn the volume down a bit. No big deal.

Timmy, on the other hand, is furious.

He yanks the computer remote from the table and cranks the volume back up. "There. That's what normal people do when they pay a ridiculous amount for rent—they watch TV however the fuck they want."

"Timmy, look, just don't worry about it. I don't want to make this into a big deal." I take the remote from him and he sighs as I turn the volume back down again.

He glares at me but doesn't argue further, his jaw working as he silently fumes.

For the rest of the night, Timmy finds it impossible to relax.

His behavior is like a pressure cooker, hissing quietly just beneath the surface. He's pacing the apartment, his fists clenching and unclenching at his sides.

Every time I hear someone walk past in the hallway, my stomach twists in knots, worried it's going to be the concierge's knock on the door with another complaint, and anticipating Timmy's reaction.

THE NEXT DAY, Timmy is still restless, but he seems happier. We manage to have a quiet day with no complaints. In the evening, I watch him walk to the balcony, completely naked, his cock swinging in the breeze.

I don't think much of it at first—we're high up on the twenty-third floor, the balconies are partitioned enough that privacy isn't usually a concern, and Timmy is just being Timmy, comfortable in his own skin. I've never seen someone do more helicopters with pure joy on their face—in fact, I don't think I'd ever seen a guy do a helicopter until I met Timmy.

But then I see him peering around the edge of the balcony, craning his neck to where the leasing agent's unit is located.

Suddenly, he's having a conversation. "Ooh, hello," I hear him say, his tone a little flirty.

"Timmy?" I call, uneasy. "What are you doing?"

He grins over his shoulder, his eyes gleaming with mischief. "Saying hi."

I inch closer, dread pooling in my stomach.

"Yeah, I'm buck naked out here right now," I hear him say, his voice low and casual. "Enjoying my evening, just enjoying the breeze."

What in the actual fuck?! How creepy.

I freeze, horrified. "Timmy," I hiss. "Get in here!"

But he just laughs. "Wow, she's really hot, your neighbor," he mutters as he finally starts to head back inside, grinning like a kid who's just gotten away with something naughty. "I think I've got a boner from looking at her."

Because he is completely naked, after all, I can see he does not, in fact, have a boner. But the fact that he said it—out loud—makes my skin crawl. The words hang in the air, vulgar and disrespectful, both to me and the woman next door.

"Are you fucking kidding me?" I hiss. "What the fuck is wrong with you? Get your ass inside. That is so gross of you to say! Why are you being like this?"

He finally steps inside, but not before shooting one last glance toward the neighbor's unit. "We should go say hi," he says, the grin still plastered across his face, making it sound like the neighbor hinted that she wanted late-night visitors.

"Oh, for fuck's sake, stop!" I plead. "Stop being disgusting!"

He rolls his eyes, but then he stops.

My heart feels heavy, sick with embarrassment and horrified by the fact my fiancé is perving at my next-door neighbor like some lecherous drunk standing on a street corner as underage girls walk past.

It makes me feel gross and unwanted, and then I feel silly for being jealous. She is pretty, but it doesn't sit well with me that he was looking at her in that way, and then had the gall to tell me about it. Gross.

We put on a movie, but I can't shake the nausea swirling in my gut. I eventually fall asleep, curled into myself, trying to make sense of the man lying beside me—the man who oscillates between sweet and unsettling at the drop of a hat, still sick to my stomach about the interaction.

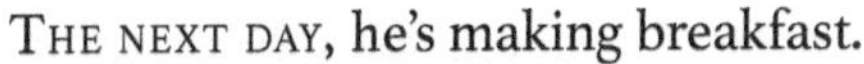

THE NEXT DAY, he's making breakfast.

I feel the need to address the situation. "Dude, you literally went outside naked and told my neighbor you were naked."

"No, that's not what happened." He shakes his head and goes back to cooking.

"Yes, yes, it is. And then you came inside and announced to me that she was hot and was giving you a boner. That made me feel weird. I didn't like it."

"That's totally not what happened. I just went outside, and we had a conversation. That's all." I feel dismissed, and breakfast is ready.

I'm distracted by his fascinating meal of eggs benedict with a curdled hollandaise creation that's strangely delicious.

A little later, I'm at my computer when my phone buzzes. It's the property management company calling, and my stomach lurches. I have a feeling I know what's coming, and I reluctantly answer.

"This is Trinity, the property manager for this building," the woman on the other end says, her tone sharp. "We've received some complaints about things happening in your apartment." My stomach sinks further.

"Oh really? Like what?" I ask, trying to keep my voice steady as my heart thumps in my chest.

"Well, it was reported that someone was howling at the moon like a wolf from your balcony at about three in the morning."

I blink, confused. "I'm sorry, but I was here all night, and I didn't hear anyone doing that." It's true, but as the words come out of my mouth, I can't help but think it sounds like something Timmy would do, given his obsession with wolves and other creatures. It's possible he did it once I'd fallen asleep, but I would have thought a loud wolf howl would have woken me up.

And despite me seeing his interaction with my neighbor, I feel defensive of Timmy. I'm sick of being picked on at this place. I feel like the concierges are used as some weird 24/7 babysitters to make sure adults make no noise at all across the building.

"Well, that's not all," she adds, her voice stiff with disapproval. "Your, uh... male guest... conducted himself in a lewd manner toward one of your neighbors, who is one of our employees." She sounds pissed and defensive right back at me.

My stomach lurches, my heart racing faster. "Oh my gosh, I'm so sorry," I stammer, mortified. "I'll make sure that never happens again."

I think of all the employees I've protected in my previous HR roles, and how it feels to have to deal with a situation like this. And now a guest in my apartment—my fiancé—is who the complaint is about. How ironic and awful.

I hang up the phone, my cheeks flaming, and I look at Timmy, whose relaxed demeanor shifts the moment he sees my face.

"Who was that?" He looks concerned. "What did they say? You look upset."

"The property manager," I say, folding my arms. "They said you stood on the balcony and howled at the moon like a wolf at three in the morning."

"What?" he scoffs. "No I didn't! That's so stupid. Man, they're really coming after us."

"Well, I told them you didn't, because I don't remember hearing you do that."

He nods, seemingly satisfied that I came to his defense. "Good. It must have been someone else."

I frown. "They also said you behaved in a lewd way."

Timmy's expression darkens instantly. "What? That's bullshit! I didn't do anything like that. I did not act in a *lewd way*!"

"Well, you did go out there naked and tell her you were." I gesture in the direction of the apartment next door.

"No I didn't!" He shakes his head, adamant.

"Well, you *were* naked out on the balcony," I remind him carefully. "And you did say you were naked—loudly. I mentioned it right before breakfast, remember?"

"That's not what happened!" he snaps. His face suddenly contorts with rage, his voice rising. "Don't twist things around. I said hello, and told her to have a nice night. That's it."

I furrow my brow. "Yeah... you did..." I say. "And then you loudly said looking at her gave you a boner. We had a little argument about it."

"That's not what happened!" he says. "No! No! No! Don't rewrite history." He shakes his head with vigor, his mouth twisted in a scowl. "That's *not* what happened. There's no way she could have seen my penis, and I didn't talk about it at all. I just said hello and I hope she's having a nice night."

I shake my head, the memory clear in my mind. I don't know why he's so adamantly denying the truth. "No, Timmy. I was right there. You said you were naked. And you said... you said she gave you a boner. I remember, because your comment upset me, and we had an argument about it."

His eyes blaze with fury, his breath quickening. "No! No, I didn't! Stop saying that!" His voice turns sharp. "You're remembering it wrong."

I flinch away, my body curling inside itself, the intensity of his anger hitting me like a wave.

"Listen, I don't think you went and poked your penis through the bars to her balcony or anything. But I'm telling you what I saw and heard. You *did* tell her you were naked. And you did make a comment about her giving you a boner, which I remember because the comment really upset me. It made me feel sick. It still is."

"Nope, you're wrong!" he says, his voice raising, his face twisting into a deeper scowl. "I would never have done that! This place is crazy. They're trying to come after you with all the noise complaints, and now they're making things up. Don't you add to it by believing their stories and making things up yourself. You were just drunk, and you don't remember shit."

The force of his denial is unsettling, like he's not just lying to me—he's rewriting the truth in his own mind, convinced that his version is the only one that exists. I know what I saw, but the force of his conviction makes me second-guess myself. *Maybe I am remembering it wrong... I did have a couple of drinks before it happened...*

I decide not to push it further. It's just not worth it. He already seems elevated about the whole noise complaint situation, which really is quite ridiculous, and this seems like a bridge too far. Maybe, when he's calm and this situation has been resolved, we'll talk about it again.

"Okay," I say softly. "Let's just forget about it, alright? How about we go take a shower and go and enjoy the rest of our day."

He nods, but his body stays tense, his mind still clearly spinning with anger.

His words needle at me, even though the events remain clear in my mind. I remember the tone of his voice, the angle of his dick as he stood on the balcony. Very specific memories. It's like he's trying to rewrite history, to fog my mind with allegations that, because I'd had a few drinks, I was imagining things that weren't favorable to him.

But deep down, I saw what I saw. And I very much remember how the interaction made me feel. Sick, and like maybe I don't really know who Timmy is the way I thought I did. The way he values and thinks about women. The way he values and thinks about *me*.

As the day progresses, he can't stop ruminating on the phone call I received.

He turns toward the wall that separates our apartment from the leasing agent's, pressing his ear against it as if listening for movement. His breathing becomes heavy, and then, slowly, he drags his fingertips along the wall.

His intensity is unsettling, and my body starts to tingle uncomfortably.

"She's going to pay for this," he growls. His voice is low and menacing, a dangerous undertone rippling through his words.

Over the course of the day, he just can't seem to stop thinking about it. I try to distract him with TV and movies and food, but he keeps coming back to it.

"I'll climb the fucking building if I have to," he seethes at one point. "One balcony at a time. I've done it before. I don't care that we're twenty-three floors up, I'll be like fucking Spiderman. And when I get to her, I'll drag her across the room with one hand, and slit her fucking throat, and enjoy the sight of her writhing in pain for what she's done. That bitch is going to bleed out."

A shiver runs down my spine. Surely he's not serious. He's just venting. Right?

"Timmy, please," I whisper. "This isn't worth it. We can just like… move or something."

He glances at the wall between my apartment and the leasing agent's again, his breath ragged. "That bitch is going to get what's coming to her," he fumes, his mouth pinched into a tight scowl.

Again, I try to distract him. But his eyes continue to be locked on the wall, his lips curled into a grimace. "She has to pay," he mutters. "For everything she's done to you. To us."

Later, he rages, his upper arms once again pressed against the wall, his ear cupped against it listening for life on the other side. His breath is ragged. "She will not do this to you! I will kill the dumb bitch!"

I shiver. Surely he's joking, not that it's at all funny. I don't know if I've ever seen someone so angry, except for in a horror movie or some kind of true crime documentary. Talk about dramatic. This seems like something that can be fixed without what sounds like parkour and murder.

"Uh, thank you for being protective of me but that's a bit over the top."

"For all that she's done to you…" He's speaking slower than usual, deeper. "Done to *us*."

"Babe, calm down," I plead, my voice soft. "Seriously. Let's just move. Find somewhere else with better soundproofing. Clearly this building sucks, and we can find something else where people don't complain at the smallest thing."

"She has to pay for what she's done." His voice is low, guttural.

"Can you please calm down? I'm upset too, but we can't do anything about it right now,"

"Look at what she's done, though," he seethes. "You've moved all the way over here, up and changed your life. And she's set you up. She's put you in the apartment next to hers, and she's making noise complaints against you for *laughing*?"

He has a point. That is pretty shitty of her. I don't know what she's playing at. But it's nothing worth causing violence over.

In a twisted way, it feels nice to have this kind of alpha male protection, even if it's also terrifying at the same time.

A more hinged individual would surely recommend complaining to her manager or the parent company. But I feel like, because of his inappropriate behavior the previous night, they now have legitimate cause for complaint. He's so angry, though, it's not the time to bring that up. That it's now his fault we can't rectify the situation properly. I get why he's mad, to a point, but now he's put us on the back foot, weakening our position by dangling his cock in her direction and telling her he was.

"Come on, baby, let's just watch a movie," I try to distract him, to change the topic. "Just… relax for a bit, okay?"

Movies generally seem to distract him, as long as they're ones he likes.

He exhales sharply, and the fire in his eyes dims slightly. "Fine," he mutters. "But we're not done with this."

He collapses onto the bed, the remote in hand, his expression still tight with anger. As he flips through the channels, I sit beside him, my mind racing. I try to steady my breath, to tamp down the fear crawling up my throat. His anger seems so over-the-top, so disproportionate with what's happened.

His words, his threats—they hang heavy in the air. I want to believe he didn't mean them. That he's just blowing off steam. But the way he said it, so cold and deliberate, leaves me with a knot of unease in my stomach that refuses to unravel.

And as we sit here, watching the screen flicker with the beginning of another movie, I can't help but feel like a fuse has been lit. And I have no idea when—or if—it will burn out.

57

PSYCHOPATHS DON'T WEAR WARNING SIGNS, THEY WEAR CHARM LIKE A SECOND SKIN

The next day, I'm hoping for peace, but enjoying our day is a lot harder than one might think, even living in a tropical beach paradise.

Timmy's thoughts just keep circling back to the leasing agent.

"She's out to get us," he mutters, his voice low and seething. "She's got it in for you. I'm going to fix this."

His words send a ripple of unease through me, there's still something chilling about them although he's not making more death threats right now. "Timmy, it's just a complaint. We'll sort it out. It's not that serious."

I want to remind him that, while the initial complaints were vexatious, he did go waggle his dick around on the balcony and tell her about it. We could have fought back if he didn't loudly talk about how she gave him a boner. He's rendered us powerless in a way.

But he's not listening, and I'm still too scared to mention it because of his demeanor.

All day, he talks about her—how she's making our lives hell, how she'll pay for messing with us. His rage is sharp and focused, and what seemed to start as protective concern seems to be transforming into an unhealthy obsession.

~

A little later

Timmy says he has to go see a friend really quickly, and slips out the door before I can ask any questions. Anxiety swirls in my gut until he returns about an hour later.

"Don't worry," he says softly. "It's been taken care of." He stands across from me, his arms crossed, a smirk playing on his lips that sends chills down my spine. His voice is low and steady, laced with a hint of satisfaction.

I shift uncomfortably. "What do you mean?" I try to keep my voice steady, but I detect a slight waver. I hope he doesn't notice it.

He steps closer. "It's better if you don't know. But she's going to regret ever fucking with you." His smile fades into something more serious. The air feels thick with unspoken words.

"Um, who did you go and see, anyway? What are you planning on having them do?" I search his face for answers, but his expression reveals none.

"Like I said, I called in a favor. She'll get what's coming to her." His eerie calmness unsettles me. He's usually so animated and loud, but his voice is low, monotone, robotic.

"Um, please don't do anything violent. That's an over-the-top response." I try to reason with him, searching for a piece of him that will share what's actually going on.

His voice becomes a growl. "How she's been treating you is over the top."

He leans in further, his voice dropping to a whisper that sends shivers down my spine. "You don't want to know the details. Just trust me, it's been taken care of."

His body language and posture remind me of the day he told me about putting bodies in a wood chipper. I shiver at the memory of his random creepy story.

"So what—.'

He puts up his hand to silence me. "It really is better that you don't know."

I feel trapped, torn between a sense of relief that my problem may have been taken care of, and that a man cares enough about me to take care of it, combined with the dread of what he might have done to achieve it.

The way he says it, so casual yet laden with implication, sends a chill through me and makes my skin crawl. My scalp shivers like worms are wiggling all over it. As he stands up, a satisfied grin on his face, I can't help but think he might have taken things too far. And that whatever he's done might well be irreversible.

Over the next few days, his obsession only grows. He snarls whenever he looks at the wall that separates our apartment from hers. He frequently presses his hands against the wall, dragging his palms slowly over the surface as if trying to get closer to her, muttering under his breath.

He continues to talk about climbing up her balcony, and fantasies of killing her. Of slitting her throat wide open and watching her crimson blood pour out.

It's creepy and disturbing and odd. But every time I try to tell him to stop, he'll play it off as being protective over me.

"She's hurting you. You're doing everything right. Paying your rent, playing movies at a reasonable volume. She's the one with the issue."

"You don't need to fantasize about breaking into her apartment and killing her, though. That's a bit much. And I don't know what you went and got your friend to do, the thing you won't tell me about."

"Look, let's just say her vehicle is flagged by a certain group of people. And if they happen to run into her, let's say she's parked at a beach, or she's at the grocery store... well, she's going to start wondering why her tires keep going flat. She's going to assume it's because of some defect. And she's going to buy more and more tires, and the same thing is going to keep happening. She won't be able to explain it, but she's going to be spending a lot of money on replacement tires."

I scratch my head. What a curious revenge plot. But I'm also quietly relieved. He didn't mention physical violence or putting her in a wood chipper. Just petty vandalism causing an ongoing inconvenience.

"Okay, well you've got that out of your system," I say, partially relieved. "You said whatever it is you're doing is in motion. Can you please just let this go, once and for all."

"Okay," he nods. "Yes, let's just have a nice night. That movie I was talking about just came out, so let's watch that."

Great, just what I need while he's acting like this. Another creepy horror. But, they do seem to calm him down. He becomes engrossed in imaginary worlds inhabited by monsters and slasher serial killers. That said, I get engrossed in dinner parties where women scream at each other and flip tables. We all have our kinks.

But his words send a wave of nausea through me. It's as if I'm watching him unravel, little by little, spiraling into a dark place I don't know how to reach. His calm is almost worse than his anger—it feels calculated, deliberate.

He tilts his head, his smile fading into something more sinister. "I'll let it go for tonight. But I won't rest until she stops fucking with you."

I LIE AWAKE, my heart pounding every time I hear someone walk past in the hallway. I hear the sounds of him pacing, still mumbling under his breath about the leasing agent, and how she deserves to die. He's spiraling, and I feel like I'm balancing on a knife's edge, unsure of what will happen if he tips too far.

The next morning, I address it.

"I can't handle this anymore. You're acting crazy about the girl next door, obsessed. Won't talk about anything else. It's upsetting me, and we're getting complaint after complaint. I think we need to get out of here, even if it's just for the night. This is all too much."

I'm at the point where I don't feel comfortable walking past the concierge desk, and the way several of them look at me judgmentally. They peek over the counter, as if they're way too interested in what

I've purchased and brought back. Some of them are just doing their job, but some of them are getting off on being a nosy neighbor without actually living here. They're like police wardens and I'm smuggling in contraband—god forbid I buy a pineapple or a new pair of shorts.

"We can go stay with Matty," he shrugs. "He won't mind you being there."

"On the floor?" I quirk a brow.

"Well, yeah. I mean, there's still a mattress."

"But we'll be sharing a room with Matty?"

"Yep. Is that a problem?" Timmy asks, as if my question is insulting.

"No," I say quickly. "At least we won't be bothered by the weirdos here."

It's me and the apartment, or me and Timmy. And he's all I have here. So I'm choosing love.

Timmy gives Matty a call, and he's kind enough to let us stay for the night. I feel like I owe him for this grand favor of being able to sleep on a mattress on his floor. It's hard to explain. This certainly wasn't the living arrangement I envisaged when I moved here, but it's only temporary, just for the night. I'm in love, and if this is what it takes, I'm prepared to do it.

Who knows? Maybe having a night away will calm Timmy down and take his mind off things.

But I just have a nagging feeling within me that we're not going to be staying in this apartment building for much longer.

As we pack to leave, a sense of deep dread settles in my gut. I know, somehow, this isn't going to end well. Yes, the apartment has its problems. But so does Timmy. And I'm starting to worry that wherever we go, this darkness will follow us.

I glance at the wall one last time, a shiver running down my spine, knowing that whatever Timmy's set in motion won't be easily undone.

58

YOU NEVER NOTICE THE PREDATOR UNTIL YOU SEE HIS TEETH

he Next Day

We go back to my apartment. I'm apprehensive, but Timmy hasn't mentioned the leasing agent as much since we left—just a couple of times here and there—and we want to enjoy some more time to ourselves.

There's a false sense of calm in the air, like the moment when the ocean pulls back before a massive wave crashes down. Timmy is quiet but jittery, as if the slightest thing could trigger him. I feel like I'm walking on eggshells, sensing that his rage is not far beneath the surface.

He's been drinking all day, and earlier he disappeared for an hour or two. He went off, wearing his stupid coconut hat, running around looking like a mentally unwell, unhoused person with dirty feet and board shorts. I was upset when he left, but figured he just needed to let off some steam, running around and doing his thing. It's nice to have a moment away from him, his wild behavior directed at my neighbor has just been so unhinged and I haven't had a chance to process it.

His boss texts me while he's gone to see if he's with me. I guess he was meant to help with some more tasks today, but he didn't mention it, and he never showed up. I explain that he's being weird. She doesn't sound at all surprised, and her automatic reply is that he's probably on some kind of bender.

When he eventually returns, things are initially fine.

He joins me on the mattress, watching a movie.

At first, it feels like everything might be okay. He's acting relatively calm, like the drinks have mellowed him out a little. That he's content to sit in silence and enjoy the movie.

The night is going fine, until it's really, really not.

After a little while, his agitation at the neighbor returns, and he's once again seething, his ear pressed to the wall, his fingertips trailing menacingly against it. "I could break through this wall pretty easily," he says, his expression darkening. "Give her what she deserves."

I shiver, very uncomfortable with his behavior, but unsure how to respond. It's so surreal. He can't really mean anything he's saying right now. He sounds psychopathic, like he might actually want to kill her. But not for one second does any of his anger seem directed at me —he's fixated on my neighbor, obsessed with doling out his own version of justice.

His obsession seems to be growing worse, though, despite my efforts to distract him. I can feel the tension continue to rise, thick and suffocating. But I just try to stay calm and focus on the movie.

Then, without anything seeming to prompt it, something snaps within him. All of a sudden, Timmy rages at me.

The man who just moments ago was lounging beside me is suddenly gone, replaced by someone unrecognizable—a monster wearing his skin.

His entire face changes.

His normally kind, blue eyes are dark, almost reptilian. And his mouth, normally smiling and relaxed and cheeky, is twisted into a horrifying grimace. It's like he's transformed into a monster out of one of his horror movies.

He charges at me, yelling. "You fucking cunt!" he roars, lunging at me. "I'm going to fucking kill you!"

The words hit me like a slap, stealing the breath from my lungs. "Timmy, stop!" I cry out, scrambling to get away, but he's too fast.

Time slows down, and everything is in slow motion.

"*You* fucking stop! Don't tell me what to do!"

I flinch away, but he grabs me by the arms, then he drags me off the bed and slams me to the floor. I cry out as my cheek smacks the smooth wood, pain radiating through my face.

"Don't you fucking move!" he snarls, his voice dripping with venom, as I try to wriggle out of his firm grasp, desperate to break free. But he's about two hundred pounds and used to fighting, and I'm about a hundred and twenty-five at the moment. Strong, but definitely not used to physical combat. It's no use. His manic fury is a monolith against my much smaller frame, still in complete disbelief at what's happening, feeling frozen in place.

I stare in terror as he grabs one of the large deer antlers from the ground and rears it back, then smashes me in the face with it, narrowly missing my eye.

I flinch away, my cheek stinging.

He rears it back again, and then aims it at my body.

"I'm going to shove this up your fucking ass, you dumb bitch!" he screams. The dull point jabs painfully at my backside, stopped only by my shorts and underwear. "Ouch, Timmy! You're hurting me!" I yell, panic rising in my throat.

Then he leans in close. "I'm going to slice your throat with this," he growls, his voice inhuman. He drags the antler across my throat, and I feel it scratching me, pressing into my flesh. I try to flinch away.

"Please don't hurt me," I whisper.

"I'll do more than hurt you," he growls, his voice dark and filled with terrifying promise.

He suddenly pulls away, getting to his feet, and for a brief second, I think it's over. I'm out of breath and in total shock, feeling like I'm inside a nightmare.

But then I hear smashing sounds coming from the bathroom—glass shattering, bottles clattering against tile. My heart races as I grab my phone, hands shaking, and fire off a desperate text to his boss:

ME:

He just tried to kill me. I'm alive, but I need help.

Her reply is instant, disbelief bleeding through her words:

HIS BOSS:

Are you serious? Are you okay?

ME:

I wish I was kidding. He just smashed me in the head with antlers.

Smashed my face.

HIS BOSS:

Oh my god! Call the cops.

He's so busy raging that he doesn't notice what I'm doing.

The chaos in the bathroom suddenly subsides, a moment of eerie silence, and Timmy stumbles back into the room, panting, his eyes wild. His face is red and sweaty, a twisted mask of fury and desperation. "You stupid fucking bitch," he hisses, leaning in close, his breath hot against my ear.

He returns to his feet and storms out to the balcony, glaring at me, and I hear more smashing. I'm frozen. My brain screams at me. *Get out. Get out.* But before I get a chance to make a dash for it, he returns inside, and he's suddenly back on me, breathing raggedly in my ear. "You stupid fucking bitch. Look what you've made me do."

"Timmy, I don't—."

He notices the phone in my hand, and he tries to yank it from me.

"Who the fuck are you texting?!" he roars, even more enraged.

Fuck. What have I done?

I don't know what to tell him, other than the truth. "Your boss. I—."

"You're texting my *boss*?" He looks even more furious now, his yelling even more guttural. "Are you fucking kidding me? I'll kill you, stupid bitch!"

"Timmy, I—."

"Shut the fuck up! Just shut your fucking stupid mouth!" he screams, cutting me off.

He brandishes his pink-handled hammer, now, raising it just high enough for me to see the malicious gleam in his eyes. "I will fucking kill you with this hammer."

He has me on the ground again, and this time he drags me across the floor.

He lifts up the hammer, as if he's about to strike me in the head with it. But then he drags it across my hip instead, and I wince as the claws scrape across my skin.

My heart hammers against my ribs. My brain screams at me to move, to run, to do something. I have to get out of here.

Somehow, I manage to wriggle free from his loosened grip, adrenaline giving me strength. His coordination is faltering, his movements sluggish and sloppy now, motor skills severely compromised, like a drunk giant stumbling through a nightmare, an elephant that's just been shot with a sedative.

I feel frozen, but I manage to fumble with my phone and dial 911.

I get to my feet and dash for the door. I open it just as he tries to drag me back into the apartment, growling like a wild animal, but I slip free. He lunges, grabbing at me again, but I'm faster. I burst into the hallway, barefoot and terrified.

My pulse pounds in my ears as I hear heavy footsteps.

"Help!" I cry out, my voice breaking with panic.

"We're here, ma'am!" One of the officers reaches me first, steadying me as I tremble. "Are you okay?"

I nod, breathless. "He's inside. Please—he said he was going to kill me."

A couple of officers rush past me and I see Timmy slipping out the exit stairs at the other end of the hall.

"I'm the one who called," I explain, in shock.

"We got several calls, ma'am," one of the officers says. "Are you okay?" He's standing right in front of me, but his voice sounds muffled, like he's speaking through a fluffy cloud, as if I'm in a dream.

"I don't know," I whisper. "He tried to kill me."

They come and take a quick look around the apartment, which by now is a mess, one of them snapping pictures.

"Do you need an ambulance, ma'am?"

"No, I think I'm okay."

"Are you sure?"

"I don't have my insurance sorted yet. I really can't afford it. I'll be fine."

"Why don't you come with us," he says. "We'll go to the lobby, and we need to ask you a few questions about what happened." I nod, in complete disbelief.

They lead me to the elevator bank, and we ride down in silence. Their expressions are solemn, and I feel like I'm going to throw up, but I manage to hold it in.

We take a seat at the long table in the lobby, several officers gathered around me, looking at me with concern.

It's not long before I see them dragging him toward the police car with his hands behind his back. I hope he can't see me through the glass. All I can see are the red and blue flashing lights.

He thrashes and spits, but I can tell that his strength is mostly gone, burned out by his manic rage. He catches sight of me through the glass. I look away, but not before his gaze catches mine—those eyes that once looked at me with so much love—now glare with hatred. My stomach twists as the lights from the police cars outside reflect off his pale, sweaty skin.

I watch from the window as they shove Timmy into the back of one of the cars. The door slams shut with a heavy, final sound. I feel a twisted mix of relief and sorrow as the car drives away. How did we get here?

"So what did he do exactly?" the officer asks, taking my statement. "Take me through it, if you don't mind."

"Well, he was very upset about my next door neighbor, and next thing I knew he was attacking me." I explain what happened with the antlers, and being thrown to the ground. I describe how he threatened to kill me, and how he was smashing items in the apartment with a hammer that he threatened to use on me. How he told me he was going to slit my throat.

They ask a few more questions—details about the attack, what led up to it. I answer mechanically, the words falling from my mouth without thought or emotion.

"Do you want to press charges, ma'am?" one of them asks. I've never been asked that before, but my brain tells me that that's what I'm supposed to do.

"Yes, I say," robotically. "Yes, I want to press charges."

The officer glances at one of his colleagues, and then he returns his attention to me.

For a moment, I feel like we're just sitting here in silence, my brain racing, my heart still thumping in my chest.

I watch as the neighbor walks past, a smirk on her face, as if she's amused by seeing me in this situation, and her presence makes my brain zap.

"Are you sure you don't need an ambulance, ma'am?" an officer asks, snapping me back to reality. I realize he's been talking to me this whole time, but his voice just sounds muffled, too, like we're in separate rooms.

"No," I whisper, numb. "I'll be fine."

"Are you sure?" he presses gently. "You've been through a lot tonight."

"I can't afford it," I mutter, my voice hollow. "My insurance isn't set up yet. I just... I just need to be alone."

The officers exchange another glance, but don't push further.

They hand me a card with a list of domestic violence resources, and say they'll be in touch the next day with more information.

~

I RETURN TO THE APARTMENT, alone, and it's eerily silent. I feel like a ghost, drifting through a surreal, nightmarish version of my life.

The apartment is wrecked—mattresses overturned, drawers emptied, shards of glass glittering on the floor. It's a physical manifestation of the chaos Timmy unleashed.

I walk to the bathroom and look at myself in the mirror, stunned. A blood vessel in my eye is popped, and it rages crimson. It's hideous, and it stings slightly, but I also feel numb.

I have bruises and scratches all over my hands, defensive from trying to prevent him from sodomizing me with the antlers, and from trying to push him away.

There's a big, multicolored bruise on my hip from where he slammed me to the ground, or maybe from when he dragged the antlers and the hammer across my body.

I grab my phone again, texting his boss:

ME:

I called them.

He promised he'd never hurt me.

HIS BOSS:

Make sure they arrest him so he learns a lesson.

ME:

They arrested him.

He promised he'd never put hands on me.

He burst my eye blood vessel earlier and then tried to kill me with an antler.

HIS BOSS:

Send him for a night in jail. He needs to sober up.

ME:

He needs to stop being abusive. Said he'd never do it.

Her reply is sharp, cutting:

HIS BOSS:

> He's not going to stop. He's done this to a
> girlfriend before.

My breath catches. *He's done this before?* My heart sinks as the weight of her words settles over me. He lied—just like he seems to have lied about so many other things. Telling me he'd never put hands on me. He swore up and down that he'd never hurt a woman.

The way he showed complete contempt for Darren hurting his ex, that he looked down on any man who would ever hurt a woman in any way.

That he was some kind of hero, the type of guy that saved people from men just like him.

ME:

> He has?

HIS BOSS:

> Yeah. He's a mess.

ME:

> Stupid asshat. He could be so awesome and
> here we are.

I feel distanced from myself, watching myself see his potential even after what he just did.

I text another friend, Sven, who's like a brother to me. That I made the worst choice. That the shithead punched me in the face and threatened to kill me. Ironic welcome to beach life. That I need to make better choices, clearly.

It's like I'm watching my life from the ceiling, that I'm disembodied, just observing myself like a third party.

I leave the apartment, needing air, needing anything but these four walls. I wander down to the corner store, dazed, not sure where else to go, and buy a bottle of whiskey and a hard seltzer. The cashier doesn't bat an eye at my injuries as I pay—just another lost soul buying booze to survive the night.

One of the cop cars is still in the driveway, and the officers watch me return with my items. I wonder if they're observing me, judging my purchases. But at the same time, I don't really care. I just need to numb myself further.

Back at the apartment, I sit on the disheveled mattress, the weight of everything pressing down on me. I sip the whiskey, hoping to drown out the thoughts swirling in my mind. But the silence is deafening, and the echoes of Timmy's rage linger in every corner of the room.

Tears well up, but I swallow them down. I don't have the luxury of falling apart—not now. There's no one to call, no one to lean on. Just me, and the bottle, and the empty bed where I once felt safe in Timmy's arms.

Sabre, who I'd usually rely on for support, still isn't with me.

I stare at the ceiling, listening to the faint hum of the city beyond the windows. How did it come to this?

And as the whiskey warms my veins, I realize I don't have an answer. I only know that I survived the night. But tomorrow is a new day, and I have no idea what it holds—or if I'll ever feel safe again.

59

____

THERE'S A FIRST TIME FOR EVERYTHING BUT THIS IS NOT ONE

*T**he Next Day*

He's in jail. *Jail.* It feels surreal, like I've been dropped into someone else's life. I've never had a partner in jail before. I don't think I've known anyone who's been in jail, actually. And because Timmy has been glued to my side since I arrived in Sunset Cay—my only real connection here—his absence is deafening. It's as if the air has been sucked out of the apartment, leaving behind only a hollow silence.

The charges are domestic violence and 'terroristic threats', a fancy legal term for 'he told me he was going to kill me'.

I sit on the mattress, surrounded by the wreckage of what was supposed to be my fresh start, trying to piece together how things escalated to this point. How we went from sharing laughs, dreams, and late-night movies to him wielding a hammer and smashing everything in sight, threatening to slit my throat.

The top of the toilet tank is shattered, porcelain shards scattered across the bathroom floor like jagged teeth. I step carefully over them, the absurdity of it all sinking in. Who smashes a toilet? What message was he sending, and to whom?

Out on the balcony, I find the remains of the potted plant—the one he insisted was special, sacred, even—the gift from Darren's now-deceased mom, something he cherished. And yet, here it lies in pieces, dirt spilled across the tiles, the pot obliterated by the same hammer he held over my head, the one he promised to use to end my life.

I notice the pink-handled hammer resting on the floor, and the sight of it makes me shiver. It looks so innocent—something you'd pick up at a craft store, not intended for use as a murder weapon.

But now it's tainted, just like everything else in this place.

It holds the weight of everything that happened last night, a symbol of what he could have done. What he almost did.

The second deer antler—the one he didn't use as a weapon—lies on the floor, discarded. The sight of it turns my stomach, and I wrap it in a plastic trash bag with trembling hands. Carrying it down the hallway to the trash chute, I fight the urge to vomit. It feels radioactive, like it's still buzzing with the malice he injected into it.

When I return, I glance around the wreckage and wonder how this became my life. I moved to this Cay for peace, for creativity, to write books and live quietly. Not to be threatened, attacked, and left in the ruins of a brand-new apartment.

The police took the other antler, and apparently his bone necklace, too.

"We thought it was a human spine at first," one officer said when taking my statement, shaking his head. *A human spine*, just like Paulo joked about when I shared Timmy's Tinder profile. I shiver again. What kind of person collects such things? It sounds like something ripped from a horror movie, the same kind Timmy loves.

And now he's in jail. Charged. Arrested. *Gone*. But not for long, apparently. The officers were clear about that—he'll likely be released in a few days. I try to wrap my head around what that means. What happens when he gets out? Will he come back, angrier than before? Will I have to move again? Will I need to watch my back every time I leave the building?

The cops warned me when they came back this morning to deliver some more paperwork, including a stay-away notice that prevents him from coming back here. "He's banned from this building," one of the officers explained. "If he comes back, even through the service elevator, we'll know. There are cameras everywhere. He can't come within 100 yards of the building or contact you for 72 hours after his release. Not by phone, not by email—nothing."

I nod, clutching the papers. "Okay," I whisper.

"And listen," he'd added gently. "That doesn't mean you should contact him once the 72 hours are up. I know there's been physical injuries as well as property damage here, but it's the emotional scars that leave the deepest wounds. Don't let him back in. And," he adds, "don't be tempted to try to sneak him up in the elevators via the marketplace downstairs. There are tons of cameras here, and we'll know."

It's odd, receiving therapy advice from a cop, but I know he's right.

Yet part of me still wonders if I'm making a big deal out of this.

Maybe I overreacted. Maybe it wasn't as bad as I thought. Maybe...

But then I remember the hammer, the antlers, the promises to kill me. I remember how his face twisted with rage, how his voice dropped into something terrifying and unrecognizable.

No. I didn't overreact. This was real.

I sit on the mattress, staring at the little yellow card with domestic violence resources printed on it. I can't bring myself to throw it away, but I also can't bring myself to call any of the numbers. Instead, I leave it on the kitchen counter, in plain sight, as a reminder. Every time I glance at it, a wave of shame rolls over me. I want to shove it deep inside a drawer, pretend this never happened, but I need it there. I need to see it. To remind myself that what happened was real, and that I'm not crazy.

I still don't know what to do next. Should I move? Should I tell someone? How do I even begin to explain this to the people back home? *Hey, just wanted to let you know my fiancé tried to kill me with a deer antler and a pink-handled hammer. But I'm okay now, thanks for asking.*

It feels too big, too strange, too surreal to say out loud. And so I sit with it, letting the weight of it settle into my bones.

I grab my phone, scrolling aimlessly, and then fixating on the latest text from his boss.

HIS BOSS:

> He's not going to change. He's done this before.

The words rattle around in my brain, making everything feel heavier. *He's done this before.* And I thought I was special. I thought I was the one who could fix him, who could be his safe place. But I was wrong, although to be fair, I had no idea what he was capable of.

I pour myself a glass of whiskey, the amber liquid burning as it slides down my throat. I follow it with the hard seltzer, hoping the buzz will numb the tangled mess of emotions inside me. But nothing can dull the gnawing fear in my gut—the fear of what happens next.

Will he call me when he gets out? Will I answer? Will I want to?

I sit on the mattress, the wreckage of my life scattered around me, and let the silence wrap around me like a suffocating blanket. For now, I am alone. For now, I am safe. But I know the clock is ticking.

And I have no idea what tomorrow will bring.

60

DEATH WISH

Dex

I will pound this motherfucker into the ground.
To treat such a lady this way.
To terrorize her.
I want to protect the shit out of her.
And the fact I can't destroys me.
It kills me on the inside.
But at the same time, I know that's how she must be feeling.
Confused. Tortured.
Like, she's the one doing wrong. Or that she contributed to what happened somehow.
But it's 100 percent this fucker. And I want to slash his heart into two hundred tiny little pieces. Because that's what he's doing to her.
And it's all that he deserves.
"Are you muttering to yourself again?"
I'm snapped out of my reverie by my colleague, Jordan. We're sitting next to each other in our surveillance van.
I laugh. Shit. I didn't know I was uttering my thoughts out loud. "Did you catch any of it?"

He laughs and shakes his head. "Just a couple of swear words. No specifics."

"Haha, that's good. I was just thinking about this human shithead."

"Are you going to take matters into your own hands, or what?"

I sigh. "I don't know, man. I just don't know yet. I have some things to figure out."

"Well, just be careful. It's one thing when we're working, but when it's personal…"

"I know, I know. I could fuck up everything."

And what I don't say out loud is that I'm prepared to… to lose everything.

To burn the whole fucking world down if I have to.

Because Margaux is worth it.

61

ALWAYS HAVE A BACKUP (& WHISKEY)

The next day, I head to the beach, as if on autopilot. I sit on the sand, staring at the waves rolling in, trying to let the rhythm soothe me. The sound of the ocean usually calms me, but today it only underscores the chaos swirling in my head. He's still in jail. What happens when he gets out? The thought grips me like a vise, tightening my chest.

I know it's messed up, but part of me feels like I need a backup, someone safe to turn to in case Timmy comes out of jail wanting to hurt me again. Not to date, just literally to know someone who is a guy who lives on the Cay. I hate that I feel guilty about it, even after what he did. But I know I can't keep sitting around waiting for Timmy to decide whether he wants to love me or destroy me.

To distract myself further, I take myself out for brunch, ordering a fancy avocado toast and sipping on a cold brew. I don't have much of an appetite, but I pick at it, urging myself to eat. People-watching usually soothes me. But even surrounded by the clink of cutlery and the chatter of tourists, I feel isolated. My mind keeps wandering back to him—locked up, alone, and simmering in rage. What if he blames me? What if he's even angrier when he gets out?

After brunch, I return to my apartment and pull one of my oracle cards. CHALLENGE.

The card shows an unsettling image—a person with their finger jammed into someone else's brain. I stare at it for a moment, a chill creeping down my spine. What does that even mean? Is it a warning? It feels weirdly fitting, as if it's foreshadowing how tangled my thoughts have become. As if it represents Timmy himself, the way he jams himself into my every waking moment, always speaking, always distracting me, never giving me a moment of calm.

Needing to burn off some of this nervous energy, and to fill the void in my mind, I head downstairs to the gym. But my workout is half-hearted. I pick up heavy weights, but they feel lifeless in my hands. I can't focus on any one exercise, and playing a full workout video in the middle of the gym feels silly, so I wing it—squats, dead-lifts, some curls. The movements feel good, but my mind refuses to quiet.

Even with music blasting in my headphones, Timmy's shadow looms over everything. No matter how loud I crank the music, no matter how many reps I push through, I can't drown out the thought of him. What's he thinking about in that cell? I can picture him pacing back and forth, fists clenched, ready to blame me for every-thing. What happens when he gets out?

I leave the gym and decide to walk along the touristy boardwalk. I weave through crowds, watching people shop and snack, soaking in the sunshine. But it doesn't feel right without him. Timmy loves doing things like this—people-watching, making silly comments, always the life of the moment. And now, instead of enjoying it, all I can think about is him.

I message a few friends from back home, hoping for a lifeline of advice or at least a distraction, including my favorite uncle's best friend, who I lovingly call 'Backup Uncle'.

BACKUP UNCLE:

Always have a backup.

The words hit differently than they normally would, replicating my earlier thoughts.

Timmy's behavior has reached a point where I genuinely fear what he might do when he's released. Having a backup isn't about a rebound—it feels like survival. So I respond to Felipe, the surfer I'd been chatting with since just before I arrived in Sunset Cay, the other guy who had offered to pick me up from the airport. I haven't been on dating apps since meeting Timmy in person, but Felipe had encouraged me to follow him on Instagram, so I still have his contact info.

ME:

It's been a mess here, honestly. Just trying to figure it all out.

FELIPE:

Let's hang out. I'll come get you. Where you at?

A shiver creeps up my spine. My trust levels are low. There's no way I'm getting in a vehicle with someone I've never met.

ME:

I don't get in cars with strangers. But I can meet you somewhere.

FELIPE:

Let's meet at the fireworks. I'll bring whiskey.

The mention of fireworks makes me laugh bitterly. Of course. Timmy never shuts up about them. He's obsessed with the ten-minute show that happens every Friday—an obsession that feels trivial now, compared to everything else.

I set off to meet Felipe, hoping the night will provide some relief. But on my way to the fireworks, I make a wrong turn down a dark alley, thinking it's a shortcut. Immediately, I know I've messed up. Shadows shift around me, men hunched over, doing drugs. Eyes flicker in my direction, sizing me up.

Heart racing, I quicken my pace, aiming for the glimmer of the ocean at the alley's end. My boots slap against the wet concrete, and when I get to what I think is safety, a wave crashes at the shoreline, splashing me with cold, frothy water. *Shit.* The tide is fully in, blocking my way out. I stifle a nervous laugh, pretending it's funny—pretending I'm not scared out of my mind.

A group of men watches me from the shadows, their expressions unreadable. My stomach knots. Then, one of them catches my eye. He looks different, and like he's helping them somehow, rather than participating in whatever they're doing—calmer, not quite part of the chaos. A large cross earring dangles from his ear.

"Hi there! I'm Margaux!" I blurt out, forcing a grin and stepping toward him, desperate to break the tension.

He gives me a slow smile. "Hey, Margaux. I'm Mack."

We shake hands, and the moment feels surreal, like I've wandered into a strange, dark dream. But somehow, the atmosphere shifts. The tension breaks. The others go back to what they were doing, leaving me alone. I let out the breath I've been holding and hurry back the way I came.

By the time I reach the beach, my heart is still pounding. But I find Felipe easily enough. He's standing by his truck, grinning when he spots me. His short dark hair is buzzed military-style, and he has tattoos peeking out from under his shirt sleeves. Unfortunately, he's not the solid wall of muscle I was hoping for, who could protect me—instead, he's about my height, around five-foot-five. Dammit. Although he is in the military, so I assume he has some form of combat training, at least.

He pulls down the tailgate of his truck, and we sit there, passing the whiskey bottle between us. He chats about his life, his job, and his culture. I listen, grateful to be out of my apartment and around someone—anyone—who isn't Timmy. But I still feel like a fugitive, glancing over my shoulder, half-expecting him to show up, even though I know he's locked up.

As the fireworks explode overhead, people cheer, but I feel disconnected from the joy around me. I take another swig of whiskey, hoping it will numb the edges of my fear.

Then, without warning, Felipe leans in and kisses me.

It's awkward. Terrible. His lips are too wet, and his timing is off. I sure don't want to be kissing anyone right now, and in a weird way, I feel guilty that this is even happening. That I somehow owe faithfulness to Timmy, even though he literally tried to kill me. I pull away slightly, but he leans in again, pressing another awful kiss against my mouth.

I freeze, unsure how to handle it without making a scene.

"Want to hang out in my truck for a bit?" he asks, his voice low.

"Um, no!" I say, panic bubbling up. "I have to go!"

"You have to go?"

"Yep! Thanks for the whiskey, though! Bye!"

Without waiting for a response, I hop down from the tailgate and take off in the opposite direction, my heart hammering in my chest.

When I finally get home, I crank up the air conditioning and collapse onto the mattress. I can't sit still. I need to move.

I pull up some shuffling videos online—the ones Timmy kept talking about, the ones that he used when he was learning to dance—and try to mimic the moves. It reminds me of the old dance routines I used to do in jazz ballet. Running man, box steps—familiar steps, but reimagined in this new style.

I dance for hours, the music blasting through my headphones, my body moving in rhythm with the beat. I can't stop. For these moments, I can forget everything—Timmy, the jail, the fear. I get lost in the movement, laughing when I trip over my own feet, letting the music carry me somewhere far away from all the chaos.

For a little while, I feel free. But only for a little while.

62

BOB THE PLUMBER

The Past

Unknown caller: This is Detective Smith from the Johnsonville police department.

Me: Oh, hello?

Unknown caller: We have a report that your car was involved in a fatal crash.

Me: Oh my god, that's awful.

Unknown caller: Yes, we're going to have to come and ask you some questions.

Me: Oh my gosh. I haven't seen that car in months. My ex kept it when we broke up. But I'd be happy to help.

Unknown caller: Well the vehicle is still in your name. So you're legally responsible for anything that occurred.

Me: Oh my goodness.

Unknown caller: (laughter) This is a joke. We wanted to give you a fright, and it clearly worked.
Me: ...who is this?
Unknown caller: This is your ex's mum, silly! (More laughter)

~

The Present

I take myself to Dock Bar. Although it's where Timmy and I first met in person, I still consider it a safe space, my space.

The bartender recognizes me, and I trust her enough to tell her what happened. "Oh my god," she says. "Can I come and give you a hug?"

I nod, and she runs around the bar and squeezes me. "I'm so sorry that happened to you," she says. "I was in a relationship like that once. And from my experience, guys like that never change."

I order some food, and I pick at it while nursing a drink. "Oops," says the bartender. "I accidentally made the wrong drink for someone. So this one's for you." She winks at me, handing me the second glass, and I accept it, grateful for the kind gesture and for her understanding.

My phone buzzes. The moment I see the call is from 'Bob's Plumbing,' my stomach churns with dread.

I don't know any contractors on this island.

Timmy works on renovations. It has to be Timmy, somehow manipulating one of his friends to intimidate me.

My hand shakes as I stare at the phone, the pit in my stomach spreading wide, threatening to swallow me whole. I let it ring out, and something compels me to listen to the voicemail.

"This is Detective Smith from the Sunset Cay Police Department. Please call me back urgently."

What the actual fuck? He's somehow sending people to pretend to be police officers, now?

My heart pounds in my chest as I dial the number, my hands trembling so hard I can barely tap the screen. This could be Timmy messing with me... or maybe it's something worse.

The line clicks.

"Detective Smith," the voice on the other end says. To be fair, he sounds like a cop. I was married to a detective, and I can usually tell. Still, I'm cautious.

"Uh, hi, I got a message to call this number?" I manage, my voice shaky.

"Is this Margaux Benson?"

"Yes, that's me."

"Oh good. I'm glad you called back so quickly. I'm just at your apartment building. Are you home?"

Every warning bell in my head goes off at once. "You called me from a plumbing number. And now you're saying you're a detective? And that you're where I live?"

He chuckles, as if this is some funny misunderstanding. "Yeah, I know. Someone's told me that before. It must be some system glitch. A number I inherited. But, yeah, I'm legit. I should probably get that changed."

A wave of nausea sweeps through me. Is this real, or am I being played? I can't tell if this guy is just unprofessional, or if I've fallen into some twisted prank.

"Can you come meet me at your apartment?" he asks again.

I grip the edge of the counter, fighting the rising panic. Absolutely not. The last thing I'm doing is meeting a strange man—real detective or not—alone in my apartment.

"No, I'm... uh... I'm down the street at the Dock Bar having lunch."

There's a pause, and I hear papers rustling in the background. "Can I come meet you there?"

"...I guess?" I say reluctantly, my skin crawling. I just want this whole interaction to be over, and my instincts are on high alert. What the hell is going on?

"Great. I'll be there in five to ten minutes," he says before hanging up.

I sit at the bar, trying to sip my drink but failing miserably, my hands shaking each time I try to lift the glass. My heart pounds, my thoughts spinning out of control. My breath feels too shallow, too fast. What if this isn't real? What if this is some kind of setup?

When he arrives, I spot him instantly. Total detective type—closely-cropped hair, business shirt, dark pants. He pulls out a badge and flashes it quickly. It looks real, but the whole 'Bob's Plumbing' thing still has my paranoia gnawing at me. I stare at him, trying to read his expression, but his face is impassive. He gestures to a table out on the balcony. "Is it okay if we sit over there? It's more private."

I nod and follow reluctantly.

"Do you mind if we tape our conversation?" he asks.

"That's fine," I mutter, feeling like I'm floating outside of my body, watching myself agree to things out of habit and fear.

He pulls out a recorder and presses the button. "Okay, let's walk through what happened last night."

His tone is calm, almost clinical, but his questions are pointed. Too specific. Every word out of his mouth feels like a trap, something designed to catch me slipping up.

"When he shoved you to the ground—did he use his left hand or his right hand?"

"Um..." I pause, struggling to recall. "I think his left... but maybe both. He came at me really fast, and... kind of shoved me hard, and I was more focused on not hitting the floor face-first."

He narrows his eyes. "So you don't remember exactly which hand?"

"I was just trying to protect myself," I say, my voice faltering. "I wasn't keeping track of his hands."

He clicks his tongue, clearly annoyed. "The more specific you can be, the more it helps."

"I just don't remember, and I don't want to make up an answer." I feel like I'm being pressed to answer something that I simply don't recall, and I don't want to lie to the police just to give them the answer he so clearly wants.

"Were you drinking?" His voice drips with judgment. "It would be helpful if you remember more than you do."

"Yes," I reply. "I'm sorry I can't remember everything about it. I wasn't expecting my fiancé to threaten, and try, to kill me."

His next question makes my skin crawl. "When he used the deer antlers on you—did they fully penetrate your anus, or…?"

I freeze, my stomach flipping violently. My pulse roars in my ears. What the fuck is happening? I feel like I've been thrown back into that nightmare from years ago—my rape trial. The cold, detached way the lawyers dissected every bruise, every rip in my body, while I sat there on the witness stand, trying not to fall apart. My instinct, weirdly, is to protect Timmy. I know what he's angling at, that penetration would take a domestic assault case into a full-on rape charge.

"They didn't penetrate," I whisper. "I had pants on."

He nods, jotting something down in his notebook. "Okay. But just so you know, we may need to document this as a sexual assault if the intent was there."

No. No. No. I feel like the walls are closing in. I can't go through that again. I can't survive another trial where my body becomes evidence, where every move I made is picked apart and questioned.

He leans back, his tone shifting slightly. "Look, I've seen this kind of thing before. I checked this guy's record, and let me tell you—it's long. It's only a matter of time before he kills someone."

I stare at him, my mouth dry. "I… I had no idea. He told me about some stuff with his brother, and that he got in trouble once for running around on the beach shouting, 'I kill you'—but I thought that was just… stupid shit."

"Yeah, it's much worse than that," he says. "And you know, when I visited him in jail to question him, he was still really out of it. Drunk, even twenty-four hours later. I had to go back a second time. And there's something really off about him. He's not right in the head."

"Seriously?" The now-constant knot in my stomach grips tighter.

The detective shakes his head grimly. "He's got a history. He's dangerous, and honestly, you're lucky to be alive."

The words hit me like a punch to the gut. I feel like I'm trapped in some twisted alternate reality. How did it get to this? How did I end up here—afraid for my life, sitting across from a detective at a bar, talking about being sodomized with deer antlers and how my fiancé, who I thought was a very laid-back surfer boy, is actually a pathological maniac with a mile-long rap sheet?

"I need you to be really careful," he says. "He's unpredictable. If he's let out, he could come straight for you."

I nod, but my mind is spinning. What if he does? What if Timmy blames me and decides to finish what he started?

The detective seems to sense my fear. "We'll make sure you're safe. He's banned from the building, and if he comes anywhere near you, you call us immediately. Don't hesitate."

I nod again, numb. My drink sits untouched on the table, the ice melted to slush. The detective gives me a small, grim smile and gets up to leave. "Take care of yourself, Margaux. And don't go back to him, no matter what."

As he walks away, I sit here in stunned silence. The weight of everything crashes over me—Timmy's attack, the fear that still clings to my skin, the uncertainty of what's coming next.

I thought I could handle this, but now I'm not so sure.

63

UNEXPECTED GIRL GANG

s I sit back at the bar, nursing my drink, I stare out at the water, trying to make sense of everything. My phone buzzes.

HIS BOSS:

Are you still alive?

What a strange question, I think, my stomach twisting again. Although, given what's happened, it sadly makes sense.

ME:

Yeah. I'm just at Dock Bar getting my head together.

TIMMY'S BOSS:

I'll come meet you?

I hesitate. I don't know her well, but she seems kind, and I'm desperate for someone to talk to.

ME:

Sure, sounds good. See you soon.

When she arrives, I'm still on edge. She sits next to me, and tilts her body toward me. There's concern in her eyes, but the smirk she wears doesn't match it. It's like she's listening to the world's most predictable story, and she's mildly amused that I've become part of it. That said, I feel like her smirk is aimed at Timmy, not me. I don't feel like she's judging me at all, just isn't surprised about any of it, as wild as it is. Given she's Timmy's ex's best friend, this just adds to my concern.

I take a deep breath and recount everything—Timmy's sudden rage, the attack, the police showing up, the antlers. I try to keep my voice steady, but the words feel heavy and absurd coming out of my mouth, as if I'm describing a dream I still haven't fully woken from.

She listens, nodding, occasionally biting her lip to stifle a laugh. It's not malicious, just... strange. Like she expected this all along.

"I'm really sorry," she says. "But, honestly? Not surprised."

Her words hang in the air.

What the hell? I think. She's acting like this is some inevitable punchline to a joke everyone knew but me.

Then, she drops the first bombshell. "So... Jennifer's downstairs."

"Who?"

"His ex. She's picking up a camera from me to install at her place because Timmy's been stalking her."

I blink, trying to process what she just said. "Wait—Timmy? Stalking her? Recently?"

She nods nonchalantly, as if she just told me it's supposed to rain later.

"That can't be right," I say, shaking my head. "He's been with me 24/7. I mean, there was maybe an hour or two when he was working on a condo, but... stalking her? No way."

"Yeah, well, that's what she says." She shrugs. "Anyway, she wants to come up here and say hi if that's okay."

I'm stunned. Say hi? Timmy's ex—who is allegedly being stalked by him—wants to meet me? The whole thing feels surreal, like I'm caught in some bizarre soap opera.

But, weirdly enough, it doesn't feel like I have much of a choice. So I nod. "Sure." What the hell else can I do today, anyway? At least nobody's threatening me with antlers right now.

A few minutes later, Jennifer strolls in. She's warm and friendly, but there's an air of curiosity about her as she sizes me up, the way you might look at a strange animal at the zoo. Not hostile—just curious. I feel like an exhibit on display. But, to be fair, I've heard so many stories that I kind of feel the same way about her.

"So... you're the new girlfriend," she says with a smile. "Or fiancée, I suppose is the technical term." There's an edge to her voice as she says the word 'fiancée', which I suppose is reasonable.

I nod, feeling awkward. "Yep, I guess so."

She settles into a chair, and I tell her a bit about what happened last night. She listens intently, her eyes sparkling with what looks like amusement, though I can't tell if it's directed at Timmy or me.

"I dated that asshole for two whole years," she says, shaking her head with a chuckle. "He never pulled that kind of shit with me, though. Probably because my kid is a giant teenager, and he knew he'd kill him if he tried anything. Plus, I've got a big community here —he wouldn't have dared."

Hearing that Timmy behaved himself with her—at least from a physical violence perspective—but snapped with me so quickly stings in a way I wasn't prepared for. It makes me wonder—what did I do wrong? Was there something about me that made him think it was okay to treat me this way?

I know it's not logical. I know I shouldn't blame myself. But the thought sneaks in anyway, like an insidious whisper.

"He owes me thousands of dollars," Jennifer continues. "And when he got mad, he used to throw my stuff over the fence. He even slashed my kid's tires."

"What the actual fuck?" I mutter.

She nods knowingly. "Oh yeah. He's crazy. Completely out of his mind. He came to my house a week ago and slashed my mattress like it was nothing. That's why I'm in the neighborhood, actually. Picking up security cameras because he's still stalking me."

I try to wrap my head around it. The timelines don't match up—Timmy's been with me this whole time. How could he possibly have gone to her house and done that?

But the weirdness doesn't stop.

We exchange numbers. A number I didn't ever think I would want or need. But it makes sense at the time.

"I bought him a truck, you know," she says casually.

I perk up. "Wait... the truck? I have the keys to that truck."

Her eyes light up. "Seriously? Do you have them with you?"

"Yeah," I say, fishing them out of my bag. "You want them? I don't want them."

"Yes!" she exclaims, her face lighting up with something close to glee.

I hand her the keys without a second thought. If this truck is hers, I want nothing to do with it. I'm happy to get the keys off my hands. The less I have that ties me to Timmy, the better.

She clutches the keys, looking triumphant. "Thank you!"

I sit back, dazed. The whole encounter feels like I'm being punked—Timmy's boss sitting with me, his ex showing up out of nowhere, the bizarre stories, the truck keys. It's like I've stepped into some parallel universe where nothing makes sense, but everyone else seems weirdly okay with it.

And through it all, deep down, I still care about Timmy. What the hell is wrong with me? He attacked me. Threatened me. And yet, I keep thinking about him—about the moments when he was kind, the way he made me feel so seen. How can someone be so many things at once?

Jennifer slips the keys into her pocket and gives me a wink. "Good luck with him," she says, standing to leave. "If he ever tries to contact you, block his ass immediately."

I nod, my head spinning, and watch as she walks away. Timmy's boss—well now, former boss, I suppose—leans back in her chair, smirking again.

"You'll be okay," she says. "I'm just glad you got out of there alive."

I don't feel okay. I feel like I've fallen into some strange dream I can't wake up from, where every twist makes me question what's real and what isn't.

And the scariest part? I still don't know what's coming next.

64

THE ONLY PEOPLE YOU'RE PURSUED BY ARE THE POLICE

Overnight, I start to think about the keys. I become scared. What if he's aggressive and angry and psycho when he gets out of jail? What if he wants to kill me? What if me giving the truck keys to Jennifer tips him over the edge?

I try to push it out of my mind, but then I receive a text.

JENNIFER:

> Hey Margaux. It was so nice to meet you yesterday despite the circumstances. Thank you for giving me the keys, but the more I think about it, the more I realize I'm actually quite scared to have them. I think he is likely to come after me if he finds out I have them, so I'd prefer to give them back to you if that's okay.

ME:

> It's so interesting you say that because I've just been through the same thought process. Where can I meet you?

JENNIFER:

I'll be at the local beach club. Let me text you
the address. Meet you there in like 90
minutes?

ME:

Perfect. See you then. Thank you.

I look up the address she sends, and it's about an hour's walk, which is really what I need in order to be able to clear my head enough to think things through. My mind is a jumble. I've never been through any of this with a person I'm properly in a relationship with. With no friends or family nearby. This is absolutely brutal.

So I get ready, and step out into the sunshine, and I crank my music through my headphones as loud as it will go.

The walk to the beach club feels both endless and too short—plenty of time for my mind to churn through every possible scenario. The idea of holding Timmy's keys and handing them over to Jennifer felt like a power shift, like a declaration that I wanted no further part in this nightmare. But now that it's come full circle, with her handing the keys back, I feel trapped in some surreal loop. What if he comes after me for the keys? The thought sends icy shivers through my veins, and I pick up my pace, hoping that walking faster might outrun the fear blooming inside me.

By the time I arrive at the beach club, the sun is high, but I feel heavy, my stomach a knot of anxiety. I spot Jennifer waving me over, and she's sitting with another woman I don't recognize. They look relaxed, like they're just two old friends meeting for drinks, but everything about this feels... off.

"Hey!" Jennifer greets me warmly, as if we're lifelong friends reconnecting over coffee. "Thanks again for meeting me."

We settle at their outdoor table, the ocean breeze tousling my hair. I try to focus on the bright, cheerful atmosphere, but all I can think about is how bizarre this situation is. I'm here, chatting with Timmy's ex and her friend, poolside, about his spiral into violence. How did my life get here?

Jennifer wastes no time diving into stories about Timmy, and soon I feel like I'm watching someone unravel a very strange puzzle—one I didn't know I was a piece of until now.

"He used to disappear on me for hours, sometimes days," Jennifer says nonchalantly, swirling her drink. "Honestly, I liked it when he did. It gave me time to fuck young guys without worrying about his tantrums."

I blink, stunned by how casually she's admitting to cheating on Timmy. Her candor is unsettling. There's something about it that feels... wrong. Too detached. As if she's playing a game I don't fully understand. I smile awkwardly, trying to mask my discomfort.

Then she drops the next bomb. "He cheated on me with that skank who keeps messaging him, the one he refers to as his 'evil twin'." She sneers. "She's been circling him for years—doesn't care if the guy's in a relationship or not. She'll always come back. She just can't stay away. And they like to do drugs together. That's part of why they're perfect for each other."

I feel sick. I'd finally managed to write off the girl Timmy mentioned as irrelevant, but now? Now it feels like a warning I should've heeded. My stomach twists, and I struggle to keep my face neutral. Was I the fool for believing him when he dismissed having any ongoing involvement with her?

"And you know what else?" Jennifer leans in, her voice dropping conspiratorially. "He stole fireworks and drugs from my son, like a damn psychopath."

I nod slowly, processing this bizarre and troubling information. I've known Timmy for only a few weeks, and yet so much of what she's saying aligns—just with slightly different details. The mood swings, the fixation on specific people, the weird power plays. It feels like déjà vu in fast forward.

"He said some things to me that were super weird," I contribute. "He kept saying that he's always the one who is pursued."

"Pursued?" She's incredulous. "Who is he being pursued by?"

"I don't know," I blurt out. "The police?"

She and her friend howl with laughter, and I join in, because we all know it's true. Other than his skanky friend who keeps coming around, there's literally no chance women are pursuing Timmy with the way he behaves. He's delusional.

Then she says something that sends a chill down my spine. "He has this routine, you know. When he screws up, he'll bring you gifts —shells, leis, maybe cook for you. He'll give you back rubs, foot rubs. It's like clockwork."

It all tracks. Nearly all of it.

Foot rubs? I frown. "Wait... he gives foot rubs?"

"Yep," she confirms. "Always has. That's part of his little apology playbook."

I blink, stunned. The back rubs, the cooking, the shells, the leis— it all felt so genuine when he did it for me. But now, knowing he's used these same gestures on someone else—and likely on every girl before me—makes it feel cheap, mechanical. Like I've fallen for a carefully rehearsed act. It's not personalized, it's not special. It's just... his method.

I feel foolish. All those moments that seemed so unique, so sweet —they weren't about me at all. They were just the next steps in a well-practiced routine. I can't shake the pit growing in my stomach.

Then Jennifer pulls out her phone, scrolling through texts with a sly grin. "When did you guys start seeing each other?"

"March 22nd."

She raises an eyebrow. "Well, here's a fun one. This is from March 23rd. It looks like you guys were at Sails down at the harbor, and it must have reminded him of when we went there together." She hands me her phone. There, plain as day, is a text from Timmy. A picture from the tropical bar he'd told me it was his first time visiting, along with the message: 'I miss your crazy aggressive ass.'

My breath catches in my throat. He told me it was his first time at that bar. I'd believed him—felt special because of it. And now I'm holding the evidence that he'd not only been there before, but used it as a backdrop to text his ex while we were sitting in the bar together.

"Wait... he told me he'd never been there," I say, feeling dizzy. "He made a huge deal about it."

Jennifer rolls her eyes. "Timmy? Please. He's a pathological liar. He probably doesn't even remember going. The guy drinks like a fish, but he's been twice with me."

My mind spins. Why lie about something so trivial? And more importantly, why text his ex the moment we started dating?

"And he doesn't have a driver's license, by the way."

I stare at her, confused. He's been driving me all over Sunset Cay. "Seriously?"

"Yeah, he's had it taken away. He's had a couple of DUIs. He's not legally meant to be driving, but he just does it, anyway."

"Oh, wow. I had no idea."

She nods, knowingly. "And he's so insane... I guess he was dating a doctor a while back. Before me. And he drove her vehicle into the ocean."

"What the actual hell?" My eyes grow wide.

She nods. "Yep."

I do remember him saying something about a Rubicon, driving it into the sea, like he was proud. And like it was a normal thing to do. But I'd just put it down to being one of Timmy's crazy stories.

"When we went to visit his parents, he got arrested because he got drunk and went crazy and threatened people."

My mind is swirling.

"And my final straw was here, in Sunset Cay," she adds. "We went over to the Juggernaut for a surfing contest. And he got obliterated drunk, like usual... made a huge scene. It was then that I knew I couldn't handle his bullshit anymore. He's so embarrassing. He's such a mess."

I exhale slowly. "Wow." This is all a lot to take in. Especially given Timmy's version of events—that this woman is his crazy, toxic ex who did nothing but drink and abuse him, slapping him around and calling him names, putting him down in front of her friends.

I don't necessarily agree with everything she's saying, but she seems... reasonable? And like a fairly normal person with good reason to be frustrated with his antics.

"He really needs to be in prison," she says. "I think he'd be very popular there… a good-looking guy with long hair. I think we all know what would happen to him. I would laugh…"

I'm disturbed by her comment, and don't know how to respond.

Her friend speaks up. "Jennifer… that's not nice," she says, her tone scolding. "Nobody should want that for anyone, even Timmy."

Jennifer shrugs. "He'd deserve it."

We all sit there in silence for a moment. Probably all visualizing Timmy locked up in a prison cell, being tag-teamed by three cell-mates. I feel numb.

"Yeah… oh, and by the way…" Jennifer smirks, savoring the moment. "He has a kid."

I blink. "I'm sorry, what?"

She shrugs. "Yep. I only found out because I got the child support notice in the mail."

The ground feels like it's shifting beneath me. I think back to all the conversations we had about kids. He was adamant—he had none, they all belonged to his exes. I feel like I've been hit by a truck.

"He didn't tell you, huh?" she says smugly, as if she's relieved to know I've been deceived, too.

I can barely breathe. How could he hide something so huge? And worse—how am I supposed to ask him about this when he gets out? I can already picture the fight it will cause, the denials, the somehow turning it all back around onto me. My chest tightens at the thought of it.

But also, why am I thinking about talking to him about anything when he gets out? I'm so confused, my brain feels scrambled.

Jennifer leans back, as if satisfied with her revelations. "You're not the first, you know. And you won't be the last."

I don't know what to say. This entire conversation feels like I've stumbled into someone else's nightmare.

"The worst part is," she says. "There will always be another woman for him to suck in with his charm. And he'll just keep repeating his cycle, time after time, until finally he goes to prison. Or… you know, he might just jump off some rocks and kill himself. That's probably what he'll do if you break up with him."

Her words slosh around in my brain, heavy and dark, like the foamy water that smashes against the rocks at the bottom of a sharp cliff face.

As we wrap up, Jennifer hands me the keys again, a knowing look in her eyes. "Good luck with him," she says. "You're going to need it. My advice is to stay far away."

I pocket the keys, feeling the weight of them press against my leg like an anchor. What the hell am I supposed to do now?

65

THEY SAY THE TRUTH WILL SET YOU FREE... BUT WHAT IS THE TRUTH, ANYWAY?

The next day, my phone buzzes. It's Jennifer, and she has some unexpected news about Timmy.

I stare at my phone, reading the text thread over and over again, my emotions in a tangled mess.

JENNIFER:

> Oh my god, I just got a voicemail from a phone number that said 'Timmy in Jail.'

> His message was all about how he needed me to bail him out. He even offered to give me back the truck and the chainsaw if I do.

Just seeing those words makes my heart race.

The part of me that knows how to survive tells me that everything Jennifer is saying is right—he's dangerous, a menace, a walking grenade with the pin already pulled. But the other part, the one who felt cherished when he cradled me and kissed me like I was his entire world, aches to reach out to him. He needs me. I can't just leave him there like that. My heart twists in conflict.

JENNIFER:

He sounds terrible. Good!

Her gleeful text snaps me back to reality. I stare at the screen, trying to decide how I feel about that. It's not that I don't get it—if anyone has a right to feel that way about Timmy, it's her. But something about the way she seems to revel in his suffering leaves a bad taste in my mouth. It's the way her words feel smug, not just relieved, that makes me uneasy. Does she want him to suffer, or does she just want me to know she's right about him?

ME:

Oh shit.

I feel guilty, even for sending that. Is it really okay to feel bad for him, after everything he's done to me? My body throbs under the weight of that thought, the bruises blossoming into angry purples and blues. I trace the edge of one absentmindedly, wincing at the sharp sting. Some of them could be from sex, sure. But the others... the ones that feel deeper, more deliberate... those are different.

JENNIFER:

Yeah, he's fucking insane.

Kept going on about how he desperately needs his medication. How he's anxious and has a sore tummy in jail. Boo fucking hoo.

Don't you worry. No fucking way in hell am I bailing him out. He's a menace to society.

And I'm going to tell Steve not to either!

The word menace rattles me. It doesn't sit right, even though she might be correct. It makes me feel defensive, as though hearing someone else condemn him stirs something protective in me. A part of me wants to argue, wants to say, 'he's not like that, not all the time.' The other part knows that's exactly what people say when they're in the thick of an abusive relationship. And yet, here I am, still trying to make sense of it.

I feel bad that he's in pain, but he kind of put himself in that situation. I've never been in jail, but from what I've seen on TV, they give you medication. I'm sure the whole desperate 'I need my medication' thing is just a tactic for him to get bailed out, a sympathy ploy. Still, I feel bad for anyone in pain, especially the people I love. And I can't help but think about him tossing and turning and experiencing heartburn and anxiety while trapped in a cell with god knows who else. And part of me feels guilty for putting him there, despite what he's done to me.

I sit back, my phone heavy in my hand, and try to piece together everything—Jennifer's stories, Timmy's promises, the tenderness, and the violence that followed.

It's like trying to fit together two different versions of the same person. On the one hand, Timmy is generous, sweet, playful—a free spirit who lights up my world with his quirky charm. On the other, he's reckless, explosive, and terrifying. And now, sitting in jail, he's hurting. And I still care about him. How can both be true?

Jennifer says Timmy slashed her kid's tires, threw her things over fences, and wrecked her stuff. She paints him as a chaotic storm that leaves devastation in his wake. And some of it matches the Timmy I've seen—the wild behavior, the unpredictability. But other parts don't fit. She claims he stalked her even while he was with me, but I know that's impossible. He's been glued to my side every second. Why would she lie, though? And then again, why wouldn't Timmy?

My head throbs. It's hard to tell where her bitterness ends and the truth begins. Maybe the timelines are blurred, or maybe this is just another manipulation—another way for Timmy to keep two women tangled in his web.

The texts feel like they're burning a hole through my phone. Why am I still entertaining this? The logical part of my brain knows I need to let go, to sever ties with Timmy and anyone associated with him. But another part clings to the hope that Timmy isn't the monster everyone thinks he is. What if he really does need me? What if, deep down, this love—this chaotic, volatile love—is something that could heal us both?

I rub my temples, as if I can physically push the thoughts out of my head. He told me I was the only one who truly understood him, that I was his person, his lifeline. And I believed him. I still want to believe him. But I also know what it feels like to love someone who hurts you—and to justify it, over and over again, until you don't even recognize yourself anymore.

I glance at the bruises again, and they feel like a brand, marking me as someone who's crossed a line that can't be uncrossed. How did I get here so fast? Just a couple of weeks ago, I was in love, dreaming of a future with Timmy, and now I'm sitting here, covered in bruises, wondering if I'm going to get hurt again when he gets out. Wondering if I'll be able to walk away.

I tap out another message.

ME:

Do you think Steve will actually listen to you?

JENNIFER:

Probably not. He's loyal to Timmy to a fault.
But I'll try.

Just stay safe, okay?

Her words feel sincere, but I still don't know if I trust her. I don't know if I trust anyone right now—not even myself. I put my phone down and stare out at the ocean, the waves crashing rhythmically against the shore. I breathe in the salt air, hoping it will calm the storm inside me.

How do I still feel like I love someone who can hurt me like that? How do I reconcile the man who made me feel seen, cherished, and adored with the man who shoved me to the ground, bruised my skin, and threatened to kill me?

The hardest part is that I still want to believe in the first version of Timmy—the one who held me close, kissed my forehead, told me I was his world and that he loved each and every one of my freckles.

The one who took me to see Sabre in quarantine. The one who made me feel like the only woman on earth.

What if everything she's saying is a lie? What if he's right, and she's the toxic, abusive, bad person in all of this? Sure, she didn't attack me. He did. But part of me feels like I need to hear his side of the story. I feel sympathy for his mental health issues, and god knows I have my own. PTSD, anxiety and depression are all a bitch that I have to deal with every day. And his condition seems more severe. No excuse to attack me, of course, or to threaten to kill me. But he says I'm his person, the one that has helped him and will continue to help him, and there's a sense of obligation in that. A sense of feeling like I might be the only one who can help him to change his life for the better.

But now, at the same time, every sweet memory feels tainted, every loving gesture a potential manipulation. It's as if the person I thought I knew was a mirage, and now I'm left wandering in the desert, desperate for water, not knowing if I'll ever find it again—or if it was all just a trick.

I pick up my phone and stare at the message thread again, my thumb hovering over the screen. I know I should block him, let him go. But I also know I won't. Not yet.

Because part of me is still waiting. Waiting for the Timmy I fell in love with to come back. Waiting for the story to make sense. Waiting for him to tell me that everything will be okay.

Even though, deep down, I know it probably won't.

66

LIAR, LIAR, SKANKS ON FIRE

ater that Day

LHis phone's still not working properly, but I'm a determined person. I want to see what I'm getting myself into. The full picture. What actual data I can pull from that's not based on an anecdote from Timmy or his ex.

Bring in the rice.

I tell myself this is wrong. Going through his phone isn't a line I've ever had to cross with other romantic partners. But it's not like I have other options now that he's in jail, unreachable. I need to know what's true, what's fiction, and what kind of mess I really might be stepping into here.

He said in his Tinder profile that he wasn't interested in drama, but I'm getting the sense that the opposite is true, and that he actually thrives on chaos. Maybe he's just got a wild streak, a harmless impulsiveness—but there's this other side I've seen now, dark and unpredictable. He threatened to kill me, and actually attacked me. And maybe this is the only way to know what I'm actually dealing with and how he might behave when he gets out.

After trying everything else I can think of, I finally manage to get his phone to work, the rice doing enough to make the screen turn on in brief, frustrating spurts. Because he's given me the passcode, I'm able to get into it.

With each minute, I feel my stomach tighten. I tell myself that it's a one-time thing, even though he's given me permission. Usually, if I did want to check something, I'd do it in front of him, not here when he can't see me doing it.

But once I get in, it's like Pandora's box, a whole new world. A sea of toxic exchanges with numerous people, the kind that feel like poison soaking through the screen.

It's mostly angry texts between him and a few friends—accusations, insults, mean jabs. A picture pops up next—a baggie of pills, sent by a number I don't recognize. I'm no drug expert, but these don't look like they were issued by a pharmacy. Is he buying them? Selling them? It's unclear. I swallow hard, feeling like I'm peeking into a world I don't belong to.

Then there's the girl. The one who he refers to as his evil twin. And she's... unremarkable, aside from the haggard look to her face that gives her away. The telltale signs of late nights and heavy hard drug use.

Okay, maybe I sound bitchy and judgmental. I own it. But there's something about her that makes me irrationally angry. She's one of those people who would be comfortable blowing up someone's relationship just for a flicker of attention, for some dick.

And she did have sex with him, right before I met him. And she won't stop blowing up his fucking phone.

I think back to our earlier conversation... not verbatim, but the general gist—

"You fucked your friend when she came to visit, didn't you?"

"No."

"Tell me the truth."

He'd sighed and scowled. "Well, yeah. Fine, I'll tell you. We had sex. It didn't mean anything, though."

"So... you pretend to like me, and then your friend comes to town. You stop messaging me for days. And it's because you're fucking your friend?"

"We weren't together yet," he shrugs. "And I had no idea if you were actually going to even show up."

"But I did show up. I asked you about it and you lied about it."

"But it was none of your business what I did before I met you."

"Listen, my friend said you're not replying because you're off fucking your female friend. And he was right. I just want to know what kind of person you are. If you can be trusted."

"Well, she means nothing to me. We got drunk and fucked. That's all."

I scroll further up, seeing the toxic messages between them.

I gasp as I see one picture of her wearing his bone necklace—the one he put on me like it meant something to him, a weird ritual of his. She's topless, her thin-lipped mouth posed in a way that doesn't do her any favors, holding the skull and antler combo to her head in some half-drunk attempt at being cute. The thought of her wearing that necklace topless, holding that skull he's obsessed with, feels like a slap. And for a second, I wonder, *how many other women has he put that necklace on?* I shiver with disgust.

Flipping through the messages, I see the desperate back-and-forth. Only a few days before I arrived, she texted him and said she needed to get her stuff from his house. He tells her only if she promises to not say a word, to swear to god she won't. And that if she says one word, she has to suck his dick. I retch. The way she's been blowing up his phone, it seems like she took it as an invitation.

Apparently, he physically hit her a couple of weeks ago. He sounds absolutely unhinged in his texts to her. And it's obvious they've both been drinking by the content of the texts. They're not... romantic... per se, but there's an undercurrent of something. A tension.

It just goes on—insults thrown like barbs, her blowing up his phone, him demanding she 'quit blowing him up'. Then him messaging her if she stops.

He told me she's a nightmare, loud and obnoxious, that he couldn't stand being around her for more than a day or two. So then, what's this? It certainly doesn't look like he's been trying to stay away.

I'm disgusted. If he fucks *that*, then... I know, I sound bitchy to myself.

But she's gross.

Now I'm having visions that he just fucks anyone in Sunset Cay who is willing.

I'm someone who has worked my ass off for so long to live my dream. And now I'm concerned that maybe he'll take what he can from me and run back to some tragedy like her, with my stuff. And leave me with nothing.

What if they're in a secret relationship? What if I'm a fucking joke to both of them? And they're just biding their time, waiting to be reunited, after he's taken everything that he can from me. Exploited what he can through pretending to care about me.

I think of his exes that I'm aware of, all older than me. Successful from a career perspective, but all with issues from a personal standpoint, at least from what he's told me.

Before we met in person, he was talking to a single mother with four children that had matching mohawks, but he said he chose me over her.

I know I'm not perfect, though. Who wants a three-times-married woman who doesn't have a family? Maybe he's the best I can ever hope for.

But if he cheated on me with... her? I'd be so grossed out.

Why do I feel like that's a risk, though? If she compliments him while we're having a fight... he's just one hurt feeling away from hurting me just to be spiteful. That's not what I want. I know that's not how relationships should work. Being worried that if you say one wrong thing to your partner, that he is so needy of praise and positive reinforcement that you risk being cheated on? That's not healthy.

But instead of pushing him away, conceptually, at least, in my mind, I pull him closer. I want him to realize why he should never want to do that. Why he should never say he had no choice but to do that. Cheat with the girl he doesn't like but will fuck.

As if on cue, his phone dings, and it's her. Selfies of them together, arm in arm, looking like she's exactly where she belongs.

For someone he doesn't like, they sure took a lot of selfies together, both of them cozy, his arm slung around her.

He looks like himself, the requisite surfer, exuding charm and confidence.

She looks all perky on his arm, but her face is still hard as nails. No plastic surgery can undo the drugs she's done.

It's funny how my anger is all directed at her. My meanness. But that's normal, right? She's the one trying to break up a relationship, or at least interfere with it. She's the one who knowingly keeps reaching out and sending him selfies. That's disgusting behavior. I tell myself that she's the one who is obsessed with him, a sad, low-value woman who can't take a hint.

But some small, insidious part of me whispers that maybe it's not just her. That maybe he's keeping her around, feeding her scraps of attention, enjoying her attention when he tells me she's nothing but a pest.

Her texts look toxic, like his, but—I have to admit—slightly more reasonable. He hurls more insults, more comments that are derogatory to women, than she does to him.

The way he talks about her behind her back feels slimy, and I can't shake the feeling I'm just the newest target of his games. Am I any different from her—just way prettier and smarter? Or am I just the one officially sitting next to him while he leads on another distraction.

The way he pleaded with her over text that they should both stop drinking because they would be 'so much better together'... it was said in what could be interpreted as a platonic way, but could easily be misconstrued by someone who's unhinged.

I'm beginning to feel like there's more to the story than the version he's given me.

Because in his version, she's a psycho who is obsessed with his dick or something.

That she's impossible to be around. Loud, jarring, gets banned from every place in town. Not very smart.

And he's the innocent one, barraged by her attention, because he's just so fucking adorable.

If that's the case, he sure does have a pattern.

My own phone dings, and it's Jennifer again.

JENNIFER:

Did you drop off his stuff at Matty's house?

ME:

Not yet.

JENNIFER:

Do it soon. Trust me.

Don't let him lure you into paying his bail.

Pretty sure he only called me bc he knows my number since he has no phone.

She has a point. There's an urgency here, and I don't know what to expect when he gets out. I feel panic rise, knowing I can't ignore her warning. There's an urgency in her words, a strange camaraderie, like she's been exactly where I am right now. And I'm feeling so flat after reading his gross messages with Skank Face.

I take all his stuff and load it into trash bags and then call an Uber to haul it all to Matty's place, hoping to put some distance between me and whatever sick trap I've walked into.

I can't figure out his keys—none of them fit in the lock—and so I leave his things right outside the front door, hoping nobody will take them. Of course, today is the one day since I've known him that Matty has a date and isn't at home watching YouTube.

When I get back to my apartment, more selfies pop up from her, and I run to the bathroom, the bile rising as I fight back these feelings of betrayal and disgust. My body heaves as I empty my stomach, retching until my eyes water and my throat aches.

I've always thought I was strong, capable of anything, but here I am, folded over and breaking.

Whatever I deserve, I'm absolutely certain that it's not this.

67

LUCKY

My chest feels heavy as I scroll through his four pages of publicly available criminal records. Who knew all this information was available? It's like a whole new world has been opened to me. Some places charge for it, but in Sunset Cay, the info is free and incredibly easy to access.

Every charge, every conviction, feels like another brick in a wall closing in around me, cutting off the air.

My heart races as my eyes dart back to the screen, unable to look away, yet desperate to close the window and pretend I never saw it. How could I not have known? The man who promised me forever—the man who kissed me tenderly in the mornings, who made me laugh with absurd jokes about tentacle porn and superheroes—has lived an entire life of chaos, and I was blissfully oblivious of most of it until now.

My hands shake, my fingers twitching as if the words on the screen are venom seeping into my skin. Assault. Theft. Domestic abuse. Each charge feels like a punch to the gut. These aren't youthful indiscretions or silly mistakes. This is a pattern. A roadmap of destruction.

I never would have thought to look at a guy's criminal record. It never even crossed my mind that I could look into someone's past this way, to proactively protect myself from someone like Timmy.

My mind races from the revelation.

Sure, I can see someone getting a speeding ticket here or there. And nearly every guy I've ever met has had at least some kind of run-in with the cops. Hell, even my cop ex-husband told me a story about how police dogs chased him and his teenage friends onto a rooftop because they were smoking marijuana. Even my very buttoned-up ex told me about how he has a metal plate in his foot from the time he skateboarded off a roof as a teenager.

Even the most sensible of guys seems to have done a bunch of dumb shit when they were younger.

It's just what they do.

But four pages worth of charges?

That requires dedication. Or a string of extremely bad luck.

I want to scream. I want to throw the laptop across the room and shatter the screen into a thousand pieces, just like Timmy smashed the top of my toilet. But all I can do is sit, frozen, feeling the walls of my apartment, once a sanctuary, now closing in on me.

How did I let this happen? My mind races through every interaction, every conversation we've ever had, replaying them with a new lens. His charm, his excuses, the way he downplayed every mistake—now it feels like it was all a script. A script designed to manipulate, to pull me in deeper, to make me believe that he was the victim, that the world was just unfair to someone as misunderstood as him. And I fell for it. I wanted to fall for it, because the alternative—the truth—is almost too unbearable to confront.

My stomach churns as I think about the detective's words: "He's a real nut. You're lucky you're still alive." Those words echo in my head like a drumbeat, constant and unrelenting. *Lucky*. I'm *lucky* to be alive.

The bruises on my body tell me how close I came to not being lucky at all. The deer antlers, the hammer, the rage—these records make it seem like it really wasn't just a bad night. It was a glimpse into who Timmy really is beneath the charm, beneath the playful exterior he used to lure me in.

And yet, part of me still wants to believe him. I can almost hear his voice, smooth and persuasive: "Margaux, baby, that's all bullshit. They're exaggerating—you know how they are. I told you about that already. It's just the system trying to screw me over. You know me— you know I'd never hurt anyone. That's why most of these are charges and not actual convictions."

I feel the heat rising to my cheeks, ashamed at what I allowed myself to believe. Of how immersed and entangled I've become with somebody whose rap sheet makes him look like a prolific offender who can't keep himself out of trouble.

Yet, part of me listened to his justifications. The way he downplays his past, like somehow he's the victim in every case. Like all the cops have had it out for him over the past two decades, and he's been on the receiving end of police targeting as a straight white man. That every woman and the one guy who has filed domestic abuse charges against him, or petitioned for a restraining order, has somehow conspired against him because he's such a nice person that they want to see him suffer.

I squeeze my eyes shut, trying to block out the imagined conversation, but it's no use. He's still there in my mind, weaving his words like a spider spinning a web, delicate and intricate. What if he really is telling the truth? What if the cops *do* have it out for him? What if his exes really *were* trying to ruin his life out of spite?

But then I think about Jennifer. I think about the stories she told me at the beach club. The way she laughed, partially with malice, but also with the exasperated humor of someone who has seen too much and is no longer surprised by anything. "He's got a routine," she'd said. "Messes up, brings you shells and leis, gives you foot rubs and back rubs." I feel my heart sink as I realize how perfectly I fit into his pattern. Maybe I was just another woman caught in his cycle—a fresh page in the same tired story he's been telling for years.

And yet, some of what Jennifer said didn't sit right with me either. The way she mentioned enjoying affairs with younger men when

Timmy stormed off in a rage—it felt off, like a glimpse into a different kind of manipulation. Maybe she isn't innocent in all this either. But does that really matter? Does it change what Timmy has done? *No. It doesn't.*

I glance at the bruises on my thighs, still vivid and angry. The one under my eye throbs with a dull ache. These are not the marks of misunderstandings or petty arguments. These are the marks of violence. Marks that shouldn't be there. Marks that he put there because he couldn't control himself, because there was something evil lurking deep inside of him.

I close the laptop slowly, my hand hovering over the screen as if shutting it will make the truth go away. But it won't. It's there, waiting for me, pressing against the edges of my mind, demanding to be acknowledged. I can't unsee it. I can't unknow it. So for now, I close the document, my heart pounding in my chest. I can't bear to see his name up on my screen anymore. To wonder what drove each and every incident. To think, in the back of my mind, about how so many other incidents have likely occurred but simply gone unreported.

I think about his actual excuses he's provided me in the past, about the incidents I was aware of, and how plausible they are. 'Oh, the cops target me because of this or that. They're just looking for an easy target, you know?' He makes it sound like everything he's done that has attracted police attention is just some trivial event, like he's the victim of some larger conspiracy.

"Oh, my sister's best friend is a dick, and he beat me up and I defended myself. People blow things out of proportion. I didn't even touch the guy, and he came at me first, you know? Cops are assholes, and they love to take guys down like me. Makes them feel important." He said it with such conviction, such confidence, that I'd believed him at the time.

His explanations have always been airtight, or carefully navigated in a manner that casts significant doubt on the veracity of any allegations against him. He knows when to be vague, and when to build in specifics. And then, on top of that, his charm disarmed any doubts that crept in.

When he talked about his exes, his tone had grown even more venomous.

"That crazy bitch," he'd say, shaking his head with disbelief, as if he's the long-suffering victim of a vindictive woman... make that many, many women. "Oh, she said she was going to do that because I wanted to leave her. She filed all sorts of false reports against me, trying to ruin my life just because I wouldn't put up with her constant drama. She had a raging drinking problem, and everything she said about me was bullshit. None of it's true, Margaux. It's all lies."

Always a reason, never an acceptance of accountability, even for the smallest citations.

"You're the only one who really understands me," he'd say, his eyes pleading. "You know I'd never hurt anyone."

His excuses were as voluminous as his charges, but he was so convincing, and I felt icky about it all, and it was easier just to push it down and believe what he told me. Because to admit I've been with someone who is a prolific, violent offender who regularly puts other people in danger is more than I can take right now.

So at the time, I believed him, going so far as to feel sorry for him —his exes all sound like unstable women trying to take him down. He always made sure to paint himself as the hero—the sensitive, kind, misunderstood soul trying to navigate a world where all sorts of people were out to get him. Exes, friends, family members, bosses, coworkers.

Always the victim.

And he plays that role so well, turning each story on its head one by one until I can't imagine it being any other way.

I despise the saying, 'there are three versions of every story: mine, yours, and the truth'. It's something my stepfather loved to say to justify my mother's terrible behavior, and gloss over everything, as if I hold some blame in how she acted while I was a child.

But in Timmy's world, he only needs one truth, no matter what evidence seems to sit in front of him. Timmy's truth. Timmy's truth. Oh, and Timmy's other truth.

It seems to vary, depending on the weather, his mood, what he said last time and whether I poked holes in any of his versions. He's adaptable, I'll give him that, but not in a good way. More like a slippery eel that weaves through rock pools, twisting and turning his words until you forget what he even said in the first place. Making you doubt your own version of events, even though you're pretty sure you know what happened.

But now, having stared at the long list of offenses, I feel ill. How could I ever have believed him? Why didn't I check this sooner? How have I ignored all the red flags that led to this moment?

My stomach churns as I think about telling anyone what I've found—friends, family. What would they say? None of them have met him in person, except for Natasja, and although he destroyed the evening we spent with her and her friends, she was fairly chill about his behavior at the time—at least to me.

Now, I can't shake the feeling that I've been played—I feel small and stupid, like I'm somehow complicit in his lies.

The worst part? He's made me feel like we're in it together, a true team. "Nobody gets me like you do," is one of his favorite phrases. His words echo in my head now, hollow and poisonous, dangerous. I feel like a fool. I was his ally, his defender, and now I'm too embarrassed to admit how deeply I've been deceived.

I can picture it now, Timmy sitting across from me feigning surprise and hurt if I bring any of these things up. He'd probably scoff and roll his eyes and say something like, "Oh, Margaux, you found a long set of charges? I told you, that's all nonsense. A string of misunderstandings. You're not actually believing any of that bullshit, are you?" I can see him leaning in, his voice dripping with condescension, his eyes flicking between 'deep, honest guy' to irritation that I might not be falling for any of this. "I really thought you were smarter than that," I can imagine him saying. "It's really hurting my feelings that you don't believe me."

And then, now, the guilt presses down on me, heavy and suffocating. The absolute shame. Because I know that, even with all the evidence in front of me, a small part of me still fears that he might somehow convince me again. That he might spin a new story, concocting an updated version that explains everything away—that calms my residual fears, by smoothing over the gouges in his backstories, like putty over the gouges he made in the walls of my apartment.

I need to tell someone. I need help. I can't deal with this alone. But the shame wraps around me like a heavy blanket, suffocating me. How could I be so stupid? How could I let this happen? I'm supposed to be smart. I'm supposed to be independent. And now, here I am, tangled in the mess of a man with a rap sheet longer than any I've ever seen, feeling guilty for wanting to help him, for still caring about him despite everything.

What if I tell someone and they judge me? What if they say, "You should've seen the signs. You should've known better."

I grip the edge of the table, the cool surface grounding me for a moment. I know what I need to do. I need to cut him off. I need to walk away. I need to be stronger than the web he's spun around me. But the thought of leaving him—of abandoning him in that jail cell, of not being there when he calls—makes my chest tighten with guilt. What if he really does need me?

I shake my head, trying to clear the fog. This isn't love, it can't be. I know that. I *know* that. But knowing and believing are two very different things. And right now, I'm still standing on the edge, teetering between the two, trying to figure out which way to fall.

I'm not ready to confront the truth yet. Not with anyone else. I need to figure out what to do next, but I need to do it alone. Without the judgment of others, I need to find a way to extricate myself from Timmy's web of lies. But all I can feel right now is guilt, shame, embarrassment, and mortification that I missed so many flags and didn't see the signs of what he was doing.

68

IF HE DID IT

I wake in a sweat, stifling a scream and gasping for air.

The images swirl in my mind—Sabre's small body, tossed over the edge of the balcony, his terrified meow silenced by the rush of air, the horrible drop, the thud far below. Too far away to hear. My stomach twists at the thought, a deep, hollow ache expanding in my chest. I clutch my sides, as if holding myself together might stop the vivid mental scenes from unspooling further. But the images keep coming, relentless and unbidden—Timmy's face, twisted with rage, shifting into that horrifying grin, the one that tells me he finds amusement in the power he holds over me. The way his mirth emerges at the worst moments, as if hurting others feeds him.

I shiver, pulling my knees up to my chest as I imagine him tossing Sabre over the edge without a second thought. The helplessness. The guilt that would consume me. Sabre isn't just my pet—he's my support, my family, my constant in a storm of uncertainty. If I lost him, there would be no coming back from that. Not emotionally. Not mentally. And the fact that part of me believes Timmy could actually do that—it's a possibility I can't ignore.

And what if he throws *me* over? The thought slides in, uninvited, making my pulse race. If he can snap the way he did—if he can turn into a monster before my eyes—what's to stop him from dragging me to the edge? One shove. That's all it would take. One impulsive second where rage overtakes him. I'd be weightless for a moment, floating, before the sheer terror sinks in, and then the nothingness. I try to push the thought away, but it lingers, like a shadow lurking at the edges of my mind.

Even now, I can hear the echoes of his laughter, that sinister glee when he smashed things in the apartment, the giddiness in his voice when he announced he'd kill me with the hammer. It doesn't feel real —none of it does. How could he, the man I shared my bed with, whispered dreams to, and fell in love with, turn into this?

His eyes, the change in his face, continues to haunt me. The way his kind, playful expression morphed into something alien—a stranger's face carved with anger and malice. It's not just the yelling or the threats—it's the transformation, like a mask being ripped off to reveal what's really underneath. That moment will forever be seared into my memory, the shift from man to monster in the blink of an eye.

I'm still in disbelief that I'm in this position. I used to be so careful, so guarded. How did I end up entangled with someone so volatile, so dangerous? I feel ashamed, foolish for letting him into my life so quickly. I feel the weight of my own choices pressing down on me, but there's no clarity, no understanding. Just confusion and an overwhelming sense of betrayal.

He spoke so convincingly about his ex—how abusive she was, how she slapped him awake, berated him, made him feel small. And I believed him. Of course I believed him.

Sure, I've had arguments where people have raised their voices and frowned. Sworn at me, even, although that's been rare. I've managed to avoid many relationships where people have called me names. But Timmy seemed like a different beast—an actual beast, when his face changed.

It's really hard to reconcile with the lighthearted, fun, carefree man I met and so quickly fell in love with.

I had no doubt he's a handful, and that he needed a bit of

coaching to be a more consistent, reliable adult. But that's very different from dealing with rage.

I hug myself tighter, feeling the weight of that realization sink in. His tears, his promises, his declarations of love—they weren't mine alone. They were tools, just like his rage, just like the antlers he tried to shove inside me, just like every lie he's ever told.

But then, there's the other side of him, the side that holds me after sex, kisses my forehead, and whispers that I'm his person. That side is real, too. Isn't it? Or am I just fooling myself again? Is anything real with him?

I think about his mental health—his wild mood swings, the manic energy that bubbles up out of nowhere, the deep crashes that leave him sullen and distant. Maybe it's too many drugs in his past. Maybe it's trauma from his childhood, or a previous relationship. Maybe he's broken in ways I'll never fully understand. And yet, I still care. I still want to help him. I still want to believe that somewhere beneath the chaos, there's a man who loves me, who needs me, who can change.

But that's the most dangerous thought of all, isn't it? The hope that he can change.

The hope that I can be the one to fix him.

TODAY IS the day I've been looking forward to—the day I get to pick up Sabre. But it's far from what I expected, and a little ironic. Sabre's getting freed from his quarantine jail, and instead of celebrating, Timmy's in actual jail for hurting me. One's getting out and the other's just gone in.

I shake my head and sigh as I order an Uber out to the quarantine facility. The journey is quiet, and it feels almost rude to look out the window at the beautiful, sunny day, and the palm trees gently swaying in the wind.

When I pick up Sabre, I'm excited to see him and can tell he is, too, but it's a somber ride back to the apartment.

When we get inside, I let him out of his carrier. "This is our new home, little buddy. I hope you like it."

He immediately wanders around, exploring his new kingdom.

I want to be excited, to enjoy this moment I've waited so long for, but instead I just feel sick and empty.

The rational part of me knows that it's not my job to save Timmy. That loving someone isn't supposed to mean putting your life at risk. But the part of me that's tangled up in him, that still remembers the way he made me laugh until I cried, clings to the idea that maybe—just maybe—things could be different.

I don't know how to reconcile the two Timmys—the one who makes me feel alive and the one who makes me fear for my life. The one who proposed to me in the botanical gardens while mongooses ate sausage in front of us, promising the world, or the one who threatened to kill me with a hammer and slice my throat with deer antlers.

As if sensing my anxiety, Sabre rubs against my leg, purring softly, and I scoop him up, holding him close to my chest. His small body is warm and familiar, a constant in the midst of the chaos swirling around me. I bury my face in his fur, inhaling the comforting scent of him. "You're my anchor, Sabre. I won't let him hurt you. I won't let him hurt us."

But even as I make that promise, the fear lingers. Timmy is still out there—maybe not right now, but soon. And when he gets out, I don't know what version of him he will be, how mad he'll be at me. I don't know if I'll be strong enough to protect myself, to protect Sabre.

I rock back and forth, clutching my cat like a lifeline, as the weight of everything presses down on me. What do I do now?

My brain swirls like it's surrounded by a pea-soup fog, unable to see a clear way forward.

Every step feels like a gamble, every decision fraught with doubt. And I'm alone in this—so terrifyingly, completely alone.

69

HARD TRUTHS > BEAUTIFUL LIES

Paulo's message hits me like a freight train. I finally texted him to let him know what happened. I needed to tell someone—someone who I know cares about me, and who wouldn't reply in a flippant way. I know Paulo is analytical, and he'll think this through logically. But even then, I'm not expecting the reply that I receive:

PAULO:

When people show you who they are, believe them.

I don't think this guy's behavior will be an isolated incident.

You guys moved very fast... and it's understandable for you to fall for someone who is offering you something you haven't gotten for 6 years... excitement, adventure, someone who is expanding your world.

And part of this new adventure in self discovery is Sunset Cay... plus some good D.

> But for you to call him your fiancée after less than a few weeks seems unhealthy, even desperate.

> And giving someone a second chance who put your physical safety at risk is not a good move.

> Ensuring your physical wellbeing and safety is at the base of our human existence, and if he can't help you achieve that you won't climb higher. Maslow's hierarchy of needs, baby.

> You know your worth and I don't want to see you diminish it with dickheads that put you in danger.

> Sorry if this comes across as judgmental or harsh, but I say it because I care for you.

He's right. Every word he says is fucking right. And he's so kind. Some of it's not nice to read, and I have a particular reaction to his use of the word 'desperate'. It makes me feel sick inside, but he's coming from a good place. Sometimes, it's easier to see signs from outside than when you're right in the middle of it. And clearly he does.

I read it once, then again, slowly, word by word, letting each sentence sink in. With every line, my stomach tightens, and I feel the familiar ache of shame rise up in my chest.

When people show you who they are, believe them.

I stare at those words for a long time. They rattle me. They gnaw at the part of me that still wants to believe in the Timmy I fell for—the one who held me under the stars and whispered promises into the night. But Paulo's right. Timmy's rage, his violence, the way he flipped like a switch—it wasn't a momentary lapse. It was who he is. And no matter how much I want to rewrite the story, to find an explanation that makes everything okay, the truth is staring me right in the face.

Believe them.

A lump forms in my throat, and I fight the urge to cry. Paulo's words aren't cruel, but they feel sharp, like a scalpel cutting through the fantasy I've been clinging to.

You guys moved very fast...

He's right. I can see that now. Moving so quickly with Timmy—it felt thrilling in the moment, like jumping off a cliff into unknown waters, trusting that I'd land safely. But the fall was reckless. And I knew it. Somewhere deep down, I knew it, even as I ignored the nagging voice in the back of my mind that told me to slow down, to tread carefully.

Excitement, adventure, someone expanding your world...

I let out a shaky breath. That's exactly what Timmy was to me— a wild ride that pulled me out of the monotony of the life I left behind. I wasn't just looking for love. I was looking for escape. A new beginning. And Timmy made me feel alive in a way I hadn't felt in years.

But Paulo's words linger, making me realize that maybe what I mistook for love was something else entirely. A distraction. A high. A need to fill a void that's been gnawing at me for longer than I care to admit.

But calling him your fiancé after a few weeks... that's not healthy, even desperate.

That word—desperate—cuts deep. It lands heavily, making my stomach churn. I don't want to think of myself as desperate. I don't want to believe that's what this was. But the truth clings to me, undeniable. I let myself get swept up in the whirlwind of Timmy because I wanted to be swept up. I wanted the adventure, the fantasy, the dopamine hit. And now here I am, in the wreckage, sifting through the debris, wondering how I let it get this far.

Ensuring your physical well-being and safety is at the base of our human existence...

I can feel the tears welling up now. Paulo's right—without safety, everything else crumbles. And Timmy has proven, time and time again, that he can't offer that to me. Especially more recently, instead of building me up, he's been breaking me down with increasing frequency. And if I don't put my safety first, how will I ever climb higher? How will I ever get back to myself?

I clutch my phone to my chest, feeling a wave of gratitude wash over me for Paulo, for his blunt honesty, even though it stings. He's saying what I need to hear, not what I want to hear. And deep down, I know that every word is true.

The weight on my chest lightens ever so slightly. I wipe the tears from my eyes, take a deep breath, and open my laptop. I type a few lines. Then a few more. The words come easier now, like a dam breaking open.

This—this writing, this space—this is what I imagined my time here would be like. Not the chaos, not the endless drama. Just me. The peaceful mornings, the sound of the ocean, the satisfaction of creating something real, something meaningful. I type until the sun rises, my thoughts spilling out onto the screen, clearing the clutter from my mind.

Later, I take myself for a long walk along the boardwalk, the warm breeze brushing against my skin. I get my steps in, savoring the simplicity of the moment. No arguments, no anxiety. Just the rhythm of my feet hitting the pavement and the sun warming my face. I stop for brunch at a little café, order a mimosa, and breathe in the joy of being alone.

For the first time since getting to Sunset Cay, I feel light. Unburdened. Free. This—this is what I came here for. To reconnect with myself, to breathe, to explore without fear. I sip my mimosa slowly, savoring every bit of it.

Later, at the gym, I move my body just for me. No pressure, no expectations. I lift heavy weights, feel my muscles burn, and let the music in my headphones drown out the lingering thoughts of Timmy. It's not a perfect workout, but it's mine. And that's enough.

When I get home, I pull out my oracle deck. I shuffle the cards, letting the tension flow out of my body, and draw one. LISTEN.

I stare at the card for a long time, the word sinking deep into my bones. It truly feels like a message from the universe. A reminder to trust myself, to hear what my intuition has been trying to tell me all along. I've been listening to everyone else—Timmy, his ex, the detective. But it's time to listen to the one person I've been neglecting: me.

Listen to the part of me that knows the truth, the part that's been whispering in the background this whole time.

It's time to stop ignoring the voice inside me. Time to stop waiting for someone else to save me.

It's time to trust myself again.

70

SWITZERLAND WITH A SECRET AGENDA

I sit at the beach once again, the waves gently lapping at the shore as the sun sinks lower on the horizon, and I tell myself, over and over again, that I've made the right decision. It feels true, mostly. The chaos of the past few weeks with Timmy has finally quieted, and I can breathe again without waiting for the next unpredictable moment. But as much as I try to convince myself, it feels more like I'm writing a mantra in the sand, knowing full well the tide is coming to wash it away.

Later, at the Dock Bar, I perch at the bar with my laptop, enjoying the sweet release of productivity. My fingers dance over the keys, and the words flow easily—more easily than they have in weeks. The happy hour wings arrive, sticky and messy—not the best option to eat while typing—so I pause to savor them. The mix of hot sauce and salty air fills my senses, and for a brief moment, I feel light. I inhale deeply, the scent of plumeria heavy in the breeze, and gaze out toward Strawberry Head and the endless coastline. The decision to step back from Timmy feels like the right one, my gut for once not in a tight knot.

A while later, I close my laptop and take a leisurely walk through the nearby shopping mall. Not because I need anything, but because I can't stand going back to the apartment just yet. The sight of the broken toilet lid and the gouges in the wall makes my chest tighten every time I see them, and I'm not ready to face it again. But even as I wander aimlessly, something nags at me—this dull ache that Timmy's absence has left behind. I miss the good times. And there were so many of them—adventures, laughter, the way he made me feel seen. I keep replaying moments in my mind like a movie reel I can't turn off.

It wasn't all bad, I tell myself, as if that thought makes it any better. His outburst wasn't like him—at least, not like the version of him I knew. There has to be more to it. People don't just change overnight. I want to believe there's an explanation, a reason hidden beneath the rage. Maybe if I could just understand it, it wouldn't feel so terrifying.

And the good stuff... oh, the good stuff. The way he helped me set up the apartment, taking pride in every little touch. How he'd played tour guide, showing me his world, filling it with excitement and adventure. How he introduced me to his friends, his boss, and spoke about a future where we'd build a life together. The way he proposed so sweetly. People don't do those things unless they care, right? There had to be some truth in all that love and affection, didn't there?

I feel a sinking weight in my stomach when I think about the other side of the coin—the growing tension, the cracks I ignored, the way I started holding my breath whenever we went somewhere new, afraid of what might happen next. That gnawing fear that he might lash out again, that he might not stop at just words or threats next time. And yet... the thought of completely walking away makes me feel like I'm cutting off a limb.

On the way back from the shopping mall, I stop at a bar recommended to me by a friend back in San Francisco. I immediately make friends with the bartender, realizing we have industry friends in common back on the mainland. This is what my life was like before I met Timmy, where I was able to make friends with ease, without there being any drama, any reservations about going some place and having my partner make a scene.

I feel a pit in my stomach at the thought of bringing Timmy somewhere like this. I can't bring him around quality people and risk him behaving the way he did in front of Natasja and her work acquaintances. And definitely not if he's ever violent again. I don't want to give up a life where I can make friends and be invited out to nice places because they don't have even a slight concern about my behavior. But with Timmy, even before the attack, I was starting to be in a constant state of alert whenever we went anywhere. And after he attacked me, I can't imagine feeling any differently when it's just me and him at home.

When I get back home, the apartment feels cold and eerie. I stand in the doorway, surveying the wreckage, my eyes flicking once again to every piece of it he destroyed. I've tidied most of it by now, but the structural pieces still remain, as well as a few things I haven't been able to bring myself to touch. The gouges in the wall. The jagged edge where the toilet lid shattered. The pot he smashed, shards of senti-mental ceramic still scattered near the balcony door. My stomach twists. I shiver involuntarily, as though his rage is still lingering in the room, clinging to the air like cigarette smoke.

My phone buzzes with a message from Steve.

STEVE: Timmy's ex keeps texting me.
There's just a lot of anger and scorn from her.
You seem to be acting like a much more sane person.
Thanks for that. Just thought you should know.

I STARE at the message for a long time. Is this meant to be reassuring? A compliment? It feels more like an odd riddle—like Steve's trying to warn me and encourage me at the same time, without taking a side. And the ambiguity only leaves me more confused.

Later, I call him to get some clarity.

"Listen," Steve says, his voice calm and even, "I've known Timmy since we were kids. I'm not going to tell you what to do—that's your relationship—but I'll say this: he's a good guy at heart. I wouldn't have stuck around this long if he wasn't. But... he's complicated. And I think you have every reason to walk away after what happened. I wouldn't blame you if you did."

His words feel like a life raft and an anchor all at once. The idea that someone who knows Timmy so well still sees good in him—that he's capable of being a good guy—makes me want to cling to hope. But Steve's neutral stance is just as unsettling. He's not telling me to run. He's not telling me to stay, either. Just that both options are on the table.

"And what about this skanky girl that keeps messaging him? The one he slept with right before he met me? Should I be worried about her?" I ask cautiously.

Steve exhales. "I can't say for sure, but Timmy's always been loyal to me. And he's been talking about you non-stop since you two met. I think he really does care about you."

I hang up, even more conflicted than before. Steve's words echo in my mind, encouraging me to see the good in Timmy, but also quietly warning me about the risk. Maybe everyone deserves a second chance. After all, people make mistakes, right? Maybe this whole thing was just a one-time outburst, a horrible fluke.

But the pit in my stomach tells a different story. The memory of his face twisted in rage, the sound of things shattering, the way I had to run from my own apartment—it all lingers, refusing to be smoothed over by sweet words and good intentions.

I miss the way he made me laugh. I miss his affection, his warmth, the way he could light up a room. But can I really trust him again?

I try to distract myself with a TV show, something light and funny. But it's not the same without him curled up beside me, making ridiculous commentary or holding me close. I close the laptop and sit in the dark, staring at the gouges in the wall. My mind drifts back to the happy moments, to the way he'd make me feel like the center of his world. How do you let go of someone who makes you feel like that?

I miss him. God help me, I really miss him.

And yet... I can't shake the fear that, if I let him back into my life, the cycle will start all over again. And next time, I might not be so lucky.

71

CRAZY, AGGRESSIVE ASSHAT

Timmy reaches out. It's technically a little less than 72 hours after he was released, but it was hard not hearing from him. I couldn't really handle the silence. He seems calm and very apologetic, and it's a relief to know he's not mad at me. He begs for a second chance, and to talk to me in person about what transpired. He's been staying at Matty's, keeping out of trouble and not leaving the apartment.

I agree to meet him in a very public place–the bustling shopping center which is about a forty-minute walk from my apartment.

While I wait for him to arrive, my heart slams in my chest. He texts me updates as he gets closer. Every logical part of me screams that meeting him again is a bad idea, but the silence these past few days has been unbearable. A knot of anxiety tightens in my stomach as I scroll through my phone, trying to distract myself. I keep picturing him—his crooked grin, his bright blue eyes. The moments we shared that felt so genuine. The affection, the adventures, the way he made me laugh until my sides ached. *Maybe it really was just a terrible mistake*, I think, as much to comfort myself as to rationalize why I'm here.

I go into a store and in a panic, I buy a pair of shoes. Self-soothing through retail therapy, something like that. When I'm in the store, I hear a familiar accent. "Excuse me, but are you guys from New Zealand?" I ask.

"Yes!" say the two guys in unison. "We're from the South Island. I'm a chef and he's a doctor. We're here on holiday with our wives, and they're trying on clothes in the dressing room."

It's such a relief to hear this familiar accent so far from home. It helps to reduce a little bit of my anxiety, and in some ways, it feels like a sign. Or maybe I'm just looking into it too much. I pay for the shoes and walk out, ready to meet Timmy.

The moment I see him, sitting on the steps in front of the mall's stage, I freeze. My body feels like it's trying to decide between fight or flight, but instead, I just stand there, trembling. I feel my mouth twitching, the way it usually does when the rest of me decides if, in fact, I'm going to cry. He spots me and jumps up immediately, his face contorting with emotion.

"Oh my god, Margaux. Oh my god," he murmurs, as he pulls me into a tight embrace.

I feel his arms wrap around me, and suddenly the weight of the past few days crashes over me. The relief, the confusion, the fear—it all swirls together as tears stream down my face. And then Timmy starts crying too, his body shaking as he holds me closer.

"I'm so, so sorry," he whispers, tilting my chin so I meet his gaze. His eyes are a deep blue, and very bloodshot, filled with regret. I can tell this isn't the first time he's cried recently. "I would never intentionally hurt you. I swear to you."

"Then why did you?" My voice is small, fragile, as if speaking the words out loud will break me all over again.

He takes a shaky breath. "I was really angry at the neighbor girl, and I could feel myself getting more and more agitated. I was trying to calm myself down, and I basically wanted to knock myself out, so I took a handful of trazodone. But instead of knocking me out... it made me go crazy. I snapped. I was trying to do the opposite, and I had no idea it was going to have that effect. I can only imagine that in my mind I thought you were her, somehow. And so I took all the rage

I had out on her onto the woman I love more than anything. My soul-mate. My fiancé. My Margaux. And I will never forgive myself. I didn't mean for this to happen, Margaux. In my twisted mind, I must have projected all that rage onto you. The person I love the most. I'm so sorry."

I blink, trying to absorb what he's saying. "So you took a handful of sleeping pills behind my back to 'calm yourself down' but it did the opposite. You drugged yourself into a frenzy and almost killed me?"

He squeezes my hands, his expression desperate. "Margaux, I could never kill you. And if I had really wanted to hurt you, to kill you, I would have, right? We wouldn't be standing here today. But I didn't. I'd never do that. I just... lost control. And I was probably just trying to scare you, or you'd be dead."

His logic makes my skin crawl, but at the same time, part of me wants to believe him. He seems so earnest, his sorrow palpable. The man standing in front of me looks like the Timmy I fell for—the one who made me laugh, who kissed me tenderly, who talked about building a life together. No sign of the monster with the dark, reptilian eyes.

"Look, it doesn't matter, Margaux. I'm here and you're here and we love each other. And I'm going to spend every day of the rest of my life making this up to you. I'm so, so sorry."

I consider his words. He says them earnestly, but he's only a handful of sleeping pills away from trying to kill me, no matter what he says. But he looks so genuine. He's clearly very upset—that part isn't an act.

"Come with me," he says softly, threading his fingers through mine. The warmth of his hand feels familiar, comforting—that didn't change because of the horrific incident—and I find myself following him without protest. "We need to avoid the cops, though," he adds. "So if you see any, let me know."

"Avoid the cops?" I ask, but he's weaving us through a crowd of shoppers and he doesn't respond for a while.

"Yeah, so I'm not technically supposed to be around you because of what happened, until after the court case. So we're just going to need to be vigilant and make sure we're not seen together. Because I'd get locked back up straight away if they did see us."

I frown. This feels like just another thing to worry about that I didn't anticipate.

The paranoia settles in, sharp and cold. What the hell am I doing? Now, I'm sneaking around Sunset Cay with a man who nearly killed me, dodging cops like some kind of fugitive.

We weave through crowds, ducking into stores whenever we spot a police officer. I find myself scanning every street corner, every store-front, hyper-aware of anyone in a uniform. The anxiety gnaws at me, and I realize I'm trapped in this strange, surreal reality where I have to be on guard constantly.

"You mean so much to me," he says, kissing me on my forehead, still holding my hand. "I'm so lucky you're speaking to me again. I can't believe you are. I can't believe I almost lost you forever, Margaux, my love. That's my worst nightmare."

WE SIT down at an outdoor table, and he pulls his chair up next to mine so we're sitting side by side, our thighs pressed against each other.

"There are a few things I need to clear up with you," I say, nervous to approach him with things that might get his back up, make him feel defensive. Because he's shown before that he can lash out when confronted with even minor issues. And even though he's very calm right now, and seems remorseful, part of my gut doesn't quite trust it. Still, I take a deep breath and decide to plow forward. I need to hear his side of the story.

"So I met your ex," I tell him. "We talked for a long time." I feel like it's better to tell him now, to get it out of the way.

"You met... Jennifer?" he asks. I can tell he's shocked. Good. He can be on the back foot.

"Yes, we spoke for quite a while."

He exhales slowly.

"You told me you'd never been to that tropical bar before," I say carefully, watching his face for a reaction. "But your ex said you had." I don't know quite why I'm starting with this, but it feels right.

He looks at me, confused.

"The one we went to on my second or so day here. When you took me to the beach and then we stopped by for some cocktails. You said you'd never been, but you have been."

He frowns. "No way. I'd never been there until I went with you."

"Well, your ex said you did...twice."

He scoffs. "She's such a liar. I would remember having gone to a place like that."

He makes a fair point. It's not some corporate nondescript bar. It's an elaborately decorated kitschy bar that people go to for far more than their potent cocktails. But why would she lie?

"But you also texted her and told her that you miss her... 'crazy, aggressive ass', I believe was the term you used."

"No I didn't."

My stomach knots at his immediate denial. "She showed me the text, Timmy. I saw it with my own eyes."

His eyes narrow. "I don't even remember saying that. If I did, it was just me being nice, trying to keep things friendly. She's a bitch, but I don't want bad blood with anyone."

I raise an eyebrow. "Texting your ex and telling her you miss her doesn't sound like just being nice."

Frustration flickers across his face. "Well, I mean, I guess I may have texted her that. But if I did, it was because I try to keep things good with everyone I know. Like, just because she's my ex doesn't mean we can't be cordial. I'm being the bigger person, I'm being nice. So I reached out to let her know that I was thinking of her."

I quirk a brow at him, glancing at him sideways. "That's really weird, Timmy. Texting your ex and telling them that you miss them? You don't think that might give her the wrong impression?"

He smirks and shakes his head. "No, you're not getting it. I was basically just calling her an asshole, in a fun way. She is crazy and aggressive. I don't miss her ass, I meant she is a crazy aggressive ass. Like I was calling her an asshole. Get it now?"

My brain is spinning. But I guess he could have meant it that way. "I suppose? But that's not the way she took it. She literally thought you meant you missed her and your relationship, and specifically, her ass."

"No fucking way," Timmy smirks, as if amused by my confusion. "I don't miss her for one second. Anyway, I'm sick of talking about her," he says, grabbing my hand and pulling me close and kissing me on the top of my head. "I'm with *you* now, and that's all that matters."

The mental gymnastics make my head spin, but I let it drop. Arguing with Timmy feels like trying to catch smoke with my bare hands.

"I talked to Steve," I say, shifting the conversation. "He's the reason I agreed to meet with you, actually."

Timmy perks up. "Really? What'd he say?"

"Well, he was neutral. Like, he definitely didn't want to betray your trust, nor did he want to convince me to stay with you or leave you. But he talked about your friendship and how long you've known each other for. And he seems so sensible and logical, and it helped to convince me to think about giving you a second chance, even though he certainly made no attempt to push me toward that."

He smiles, his face softening with relief, and he leans forward to kiss the top of my head. "Thank you," he murmurs. "That's so nice!" His face clouds. "I spoke about you with him, too. Back after our first visit to see him. He wondered if you're the best person for me... you know, because we both like to drink and have a good time."

Suddenly, I feel on the back foot, like he's been getting evaluations of *my* suitability from his friends. I guess that's normal to a certain extent, but isn't Timmy the one way more likely to go off the rails and leave a trail of destruction in his wake?

I'm getting a little resentful of Steve, like he's playing Switzerland to me, but giving Timmy an earful on the back end, spilling the real tea. But I suppose that's what some good friends are for.

As we sit there, I feel a strange push and pull inside me—a war between logic and emotion, between fear and longing. I know that staying with Timmy could be dangerous. But the thought of losing him—losing the version of him I fell in love with—is just as terrifying.

"By the way, my evil twin came and got her suitcase finally." By now, we're wandering through stores hand in hand while he looks at surfwear, and he mentions it casually.

My stomach clenches at the mention of her.

"You hung out with her?" I'm devastated.

"No, no," he says quickly. "She randomly called me, and I asked her to please finally come and get her suitcase. I know it was upsetting you that it was there. And so when I got back to Matty's, she was there, picking it up. I told her that you mean more to me than anything, and that I couldn't talk to her anymore. That we were going to have a fresh start."

I quirk a brow. "Oh? And how did she react to that?"

"She was like 'really? We can't be friends anymore?' And I told her 'yep, exactly.' And then she left."

"And that's really all that happened?" I scrutinize his face for any signs of deception, but see none. Just honesty and transparency, his blue eyes earnest and clear.

"Yes. She left right after that. A car was there to pick her up."

I feel relieved, knowing the suitcase won't be sitting at Matty's like a constant reminder, something continuing to link them together. And relief that he's set a boundary with her, letting her know that she's no longer welcome in his life. Better late than never, I suppose.

Oblivious to my complex thoughts on this topic, and unaware that I've reviewed their correspondence on his phone, he launches into stories about his time in jail, laughing about how the cops know him by name. "They always recognize my hat," he grins. "It's like I'm a local legend."

"'O'Malley's here again,' the cops will say," Timmy says proudly.

I frown. "They shouldn't. Why would they?"

"Well they know my hat I used to wear. And then one time I set off fireworks and they were running around looking for me. And then there was the time they arrested me for saying 'I'll kill you' in a funny voice."

"That's... not something to be proud of," I say, frowning. "Timmy, you're too old for this shit. That's stuff like my dad used to do when he was around fourteen years old—the fireworks part, I mean. My dad didn't run around threatening to kill people. And you shouldn't be proud of the cops all knowing you by name. That's not a good thing, unless you like... work with them or something. Not because you're someone they're having to arrest all the time."

Timmy shrugs and laughs. "Don't be so uptight. None of it's a big deal."

And just like that, I feel the pit return to my stomach. It's like something's not connecting in his brain, for him to be proudly bragging about being well-known to the police.

The conversation quickly changes to how he entertained all his cellmates, and how he almost made them all vomit with his noxious farts.

I feel uneasy about his apparent lack of shame or remorse for any of this, but he makes his behavior seem so... normal, so justified.

So harmless. Part of everyday life growing up in Sunset Cay, and continuing into adulthood.

Maybe he's right.

Maybe I'm just way too uptight.

I love him. God help me, I do. But I also know, deep down, that loving him might be the most dangerous thing I've ever done.

EVERY TIME we notice cops driving past, of which there are many, he'll turn us in the opposite direction or pull me toward him so our faces are obscured. It takes me back to the first day he kissed me, when he said a cop was going past and pulled me to him.

What the actual fuck? I moved here for the quiet life and to enjoy the beach, and now I'm not allowed to be out and about with my fiancé on this beautiful island. It feels like we're Bonnie and Clyde, running from the cops, hiding in the shadows, and creeping around corners. But in this case, I didn't do anything wrong.

One time I'm in the grocery store alone, near Matty's house, when I notice three cops enter the store. I resist the urge to run out of there because I realize it would only serve to draw their attention. Instead, I put my head down, and go on about my shopping. As I exit, I take a deep breath and exhale slowly. Surely they don't know everyone that has a restraining order by sight. Having bright red hair doesn't help, but at least I'm wearing a cap. Note to self: maybe don't wear the leopard-print overalls and bright pink bikini top I was wearing when he was arrested. It's a cute outfit, but also like the most conspicuous one ever. I'll just tone it down a bit for now, especially when we're in this neighborhood where they know he's staying.

I hate that Timmy attacked me, of course... hate that the night ever happened. But I'm also upset that there's an after-effect of it all. That it's impacting our life going forward. And that Timmy's behavior is having consequences long beyond the event itself.

72

UGLY DUCKLING SYNDROME

I'm unofficially moved into Matty's apartment. I already had a ton of my stuff here, but we'd been spending most of our time at mine. Now that it's not an option for Timmy to be there, we're spending all our time at Matty's.

"What about Sabre, though?" I'd asked when Timmy insisted I come and stay with him.

"Bring him," he grins. "Matty will love the company. It'll be the first pussy he's had in ages."

"Okay," I'd said, unsure, but I didn't really see another option if I wanted to be with Timmy.

And, now that we're at Matty's, we're not leaving the house much. When we do, Matty seems eager to tag along.

It's food stamp day, so we go on a group trip to the grocery store, and Matty and Timmy pick out a bunch of bacon, sausages, steak, hash browns, milk and eggs. I wander over to the produce department, marveling at the prices of fresh fruit and vegetables on Sunset Cay. Picking up a tiny punnet of raspberries, I let out a low whistle and put it back down when I see the price—nearly ten dollars. I used to think San Francisco prices were high, but damn.

After, we all go and see the dolphins over at a nearby hotel, and we've arrived right at feeding time. It's cute, watching them open their mouths wide, eager, so their handlers can drop in handfuls of fish.

Timmy takes some really picturesque photos of them as they zoom underneath us as we stand on the bridge over their enclosure.

I love watching him when he's being artistic. He gets so engrossed in what he's doing, and he's so talented at picking out the right lighting and angles, adjusting the settings in his phone to make the image come out... special, somehow. I take decent photos myself, but his blow me away.

I find creativity incredibly sexy, especially when it comes to visual and graphic design. There's something about a man who can take something ordinary and turn it into something beautiful before my eyes. Maybe I have some kind of an ugly duckling complex—in fact, I'm more than sure I do—and so someone with that kind of power totally feeds into my kink.

THE NEXT DAY, I wake up with a thrill of anticipation.

Timmy has planned a hike for us to Wriggler Falls, a chance to escape the apartment and get some fresh air and sunshine, just the two of us. I've been craving something like this—physical exercise, being out in nature, away from the suffocating routine of sitting around binge-watching movies. I'm eager to feel the sun on my face, the thrill of a workout, and to visit a place I've never been. And of course, to share it with Timmy. It's going to be perfect.

Timmy takes great care to pick out snacks he knows we'll both enjoy. He fills his insulated backpack with an assortment of grapes and mandarins and sharp cheddar cheese, as well as crackers and even some dried fruit and nuts. He fills up the Hydro Flask with icy cold water.

We're getting ready to head out, and I can feel lightness in the air for the first time in a while, like we're finally doing something for just the two of us. But, as we're about to leave, Matty pops out from his room, grinning. "Where are you going?"

I freeze for a second, glancing at Timmy, hoping he might deflect the question. But, of course, Timmy's easygoing and inclusive nature kicks in.

"The waterfall," says Timmy. "Margaux hasn't been to Wriggler Falls yet."

"Oh my gosh!" Matty's face lights up. "Mind if I join you? I love waterfalls."

I blink, the excitement deflating from my chest like a sad balloon a few days after a child's birthday party. I turn to Timmy, still hoping he'll say something, but he just looks at me with that neutral expression, waiting for my response.

I give a subtle shrug, trying to mask my disappointment. "Sure, why not? Come along. The Uber will be here in a few minutes, though, so hurry."

Matty rushes off to his room to change, and I let out a quiet sigh. This was supposed to be our day, just Timmy and me. But now, well.. it's the three of us. Again.

It's not that Matty is awful, or even particularly annoying—he's actually okay to be around when he's not drunk, which is when he tends to say stupid things. But it's starting to feel like Timmy and I are not getting any time to ourselves. We don't really go anywhere, and Matty is always... there.

It's his apartment, so I'm not complaining—it's not like I could ask him to leave. But I can't help but feel trapped. I'm paying insane rent for an apartment we can't escape to for couple time, because Timmy's no longer allowed there.

I'm resenting it. Resenting Timmy for not making more of an effort to make up for the consequences of his attack on me. I'm resentful that my gorgeous life is being reduced to this.

And now, when Timmy makes an effort for us to actually leave the house so we can have some alone time doing something that makes me happy, Matty is a third wheel. It makes the whole outing feel less special, defeating the purpose of just Timmy and I spending time together alone.

I shake the thought off, feeling guilty for even thinking it. It's not *that* big of a deal, is it? I mean, it's just a hike. The more the merrier. But, deep down, I know that's not what I want. What I want is alone time with Timmy—time to connect, to talk, to just *be* together without anyone else. Our relationship needs that space, especially after everything we've been through. But instead, it feels like there's always this extra person there that prevents us from expressing our true selves the way a couple normally would.

Hell, I'm resentful that Timmy and I can no longer walk around my apartment naked, enjoying each other and having sex whenever we want without timing it around Matty's cigarette breaks. But I feel like a terrible person for resenting any of this. I've signed up for this relationship, and this is the price for now. And at least he's not dangling his dick off the balcony over here.

When we get to the trail, the hike is beautiful. A lush path, lined with gorgeous native ferns and giant trees that seem to stretch up into the heavens. Roosters walk along near the entrance, and the sounds of other birds and loud insects can be heard all the way to the water-fall. I get frustrated, because Timmy keeps running ahead, jumping up into places I don't feel comfortable going, so he can snap pictures, leaving me with Matty, who chats away. He makes jokes, and I try to smile, but each step feels heavier than it should. The whole time, there's a gnawing in the pit of my stomach.

The falls themselves are stunning, water thundering down a rugged rock face into a clear pool lined with stones and larger rocks. We all jump in, frolicking under the falls and just bathing, enjoying the time in the water beneath the golden sun.

Timmy and I contemplate having sex up a side trail, and ask Matty go on ahead, but call it off at the last minute because there's too much of a chance of someone walking past.

When we're back in the apartment, Matty starts cracking open beers like he's letting off fireworks on the Fourth of July.

"Oh, your girlfriend Lila from high school wouldn't like that," Matty says out of nowhere, smirking at Timmy.

I glance over, confused and irritated. What is he even talking about?

Timmy shrugs, not paying attention, but Matty keeps going.

"And remember when you saw that one girl and she stayed over? She was really nuts. Left several pairs of panties here. I found them in the closet."

I feel my stomach twist. Why the hell is Matty bringing this up? It's like he's trying to stir the pot, to wedge himself into our relationship and make me uncomfortable. And it works. Every time he mentions some random girl from Timmy's past, it feels like a little jab. Like he's reminding me that I'm not the only one. And firmly establishing that Matty knows lots of things I don't know about Timmy's life before I entered the picture. And Timmy just seems to let it happen, brushing it off like it doesn't matter. But it does matter to me.

This entire apartment is becoming like an eggshell for me. One wrong move, one wrong word, and everything will crack open. I'm walking on thin ice, trying to keep the peace, trying to pretend like everything's fine when it's really, really not. And I'm tired. Tired of having to constantly navigate this frustrating, awkward dynamic. Tired of never having a moment to myself, and never having a moment alone with Timmy.

I glance over at Timmy, hoping for some glimpse of understanding or reassurance, that maybe Matty's pushing things too far. But Timmy's just sitting there, smiling, totally unfazed.

And I feel trapped.

Timmy is drunk, and he's acting insane.

He stands by the doorframe, waiting for Matty to re-enter the room.

His body is rigid, and as his arm moves back, his elbow bent, I see the flash of his knife blade angled and ready to strike.

Oh my god, he's going to stab his roommate when he comes out of his bedroom.

And for what? Because he's mildly agitated over something stupid?

Jesus.

"Timmy," I hiss. "Timmy! What are you doing?"

"Shhh," he growls. His posture is off, and he doesn't turn to look at me, but I don't have to see his face to know it's changed.

He's that other person, the one who attacked me in my apartment.

I stay down low, not wanting to draw his wrath.

I can't let this happen, but at the same time, I feel relief that I'm not his target.

But I also don't want him to kill anyone. So I remain alert, watching him.

After what seems like ages, but is probably only a minute or so, he turns around, distracted, and places the knife down on the arm of the overstuffed armchair.

He goes to the kitchen to continue cooking, as if he wasn't just about to shank his roommate.

I quietly grab the knife and move it underneath the armchair so he can't see it, so he can't instantly retrieve it when he remembers what he was planning to do.

Part of me considers running away, but his behavioral shift was so sudden. I peer over at him, and his face has returned to normal. To the cute, sparkly-eyed surfer, not the reptilian demon who almost murdered someone.

I sigh with relief, exhausted, still in a fog. Trying to parse apart how someone can act so calm and loving and funny and fun could also be this completely other person. It doesn't make sense, and my brain just won't process it.

DAYS LATER, it's just me and Matty in the living room.

"I'm sorry he tried to stab you the other day. That was a bit crazy," I say. "I moved the knife when he wasn't looking, so he couldn't see where it was."

Matty shrugs. "It's fine. I'm fine." His voice is casual, as if it's the most normal thing in the world.

"He tried to shank you, though? He was waiting for you to come out of the room, with the knife in his hand. He stood there for ages, waiting, but thankfully you didn't come out."

"Eh, no worries," says Matty, as if I'm saying someone accidentally ate something of his from the fridge.

Everyone's acting like it was just normal. Everyone except me. Maybe I'm too uptight. Maybe this is normal behavior. Everyone around me seems to think it is.

I'm the only one with the problem.

73

TRAUMA BONDED TO A BOMB

Dex

She's trauma bonded to this monster.

She doesn't see it, but I sure do.

There's literally nothing he's providing to benefit her, except for dick. And even that's questionable. She could get good dick anywhere.

I see why she's in this position, though. Her last ex was fine, checked all the boxes except for the dick part. But she wasn't in love with him. She loved him. That sounds super corny and cliché, but it's true.

And then she finds this guy, and he seems exciting. And he is, to a degree.

But it's because he's steeped in instability. And he's a dangerous, unhinged manipulator who will destroy her life. That's all he knows how to do.

But I can't just walk up to her and say that, as tempting as it may be.

I'd be the villain then. They'd unite against me, the common enemy.

He's written off all of her other friends who have tried and failed to come between them.

And it just builds her image of him, that he's a protector. That he will save her.

When he's really the only person who wants to destroy her.

It's sick. He's sick. I'm sick about it.

"Is she still dating that dickhead?" Jordan asks, reading my expression and knowing I'm thinking about her.

"Yeah," I frown. "They're engaged."

"Jesus, that didn't take long."

I scoff. "He proposed within ten days. He knew she was better than him and he locked that shit down."

"Probably made her feel really special."

"That's what love bombers do." I shrug.

"So... what are you going to do about it?"

I sigh. "Nothing for now. I need the timing to be perfect. It's a fragile situation."

"Like you're detonating a love bomb." He smirks.

"Kind of. For real."

"Well, be careful. Because you know that the person sent to detonate the bomb risks being exploded along with everything else. Shooting the messenger, if you will."

"That's what I'm afraid of."

74

SOMETIMES YOUR BODY TELLS YOU THINGS YOU DON'T WANT TO HEAR

I head back to my apartment to gather some extra clothing. The moment I step inside, my body betrays me. The familiar wave of anxiety washes over me, and my bladder tightens like a clenched fist. *Not now, not again.* I squeeze my thighs together, clenching, but it's no use. The second I hear the click of the door closing behind me, my body gives in. Hot, humiliating wetness spreads, and I stand frozen in the entryway, mortified by my own body's response. What the hell is wrong with me?

I've had UTIs before, where you have to pee suddenly and furiously, even if barely anything comes out, but this is not that. It only happens when I get to this apartment, the place where Timmy tried to kill me.

This is my space, my home. But now, every time I walk through the door, my body reacts like I've just stepped into a war zone. I wipe my hands across my damp shorts in frustration. I've fought through tough situations before, lived through trauma—but never has my body betrayed me like this.

Once I'm in the bathroom, I sit on the cold toilet seat and search for answers. *Trauma-related incontinence*, the screen reads. The words sting, but at least I'm not imagining it. It's real. My body is screaming at me, telling me something isn't right.

I glance at the broken toilet lid—Timmy's handiwork. I sigh and carefully reach for the shattered ceramic piece. The jagged edge catches my finger and rips through the skin before I even register what's happened. Blood spills out fast, hot, and red.

"Fuck!" I scream, clutching my hand as the pain blooms. I press a paper towel to the wound, but the sight of the blood makes me dizzy. It's like this apartment won't let me forget. I slam the broken lid back down on the floor, the sound loud and jarring in the quiet apartment. I hold the towel against my hand and storm into the kitchen, my pulse roaring in my ears.

As I grab another paper towel, one of my precious cat carvings— the ones that mean so much to me—tumbles off the counter with a dull thud. The sound of wood splintering hits my ears, and when I look down, a jagged piece of its little paw lies on the floor.

"You've got to be fucking kidding me!" I cry, my voice breaking. I crouch down, cradling the broken carving in my hands. The tears hit me all at once, hard and hot, and they don't stop.

It's not just the carving. It's not just the lid. It's everything—the piss, the blood, the shattered remnants of what this place used to be. It's the ghost of Timmy's rage that still lingers in every corner, as if his energy never really left. It's like the evil that possessed Timmy the night he attacked me still lurks here. It's hiding in the corners, mocking me as I try to make sense of everything. And I don't know how to make it stop.

I yank off my shorts and underwear, throw them in the washing machine and turn it on.

I collapse onto my bed and bury my face in the pillow, inhaling deeply, trying to calm the shaking sobs that rack my body. For a moment, I let myself surrender to the exhaustion, closing my eyes. I don't fall asleep, but the simple act of lying still—of retreating into myself—offers a small, fleeting comfort.

Then my phone buzzes in my hand, pulling me back into the harsh reality. I swipe the screen and see a message from Timmy.

TIMMY:

> Everything okay? You've been gone a while,
> and I haven't heard from you.

I hesitate, my thumb hovering over the screen. I don't want to tell him I just pissed my pants. But what's the point in pretending? He's the reason it's happening. So I tell him the truth.

ME:

> Cut myself on the toilet piece when I lifted
> it up.

> Peed myself, because that's what I do when I
> get to the apartment now.

> And one of my carvings flew off the counter
> and broke.

His response comes quickly, almost as if he'd been waiting for the chance to say something right.

TIMMY:

> Oh my god, I'm so sorry, Margaux.

> I wish I could be there to help you with
> everything.

> I hate that I created this situation for you.

> I love you so much, and I'm going to give you
> the longest, best back rub when you get
> back.

I stare at the message, feeling the familiar, toxic mix of emotions welling up. His words are like a balm—temporary, fleeting relief. He sounds like he means it, and part of me wants to believe him. But how can I reconcile the person who smashed my toilet, broke my things, and tried to hurt me, with the one who promises back rubs and love? The one who says all the right things when he knows I'm at my most vulnerable?

TIMMY:

Remember to send me a picture of the toilet lid I broke so I can get a new one.

It's refreshing and a relief to see Timmy holding himself accountable. I still don't know how he expects to pay for the replacement items, but he seems to think he'll be able to. And so he should. If someone comes to your home and breaks things, they need to pay for the repairs. It's simple.

He can't come and do the repairs himself, of course, seeing he's banned from the property.

"I'll send Matty or someone else to come and fix it. There's a guy I used to work with who I'd trust to do a good job, and he won't charge much."

It feels like he's taking responsibility and ownership for what he did, and trying to make it right. Of course, I'd love it if he could just come here and get all the information and fix it himself, but obviously that's not an option in this situation.

I push off the bed slowly, my limbs heavy with fatigue. As I move toward the door, I pause, spotting my deck of oracle cards on the counter. It's a strange ritual, but one that's been grounding me lately. I shuffle the deck, and as if guided by something beyond me, I pull a card. CRY.

The simplicity of the word hits me hard. *I already am*, I think bitterly. But the card isn't just about tears. It's telling me to let go—to release, to grieve, to feel every emotion I've been bottling up.

I place the card back in the deck and stuff it in my bag, grab the rest of my things, and head toward the door, for now leaving the shattered ceramic, the broken carving, and the haunted memories behind me.

75

UNNECESSARY GUILT

The fireworks crackle overhead, painting the sky with brilliant streaks of gold, red and violet. After the display is finished, Timmy takes my hand, squeezing it gently as we stroll through the fragrant gardens of the resort. The air smells of jasmine and saltwater, and the sound of waves crashing in the distance adds to the magic of the night. It feels peaceful, like we belong here, walking side by side.

As we wander along the pathways, he points out native flowers and plants, describing each one with admiration. "These plumeria only bloom here," he says, brushing his fingers lightly against a blossom. His attention to detail is mesmerizing. I've never met someone who notices the little things like he does, who makes the world feel vibrant and alive by simply observing it.

I glance at him, feeling both grateful and guilty. His expression is peaceful, but the weight of what I need to tell him sits heavy on my chest. "I have to admit something," I say quietly, my voice barely audible over the night breeze. "While you were in jail, I met up with someone—here, at the fireworks."

He doesn't react immediately, just nods slowly, as if giving me space to speak without judgment. I tell him about the kiss—how it happened suddenly, how I panicked and ran away. My heart thuds in my chest, expecting anger or hurt, but Timmy remains calm. He rubs the back of my hand with his thumb and says, "Thank you for telling me." That simple sentence feels like an olive branch, and I can breathe again.

THE NEXT MORNING, Timmy and I take a drive to a trendy part of town. The streets are filled with vibrant murals splashed across brick walls—sunsets, oceans, mythical creatures—the energy of the neighborhood is contagious. The sun warms my skin as we sip iced coffees under a bright blue sky, the buzz of people chatting and laughing around us.

We explore the shops together, and Timmy picks out bikinis for me to try on. I'm skeptical at first, but he seems to know what will flatter me better than I know myself. He selects colors I would have never considered—pale yellow, coral, deep purple. I slip one on in the dressing room, and when I see my reflection, I barely recognize myself. I feel radiant. He's right. How does he see me in a way I can't?

At an indoor arcade, we find a 3D wall made entirely of paperback books, their pages springing out like wild paper sculptures. Timmy pulls me close, posing me for pictures. "Your readers are going to love this," he says with a grin, snapping shots of me against the whimsical backdrop. It's the kind of thoughtful gesture I've always longed for—someone who not only shares my joy but enriches it.

In these moments, it feels like I've found something rare. This kind of partnership, where creativity and love intertwine effortlessly, seemed out of reach for so long. But here it is, unexpected and beautiful, unfolding before me with each passing day.

Later, we gather groceries, and Timmy meticulously selects the freshest produce. I've never seen someone so painstakingly make sure they're getting the most perfect tomato, the firmest onion, the way he does. He sees objects differently from me, noticing the beauty and imperfections in each. I'm more of a 'turn it over and if it clearly has a bruise pick another one' kind of girl. He's the 'go through every single one in the store and I'll have only the best' kind of guy. I'm learning from him, to not just accept what's given on the surface. To dig deeper, to look deeper.

He picks ti leaves and makes me a magnificent headpiece, with flowers picked out to complement my hair. He takes pictures and smiles at me with kindness in his eyes. "You're so beautiful," he says, with warmth in his voice. "I'm so glad we found each other. You really are my soulmate."

And I feel it too. I've never been with someone so kind, so considerate. Someone so fixated on the little details about me. Who listens carefully to nearly every word I say. Who squirrels the little details away, and then surprises me later when I least expect it, remembering even things said briefly in passing. This is the love I always dreamed of but hadn't experienced until I met Timmy.

He strings together a delicate lei of plumeria flowers and places it over Sabre's tiny head and drapes it around his neck, snapping a photo of my cat adorned like a king. "Look at him!" Timmy laughs, his eyes sparkling with pride. "He's a natural."

I laugh with him. Timmy is once again making life feel vibrant, full of art and whimsy.

He lets me braid his hair into little Princess Leia buns, running around like a kid while I double over with laughter, tears streaming down my cheeks. How could someone like this ever be dangerous?

And yet, the gnawing doubt creeps in, curling at the edges of my joy. His rage still lingers in my memory, a shadow that refuses to leave. I want to stay in this love bubble forever, but I know deep down that love isn't supposed to feel like a rollercoaster of exhilaration and fear.

I clutch onto the good moments, hoping they'll be enough to drown out the bad. But in the quiet spaces between, the anxiety claws at me. And I wonder how long I can live like this—teetering on the edge between euphoria and disaster, praying the bubble doesn't burst.

The next day, I see something as I'm scrolling through my phone that stops me in my tracks—a meme that reads:

'Your nervous system will naturally feel calm around people with pure intentions and authentic energy - trust it.'

I don't feel calm around Timmy. I feel constantly exhilarated and on edge.

I used to think of it as a giddy kind of excitement, but now I'm beginning to wonder if the constant butterflies mean something else, that my body is trying to tell me something.

My anxiety is peaking, but he makes us breakfast, distracting me, and I push the thoughts down.

There's an ANZAC ceremony at the military cemetery, and I really want to go. Timmy agrees to go with me, and we take an Uber up the winding mountain road. The military ceremony to commemorate the New Zealand and Australian soldiers killed in Gallipoli is somber and reflective, and Timmy stands calmly, holding my hand and taking it all in.

It's a rare moment to see Timmy this serene and grounded, behaving appropriately in a formal situation. For once, I have no concerns about how he's going to act or what he's going to say. I can tell he gets the memo that this isn't a place to joke around, to stand out, to draw attention, to make a spectacle. We're here to honor the dead, the fallen, and he's taking it seriously.

"That was so moving," he says after the ceremony, wiping a tear from his face. "I used to really want to be in the military, but I wasn't allowed in because of my back injury. I felt like I was letting my dad down. So I'm so glad my nieces and nephews are following in his footsteps."

I'd never really thought about it, how it must be to be the child of a respected veteran, and not choose the same career, especially as a male. I get the sense he feels deficient in some way, that he felt the weight of others' aspirations for him to do it, too. That's a lot of pressure, I imagine.

In the afternoon, we visit a bar where one of my friends from back on the East Coast is visiting to deliver a presentation on agave-based spirits. Timmy doesn't drink the entire time, and gives me his tasting samples. He's social, but appropriately so, and just relaxes and enjoys learning about the different forms of spirits. He asks questions and chats with the people around us.

In the bathroom, the walls are lined with blackboard paint and chalk is provided. He gets me to go into a stall after he vacates it. He's written 'Timmy <3 Margaux. She said yes!'

My heart flutters when I read it. This man is helping me to experience pure joy, pure love for the first time. I grab my own piece of chalk and add 'I did <3 :)'. He smiles when I show him, and pulls me to him for a passionate kiss.

I am *living* with this man. Truly living. The way I've always read about, but never thought would be possible for me.

What a talented, creative individual. And he loves my cat, too. There's literally nothing more I could ask from this man. I never want this love bubble to burst.

76

THE MASK BEGINS TO FALL (AGAIN)

After a couple of weeks, something changes.

At first, I try to ignore the shift. I tell myself that everyone has off days, moments where they just need to recharge. But this feels different. Something in Timmy has switched off, and I can't pinpoint exactly when it happened. One moment, we're making plans for hikes, art exhibits, and lazy afternoons at the beach, and the next, it's as if a curtain has fallen between us and the outside world.

"I don't feel like doing that today," he mutters when I suggest going out for coffee, his voice flat, eyes glazed as he flips through movie options on the TV.

"Maybe next week," he mumbles when I bring up a trail we'd been excited about for weeks.

It's not just that he doesn't want to go—it's the sudden apathy, the way every idea seems like too much effort now. Every plan I float fizzles out before it even has a chance to form. There's always a reason, a vague excuse:

"I didn't sleep well."

"I think I might be coming down with something."

"Matty's expecting us to hang out later."

"I have a sore tummy."

"I had a nightmare."

And so we stay, trapped inside Matty's apartment like caged animals.

I start to feel the walls closing in. "I feel trapped in here," I blurt out one day. I try to keep my voice steady, but the words wobble on the edge of frustration. I don't mean for them to sound accusatory, but I can't hold it back anymore.

Timmy sighs, rubbing his temples. "It's not like I *want* to feel like this," he says, his voice defensive. "I just... I don't know. I'm not up for it right now, okay?"

It feels like I'm talking to a stranger. Where's the guy who bounced with excitement at the idea of exploring every corner of Sunset Cay? The guy who dragged me out of bed to whisk me off to show me around? He's here physically, but emotionally, it feels like he's slipped through my fingers.

In some ways, I tell myself, maybe this change isn't such a bad thing. I can't keep funding our outings—my savings are dwindling, and the constant shopping and dining out were never sustainable. But the silence is oppressive. There's only so much greasy food cooking and movie-watching I can take before I start to feel like I'm losing my mind. Every suggestion I make to leave the apartment is met with resistance, and I can't write in this cramped environment.

Timmy's mattress is shoved in a corner in a room with no natural light, and when I try to work in the living room, Matty blasts YouTube videos about home-built machinery or bizarre DIY projects at max volume. It's unbearable. The low drone of people explaining driveway leveling techniques grates on my nerves, and I find myself grinding my teeth as I try to concentrate on anything other than how much I want to scream.

Meanwhile, Timmy sinks further into lethargy. He sleeps in late, cocooned in blankets, only waking up when he feels like it—usually well past noon. When he does stir, it's only to suggest we watch yet another movie, eat, or occasionally, have sex. He's exhausted the catalog of streaming services, and the few new films he does find are interspersed with rewatching ones we've already seen. It drives me crazy. I've never understood the appeal of rewatching things, and now it's become a point of tension.

"We literally just watched this a couple of weeks ago," I say, exasperated, as he queues up a movie we'd already seen.

"Yeah, but it's good," he says, walking out to the balcony to light a cigarette. "You'll like it more the second time."

I groan quietly, but don't fight him on it. Fighting takes energy I no longer have.

The hours blur together in an endless loop: wake up late, watch movies, cook, sometimes have sex, eat ice cream, he'll smoke cigarettes, and then we'll fall back asleep.

If I suggest going outside—taking a walk, getting some air—he continues to wave me off with excuses. But if I mention picking up alcohol, he perks up, suddenly willing to leave the apartment. I feel a flicker of bitterness at how easily the promise of booze shifts his mood.

The worst part is the resentment simmering just beneath the surface. I can feel it radiating off him, especially when I bring up doing something, anything, outside the apartment. His responses carry the weight of irritation, as if I'm nagging him simply by existing, by wanting more from this experience than just sitting around.

And so, the dynamic changes—slowly at first, but unmistakably. The man who used to be a whirlwind of energy, dragging me from one adventure to the next, now feels like a dead weight. It's like he's resigned himself to this dull existence, and I'm being dragged down with him.

I find myself walking on eggshells, carefully choosing my words so as not to trigger his frustration. But the frustration builds inside me instead, bubbling up like a slow-boiling pot. How did we end up here? How did I go from being head over heels for someone who felt like the love of my life, to feeling suffocated in a dimly lit apartment where the air is thick with cigarette smoke and disappointment?

I try to convince myself that it's just a phase, that Timmy will snap out of it. But deep down, a voice whispers that maybe this is who he really is—a man who only thrives in the highs, but can't sustain the everyday. And now that the initial rush has faded, we're left with the truth.

77

IMPROVISED PRISON CELL

There's something both ironic and soul-crushing about living in a tropical paradise surrounded by sunshine, beaches, and swaying palm trees—yet feeling like you're stuck in a slightly larger prison cell.

That's how it feels at Matty's.

Yes, the air conditioning is nice, a relief from the relentless heat, but it's the only luxury. The windows stay permanently closed, shutting out any hint of natural light or fresh air. The tiny, fenced-in patio smells like stale cigarette smoke, the scent so thick it seems to cling to my skin even after I shower. It's a grim little space, like an open-air ashtray.

At first, I half-joked to myself that this place reminds me of Charlie and the Chocolate Factory—a quirky, chaotic place, Timmy and Matty playing the oddball grandparent characters. But as the days drag on, I can't shake the unsettling realization—Timmy is unconsciously recreating prison for himself.

The parallels are striking.

He and Matty sleep in beds lined up side by side like cellmates. They rarely go outside except to smoke. The concrete walls, devoid of art or color, seem to absorb any joy I bring in with me. Timmy barely exercises or leaves the apartment unless I coax him out, and even then, it's a struggle. Their biggest indulgences are movies on repeat, streaming endlessly, and the occasional fried meal cooked in so much oil it sets off the smoke detector.

It's a bizarre halfway existence—not quite free, not quite imprisoned. The only real difference from an actual jail cell is the ability to cook and surf channels on TV. But somehow, this feels even sadder. There's freedom all around us—on the beaches, in the mountains, under the clear blue skies—and yet here we are, holed up in a dark, musty apartment, like the outside world is too much to bear.

I understand that for many people, even this modest apartment would be considered a luxury. Sunset Cay isn't exactly affordable. Foreign investors have transformed it into a playground for the wealthy, with overpriced Airbnbs and luxury villas that sit empty most of the year. Locals can barely afford to live here anymore. I get that. And I know it's not entirely Timmy's fault that this is where we ended up—even if he hadn't attacked me or swung his penis around the balcony, vexatious noise complaints were flowing thick and fast, and that building was never going to be a long-term solution.

But I still can't ignore the gnawing resentment that rises inside me. I left behind a beautiful, bright apartment with a view of the ocean, easy access to the beach, and a pool. I had natural sunlight pouring in every morning, a place where I could sit and write with peace of mind. And now, because of Timmy—because of his impulsiveness, his inability to control his rage—I lost it all. He took it away from me with no real understanding of what he was taking.

He says he's sorry, and maybe he is. But words are easy, and I've learned they don't mean much unless they're backed by action. And he's not exactly making an effort to fix what's broken—not with the apartment, not with me. He apologizes, but the weight of everything still rests on my shoulders.

I'm the one who gets up early every day, puts on my shoes, and walks to the beach for the sunrise. I'm the one finding ways to escape Matty's suffocating apartment, taking long walks in the sunshine, getting my heart rate up, and breathing in the fresh, salty air.

I'm the one buying healthy groceries and preparing meals with fresh ingredients, trying to nourish both of us. Meanwhile, Timmy spends his food stamps on processed, greasy junk food, which he and Matty devour without a second thought. They bond over bacon and fried hash browns while I try to remind myself that love is supposed to be about compromise.

I try to reframe things, to keep the resentment at bay. I tell myself that Timmy has his good moments, too. He shows glimmers of understanding that make me believe, just for a moment, that he gets it. Like when he takes me out occasionally to work away from Matty's, finding coffee shops where we can sit side by side and dream about the future. Or when he encourages me to watch my own shows now and then without complaining. Those small acts of kindness remind me that he does care, that he's trying in his own way.

He praises my food, saying, "I actually like salads now. You've changed me." He brings me ice cream, cuddles with me, and tells jokes that make me laugh so hard I forget the frustration for a little while. Those moments feel like gold, fleeting but precious, and they keep me tethered to him.

So I try. I try to convince myself that this is exactly what I need—a slower pace, fewer expectations, less perfection. Maybe it's good for me to learn how to live without all the things I thought I needed. Maybe this stripped-down version of life is what I was meant to experience all along.

But the resentment lingers, simmering beneath the surface. And I know it's only a matter of time before it bubbles over.

And the truth is, I love him. I could live in a cardboard box with Timmy and still feel happy, as long as we're together. When he's good to me, when he holds me close and tells me he loves me, there's no question in my mind. I'd choose him over material things every time. Because that's what you do when you love someone. Right?

But deep down, I know it's not that simple. He took something important from me, and I'm not sure he even realizes how deeply it hurt. The sunlight, the view, the freedom—I'm mourning those things in ways I never expected. And what hurts most is knowing that

I'm the one making the effort to adjust, to make things work, to keep moving forward. He's content to stay where he is, trapped in his own little world of movies and cigarettes.

At the same time, whenever I think about this, a little voice says to me, *If you stick with Timmy, living in a cardboard box might not be so far-fetched*, a thought that makes my stomach churn.

78

—————

TRAPPED IN PARADISE

Over the next month or so, the pattern with Timmy becomes clearer each day, though it's not one I like admitting to myself. But it's becoming harder and harder to deny.

He's definitely not a morning person—fine, not everyone is. But it's more than that. It's like the motivation that once seemed to drive him evaporated overnight and somehow continues to drain further with each passing moment.

I tell myself it's okay. Maybe he just needs to adjust to our new environment. But there's a gnawing discomfort that settles deeper.

I decide not to let his moods and his lethargy dictate my life.

Nearly every morning, I continue to slip out of bed and make my way to the beach to catch sunrise and write. It's become my sanctuary —my escape. The sky shifts from indigo to a swirl of pinks and purples, the sunrise painting the horizon in gentle strokes. The air is crisp, quieter than the bustling daytime. I savor the peaceful lull before Sunset Cay wakes up—the soft clink of cutlery from hotel guests enjoying an early breakfast at the hotel restaurant behind me, the rhythmic rustle of the surf as it kisses the shore, and the beach boys setting up their cabanas and surfboards all around.

This is the part of my day I cherish most. I've developed my own routine—I stop by the hotel coffee shop, order a strong iced coffee, and then find a spot near the water to settle in. My backpack becomes my makeshift desk, and between bursts of writing, I let my gaze wander to the horizon. This is what I came here for—time to reflect, to create, to feel inspired by the simple beauty of the ocean.

But each time I return to the apartment, it's like I've stepped into a different world. Timmy is almost always still in bed, cocooned in the blankets, oblivious to the sunlight pouring through the curtains. On the rare occasion he's awake, the smell of frying bacon or steak fills the air. His routine remains the same. Matty's already camped out in the living room, usually having slept on the couch the night before, glued to YouTube videos about obscure machinery or DIY projects. The noise of his tedious videos fills the apartment, chaotic and relentless. It's still impossible to write here, impossible to think or be remotely creative or inspired.

The apartment feels more and more like a cave, dark and stifling. The air conditioning blasts continuously, the curtains drawn to block out any sign of the vibrant tropical world outside. I keep trying to nudge Timmy into action, despite his resistance.

"Can we do something today? Take a walk, grab a coffee?" I ask, trying to keep my tone light, coming up with more and more plans in the hope that one of them will pique his interest.

"I don't feel like it," he mumbles, still buried in the blankets.

The same apathy, the same excuses. It's as though the man who once brimmed with excitement for every little thing has checked out completely.

Frustration bubbles to the surface, me now the one full of resentment.""I didn't move all the way to Sunset Cay just to sit in a room with the curtains closed, watching movies," I snap one day, the words spilling out before I can stop them.

His expression shifts instantly, a flicker of annoyance flashing across his face. "I'm sorry this isn't good enough for you," he says coldly. "You could just go back to your apartment if you wanted. You don't have to be here. I'm not the only reason we got kicked out."

The audacity of it takes my breath away. I know the real reason, and so does he. But in Timmy's world, truth is a slippery concept. It morphs and bends to fit whatever narrative suits him. And somehow, he's found a way to share the blame with me. I can feel the shame creeping in, even though I know better.

"Would you at least come with me to see the sunrise?" I ask him. "It would be nice if we could go together."

He groans. "And do what? Watch you type? What am I supposed to do, just sit there?"

"Swim? Collect shells? The same things you love doing at the beach?" I say, exasperated.

"Yeah, I guess," he mutters. But his tone tells me everything—I shouldn't hold my breath.

Then, one morning, he surprises me. "Let's go to the beach," he announces. I'm caught off-guard but excited. Maybe this is the turning point.

He drives Matty and me down to the water, but when we arrive, it's not the beach I love—the one where I write, where I feel at peace. It's a different spot altogether. I sit in the passenger seat, confused and a little hurt.

Without a word, Timmy jumps out of the car and heads straight for the ocean, Matty in tow. He dives in, swimming effortlessly, completely ignoring me. No invitation, no acknowledgment. I remain sitting in the truck, feeling foolish and abandoned, watching him enjoy the water on his own while Matty wanders off to the other side of the parking lot.

I want to follow Timmy in, but something stops me. The hurt festers, turning into bitterness. This wasn't what I imagined—this wasn't the romantic sunrise swim I had hoped for. I stay in the car, arms crossed, feeling angry and sulky and alone.

When he finally returns, droplets of seawater clinging to his skin, he looks at me with a mixture of confusion and frustration. I'm clearly agitated. "What's the problem with you?" he asks, brushing water from his hair.

"This isn't where I wanted to go," I admit, trying to keep my voice steady. "I like going down to the hotel beach. That's where I write. You know that."

He frowns. "I thought you'd like to try something different. I didn't think it would be such a big deal."

"But we didn't talk about it at all," I complain, on the verge of tears. "You just made the decision without me," I say, my words heavy with disappointment. We so rarely go anywhere anymore that this choice of beach is a big deal for me.

He sighs, exasperated. "So I made a call. Big deal. You're really going to ruin the day because we went to a different beach?"

"You ran off without me," I add quietly. "I felt... left out."

He softens slightly. "I'm sorry, you're right. I should've waited for you. I just wanted to get in the water."

His half-apology hangs in the air, and I realize how ridiculous I must sound. I wanted him to hold my hand, lead me into the water like a child. It's embarrassing, and I hate myself for being upset over something so small.

"It's okay," I mumble, brushing it off, though the sting still lingers.

We return to the car, but the weight of unspoken tension follows us. This little moment—the unmet expectations, the miscommunication—feels like a microcosm of something bigger. Something is unraveling between us, and I can't quite put my finger on it, but I feel like I'm losing every aspect of us that I used to love. As well as everything I loved about Sunset Cay.

I try to tell myself it's just one of my moods, that I'm overreacting. But deep down, I know it's more than that. I'm clinging to the hope that things will go back to how they were at the very beginning, that this slump is temporary. But hope is a fragile thing, and with every small disappointment, it feels like it's slipping further out of reach.

79

CIGARETTE SMOKE & SCREAMS

Dex

Growing up with parents suffering from addiction is hard. And my mom's issues were no fucking joke.

She overdosed when I was young, leaving me in a car filled with cigarette smoke and most of our worldly belongings. A good samaritan happened to be walking past and heard my screams and rescued me. We'd been evicted the week before.

I guess it was only a matter of time before it happened, based on what I've been able to piece together over the years.

And honestly, maybe that saved my life. Having her go when she did.

A revolving door of stepfather types... that's what she'd call them all, even if they'd only been dating for a few weeks. I was starting to get to the age where the way they treated her was kicking in some kind of protective instinct. I was always a tall kid for my age, but I would have been no match for some of these guys she'd have around. They were tall, too, and had filled out and easily had a solid hundred pounds on me.

But I have, let's say, an intense problem with men who hurt women, and that's never really gone away.

In fact, if anything, it's intensified.

And everything is magnified when it comes to Margaux.

80

___

NOT WHAT I'M HERE FOR

few days later

A The greasy smell of bacon hits me before my eyes are even open, thick and cloying. At first, it's not entirely unpleasant—I love bacon as much as the next person. But there's something about the way it's being cooked now that twists my stomach, making it hard to breathe through the heaviness in the air. I pull the blanket over my face, trying to escape it, but it's already in my nose, clinging to the walls and fabric of the apartment.

The distinct scent of hash browns joins the mix, and for a brief moment, my heart lifts. I adore hash browns. But then I remember where I am. The hope dissipates. I already know what I'm going to find when I walk into the kitchen. It's not crispy, golden nuggets of potato cooked to perfection. It's going to be something drowned—no, suffocated—in unnecessary oil.

I rub my eyes, stretching as I rise reluctantly from the mattress. The air conditioning hums softly in the background, the room dim because the curtains stay perpetually drawn. My feet shuffle across the cool floor as I make my way to the kitchen.

And there it is—exactly what I expected. Matty is swaying next to the stove, humming to himself as if he's headlining some concert only he's attending. The pan in front of him looks like a death trap—half full of shimmering grease. Flaccid bacon curls at the edges and sputters along the sides, swimming lazily in oil. Hash browns sit in the center, bloated and lifeless, like tiny fried corpses.

Not to be dramatic, but it's one of the most disgusting things I've seen cooked in my life. The oil reaches halfway up the pan, the entire setup one wrong move away from an apartment fire. It's not even deep frying—it's some bastardization between shallow frying and pure chaos. I shudder, imagining flames licking the cabinets while Matty, oblivious, sings along to his own drunken soundtrack, even though it's only morning.

He catches me standing there and offers a lopsided grin, bobbing to a rhythm only he can hear. His cheeks are flushed, his eyes glassy —definitely still drunk from last night. I lean against the doorway, trying to mask my disgust, but the greasy air presses against my skin like a sticky film.

"Morning," he says cheerily, flipping the bacon with a spatula that sends tiny drops of scalding oil flying across the stove.

"Morning," I mumble back, trying to ignore the wave of nausea building in my stomach.

I want to be grateful. I *am* grateful—Matty didn't have to let us crash here. But God, it's getting harder every day.

The toilet seat always has a puddle of urine on it, the seat often left up, and I've fallen partially into the bowl more than once in the middle of the night.

The incidents where Matty shits his pants in the middle of the night are becoming more frequent than anyone should be comfortable with.

And the mean-spirited jabs—half jokes, half serious—are starting to wear me down. It's the way Matty snickers while making cutting remarks about everything from the skanky girl Timmy used to sleep with, to his first girlfriend from high school, as if it's all one big joke. Over and over again. A joke I'm supposed to laugh at, even though I hate every second of it.

And then there's this—his greasy, heart-clogging monstrosities that turn my stomach. I stare at the mess on the stove and feel my resentment bubble up, just like the oil in the pan.

I think about my apartment—the nice one I was so excited to move into. The one Timmy got us kicked out of. I gave that up. For him. For this. For greasy bacon mornings and shart jokes, comments about other girls Timmy's been involved with, a shared room, and a mattress on Matty's floor.

And it's not just the apartment—it's everything. I gave up the peace I thought I'd find on this island, the dream of mornings spent writing by the ocean and evenings sipping cocktails at sunset. Instead, I'm here, marinating in frustration, inhaling secondhand grease and regret.

And the worst part? I let it happen.

I get so wrapped up in this need to prove to myself and others that I'm not materialistic. That I can live simply, without the trappings of comfort or luxury. That *things* don't matter to me, and money doesn't matter. But maybe they do. Maybe it's okay to want nice things, to live somewhere peaceful, to feel like I deserve more than this chaotic mess.

Timmy sees this conflict in me—I'm sure of it. And I think he plays on it. He knows exactly how to push the right buttons, to make me feel guilty for wanting more, for craving something better.

"Food's almost ready if you want some," Matty says proudly, oblivious to the war waging in my mind. He plops another soggy hash brown into the pan with a splash, and oil splatters across the stove and the countertop. It's everywhere—like my feelings, leaking out in ways I can't control.

I swallow the lump rising in my throat. I hate that I'm so affected by something as simple as breakfast. But it's not just breakfast—it's the whole picture. It's the weight of everything I've sacrificed, everything I've settled for, and the creeping realization that I don't even recognize myself in this life I've chosen.

The oil pops again, and Matty laughs as though nothing in the world is wrong. As if this is just another day, another breakfast, another joke. But to me, it feels like the culmination of every bad decision I've made since meeting Timmy. And it's becoming harder to convince myself that this is the life I want—or that I can keep pretending it's enough.

81

YOU CAN'T JUST RELY ON THE ROSE, BRUH

Timmy's obsession with sex when we first met was new territory for me. And I can't say I disliked it—far from it, actually. But something in that aspect of our relationship has shifted now, too.

It doesn't help that we have to share a room with Matty, which limits when we can engage in intimacy. But it's about more than that.

From the time we first met, it's obvious Timmy has consumed a lot of porn. I can tell from the way he talks about certain websites, dropping names casually into conversation like they're common knowledge. His references to specific videos and genres are so offhand, it's as though everyone has a mental catalog of scenes, plots, and performers. And there's the way he interacts with me in bed—like someone who's absorbed years of adult content and brought it all into our bedroom, turning fantasy into something tangible.

Some of it used to be hot, but now I sense that he's recreating his favorite scenes more than trying to bring me real pleasure.

There's the way he smacks my pussy—not hard enough to hurt, but hard enough to surprise me. At first, I flinched, but then I found myself laughing, almost amused by his audacity. He's unapologetically bold, and that turns me on in a way I didn't expect. But I have told him before that I don't find that particularly enjoyable, yet he keeps doing it.

Then there's how he insists I stick my tongue out when he's about to come so he can spray his jizz all over my face. I'm not judging that part, but I know where it comes from.

I've noticed that he's obsessed with the idea of covering me—my chest, my face—marking me in a way that feels primal. He mentions it frequently, like it's not just a desire but a deep-seated need, and the sheer enthusiasm he brings to the idea makes it difficult not to get swept up in it.

There's no hesitation in him, no shame. If this is his kink, then so be it—I'm more than happy to oblige. There's a certain freedom in surrendering to his desires, knowing he's completely consumed by me in these moments.

Because sex with Timmy? It can be really fun.

It's not just a physical thing—it's a game, an adventure. With him, sex isn't something that fades into the background or becomes an afterthought. It's electric, a core part of our relationship. And compared to past relationships where sex felt like a non-thing— sporadic, awkward, or something we barely discussed—being with Timmy is a revelation.

But slowly, something has shifted. A while ago, I started to notice that what used to feel like a two-way connection—this sensual dance of both of us getting lost in the moment—has become more one-sided. Timmy's attention, once firmly locked on my body and my pleasure, has started to dwindle.

What was once a shared experience, with whispered praise and guiding hands, has turned into something more routine, something mechanical. It's been months since he last went down on me, or brought me to orgasm with his fingers.

At first, I brushed it off, thinking it's maybe just a phase. Relationships evolve, after all. People get comfortable. But now that the pattern has continued—now that he's begun to skip the foreplay entirely, rushing through the motions—I've found myself feeling hollow and disconnected.

He used to care so much about whether I came, and seemed almost obsessed with making sure I got there. Now? His focus is entirely on finishing himself off.

It's fine, I tell myself. He still loves me. *Sex isn't everything, and when we have it, it's still fun.* But I can't deny the frustration simmering beneath the surface, the subtle disappointment that grows every time he rolls off me, satisfied, without so much as a second thought for whether I was satisfied, too.

Also, he's kind of stopped getting on top of me, preferring me to be on top or do what he calls a 'side bang', bragging that it's all 'less work' for him. I enjoy all the ways, but the fact he wants to get off for the least effort feels a bit unfortunate.

I decide to take matters into my own hands—literally. I order a rose vibrator, determined to reignite my own pleasure without needing to rely on him. When it arrives, I pull it from its sleek packaging, feeling the cool silicone between my fingers. It's a small, flower-shaped thing—innocent-looking but powerful. In soft lilac, his favorite color, of course, because I figure that way he might be more inclined to use it, and because it's now become habitual for me to purchase everything in that color.

I show it to Timmy, bracing myself for how he might react. I half-expect him to be defensive, maybe a little offended, like I'm pointing out some deficiency in him. Instead, his face lights up with curiosity. He takes the toy from me and turns it over in his hands as if it's some kind of ancient artifact, his expression full of childlike fascination.

"Whoa," he says, grinning. "This is cool."

Relief washes over me. He's not offended—if anything, he's intrigued. And when we're in bed later in the evening, he eagerly grabs the rose and sets to work, holding it against me with almost scientific precision.

His eyes are glued to my face as if waiting for some grand reveal— like he's discovered a cheat code to pleasure that requires minimal effort on his part. He watches me intently, his expression a mix of satisfaction and amusement.

And to be fair, it does work. The rose is incredible, a small miracle of technology that brings me to climax faster than I expected. But something about the way he wields it makes me feel... off. It's as though my orgasm is no longer something he wants to help me achieve—it's something to tick off a checklist.

"That was good, wasn't it?" he says with a smug grin, walking off to the bathroom to shower as soon as I'm done. No more lying tangled in each other's limbs, whispering sweet things to each other.

Instead, I lay here, panting, alone, trying to process the moment.

It's not that I'm unsatisfied exactly. The orgasm was good. Great, even. But it feels transactional—like he's more relieved than pleased that he's managed to get me off without having to engage too deeply.

And there's a growing awareness that this rose has become a substitute for effort. He now reaches for it almost automatically, like it's a tool to finish a job he doesn't feel like doing by hand, cock or tongue. The intimacy that once existed between us feels like it's slipping away, replaced by something colder, more utilitarian.

And every now and then, I get there without it—like sometimes when I ride him. It's those moments, the ones where I find my own rhythm on top of him, that make it clear he's not entirely selfish. He enjoys the way I move, the way I lose myself in the moment. I can tell by the way he watches me with a mixture of hunger and awe, his hands gripping my hips like I'm the only thing in the world that matters.

Sometimes, he even preempts me, asking, "Do you want your toy?" with a grin that's more sweet than smug. Those little gestures show that he cares, in his own way. He might not be the most intuitive lover anymore, but he's willing to make the effort, and that counts for something.

So even though the way I get there is often a little anticlimactic compared to the fireworks he seems to experience every time, I still end up feeling satisfied.

Still, being with Timmy makes me feel sexy—alive in a way I didn't realize I'd been missing. There's a charge between us, a sense of adventure, even if it's a little reckless. It's not perfect, but it's ours.

I tell myself it's fine. At least I'm getting what I need, right? He's open to using the toy. He's not dismissive or rude about it. But still, there's a nagging feeling—something quietly eating away at me, whispering that this isn't quite right.

I try not to dwell on it too much, focusing instead on the moments where things still feel good, where he still feels like us. But I can't help wondering—is this just the natural evolution of sex in a relationship? Or is it a sign of something deeper—a widening gap between us, one that a tiny soft lilac vibrator can't quite bridge?

It's not like he doesn't care about me. I know he does. But his eagerness to hand off my pleasure to a machine leaves me feeling... lonely. Like I'm slowly becoming a spectator in my own intimate moments. And the worst part? I'm not sure he even notices the difference.

After all, from his perspective, he's still delivering what he thinks I want. And maybe that's enough—for now.

But as I lie in bed, listening to his soft snores as he drifts off to sleep, I wonder how long it'll be before this quiet disconnection becomes something I can't ignore. Just another thing that started off beautiful, but has very quickly eroded.

82

THE ONLY THING HE SURFS IS THE INTERNET

At this point, the resentment of having to be at Matty's isn't just simmering beneath the surface, with the occasional sputter where it rears its ugly head. It's cascading, frothing over, constantly. Each day, I seethe, feeling like something precious has been stolen.

My routine is still my salvation in the earlier parts of the day—yet, by the afternoon, like clockwork, I feel the need to speak up, and it inevitably creates a daily conflict.

Timmy is resentful that I'm resentful.

I try to drink it away, numbing myself with booze, trying to stop caring that this is my new life. But it doesn't work. Sitting in the dark room, nursing vodka or whiskey or hard seltzer, does nothing to satisfy my craving for sunshine, fresh air, writing, and joy.

My resentment just continues to brew from an endless supply, as if pouring from a limitless cup of poison.

"Timmy," I say, on yet another afternoon, "we can't just sit around here every day. I feel like I'm losing my mind."

Usually, his mouth just twists into a scowl, ready to hiss projectiles defending the situation, as if my discontentment is the problem, and my problem alone.

But one day, instead of yelling at me, he just sighs, as if my request is a burden. "I get it, Margaux. I'll try harder."

I blink in surprise, not sure if this is some kind of cruel test.

I can't stand it. "Timmy," I plead, "can we please go somewhere? Just the two of us? Matty's very kind to let us stay, and I don't mind him coming along with us on some outings, but I need time just with you. To focus on us."

He looks at me, guilt flickering in his expression. "Okay," he says. "I get it. I'll do better."

And, once again, to my surprise, he does. We find a small café a few blocks away—a Starbucks, of all things, nestled inside a hospital. It's well-lit, has plentiful tables, wi-fi, and even a cute little outdoor area.

It becomes our new temporary workspace, where he designs graphics and I write. Sitting beside him, working together on our individual projects, feels almost like a dream—a glimpse of the life we talked about, the life I thought we'd have. He's focused and creative, and it's infectious. His excitement for his designs makes me feel more motivated, more alive.

It's not perfect, though. Every few days, I have to remind him not to slip back into old habits. But it's progress, and I tell myself that progress, no matter how incremental, is still worth celebrating. Two steps forward, one and a half steps back—but forward nonetheless.

As frustrating as it can be, I also wonder if this slower pace is teaching me something. Maybe the relentless urgency I've always felt isn't sustainable. Maybe I need to slow down, to embrace this more relaxed rhythm of life. Maybe the universe brought me here to learn exactly that.

And so I try to be patient, to appreciate the little victories. The coffee shop afternoons, the moments when he listens without defensiveness, the rare times he wakes up early enough to see the sunrise with me—just kidding, he never does that. But I remind myself that change doesn't happen overnight, and maybe I just need to give him —and myself—more grace.

But deep down, I can't ignore the restless itch beneath my skin, the nagging voice that whispers this might not be enough. That no matter how many steps forward we take, we're always teetering on the edge of sliding back—and, like a game of chutes and ladders, maybe it won't be just half a step back, the setback could be huge.

Because, while it is a form of progress, let's be real—we're sitting in a chain coffee shop inside a hospital—not on the beach or by a pool enjoying what the Cay really has to offer. Not surfing, or swimming, or walking hand in hand along the boardwalk, all of which now feel like a distant dream.

And I wonder how long I can hold on, hoping for the life I imagined, while the reality of life with Timmy pulls me in the opposite direction.

83

OFF-LIMITS (BUT IT DOESN'T STOP ME THINKING ABOUT YOU)

I find myself randomly wondering about Dex. What he's up to. If he's still dating the girl he's been with for a couple of years.

I've always felt this weird kind of jealousy ever since they got together, same as when he was engaged. Like I'd missed some delusional chance of being with him.

Not that it would make any sense. You just don't go around dating your brother's best friend. And there's a big age gap, and he's happy. Ugh, why can't my pussy just behave and realize he's off limits.

As far as I can remember, he was always dating someone, like a serial monogamist. Delaney or Brooklyn or the one I used to call Bobble Head. Which was mean in hindsight. But they were all these very attractive women who seemed to have their shit together. The exact opposite of me, an awkward little kid.

And Dex himself, like some sort of god. The way he can look at me and make him feel like I'm the only person in the room. The details he remembers that nobody else would give a second thought to. The little gifts he used to bring me back from his travels, some of which I've kept in a cherished box of trinkets in my room.

The complete opposite of my brother, who couldn't even find the time to see me in my school play, or who would invite me to a concert when I was a teenager as a gift, and then turn around at the last minute and try to charge me for it.

But that's all silly. It probably didn't mean anything to Dex anyway, even though it meant a hell of a lot to me.

I get the sense that Dex would never tolerate behavior like Timmy's. He'd never sleep in all day and laze around. He'd be off doing things, whether it be his mysterious job or just keeping himself busy—working out, working on his motorcycle, tinkering around with something, anything, to keep his mind busy. He has ambition, goals—always has.

Besides, I'm in a relationship myself. And I'm fine. No need to go and be some kind of home wrecker. Everything is fine-ish here, and I truly hope he's doing well. It's just some weird schoolgirl fantasy I have when it comes to him, and I need to leave well enough alone.

And maybe that's what chosen family means. Maybe I love him, but in the way you might love an older sibling. Although, I don't dream about my older siblings the way I dream about Dex.

Thank god. That would be really fucked up.

84

A BIT OF A DOUCHE

Timmy's phone buzzes loudly, shattering the lazy stillness of the day. Timmy answers with a grin, launching into rapid chatter. From the way his face lights up, I know it's Steve. I can only catch half the conversation, but whatever Steve's saying has Timmy buzzing with excitement.

When he hangs up, Timmy beams at me, his energy already surging. "Steve's coming to pick us up! We're going on an adventure!"

Truth be told, I feel a flicker of excitement too. I've been itching to get out of the house, away from the same walls and routines. And Steve seemed decent enough—or at least helpful—when Timmy had that stint in jail. It'll be nice to break the monotony.

When Steve pulls up, Matty decides to come along, and we all pile into Steve's car, with me riding shotgun.

At first, everything seems fine.

We head up to a scenic lookout with sweeping views of the coastline, the kind of spot that feels like it belongs in a postcard. The ocean shimmers in the sunlight, and I snap photos, grateful for the brief peace. The guys chat aimlessly—surf spots, old friends, random gossip—while Timmy cracks open a hard seltzer.

At first, I sip mine slowly, letting the cold fizz settle on my tongue, but Timmy downs his like a man stranded in a desert. One can, two cans, three—all within minutes. His hyperactivity, always present to some degree, skyrockets in Steve's presence. He fidgets in his seat, his words coming out in rapid bursts, his thoughts scattered like confetti. It feels like he's performing for Steve, trying to impress him, and the manic energy is unsettling.

Something in the air shifts as Steve cracks a crude joke about an old classmate. "Remember Cindy at school? Ooooh man. Her tits were fire. Damn, I wanted to fuck her so bad. And Chelsea? Goddamn." His voice is laced with lecherous nostalgia.

A pit forms in my stomach. *This* is the guy I thought was the mature, responsible friend? I thought Steve was a career guy, a horse-back park ranger with a family. But here he is, talking like a horny teenager. It makes me uncomfortable, the way he talks about women like they're objects from a buffet line. Instead of the good guy I thought he was, he's actually turning out to be quite a douche. If I misjudged Steve this badly, what else have I misread?

We drive past a bar, and Steve leans forward, grinning. "Oh my god, remember Emily? Met her here once. Hottest thing I've ever seen." He groans in his seat, like just the memory is enough to make him swoon or potentially jizz his pants. It's pathetic.

Then he swerves the car toward a random woman walking along the street. "Ooooh, look at her." She's just an ordinary person minding her business, but the way Steve gawks makes it seem like she's some kind of goddess descended from the heavens. It's over the top, crass, and chauvinistic.

For once, Timmy stays cool. He glances at me, noticing my discomfort. "Keep your eyes on the road, Steve," he mutters, sounding exasperated, although his face is plastered with an amused grin. I breathe a small sigh of relief. At least Timmy isn't feeding into Steve's nonsense too much—yet.

We stop for pizza, and it's the kind of pizza that makes you want to close your eyes and savor every bite. Perfect crust, bold flavors—easily one of the best I've ever had. But while I'm enjoying the food, I notice Timmys' seltzer buzz has now escalated into full-on drunkenness. His movements are a bit wobbly, and he's saying increasingly silly things.

Steve, noticing Timmy's intoxication, tells him he can't have any more beer, and insists that he can only take sips of mine. I'm grateful for Steve's moment of responsibility, so I let Timmy steal a sip—but then he takes another, and another, until half my beer is gone.

Timmy leans in for a selfie, his lips crashing into mine in a sloppy kiss. He's in one of his drunken, affectionate modes, where every kiss is supposed to feel passionate but ends up sloppy and overwhelming. It's an odd combination—feeling cherished and grossed out at the same time.

At least he isn't being crude like Steve. If there's one thing I can say for Timmy, it's that he seems to know where my line is when it comes to talking about women. He might need to dial it back in other areas, but at least he seems to understand that kind of disrespect would be a dealbreaker for me.

Or so I thought.

As we drive back, Steve brings up one of Timmy's exes for no apparent reason. "Hey, remember Barbara? Kicked you out of the house with that eviction notice?" Steve chuckles like it's the funniest story in the world. "And remember her super hot friend, Madison."

Timmy's eyes grow dreamy, a grin spreading across his face. "Yeah, Madison," he murmurs, his voice thick with the same lecherous nostalgia Steve has been displaying throughout the outing.

At first, I roll my eyes and laugh it off. But he keeps going, recounting every detail with more and more enthusiasm. "She tricked me into letting the cops in," he says with a grin. "But man, she was so fucking hot."

My stomach tightens. "Stop, Timmy. Please."

I'm quickly realizing that Steve has this uncanny ability to trigger Timmy's spectrum of inappropriate emotions, in this case taking him from anger at an ex to perving about some girl.

Although, I guess I have the same ability to push his buttons, too. He's told me so a few times now. Under the guise of "we're connected on such a deep level that I feel what you feel and vice versa. And you really know how to upset me and use things I told you in confidence against me." Both things I don't believe I've ever done, although the opposite could be said about him.

"Oooh yeah," grins Timmy, continuing the conversation about 'hot Madison'.

"Stop, please," I plead.

He laughs, ignoring me, caught up in his own story. "I would've let her stay in my apartment anytime," he leers.

"Timmy," I say, my voice sharper this time. "Please—stop."

But he just keeps going, encouraged by Steve's laughter. It's like watching a train wreck in slow motion—every word a new collision, every laugh a reminder that they don't care how uncomfortable I feel.

I've never, in my history, had to ask a partner to stop speaking so disrespectfully in front of me about another woman.

"Shut the fuck up, Timmy!" I snap, my voice rising. "Just shut the fuck up!"

The car falls silent for a beat, the tension thick enough to choke on. Steve glances at me in the rear-view mirror, and then at Timmy, a smirk playing on his lips, as if he finds my outburst amusing. Like this was all some sick game to him, and he's enjoying the fallout.

The realization hits me like a punch to the gut—Steve knew exactly what he was doing. As if he intentionally lit a powder keg to watch it go off.

He baited Timmy, knowing he'd take the bait, and now I'm the one who looks crazy. The insecure girlfriend. The jealous nag. Which only makes me feel even more crazy. Because I know that's how the guys would all paint it. "Oh, look at Margaux being all jealous. Raising her voice. Screaming. What a crazy bitch."

And yes, maybe I am a little jealous. But when I tell my partner to please stop saying something because it makes me feel uncomfortable, I expect them to respect that boundary and stop. Not to double down and have their friends encourage them more.

And the worst part? Timmy doesn't seem to care.

Steve drops us off, thank god. And I think it's over, but I'm wrong.

Back at Matty's, I head to the bathroom, needing a moment alone.

But the window is open, and I can hear Timmy and Matty's voices outside on the porch while they have a cigarette.

"So, as I was saying," Timmy slurs, "that girl showed up at my apartment, and she was so fucking hot—"

He never talks like this in front of me, but an hour or two with Steve and he's turned into some disrespectful, pervy piece of shit.

"Are you fucking kidding me?" I scream, mid-stream. I finish up as quickly as I can and exit the room, slamming the bathroom door behind me. Fury bubbles over, and before I know it, I'm on the porch, confronting them. "You got home and kept this conversation going? How many times do I have to tell you not to be disrespectful, and to stop with your gross story?"

Timmy sneers at me, his drunken grin twisted and mean. Matty stands off to the side, silent and useless.

"Fuck you!" I scream, slamming the door to the porch, grabbing Sabre and storming out of Matty's apartment. I need space—away from Timmy, away from his disrespect, away from the toxic dynamic that Steve created, and that Timmy is now perpetuating. We take an Uber back to my apartment.

Later, my phone buzzes with a message from Timmy.

TIMMY:

> Please come back, Margaux. I love you. I'm sorry. I don't really know what happened, but I hate it when you're mad with me.

I sigh, the exhaustion settling deep in my bones.

ME:

> Fine. But please think before you speak next time.

TIMMY:

Okay. I promise.

When I return to Matty's, Timmy greets me with wide, apologetic eyes.

"I want to talk about what happened earlier," I say, my voice steady but tired. "You were being really disrespectful in the car. And then back at the house."

He frowns. "No I wasn't."

"Yes, you were making pervy comments and I asked you to stop."

He scrunches up his face, confusion clouding his features as he tries to remember. "What did I say again?"

I remind him of the entire conversation, and to my surprise, he doesn't argue.

"You're right," he says, nodding slowly. "It probably was a really pervy comment. I should've listened to you and stopped. I shouldn't have said it in the first place. I agree with you. And even if I disagreed, I should have acted respectfully enough toward you to stop, and then we could have discussed it in private, after. I'm sorry."

Relief washes over me. For once, the defensiveness isn't there. He's actually listening and taking accountability, coming up with a way to avoid it happening again in the future. "Well, I appreciate you acknowledging that. Thank you."

He pulls me into his arms, his embrace warm and solid. His gaze meets mine, his eyes soft. He tips my head up and kisses me on the forehead. "I'm really sorry, Margaux. I wouldn't like it at all if you did that to me. I won't do it again."

For a moment, I let myself believe him. I let myself sink into the comfort of his apology. "Thank you for your apology. I'm sorry, too." I hug him back.

It feels like we're making some progress on having adult conversations about difficult things. I felt heard and seen in this situation. In the big scheme of things, it's not a big deal, anyway. I was just being a bit jealous, because he was being a bit pervy and disrespectful. We were both at fault. Everything's going to be fine.

"I love you, Margaux," he says, kissing me.

I kiss him back. "I love you too, Timmy."

With that, it's like the tension that had been building all evening evaporates into the humid night air. His words, his apology—everything sounds genuine. This is the Timmy I fell in love with. The one who can make me feel cherished, heard and safe. Maybe we've really turned a corner, and we're finally figuring out how to communicate in a way that isn't chaotic or hurtful.

But even as I kiss him, a small voice in the back of my mind whispers: *How long until the next time?*

We head inside Matty's apartment, the heavy night settling around us like a blanket. Timmy stretches out on the mattress, tugging me down beside him, and I snuggle into him, hoping the closeness will stave off the doubts swirling in my mind.

But as I lay there, I replay the evening in my head—the way Steve egged Timmy on, the smirk on his face as if he was reveling in the chaos he'd caused. And Timmy, leaping right into the trap, letting himself be baited, even though he knew better.

It's not just the pervy comments that sting. It's the fact that I had to beg him—multiple times—to stop. The way he seemed to enjoy the discomfort it caused, doubling down instead of dialing it back. And that's not something I can easily forget.

Still, it's hard to stay mad at him when he looks so peaceful lying next to me now, like all the tension from earlier never happened. His lips brush against my forehead again, a soft kiss that feels both like a promise and a plea for peace.

"Everything's going to be fine," I whisper to myself, trying to believe it. Trying to convince myself that this isn't part of some larger pattern—one where the apologies flow easily, but the behavior never really changes.

THE NEXT MORNING, things are calm again. Timmy wakes up before noon for a change, and there's no mention of the previous night's drama. It's like he's reset, as if our argument dissolved into thin air the moment we made up.

I wish I could shake off things that easily. I wish I didn't carry the weight of every hurtful word or dismissive action.

"Let's get breakfast," he suggests, his voice bright, as if nothing had ever been wrong.

I hesitate for a second, feeling the weight of my own emotions still lingering in my chest. But then I tell myself that it's okay to let it go. Not every moment needs to be dissected, not every issue is a sign of impending doom.

"Yeah," I say with a small smile. "Let's get breakfast."

We head out to a little café by the beach, the ocean breeze cool against my skin as we walk hand in hand. Timmy's thumb traces slow circles on the back of my hand, and I lean into him, enjoying the simple pleasure of the moment.

He orders pancakes, I get an açai bowl, and everything feels almost normal. Almost.

And yet, beneath the surface, there's an undercurrent—a tension I can't quite name.

I know I should be happy with how things are right now. He's here, he's apologetic, he's holding me like he means it. We're eating breakfast by the ocean on a beautiful day.

But I can't stop the thought from creeping in—how long until the next time?

Because that's the thing with Timmy. The apologies come, the tenderness returns, but the cycle keeps spinning. It's a ride I didn't realize I'd signed up for, and now I'm not sure how to get off without crashing completely.

And will this be the same thing every time we hang out with Steve? I thought he was a sensible, mature guy—but the way he talks about women is juvenile and misogynistic. Even Timmy knows how to reel it in better, as long as he hasn't had too much to drink.

For now, though, I sip my coffee, soak in the sunlight, and try to convince myself that things will be different. That love is enough. That Timmy can be the person I see glimpses of in these quiet, good moments—the person I want him to be all the time.

He leans over, kissing me on the cheek, and my heart does that frustrating thing where it skips a beat, just like it did the first time we kissed. I smile at him, and for now, I let the doubt fade into the background.

85

EXIT OF THE SKÖLDPADDA

The weight of Sven's message sits heavy in my chest. I stare at my phone, the screen still open to the last few texts before one of my closest friends from the East Coast blocked me, reading them over and over again, hoping I missed some context that might make this feel less gut-wrenching.

SVEN SKÖLDPADDA :

You had this all planned out.

I would kill him if he were any closer, after what he did to you.

I'm going to block you now.

Gone. Just like that.

One of my closest friends—someone I always thought of as a brother—has cut me out completely. I sit there in stunned silence, the phone slipping from my hand.

"What's wrong?" Timmy's voice pulls me out of my thoughts.

"Sven... he just blocked me." My voice cracks, barely above a whisper. "Because of you."

Timmy shrugs, his expression remaining maddeningly neutral.

"Fuck that guy," he says, his arm draping around my shoulders with a casual possessiveness. "He just wanted to bang you, anyway. I didn't like you talking to him. It's much better this way."

His words twist inside me like a dull knife. I know Timmy doesn't like Sven. That much was obvious. But hearing him dismiss someone who meant so much to me—someone I thought would always have my back—feels surreal.

Timmy's hand moves to my chin, tilting my face toward his. "Now at least you know who your real friends are. Like me." He smiles, his blue eyes sparkling, as if Sven blocking me is some sort of gift. "I'm your real best friend."

A lump forms in my throat, and I try to swallow it down. Part of me knows this is all wrong—knows that a best friend, a real friend, wouldn't try to isolate me from the people I care about, wouldn't relish in me getting cut off by yet another member of my support system. But the other part of me is so exhausted, so worn down by the constant push and pull, that it feels easier to let Timmy's words sink in.

Sven did overreact—there's no question there. Maybe Timmy is right—maybe Sven had ulterior motives, and maybe it is better to cut ties with people who can't accept the choices I'm making. But it still hurts. The wound feels raw, and I know it won't heal easily.

Timmy pulls me closer, planting a kiss on the top of my head. "It's just you and me, babe. We don't need anyone else. I've got you, and you've got me. That's all that matters."

The warmth of his arms around me should feel reassuring, but instead, it feels heavy. Suffocating. Like a weight I can't seem to shrug off, no matter how hard I try. I sit, frozen, trying to convince myself that this is okay.

That I don't need anyone else. That Timmy is enough.

But deep down, something feels fractured. Sven's words echo in my mind—"I'm so upset with you." And all I can do is sit with the uneasy knowledge that the people I love are slipping away from me, one by one, and I don't know how to stop it. I get the sense that they feel helpless, with me so far away, knowing I'm in a situation that maybe isn't as good for me as it once felt. Powerless to do anything but watch from a distance and hope for the best—that I either snap out of it myself, or that they were wrong in their assessment and things are better than they fear.

I shift slightly under Timmy's arm, and he tightens his grip, as if sensing my discomfort. "We're good, Margaux," he whispers. "It's just us. That's all you need."

I nod, more for his benefit than mine. But inside, I feel like I'm slowly disappearing, fading into the version of myself that Timmy wants me to be. And I wonder how much of me will be left by the time this is all over.

I find myself pulling away from all but my closest friends.

I'm embarrassed about what happened, nervous about anyone knowing that the person who attacked me is still in my life.

I don't post many pictures of us together online, preferring to keep them private. As if—instead of being someone I'm proud of and want to share with the world—Timmy is my guilty secret.

This is out of my typical behavior—I'd usually be blasting my love far and wide.

But nothing feels very typical anymore.

86

A LEAP OF FAITH

We take a drive to the opposite end of the coast, because Timmy wants to show me a few new beaches and maybe check out some board shorts and hats in the surf shops to understand the trending designs.

As soon as we get to the small town, I notice Timmy staring intently at a metal bridge right beside the welcome sign. The sun is already dipping low in the sky, casting long shadows over the water. The bridge's high arches loom over the rippling surface. Usually, seeing water brings me calm, but Timmy's been agitated, edgy today, as if something is on his mind.

I see Timmy staring at the bridge with an intensity I haven't seen since he first met me, and with a sinking feeling, I realize I know what he's about to say before he says it.

"Can I jump off the bridge?" He points to a little space to the side of the road where the truck could fit. "Please? We could just park over there. I'll only take a minute." His voice carries a familiar hint of excitement.

"No, Timmy," I frown, my stomach twisting into a knot. Not this again. Not now. "You said you'd stopped jumping off bridges now.

That it's dangerous, remember? You said that now you're with me, you valued your life more and so you wouldn't do it again."

I truly believed him when he said those things. That being with me was more important than a reckless fixation.

But he pouts as I speak, his brow furrowing like a two-year-old being denied a second cookie. "You're so fucking controlling. I'm a grown-ass man. I should be able to jump off a stupid fucking bridge. Plus, it's not even that big of a bridge. And I brought my Superman cape and everything."

He says it so matter-of-factly, like the cape is going to somehow make him fly.

I shake my head. "No I'm not. You promised me you wouldn't do something. That thing happens to be really dangerous. I believed your promise, and so—no. I'm not going to be complicit in you breaking that promise. You need to respect my boundaries, or why tell me anything at all? I'll just stop believing a word you say."

This is about so much more than jumping off a stupid bridge—it somehow feels symbolic of our entire relationship.

He mocks me, mimicking my tone. "I'm not going to be complicit in you breaking that promise." He glares. "Don't use your big fucking words to be a bitch, Margaux. You're no fucking fun."

"Yes, I am. I just don't want you to die." I keep my voice gentle and steady, even though I feel like I'm about to vomit. "Because you're amazing and I love you."

Maybe if I appeal to him with how special he is to me, he'll get over this sudden, spontaneous impulse. I mentally cross my fingers that this will placate him, at least for now.

He sighs, looking at me. "Okay. I won't jump off the bridge today."

I breathe a sigh of relief.

~

TWO HOURS *later*

"Can I jump off the bridge *now?*"

It's been two hours, and Timmy has had a hard seltzer, and seems to have forgotten our prior conversations.

"No," I frown. "We talked about this. You promised you'd stop asking."

Timmy lets out an exaggerated sigh. He mutters under his breath. "Oh my fucking god. It's not even that high. Way to make a big deal out of nothing." There's something dangerous underneath his words —something that sets me on edge.

For a moment, he just stares at me, as if he's really having a problem with why I don't want him to break yet another one of my boundaries. "Of course," he continues to complain. "You're always such a fucking killjoy. God forbid I'm ever allowed to do anything fun."

We get to another beach. "Here, let's park in this parking lot," he says. It's busy, and we have to wait a while, but eventually someone pulls out.

"I'll be right back!" Timmy says, jumping out of the car in a hurry. "I just need to jump off something."

"Wait, wha—."

"You're so fucking controlling," he scoffs, cutting me off. "I'm going to go jump off that rock over there. It's not as high as the bridge. And you'd better still be here when I get back. You always act like I'm some reckless child you need to babysit. God forbid you'd ever allow me to do anything exciting. I'm fucking going."

I try to plead with him, but he's already gone. And I see him off in the distance, clambering up a rock face and joining the queue of tourists eager to get their vacation stunt moves snapped. And hopefully not their backs.

Actually, this jumping area looks a lot safer than some random bridge.

But still, I feel like he was being duplicitous. Getting me to park here under the guise of taking me to a new beach, when really he was planning to get his way and jump off something.

It feels like he's found a way to disrespect a boundary, to push a little further, by sidestepping the specific thing I didn't want him to do and doing something very similar, but not exactly the same. Semantics, in a way.

He's right, though. This is something I'm uptight about and I don't really understand. I spent so many years hearing my mother saying 'never jump into random bodies of water. There could be a rock. I know so and so broke their spine doing that'. I'm probably being neurotic, passing along my own issues because my mother is overprotective and tends to spew random myths like they're absolute truths. That's not his fault. I just need to calm down.

But the way he's gone about it has me feeling a type of way and I can't one hundred percent figure out why. Jeez. Maybe I'm the one with the mood disorder.

I just want him to be safe. His words still sting, even after a few minutes. I'm truly not trying to control him. I just don't think risking his life is 'exciting'. And I'd like to think that if my partner promises me he won't do something because it makes me feel uncomfortable, that he'll stick with that. Not nag at me until I give in and 'let' him do that thing. It just doesn't feel respectful of me or my boundaries.

He comes back, and he's thrilled.

"Man, that makes me miss the bigger jumps!" he says, his eyes sparkling.

Then he turns to me, his expression growing serious. "And I'm sorry, Margaux. For what happened earlier. I really appreciate you letting me do this here. It makes me really happy. And this one was safe. I appreciate you caring about me. And I love you."

His words throw me. I was expecting him to be more aggressive, more arrogant about going against what we'd talked about.

"Oh, well, I'm glad you had a good time." I feel defeated, unable to talk to him about how I truly feel. And somehow, deep down, I have a feeling he knows that, and that he's enjoying every minute of making me squirm.

Because somehow he's done it again, spun the narrative against me. Turning my concern into control, and my love into suffocation.

Making it seem like I'm toxic for expecting him to keep a boundary that he promised. Jumping off a cliff might seem like a little thing, but to me, it's not about the cliff.

And it feels like there's no point forcing the issue.

Because Timmy's already lost too deep in his own storm.

87

I CAN'T DO IT AGAIN

Ultimately, I decide that I want to drop the charges against Timmy.

I think about it over and over again, and I can't bring myself to be victimized through another court process. Given the way the detective behaved when he interviewed me, I can only imagine how traumatic this situation would be—the shit that Timmy's defense team would likely make up about me, even though of course unlike my rapist he wouldn't be able to afford the most expensive defense lawyer in the country.

From experience, I know that defense lawyers have tactics which include ripping an innocent victim's testimony and credibility to shreds. And if there's any alcohol involved? Forget about it. There's just no point.

I call the prosecutor's office at the number given, and she just never gets back to me. So I sit and I wait and I toil.

While I wait for a response I never receive, a wave of conflicting emotions floods over me. Relief, regret, anger, and confusion all twist together in a tangled knot in my chest. Dropping the charges feels like the right thing, but also like surrender. Like I'm letting Timmy, and maybe even the system, off the hook.

I end up going into the prosecutor's office in person, so they won't have the opportunity to continue ignoring me. They make me wait in a lobby covered with cameras, and I squirm uncomfortably, feeling scrutinized. Someone eventually comes out to see me—an advocate —and she sits with me and speaks in hushed tones about what I'm trying to do.

She explains that someone will be out shortly with the form that will officially record my request to drop the charges.

The woman is nice and asks some standard questions about domestic violence and how safe I feel. I answer without giving too much information, definitely not letting on that Timmy and I are still together.

But I do take the time to explain that I want to drop charges because I can't bring myself to go through the court system again as the victim of a violent crime. She's empathetic, and seems unsurprised to hear that part of the reason for my hesitation is the unprofessional, accusatory way I was interviewed by the detective.

When I explain that if the person investigating the case was so judgmental in his questioning, how could I possibly expect the judge and jury to treat me with any fairness—let alone the defense counsel?.

I know people in her role are meant to remain neutral, helping victims to navigate the system while also supporting the institution they work for, but she seems oddly detached by what I have to say. As in, I don't feel judged, but she doesn't seem at all shocked by my feedback. The advocate listens kindly, her nods almost too familiar, as if she's heard this story from dozens of other women.

In this moment, I see the process for what it is. I'm not being paranoid. This is how it is for victims, and I stand strong in my resolve not to put myself through that ever again.

"He'll be out with the form soon," she reiterates. "We'll get it taken care of."

And then a large, intimidating man with a stack of papers steps in, like a hunter cornering prey. The subtle threat in his body language makes me feel trapped. My throat tightens when I realize what he's trying to do.

"Are you trying to serve me?" My voice squeaks with outrage, blood pounding in my temples. My body starts that same familiar buzz signaling flight or fight.

"Yes," he says calmly. "If you'll just step into this room..." He gestures at the door behind him.

It's a moment that sharpens everything—reminding me of how broken the system is, how victims are not just expected to survive trauma, but to fight through it again in court.

"No, absolutely not!" I snap at the man, standing my ground. "I don't feel comfortable."

When he sighs in frustration, it's clear how little my comfort means in this equation—to them, I'm just a tool to add to their stats, a case file they can check off as a successful prosecution.

After more back and forth, I snap. "I will leave the fucking *country* if I have to, but I will *not* be going to court!"

My words punctuate the fact that I'm not playing around, and the energy in the room shifts.

With a sigh, he finally hands me the form I came for—confirmation that the charges against Timmy are dropped on my end, at least. But the threat lingers—the prosecutor could still pursue the case whether I want them to or not. It's the state's case, not mine, and as such, it's their call. One thing is clear, though—I would prove to be a very hostile witness, and they know it.

During my rape trial back in New Zealand, I felt very strongly that I wanted to stop the rapist from hurting another woman ever again. By having him locked up for what he did. But instead, I was dragged through a humiliating, soul-destroying process, and then he got off scot-free, with what? One night in jail? There's no way I could go through that again, knowing it likely wouldn't help anyone, anyway. Bad guys get off either way, based on my experience.

And, since my trial, I've realized that it's not actually my responsibility to stop a man from harming a woman. It's a broad societal issue and a victim can't be expected to take responsibility and feel the burden for his actions. So I don't feel great about refusing to go through the process, but I refuse to let myself feel guilty.

The way Timmy explains the attack away as a one-off incident plays a part as well. "I was protecting you. I really was angry at what that person has been doing to you, tormenting you in your nice new apartment. And I needed to calm myself down, so I took a handful of trazodone after I'd been drinking, and I thought it would make me fall asleep straight away. But instead, it made me insanely angry and full of homicidal rage, and I took it out on you, the person who is most important to me. The person I love and most want to protect. And I'll never forgive myself for that."

"That was a really dumb and dangerous thing for you to do, Timmy," I'd said, on one of the many times we'd discussed it. "And you didn't mention it to me before you did it. Please promise me you'll never do that again."

"Oh, believe me. I promise with my whole heart. I love you so much, and the fact that you're agreeing to speak and meet with me again is far more than I deserve."

"You tried to kill me, Timmy," I'd pleaded with him. "That was really terrifying for me."

"Oh no," he'd shaken his head, adamant. "If I'd tried to kill you, you'd be dead."

His words chilled me each time he'd reiterated this, and he'd continued, oblivious. "I was just trying to scare you."

I'm not quite sure how he intended his words to make me feel better, and they didn't—it was as if he was simultaneously trying to reassure me while also minimizing his behavior. As if it's better to make your partner think you want to—and could—kill her, than actually committing the murder. I suppose that's technically true. I prefer the former over the latter, but it's also kind of a crazy thing to tell someone.

But he'd followed up with the love and affection he'd promised this whole time.

"I'm beyond sorry," he'd said, his voice eager, his eyes meeting mine. "I would never ever fuck this up again. I can't believe things got that far. I truly love you, and I will spend the rest of my life making it up to you."

Based on his words, and everything else, dropping charges seems like the right thing to do. So I'm prioritizing my mental health, trusting his word, and pushing down any sense of regret.

I leave the office, my heart pounding, and it feels like I've run a marathon through my own worst memories. It's not just what Timmy did—it's the looming specter of my past trial—the soul-crushing process of being shredded on the stand, accused of being the architect of my own abuse. And I know, deep down, that the same tactics would be used this time, too. The detective's smug, accusatory tone still rings in my ears. I know exactly how it would play out. And I just can't put myself through that again.

WHEN I GET BACK, Timmy is waiting, impatient and tense, clearly eager for an answer. His gaze follows me as I walk through the apartment like a ghost, every step heavy with the weight of what just happened.

"What happened? Did you drop the charges?" he asks, trying—and failing—to mask the urgency, the desperation, in his voice.

I look at him, the words tangled on my tongue. I need space. I need time to process. "I'll be right back," I mumble. "I need to go to the store."

I leave without further explanation, my mind a storm of anger, sadness, and exhaustion. I pull my headphones over my ears, blasting music loud enough to drown out my thoughts. As I walk to the convenience store, I focus on my breathing, trying to ground myself in the rhythm of each step. The trauma feels like it's clawing at the edges of my mind, threatening to overwhelm me.

And maybe, if I'm honest, there's one tiny sliver within me that makes me feel like—by delaying telling him for just a few more minutes—I get to feel less out of control about everything. That for once, I have a piece of information that he doesn't. That I get to anchor to what happened without anyone else having the upper hand. That I know what truly happened before I tell Timmy, before he gets the opportunity to rewrite history, recasting the narrative so he becomes the hero of this story once again.

I buy a bottle of Irish whiskey, knowing it's not the healthiest coping mechanism, but it's the only thing that feels like it'll help right now. When I get back to the apartment, I take a shot straight from the bottle, the warmth spreading through my chest like a buffer between me and the chaos swirling in my head.

Finally, I sit down across from Timmy, ready to tell him what he's been waiting to hear. "I dropped the charges," I say flatly.

His response comes immediately, relief flickering across his face, followed by irritation. "What took you so long to tell me? Why couldn't you just say that in the first place?"

I feel a surge of frustration at his impatience. "Because it's not that simple, Timmy. The guy tried to serve me. It was a trap, and it brought up a lot for me. Flashbacks. Stuff from the trial. I needed a second to get my head together."

His expression softens slightly, though not entirely. He pulls me into a long hug, his arms wrapping around me in what feels like both relief and possession. "Thank you so much for doing that for me, baby," he murmurs into my hair.

I close my eyes, torn between the comfort of his embrace and the unease that still lingers. "You need to live up to the promises you made, Timmy," I whisper. "This can't happen again."

He pulls back just enough to meet my gaze, his blue eyes filled with what seems like sincerity. "You can bet on it," he says, his voice soft and earnest. "I'm ready to become a better person—with you by my side."

I nod, though deep down, doubt gnaws at the edges of my resolve. He's so convincing, so good at saying all the right things. But words are easy. It's the actions that follow—or don't—that tell the real story.

And I don't know if I have the strength to wait and see which story Timmy decides to write next.

For now, though, it's easier to let myself believe him. To lean into the warmth of his arms and hope, desperately, that this time, he means it.

88

ACTUAL WTF

Few Days Later

A My heart pounds in my chest as Timmy's accusations ring through the apartment, sharp and relentless and irrational.

His face is twisted with rage, and his blue eyes blaze darker as he points a finger at his slightly deflated, sagging foil baby shark balloon—the same balloon that he kept from a friend he'd mentioned once in passing. He hasn't gone into details about who or why, but he's made it clear it holds some sentimental value.

"I know what you were trying to do, Margaux!" He screams, his voice cracking. "You were going to pop it because you know it's important to me, weren't you?" His words are venomous, filled with a fury so disproportionate and so inaccurate it leaves me breathless.

I stand frozen, my hands raised as if surrendering. "I wasn't trying to pop it, Timmy! I told you, I was trying to move it so it *didn't* get squished, because you had it between me and the hard concrete wall! I—".

"Bullshit!" he yells, cutting me off, his eyes narrowed into tiny little slits. The veins in his neck bulge as he storms over to me. "You always do stuff like this! You think it's funny to mess with my stuff, to threaten the things that matter to me!"

I stare at him, stunned, the air around us thick with tension and disbelief. Every word out of his mouth feels like a slap in my face, and all I'd been trying to do was *help*. Something deep inside me fractures under the weight of his rage, and the realization hits me like a punch to the stomach, rendering me breathless—this isn't just about a foil baby shark balloon. Surely not. Nobody could possibly be so irrationally upset over something suitable as a cheap decoration for a child's birthday party.

Tears sting the back of my eyes, but I try to fight them back. I don't want to let him see the effect his behavior is having on me. Not now. Not after everything.

"I can't do this," I whisper, more to myself than to him. My voice wavers, but I steel my spine, gripping the bottom of my shirt as if it's holding me together somehow.

Timmy keeps ranting as I gather what I can in a hurry and shove it into my backpack—my phone, a few clothing items and my charger. Sabre is spending the night back at my apartment, so I don't need to grab him. I don't stop to check if I've forgotten anything.

The apartment door slams shut behind me as I stumble into the night, my breath coming in shaky bursts. "Yeah fuck off, you dumb bitch!" I hear him call after me, and it feels like another slap in the face.

The street outside is dark, the streetlights buzzing faintly but offering little comfort or visibility in the inky black night. Shadows stretch across the cracked pavement, the overgrown weeds that line the alleyway elongating into creepy shapes that make me shiver despite the warmth of the humid air that envelops me like a suffocating cloak.

Distant sounds—a car horn, an alarm, laughter, the hum of engines—make the night feel uneasy, threatening even. I hug my bag close, scanning my phone and the street on either side for signs of the Uber.

My phone buzzes, and I see the car icon moving closer, just a block away.

Hurry, I plead silently.

The seconds feel like hours as I shift on my feet, rubbing my arms as I feel a chill despite the warmth of the night. I can't stop the tremble in my hands—whether from hurt, fear, anger or exhaustion, I'm not sure.

Just as the car's headlights come into view, I hear a voice from behind me and I jump.

"Margaux! Margaux, please wait!" I hear Timmy's voice, ragged, as if he's been running. I see him coming toward me, wild-eyed, his hair a tangled mess. Shirtless and shoeless as usual, wearing only board shorts.

He drops to his bare knees right in front of me, onto the dirty sidewalks, his breath coming in uneven gasps, his hands in prayer position. No man has ever got on his knees for me. In public, I mean.

"I messed up! I really messed up." This time his voice cracks, not from anger, but from something that sounds like desperation.

I step back instinctively, my heart racing. I'm not sure whether I should feel fury or relief, or both.

"Matty..." he sucks in a deep breath, trying to gather himself. "Matty told me I was being a complete asshole." Timmy looks up at me with eyes that now seem haunted, hollow with regret, pleading for me to listen. "He's right—I misunderstood, and I took things out on you. And that's really not okay. None of it was okay."

I stare down at him, stunned and silent.

"You're the best thing that's ever happened to me, Margaux," he pleads, his voice raw, breaking apart. "Please... I don't know what the hell I was thinking. I don't want to lose you. Not like this." He bursts into tears. "I never want to lose you. Ever."

The Uber idles by the curb, waiting.

My hands grip tightly around the handles of the backpack. Everything inside me is swirling—anger, pain, rage, love, confusion, frustration, betrayal. The man I thought I knew now kneels on the cold pavement, begging for forgiveness, drawing curious glances from passersby, his earlier rage dissolved into remorse.

"Margaux, please. I beg you to forgive me. Matty was right. You're the best thing to ever happen to me. You're the best thing in my life. I'm so lucky to have a chance to be with you, and I'm acting like an idiot. Will you please give me one more chance? You're my everything, my universe. I'd be lost without you. I love you so much."

His eyes are kind and blue, pleading. And we're on a dodgy street, but it's as if everything around us fades away and all that is left is me and him and his pretty words.

"Please," he adds. "I'm so sorry. I'll make it up to you. I promise. I'll treat you like a queen, just the way you deserve."

I could get in the car and leave. I could close the door on all of it —the stupid balloon, the screaming, the wild accusations. But as Timmy kneels there, trembling under the weight of his own guilt, I realize something important—forgiveness, like love, is complicated. It's messy and painful and non-linear.

"Please," he pleads again. "I'll make it up to you, I promise."

My fingers hover over my phone as the Uber driver glances at me, as if waiting for my signal. The easy thing would be to drive away, escape the mess and hurt. Timmy's behavior was completely out of line, and a nagging feeling in my gut worries it's a sign of things to come.

But he's also taking accountability for his actions, apologizing, promising me that he realizes he created this situation. Telling me I'm the best thing that's ever happened to him. Something in his voice pulls at me—a combination of guilt, remorse and genuine fear.

I exhale slowly, as if I'm deflating like the baby shark balloon. And I press the cancel ride button on my phone. The driver pulls away, giving a slight shrug, satisfied no doubt with his cancellation fee. The hum of his engine fades as his taillights disappear down the street, leaving me wondering if I just made a huge mistake.

I take a deep breath, and for the first time since the fight started, I speak.

"I really was trying to make sure we didn't accidentally pop the balloon," I say, my voice low. "I would never, ever destroy your things. Especially when I know something means a lot to you."

Timmy nods, grabbing my hand that's not holding my phone. "I know that now, Margaux. I really am so sorry."

He rises to his feet, watching me cautiously, as if he's afraid I might change my mind at any moment and order another Uber.

I put my phone in my fanny pack, zipping it up and clutching my backpack tighter, still unsure whether I'm making the right decision —but at least the anger and venom in his eyes is gone, replaced by something softer and more familiar.

"Come on," he says, taking my hand and leading me back to Matty's apartment. He opens the apartment door and guides me in. "Let's go inside."

I follow him back in, the space feeling strange now—quieter, calmer, like the storm has passed, but also left everything slightly off-kilter.

Timmy rubs the back of his neck, his eyes flickering with guilt. "I really am sorry, Margaux," he says. "I promise I'll make it up to you, starting right now."

He takes my bag gently from my shoulder, and places it on the ground by the couch, and pulls me into a hug. His arms wrap around me tightly, as if holding me will stop everything from unraveling.

I exhale heavily again, pressing my forehead against his shoulder —still unsure if I'm ready to forgive, but relieved the rage has dissolved, and he seems to be trying.

"Do you want some ice cream?" he asks, pulling back enough to see my face, a sheepish smile forming at the corners of his mouth.

I nod, feeling the tiniest flicker of warmth in my chest. I'm not hungry, but my acquiescence is more about the gesture than the ice cream itself. "Sure, ice cream sounds good."

He rummages through the freezer, returning with one spoon and a pint of Half Baked ice cream, and guides me into the bedroom. We settle on the mattress, together, me tucked under his arm, the duvet draped around both of us. We take turns devouring big spoonfuls of ice cream.

As the movie starts, Timmy rubs slow circles into my back, murmuring soft apologies between scenes. I feel the tension in my body ease, little by little, as the night unfolds with an unexpected gentleness. His attention feels genuine now—as if he's trying to undo the damage he caused, bit by bit.

Matty stays out of our hair and gives us space.

Timmy rubs my back and my feet. He brings me wine and sparkling water. And he makes me feel like I really am the only thing in his universe.

"I really thought you were going to pop my baby shark," he says, his eyes pleading.

"I said 'let me move this so I *don't* pop it by accident', because I know it has special meaning to you. I would never damage anything of yours. That's not how I am as a person."

Timmy frowns and nods, as if everything is sinking in. "I understand that now. I'm sorry that I got my wires crossed. I'll listen better. Thank you for making sure you didn't pop it."

"Also, it's a fucking balloon, Timmy. I can't believe you got so upset over this, even though it has sentimental value which I totally get. You literally went crazy because of a foil, helium-filled baby shark. Can you please assume positive intent? There's no way I would intentionally damage your belongings. Ever. I'm not vindictive. I'm not spiteful. I can be low-level petty, but not in a malicious way, and not with you. Okay?"

"Okay, I promise. I'm just so grateful for you giving me a chance. I love you so much."

I look at him and his gorgeous blue eyes. He smiles at me hesitantly. God, that smile.

"I love you too, Timmy. I love you so much, too."

I'm not sure whether I've made the right choice by staying. But as Timmy kisses the top of my head and offers me the spoon again, I feel the tiniest spark of hope.

Maybe, just maybe, that was a one-off explosion, and things will be better from here.

89

NOXIOUS & OBNOXIOUS

It's quiet in Matty's apartment, the hum of the air conditioning filling the space. For once, Matty isn't playing YouTube videos or movies at top volume.

Timmy and I are sitting on the mattress in the bedroom, googling what movie to watch next.

Suddenly, there's a knock at the door—sharp and deliberate, echoing through the room like a subtle warning.

Matty's footsteps thud from the living room to the bedroom, where he glances in at Timmy, a silent exchange passing between them, quick and intentional. Without saying much, Timmy rises from the mattress and gives me a quick, almost absent, smile. "We'll be back in a few, babe," he says, as if to downplay the sudden shift in energy. "Just gotta meet someone real quick. Be right back."

"Wha—." I go to ask who it is, but it's too late. Timmy and Matty have both left the room and slipped out the front door, headed out into the night.

I hear faint murmurs through the door—a muffled conversation happening just out of earshot. And then all goes silent, leaving me alone with my thoughts. My curiosity sharpens as the minutes stretch on. I fidget with my phone, checking it every couple of minutes. After what feels like an eternity, but must have been no more than twenty to thirty minutes, I hear the door click open. They're loud and joking, their laughter echoing around the apartment. I feel relieved they're back, but uneasy about what took place. Why didn't they want me to go with them? Why didn't they want me to meet their friend?

"Hey babe," he grins nonchalantly.

"What was that about?" I ask, my brow furrowed.

He glances at me, his expression unreadable, an awkward mix of casualness laced with something heavier. "Just an acquaintance," he says vaguely, rubbing the back of his neck, his eye contact almost too direct, as if he's trying to avoid a tell-tale flicker that could catch him in a lie. "We were just saying hey."

The pit in my stomach deepens. "Why didn't you want me to meet them?" I ask.

Timmy exhales, as if trying to find the right words, but at the same time not giving away too much. "Look, it's not that I didn't want you to meet them. It's just...," his tone is careful, measured. "He's not a good person," he shrugs, the gesture coming out forced. "Someone you don't need to get involved with. I was being protective of you."

My unease sharpens. "What were you guys doing out there?"

He shifts uncomfortably, running his fingers through his hair. "Nothing much," he says. "Like I said, he was just saying hey."

His nonchalance feels so forced, like a curtain hastily drawn over something ugly. I want to just believe him and let it go, but the whole situation feels so strange, and instead my nagging unease remains, heavy and persistent.

I sit back, trying to process the minimal information Timmy has given me. It's like a little door has cracked open to a side of him I've never seen before.

I want to trust him, but his lack of transparency gnaws away at me, leaving me suspended in the strange limbo between wanting to push for answers, fearing what those answers might reveal, and fearing how he might react if I continue to push.

The baby shark balloon incident is still fresh in my mind, and I definitely don't want a repeat, even though he assured me it would never happen again.

The night goes on, but the weight of his earlier absence lingers between us, thick and unsettling. And as Timmy settles down onto the mattress beside me, draping an arm around my shoulders, I can't help but wonder what—or *who*—I'm really sitting next to.

LATER IN THE evening

The noxious farts begin.

At first, it's one. And he apologizes. "I'm so sorry. My stomach is a bit messed up."

But then they just keep coming.

They're noisy and they stink like the worst stench I've ever experienced. How a human can produce the smell is unfathomable.

"I'm sorry!" he says. "You make me nervous and it gives me an upset tummy! I only do this around you!"

"Why do I make you nervous?"

"I don't know. You tell me what to do, and you get mad at me. And my ass responds."

"Well, that's weird, but okay," I say. He does have a tendency to blame things on me, I've noticed. Now I guess bodily functions can be added to the list.

I don't think it has anything at all to do with the secretive visitor. And maybe I do make him nervous. I think he can tell I'm getting a little suspicious of his antics, his excuses. If I were him, I'd be a nervous, too.

Over the next few days, the flatulence continues and seemingly starts to bring him joy.

The apologies stop, and his reaction becomes laughter. Not like a lighthearted 'oops' type laughter, but something approaching a gleeful cackle with an edge to it.

He's quickly figured out that it irritates me, and that seems to make him want to do it more.

I have to leave the room more than once, and a couple of times it makes me actually retch so hard I vomit.

In the entire six years I was with my ex, I don't recall hearing—or smelling—him do it once.

Maybe Timmy's sharting out his personality. Hopefully all the bad parts, so he can be the sweet, nice guy I'm in love with on a more consistent basis.

But for now, he's beginning to stink in all the ways.

90

—————

THE ONES WHO GAS YOU UP

he Next Day
He pulls me close, his arm firm around my waist, and with his free hand, he gently tilts my chin until our eyes meet. There's a softness in his gaze I haven't seen in a while, as if he's stripped of his usual bravado and standing before me, vulnerable and bare. His voice lowers, sincere and warm.

"Baby, I know you're such a good person," he says softly, out of the blue. "An amazing person. I want nothing more than to spend the rest of my life with you. You're funny, smart, so beautiful, and insanely talented. You're an incredible writer."

The words, spoken so smoothly, hit me right in the chest. His compliments feel like raindrops on dry soil, sinking deep into places where I've felt starved for validation. And his eyes—those deep blue eyes—reflect nothing but tenderness.

He draws a deep breath, as if gathering his thoughts, and continues, "I know I've done some shitty things, been caught up in stuff I shouldn't have. Made stupid choices." There's a heaviness to his words, but also hope, as though admitting this is a step toward becoming the person he wants to be. "But I know I have so much potential. I really believe that. And I want to live up to it. You know my plans, my designs—I want to bring them to life. I really believe I can do it—with you by my side, supporting me. And I want to be there for you, supporting your dreams, too."

"But... it feels like you're pulling away from what's important to me." My own voice falters for a moment, and it's hard for me to say. "And it's for reasons that don't really matter, things that don't need to get in the way."

His eyes shimmer as they search mine, brimming with unshed tears.

I continue. "It's starting to feel like... like you haven't really changed at all."

A tear slips down his cheek, and before I can respond, he pulls me into a tighter embrace, burying his face in the crook of my neck. His voice becomes thicker with emotion.

"I just... I want you to help pull me up. I never want to drag you down. I know you're better than me, and I want to be better, too. For us. I need your support. With your love, I know I can do this. I love you so much, Margaux. I want to be with you for the rest of my life."

The rawness in his words hits me harder than I expect. I think back to the moments when his excitement about his designs was infectious, how he'd light up talking about the future he wanted to build. Maybe this conversation, difficult as it is, is his way of acknowledging where he's fallen short—and that he knows what needs to change. I start to wonder if he really could shift gears.

Because the truth is, part of me still believes in him. The part of me that fell in love with his passion, his charm, the way he made me feel like we were on the cusp of something incredible. He's right—he can achieve what he wants, if he just puts in the effort. And I've always wanted to help him get there. Maybe that's why I've stuck around through all the chaos, why I've clung to the good moments, believing they outweigh the bad.

"You really mean all of this?" I whisper, my voice barely audible. I want to believe him so badly.

His hand shifts to cup my cheek, his thumb gently stroking my skin. "I've never been more serious about anything in my life. This relationship... it means everything to me. You're my whole world. And I swear, I'll stop doing stupid shit to mess it up. I won't hurt you again. I promise."

For a moment, I search his eyes, looking for even the smallest flicker of insincerity. But all I see is a hesitant, hopeful smile—the kind that makes me think that, for all his flaws, he truly wants to do better, to be better. His arms around me feel solid, like a lifeline pulling me from the undertow of doubt. There's a safety in this embrace, even if it's fragile.

"Okay, baby," I say softly, my hand resting against his chest. "Let's do this. But please... please follow through on what you're saying. If you don't, it'll break my heart."

He presses his forehead against mine, his breath warm and steady. "You have my word. I'll show you how serious I am. No more excuses."

91

TWO-SIDED LOVE TRIANGLE

few days later, Timmy insists on getting into his old Apple ID so he can 'download important media.' He's fixated—it's all he can talk about—and it makes me feel sick. The whole purpose of getting rid of that ID was so people couldn't contact him, including the annoying girl he slept with right before we met. It was his idea in the first place, and it was kind of extreme, but I appreciated the gesture. And now it's like he's trying to undo it. What's so important for him to access in there?

After a rigmarole that consumes our lives for the next week or so, because he manages to lock himself out and neither his cell phone provider nor Apple are able to help him for a while, he finally gets access to his old ID.

There's immediately a ding, and waiting for him is a text from Desperate Girl, announcing it was her birthday the day before, saying how much she wants to meet me and how happy she is for him that he's found his soulmate. This is followed up by a picture of the two of them together. Another where she has her arm around Timmy and they're both smiling.

What gives with this girl?

Timmy told her not to contact him anymore. That he was getting his number changed, and to please respect that. And, less than a month after that conversation, she's sending attention-seeking texts to a 'friend' she knows is engaged. Why would you send a picture of yourself and a guy to that guy when he has a new girlfriend. I can't trust her as far as I can throw her.

Timmy tries to justify it at first. "Oh, she must have been lonely and just reaching out to friends."

But I remind him of the boundary he set, asking her not to contact us, and how she had violated his wishes. That, coupled with her reaching out to people on *her* birthday. Who does that?

He seems to take this at face value. "Yeah, you're right. I guess that is kind of quite a weird thing to do. Well, I'll just ignore it. Here you go, see? Deleted. Are you happy now?" He deletes the messages right in front of me.

"As soon as you snap that SIM card," I say.

"Wait—" he says, frowning, then he shrugs. "Okay, do it." He hands it to me, looking annoyed and tentative, like there's something on it that's really important to him but he can't quite bring himself to say it.

And I snip that SIM card into tiny little fragments. There's no way we're having one more fight about that thing. It was *his* idea to give up his old number, his old Apple ID, to start afresh, away from his bad influences. But he's done nothing but make me feel bad for his own decision. Like somehow it's unfair, that it's something I demanded he do in the first place. I'm making him stick to his self-imposed boundary, though. No more discussions about this stupid SIM card or Apple ID.

I also don't live under a rock, and I'm not a complete moron when it comes to technology. And I know, from experience, that some of your contacts are somehow kind of perpetually stored in the cloud, so even if you've deleted them, their number can show back up. Plus, he does have social media, so anyone from there could contact him on messenger, or Instagram, or even call him via Facebook.

So I'm feeling a bit defeated. So many fights over something that really is a bit of a non-issue.

And I realize a few things. It's great that he's changed his number to avoid certain people reaching out, but his fixation about getting back into that account was way more intense than was normal. Kind of obsessive, even. It's been all he could talk about for a couple of weeks.

What was in there that was so important, that he decided to disregard but then suddenly needed it back?

I have this weird nagging feeling that there's more to his relationship with this hideous girl than he's sharing, or maybe there are others he feels he needs to get in contact with.

It feels like he's omitting something—that something doesn't quite add up. But, from experience now, I know that Timmy has a habit of 'protecting' me from information he thinks would hurt me. And protecting himself by not sharing information with me that I should probably know, that doesn't make him look good.

And then there's just the simple fact that this boils down to trust. There are always ways to betray and lie and deceive, if that's who you are as a person.

If I can trust this guy, my future fiancé, then I don't need to worry about who reaches out to him. He'll always be transparent, like he promised me he would be.

I feel like my trust in Timmy is eroding, that he's given me reasons already to be working from a low base.

But he also tells me that he's everything that mirrors what I want in a relationship—a partner who I can trust, and they respect me, and who I can grow together with. I just need to make sure his actions line up with his words.

LATER IN THE week

Timmy takes off while I'm asleep. Simply up and leaves. He's just gone, no text or anything.

I wake up to an empty bed, and Matty sitting on the couch watching movies. Matty seems to think he's gone to some drug dealer's house, the guy who owns the club we went to when I first moved to the Cay.

It feels so sneaky and underhanded. But when he returns, he makes me feel stupid about it.

"I just wanted to pop down to the Irish bar to see some friends," he says, nonchalantly.

"You drove to the bar after drinking all day? While I was asleep?"

"Yeah," he shrugs, a smirk on his face. "What's your issue?"

I feel like I'm going to explode. Blood pounds in my head and my body hums with discomfort. "It's inappropriate on so many levels!"

He smirks, a cruel gleam in his eye. "I should be able to go out without you, Margaux."

"I agree! I should be able to go out without you too."

He narrows his eyes at the implication.

"But this is something we should be talking about before," I explain. "This is something we should be planning in advance and setting boundaries. Not taking advantage of someone being asleep to decide you want to go. Who the fuck were you talking to, anyway?"

He shrugs. "Just some friends."

My eyes narrow. "Girls?"

"No, all guys." He rolls his eyes. "Man, you're so jealous and inse-cure. It's really unattractive." His eyes are still narrowed, and he just about spits the word out at me.

Suddenly, I feel like I'm on the back foot. Even though he's the one who snuck out of the house and went to the bar while I was sleeping.

Is he fucking kidding me? I feel like ripping my hair out.

I've gone for a walk in the middle of the day before and he's accused me of being on a date, even when I've told him where I'm going beforehand, and I always reply to his deluge of texts and emails and phone calls the entire time I'm gone.

But I go to sleep and he leaves the property, in a vehicle, intoxi-cated, and goes to hang out with other unknown intoxicated people? Supposedly at a random bar?

Talk about a double standard.

But he's drunk, and he's unable to be reasoned with at the best of times, when it comes to him doing something wrong. When it comes to holding him accountable.

I take a deep breath and a very slow exhale.

This will have to wait until morning.

92

MOVING THE PROBLEM, SHIFTING
THE BLAME

"Listen, I have an idea," says Timmy. He pitches it perfectly, his voice smooth and reassuring, like he's thought everything through just for me. "I know that me being around bad influences bothers you," he says, squeezing my hand. "And I get it. I want to do better—for you, for us. So, I've been thinking.... we could move to the other side of the Cay. It's quieter, cheaper over that way. We could probably even swing a beachfront place. And the surf is amazing... it'll be a great place to teach you." His face softens as he leans in closer. "We could work on our stuff—your books, my art, really focus on our relationship without all the other distractions. Just us."

The idea of moving to the other side of Sunset Cay feels like a lifeline. It sounds perfect. Almost too perfect. But I push that nagging thought aside. What writer doesn't dream of a peaceful, visually inspiring place to focus on their craft, far from the noise and distractions? This could be the reset I need—the reset *we* need. And I sure as fuck know we need to get out of Matty's apartment.

We spend the next few hours scrolling through listings together. He's right—rentals on the other side of the Cay are not only affordable, but beautiful. Beachfront units with views of the ocean, the kind of place I've always wanted to live. And it's flattering that Timmy is so eager to start fresh with me, uprooting his life and leaving behind whatever bad influences still tug at him from this side of the Cay. It feels like a new chapter—a chance to escape the noise and chaos. A chance to embrace creativity, time together as a couple. Even a bit of romantic solitude. *Teamwork.*

But a small voice whispers in the back of my mind: *What if it's super lonely out there? Far from everyone and everything you know? What if Timmy acts out?* I push the thought down. This is an opportunity, and I want to believe that Timmy is sincere about making things work between us.

WE CATCH the bus the next morning, excited to see a few of the more promising apartments in person. The ride is long, winding through lush greenery and cliffs that drop into sparkling, turquoise water. We hold hands on the trip, sharing headphones and playing songs for each other. By the time we arrive, the salty breeze feels like a promise. I can already picture us here, far away from the stress, distractions, and judgmental neighbors. And, of course, Matty.

The first apartment we see is in a charming little condo building with a nearly private, pristine beach out back. It's an older building, but the upgrades give it character—a blend of rustic charm and modern touches.

Timmy lights up as we walk through it, bringing the space to life with his ideas. "We'd put the bed here," he says, pointing toward the large window that faces the ocean. "And we could even sleep out on the balcony some nights, under the stars."

I can already see it—us lying under the night sky, listening to the waves crash, Sabre curled up beside us. It feels like magic.

Then we tour a larger apartment community right on the beach. The place is practically a mini-resort, with a giant pool, a fitness center, and even a little convenience store tucked near the lobby. Timmy holds my hand tightly as we walk through the grounds, both of us buzzing with excitement. The apartment itself is quite run down, and the leasing agent explains that it's in foreclosure and the bank may seize it at any time. So while we like the complex, the particular unit doesn't seem like a great fit.

We apply for the first place we saw. I'm already picturing us living there, imagining morning swims and quiet nights under the stars. But the call comes later that afternoon.

"I'm sorry," the leasing agent says. "We just rented it to someone who came to see it a few days ago."

My heart sinks, disappointment heavy in my chest. "Okay," I say, trying not to let it show. "Thanks for letting us know."

Timmy pulls me into a hug, kissing the top of my head. "Don't worry, babe. We'll find something better. I promise." His optimism is contagious, and I allow myself to believe him, even though there's a knot of unease forming deep in my gut.

THE NEXT DAY, we look at another set of apartments in the larger complex. One is on the upper floor, but the moment we step inside, I'm overwhelmed by the clutter—it's furnished, but in a way that makes me think the landlord has just packed it to the brim with all their spare furniture that they don't want, random knick-knacks strewn across every surface. And the bathtub is filled with at least half a dozen very large—thankfully dead—cockroaches.

I wrinkle my nose. "I'm not too sure how Sabre will fare with this upstairs balcony," I say, gesturing toward the railing and the decent-sized drop to the ground floor below. "I can see him zooming out there when he's being silly, thinking he could fly."

Timmy laughs. "Totally. Let's go check out the one downstairs."

The moment we walk into the lower unit, it feels different. This one is much nicer. It's been newly renovated—modern fixtures, fresh paint, and sleek granite tiles throughout the floor plan. The landlord has even added little touches like built-in shower nooks, and a stylish, deep square sink. But it's the view that steals my heart.

Just beyond the sliding door is a patch of grass, a tall chain-link fence, and then the ocean stretching out as far as the eye can see. It feels perfect.

Timmy grins, wrapping an arm around me. "Look at this view, babe. Sabre's going to love it."

My heart swells with excitement. "We have to get this place," I whisper, already picturing Sabre basking in sunlight by the door, watching as the waves roll in and birds frolic in the grass.

I call the landlord immediately, eager to submit our application.

But just as I'm about to fill out the form, Timmy hesitates.

"Um... I don't think you should put my name on the lease," he says, shifting uncomfortably.

"Why not?" For a moment, I think he's planning to have me move out there and then say he's not coming anymore.

He frowns. "My credit's really bad. And if they see my criminal record, we're screwed. It's mostly traffic stuff, but there's some violence stuff in there, and it looks bad."

I've never had to worry about a partner not being able to be on a lease application. For as long as I can remember, whenever I've been in a domestic relationship we've both gone on the lease, no questions asked. I did have someone request a co-signer when I was married to husband number three, but that was on the basis of his credit.

I've never had to worry about a serious partner having four pages of criminal charges and several convictions against them. Just like I've never had to worry about how a serious partner would behave in public—or at least if they weren't having their best moment, my biggest concern would be that they'd just remain sullen and aloof. This is the first time in my entire life that I'm worried about how someone might react to a perceived slight, and whether he might randomly start a fight with someone. Or with me.

My time with Timmy is proving to involve a lot of firsts, some of which are much more fun and interesting than others.

The unease that had been quietly simmering flares up again, but I push it down. I put myself as the primary tenant, and list Timmy as secondary, which means I'm the one who'll go through the intensive screening. It's a workaround, but I figure it will be fine. I hope so.

THE FOLLOWING DAY, we get another call.

"I'm sorry," the landlord says. "Another applicant beat you to it, and I think it's only fair to approach it on a first-come-first-served basis."

I feel crushed. "Okay," I manage, although my voice cracks slightly. "Thanks anyway. And if anything changes, please keep us in mind. We love what you've done to the place."

Timmy pulls me into his arms. "It's okay, babe. We'll find something better," he murmurs into my hair. His words are soothing, and I lean into him, trying to believe it.

But the truth is, I'm starting to feel trapped. We can't stay at Matty's place much longer—my sanity is hanging by a raggedy thread —and the longer this search drags on, the more anxious I become. I can no longer rely on my income statements from my former employer, and I'm going to have to find a landlord understanding of our situation, that I'd be funding the rent through my savings until my writing career starts producing more consistent income, and until Timmy finds a new job.

"I just want to find a place soon," I say quietly. "I'm losing my mind."

"I know, baby," he replies, brushing a strand of hair from my face. "But as long as we're together, everything's going to be fine."

His words are like a balm, soothing the unease clawing at my insides. *He's my partner. My ride-or-die.* And even though the doubts linger, I let myself believe him. Because, at this point, what else can I do?

We have to find a place. And I have to believe that this move will be exactly the fresh start we need. A chance to focus on my writing, to rebuild and augment our relationship, and to escape the chaos.

But, beneath the excitement, burrowed beneath the anxiety, a quiet dread hums, reminding me that isolation can be a dangerous thing. And I can't quite shake the feeling that Timmy knows exactly what he's doing.

93

WHAT DID I JUST DO?

The approval for the apartment feels like a huge relief—at first.

"Good news! Well, for you two and me," the landlord says with a satisfied grin that I can hear through the phone. "The other tenant backed out, as unfortunately they're no longer going to be able to move here from overseas. The place is yours if you still want it."

Timmy beams, wrapping his arm around me. "See, baby? Things are starting to fall into place for us."

I smile back, but it feels tight, forced. Inside, my gut twists into knots. My thoughts are spinning, riddled with what-ifs and worst-case scenarios.

I try not to let Timmy see the flicker of doubt in my expression. The last thing I want is for him to think I don't believe in him—or in us.

Later, in the quiet of night, the anxiety creeps in like an uninvited guest. I wake up in cold sweats, my heart racing as fears crowd my mind.

I lie in bed, staring at the ceiling, Timmy's breath steady beside me, and I try to soothe myself with reason. He promised he won't run away—he's said it over and over. He swears this will be a fresh start for us, away from the distractions and bad influences that seem to follow him on this side of the Cay.

But my gut is tickling at me. I wonder what happens if we break up out there? If it's actually safe to live out there. What if Timmy does run away even though he promises he won't?

But then, if we stay here, he's just around the same old bad influences, and it'll take longer for us to find something else. It'll be far easier for him to get in trouble here, he keeps reassuring me. What he says makes sense. He keeps reminding me that it's easier for him to find himself in trouble on this side of the Cay. The problems out on that side of the coast seem to be things he hasn't gravitated toward to my knowledge, like meth and heroin. I doubt he would be involved with those things after observing their impact on acquaintances and family members, including some of his siblings.

"I've seen what meth and heroin do to people," he says. "That's not me. That'll never be me."

I believe him, mostly. He's never given me a reason to think he'd slide down that path. But still, the worry gnaws at the edges of my mind. What if? What if this isn't the fresh start we need? What if the distance just becomes another hurdle? I shove the thought down, reminding myself that doubts can't build a life—only actions can. And he's been trying, he really has.

Then there's another flicker of hope—I've finally sorted out my health insurance, after weeks of confusion and stress. It's a small victory, but one that makes me feel lighter. I no longer have to panic every time we're driving, worrying that an accident or emergency could leave me bankrupt. It feels like a safety net beneath my feet, a step toward some semblance of stability.

I pull an oracle card. GROW.

It's fitting. Like the universe is nudging me forward, telling me that this is the right path. I need to embrace the change, take the risk, and trust that we'll grow through whatever comes next.

Tonight, things take a rare and sensual turn. Matty, miraculously, is out on a date—something involving a boat ride and dinner, so we know we'll have the apartment to ourselves for at least a few uninterrupted hours.

Timmy's eyes light up with mischievous excitement, and I feel my pulse quicken in response. He's always talked about wanting to try shibari—Japanese rope bondage—and now, finally, we have the time and space.

He pulls out the soft lilac ropes, his hands deft as he begins to tie intricate knots around my wrists, the strands winding their way along my body. The tension is perfect—snug, but not painful. It feels intimate, almost meditative, as he focuses completely on the task at hand, drawing on his experience with ropes from his time as an offshore fisherman. There's something soothing about surrendering control to him in this way, letting the ropes bind me and hold me in place. He snaps a couple of photos with the rope expertly knotted around my breasts.

"You look so beautiful like this," he murmurs, brushing a thumb over my cheek. His voice is low, filled with reverence as he shows me the photo—I have to agree, it looks hot as fuck—and for a moment, I feel like we're the only two people in the world.

With Matty gone and the apartment quiet, it feels like a pocket of peace amidst the chaos. Just us, no distractions. The ropes secure me in place, but for once, I feel free—free from the weight of my worries, from the uncertainty about the apartment, from the fears about what the future holds. It's just me and Timmy, tangled up in something that feels as fragile as it is meaningful.

Afterwards, we lie together, our limbs still intertwined, the ropes loosened but not fully removed. His fingers trace lazy patterns on my skin, and for a brief, fleeting moment, I feel like everything might be okay.

But life, as always, presses on. The next day, it's back to reality—dealing with the truck, getting the paperwork sorted to transfer it into my name. To park the truck in our new building's parking garage, we need to provide a driver's license to match the ownership details, and Timmy doesn't have a license. Plus, he's offered to give the truck to me as a gesture of goodwill, a contribution toward our first couple of months of rent. Of course, being Timmy's vehicle, back payment is owed on the registration, and it needs safety tags which is a challenge with a beater like that. It's another task I take on, knowing that Timmy is leaning on me to handle the logistics. It's exhausting, but I tell myself that it's worth it. That we're building something together, even if it's messy and complicated.

He promises to pay me back. He always does. And I want to believe him, but there's a small part of me that wonders how long I can keep carrying the weight of us both. How long I can keep filling in the gaps, smoothing over the cracks.

Still, I hold onto the moments like last night—the tender ones, the ones where it feels like we're both trying.

94

HOPE FEELS BETTER THAN DOUBT

The barbecue with Rebecca and Jetson feels like a breath of fresh air, a reminder of what normal life can look like. Their beachfront home is nothing short of paradise—a sprawling balcony that stretches right over the water, where the waves crash so close that the mist occasionally drifts over the wooden railings. The air is filled with the mouthwatering aroma of grilling meat, the sweet-and-salty scent of the ocean, and the faint hum of laughter as friends chat and unwind around the fire pit.

It's an eclectic mix of people—locals and visitors, surfers and artists, entrepreneurs and digital nomads—giving the gathering a vibrant energy. There's a sense of community here that I haven't felt in a while, and it feels good to be among people who seem genuinely happy.

Timmy slips seamlessly into the fold. He beams with excitement at the grill, his element, as he pulls out some venison from the freezer bag he packed. "You guys gotta try this," he says, proudly displaying the cuts of meat from the deer he hunted over at Steve's place on Solvana. Watching him light up, sober and engaged, fills me with a sense of relief I didn't realize I needed. It's a glimpse of the man I hoped he could be, the one I still believe in.

He laughs easily, making conversation with everyone, and for once, I don't feel the familiar tightness of anxiety creeping in. He isn't drunk, slurring words, or crossing boundaries. He's just Timmy—playful, social, and full of stories.

Midway through the evening, he wanders off and, after about twenty minutes, comes rushing back, a grin plastered across his face. "There's a bunker under the house!" he announces, his eyes sparkling with childlike wonder. He scrolls through his phone, showing everyone grainy photos of the bunker's dusty interior and cobwebbed corners. His excitement is contagious, and soon people are talking about apocalypse scenarios and the usefulness of secret bunkers. It's one of those silly, spontaneous moments that make gatherings like this so memorable.

Later, we gather around to play some cornhole, and at first, everything is lighthearted. But after I beat Timmy three times in a row, his mood shifts just slightly. It's subtle, but I know him well enough to see it. His eyes narrow ever so slightly, his smile tightens at the edges, and he starts making little jabs.

"You always cheat at everything," he says with a playful grin, but there's something lurking underneath the humor. "Fucking cheater." His words feel like the beginnings of a sulk—like a kid at a birthday party, irritated that things aren't going his way. It's not a tantrum, but it's close enough to make me brace myself for more.

I expect him to escalate, but—whether it's the absence of alcohol or just a good day—he lets it go. The moment passes, and he even manages to laugh it off, throwing his arm around me like a good sport. "You're actually really good at that. I'm so impressed by you. You're good at literally everything you do." He kisses me on the cheek.

For once, the day ends on a high note. No big blow-ups, no arguments, just a pleasant, peaceful day by the beach with friends.

In the days that follow, I throw myself back into my routine—walking to the beach at sunrise, writing, working out. Each morning feels like a small victory. I'm carving out moments of peace amidst the chaos, and it makes me proud that I'm sticking to my goals, especially when Timmy and Matty seem so content to laze around.

When I swing by my apartment to grab a few things, I pull an oracle card. TRUST.

I turn the word over in my mind, contemplating what it means in the context of my relationship with Timmy.

It's been a few good days. Timmy hasn't had a drink, and he seems calmer, more centered. I can see the effort he's making, even in the little things. He's been cooking more, and not just greasy breakfasts, but healthier meals with me in mind. He's started picking flowers again, weaving them into beautiful leis like he used to do when we first got together.

It's only been a few days, but in the grand scheme of our chaotic relationship, a few days without conflict feels monumental. Each small gesture, each sober day, feels like a step in the right direction. And while I know it's too soon to let my guard down entirely, I can't help but feel a flicker of hope growing inside me.

A few days later

The St. Patrick's Day celebration with Rebecca and Jetson cements my hope a little further. It's a cute, festive community event —food stalls, art exhibitions, live music. The kind of laid-back evening that reminds me why I moved here in the first place.

There's alcohol everywhere, but Timmy doesn't touch a drop. He doesn't even seem tempted, which is a relief. Rebecca and I indulge in a few whiskey shots, giggling as the warmth spreads through our chests, but Timmy stays steady, smiling and relaxed.

He even encourages me to enjoy myself. "You deserve it," he says, wrapping his arm around me as we sway to the music.

In this moment, I start to believe that maybe there's real hope for us. Maybe he's turning a corner. Maybe this time, his promises will stick.

His actions, though small, are beginning to align with his words. I remind myself that growth takes time. Maybe love is about seeing the effort, even when the progress is slow.

And for now, I see effort. I feel love. I feel hope.

95

WHO IS BEING PLAYED?

Just after my birthday, I feel compelled to look at his phone again.

And I'm glad I do, because I see that just over a month earlier he texted the tragic girl that wouldn't leave him alone. As in, while he and I were together.

TIMMY:

Yo ho.

I'm out of jail and miss you.

I was bitter that you flew back then dipped… but I was being a dick and sorry

I hope everything is good and my phone has drowned so call Matty.

K love you bye bye.

If you need any of your stuff tell Matty to get a hold of me.

My stomach once again sinks like a stone, my chest feeling crushed. I retch.

From what I can see, she didn't reply directly to his messages.

Four days later, she'd sent him a video. A random GIF, not at all suggestive.

For someone he apparently can't stand, who he says he kicked out of his place, things just aren't adding up. Did he actually kick her out for being 'annoying', or did she leave and he's bitter about it? Both can't be true at the same time. He told me one thing, and texted her another.

I feel upset, I feel betrayed. And I also feel like maybe that's what I deserve for going through his phone. But, he said I could, and if he went through my phone he'd never find anything like this.

The difference is that I mean what I say and am open about things, and yet he seems to live in a world of deception and lies.

I confront him about it.

"What the fuck, Timmy?" I hold out his phone.

He looks at the message and seems genuinely surprised. "I don't even remember sending that. I don't know why I'd even send that to her because it makes no sense. That's not what happened. I kicked her out, she didn't dip out on me. I must have been drunk to send that. I just wanted her to pick up her fucking suitcase because it's been here for ages and has caused enough problems between us already. I just wanted it gone."

"You said you kicked her out for being annoying, but now you miss her? And you're sad that *she* left? After you fucked her?"

"Well no. I don't miss her at all. She's a pain and I don't like spending time with her. But I guess I was trying to be nice, and I figured you can attract flies with honey. If I sent her that, I figured she might finally come and pick her suitcase up." He shrugs. "And, as you know, she did end up picking it up right after I got out of jail. So it's not an issue anymore."

I feel sick, but I also feel sick at myself for being in a relationship where I feel compelled to check my partner's phone on the regular. But it's because of the way he's behaving. Sure, I've taken a peek at prior partners' phones here and there in the past, just in case. But Timmy just seems to embellish and withhold information, and it's in my nature to need to be well-informed. It's also a protection mechanism. I don't trust this situation between him and this person he allegedly can't stand.

"You still messaged her behind my back."

"Sorry, again, like I keep saying, I must have sent it to her when I was drunk. And I was just trying to figure out a way to convince her to get her stuff. I try to be nice to people. I figured that was better than saying 'hey bitch, pick up your things or I'll throw them out on the street.' He rolls his eyes, as if I'm inconveniencing him by asking for the truth. As if I'm being the unreasonable one.

"By changing the course of history in your text? Did you actually kick her out, or did she leave you? Please be honest."

"Oh, I *definitely* kicked her out." He laughs, and there's a cruel edge to it. "She's so fucking annoying. Believe me, I didn't want her here any longer. I can't stand her, actually."

"And you said if she did come back to get her stuff she'd have to suck your dick. That's what you said in an earlier message."

"It's a figure of speech." He rolls his eyes. "I say it to my guy friends, too. Shut up or suck my dick."

I furrow my brow. The words coming out of his mouth aren't computing for me. "I have never ever told any of my friends to suck my dick—or eat my pussy—if they talk. Especially if they're someone I'd actually slept with. That's just insane."

He lets out a frustrated sigh and shakes his head as if I'm a complete idiot. "It's a common saying around here. Calm down."

Now I feel crazy. The rest of the day has been fine. Maybe I shouldn't have said anything.

He hasn't been running off behind my back or anything, and there's no way they've been spending time together. I don't see texts from her saying anything inappropriate. I'm just really hurt that Timmy reached out to someone who he—based on what he told me —can't stand, telling them he misses them. And who he—based on his recounting of events—kicked out of Matty's apartment. But to her, he tells a completely different story.

"So she's this insane that you think you can half suck up to her and she'll do what you want?"

"Something like that," he says, shrugging. "I just wanted her to get out of our lives."

"By proactively contacting her and saying that you miss her, and you were angry because she left your apartment?"

He sighs. "I know, I know. Again, that all made sense to me while I was drinking. I'm sorry. Believe me, if I never see her again I'll be very, very happy. Why would I do anything to fuck up what you and I have? You're the only one for me, and she's a complete mess. I wouldn't touch her ever again with a ten-foot pole. Believe me."

I look at him, but his face reveals no answers. "If you say so."

THE MORNING after I see the message on Timmy's phone, I wake up with a knot in my stomach that feels like it's taken up permanent residence. I try to shake off the lingering sense of betrayal, but the words I read—*"I miss you"*—keep looping in my mind, like an earworm I can't dislodge.

I get out of bed quietly, leaving Timmy sleeping soundly beside me, and shuffle into the kitchen to get a glass of water. Usually, I find it refreshing, but today it does nothing to cut through the fog of unease. I stare out the window of Matty's apartment, watching the world wake up, people going about their business as if everything is normal. But nothing feels normal for me anymore.

Timmy's excuses echo in my mind:

"I was drunk."

"I just wanted her to get her stuff."

"It's better to attract flies with honey."

The words swirl in my thoughts, pulling me deeper into confusion. If she's as annoying as he says, if he really kicked her out and can't stand her, why did he reach out to her? And why does it seem like he's still holding onto some kind of lifeline with her, even if just to keep the door slightly ajar, keeping her on the back-burner in case things don't work out with me? The dissonance between his words and actions is starting to scrape against my sanity like nails on a chalkboard.

When Timmy wakes up, he immediately senses my tension.

He pulls me close, pressing kisses into the crook of my neck, murmuring sweet things that usually make me melt. But today, they feel hollow, like he's trying to smooth over a crack in the foundation with cheap plaster.

"You're still upset, aren't you?" he asks softly, his arms tightening around me.

I nod, not trusting myself to speak without my voice cracking. "It just... it doesn't make sense, Timmy. If she's out of your life, why did you need to text her and say you miss her?"

He pulls away, rubbing his eyes like a child who's woken up too early. "I already told you. I was drunk. It was just to get her to pick up her stuff, babe. That's it." His tone carries a trace of frustration, like I'm overcomplicating things.

"Okay, but it just feels... off." I pause, trying to find the right words. "If I did that—if I texted some guy from my past and said I missed him—you would lose your mind. And you know it."

He stiffens, his frustration now visibly bubbling to the surface, as if I've caught him in an awkward truth. "You're really going to hold that over me forever?" he asks, as if it happened years ago, as if I hadn't just noticed it the day before. "It was a stupid text. It meant nothing. I thought we were past this."

It feels like every time he's upset about something, he gets to keep mentioning it over and over again. But if I dare to bring something up, I have like a five-minute window before I'm 'going on about something that happened ages ago' and 'rehashing the past'.

I swallow hard, feeling the familiar push and pull—the yearning to let it go versus the nagging suspicion that letting it go means ignoring my gut. Part of me wants to believe him, wants to push away all the discomfort and just enjoy the good moments. But the other part of me, the part that's been burned before, knows that ignoring the signs only leads to deeper wounds.

He senses my hesitation and changes tactics. He picks up Sabre, showering him with exaggerated affection. "You know what you need? Bacon and eggs," he announces, setting Sabre down gently. "Let's start the day off right."

I nod, grateful for the distraction, even though the pit in my stomach hasn't gone away. "I'll get it this time," I say. As I crack eggs into a hot pan, I focus on the hiss and pop of bacon. Cooking feels like the only thing I can control right now. The food sizzling in front of me, at least, follows predictable rules.

LATER, we decide to drive up to the other side of the Cay. The scenic route is supposed to relax me, but the car ride becomes yet another battle. I can't play the music I want without him making snide comments. He complains about my choices, saying I have 'terrible taste', that I 'always play the same songs', and acting like he's doing me a favor by tolerating them. When I refuse to stop at bridges for him to jump off, his irritation deepens, the air in the car thickening with tension.

Then, at a surf store, he tries to shoplift right in front of me. I catch him about to slip a pair of sunglasses into his board shorts. "Timmy, what the hell are you doing?" I hiss, my heart racing.

"Relax," he mutters. "It's no big deal."

"Yes, it is!" I whisper fiercely. "Put them back."

He rolls his eyes, but reluctantly returns the sunglasses to the display. "You're such a buzzkill," he mutters under his breath, and I bite my tongue to keep from snapping.

At the next stop—a coffee shop—he tries again. This time, it's a cute espresso mug he has his eye on. I grab his arm before he can casually wander out of the store with it.

"Seriously?" I whisper, glaring at him. "What's wrong with you?"

His eyes darken, his expression shifting into that familiar look of irritation mixed with defiance. "You're overreacting. I know you like to drink out of cute coffee cups."

"That I pay for," I say, through gritted teeth.

Apparently, me asking him not to shoplift is wildly offensive, and he spends the rest of the time being sullen and sulky, snipping at me over everything he can find to cause dissatisfaction.

I feel the urge to scream, to jump out of the car and run as fast as I can away from all of this.

It's becoming all too much—the texting, the lying, the petty theft, the constant conflict. We've never been able to come to this side of the Cay without having a big fight.

The chaos clings to me like a second skin, suffocating and relentless. And no matter how hard I try to keep us afloat, it feels like Timmy is dead set on tearing our flimsy raft apart piece by piece.

WHEN WE FINALLY GET BACK TO Matty's, I'm emotionally drained, teetering on the edge of collapse. I don't even have the energy to confront him anymore. Instead, I retreat into the bathroom, close the door, and sit on the toilet with the lid closed. Tears sting my eyes, but I force them back, refusing to cry.

This is all too much. The jail situation, the courts, an apartment I'm paying for but can't live in, having to stay at Matty's if I want to be with Timmy, and now some skank that he's reaching out to behind my back. This has taken a wild turn and not in a good rollercoaster kind of way. My gut is churning, I'm grinding my teeth, and I feel on edge.

And whenever I stick up for myself, he gets even more enraged. I'm already upset about this texting situation, and he's mad at me for being mad at him about it. So now he's piling on thing after thing. Trying to engage in risky behaviors, putting me down, making excuses for himself, and getting mad at my reaction to his very questionable actions. I can't even imagine how he would react if he saw a text where I said 'I miss you' to some guy I'd just slept with right before we met, and then made the excuse I was drunk. He'd completely lose his mind, more than he already has.

But I'm just meant to sit here and take it. And smile sweetly. And believe the words coming out of his mouth that his actions don't match. I'm supposed to believe that he really cares for me and nobody else, and that the message had no feelings behind it. I'm supposed to believe that everything is fine.

And part of my body and my brain want to believe that. Because it's so much more comfortable than constantly being on edge. About worrying about what he's doing, and how he might not be acting in my best interest. Because every thought I have about him, about us, is how to keep strengthening our relationship. How to let these feelings go. Building us out of this hole that's started to be dug. And it's starting to feel like he's standing right behind me with his own shovel.

I take a deep breath, pull out my phone, and scroll mindlessly, searching for anything to distract me from the turmoil swirling inside. But no matter how hard I try, the weight of everything—his lies, his temper, his risky behavior—presses down on me like a heavy fog.

When I return to the living room, he's sitting on the couch, scrolling through his own phone as if nothing is wrong. He looks up and gives me a half-smile, as if to say, *See? Everything's fine. Why are you making a big deal out of nothing?*

But everything isn't fine. It hasn't been for a long time. Maybe it never really was.

And yet, I cling to the hope that the move will change things. Maybe being away from Matty's influence will give us the space we need to rebuild. Maybe things will calm down once we have our own place, once the distractions are gone, and it's just us, working on our shared future.

Because if I don't believe that... what else is there? If this relationship falls apart, what will I have left?

96

HEAVY LIFTING

Because Timmy is banned from my apartment building and the hundred-yard radius around it, I have to move, well... everything, myself. And I don't really know anyone else who could help, unless I want to hire an expensive moving company, so it's on me. Luckily, I still don't have too many belongings, so I repack my four suitcases, as well as a couple of backpacks for the additional items.

The mattresses are big and bulky, and they're a pain to move by myself.

I slide the top one off, and sitting on the lower mattress is Timmy's stupid bone necklace. The one that looks like a human spine. I thought the cops had taken it, but I guess it's been here all along, secretly taunting me. My stomach churns at the sight of it, and I feel bile rising in my throat.

That stupid fucking thing.

I immediately think about the picture of his skanky 'friend' wearing it around her neck with nothing else.

Disgusting.

I wrap it in a trash bag and immediately throw it out.

It has bad juju all over it, and I want nothing to do with it.

I feel slightly guilty as I do, despite everything that transpired. He really liked that stupid thing. But he also let random skanks wear it while topless, and he wore it the day he attacked and nearly killed me.

So, it really did have to go.

I yank the mattresses to the door one by one and load them onto the luggage cart. It's almost impossible to get them balanced and stable on the cart. On more than one occasion, the mattresses tilt sideways and completely block the hall.

The bone necklace flashes through my thoughts again—that stupid fucking thing tangled in all its symbolism. That tragic girl's smug, half-naked grin sears into my mind, Timmy's necklace hanging between her breasts. My fingers itch from just having touched it, and I sanitize my hands. Tossing it into the trash felt like a small exorcism, a desperate attempt to cleanse something rotten between us.

But still, a tiny voice in the back of my mind needles me—what will he say if I confess that I found it and that I threw it out? What if the absence of that dumb thing becomes yet another wedge between us?

It's not just the necklace—it's the fear of what it represents. A secret world he carries with him, made up of bad decisions, reckless behavior, and ghosts of women he swore meant nothing.

I shake the thought away, nearly losing control of the cart in the process. The mattress shifts again, tilting dangerously to one side, blocking the narrow hallway. I grit my teeth, pushing it back into place, my arms burning from the strain. There's no one here to help —just me, doing this ridiculous move alone. A neighbor peeks out from their door, but they quickly retreat back inside without offering a hand. Typical.

I stop a couple of times, willing myself not to give up, but eventually I get them all loaded up and I wheel them down the hallway. Somehow, I manage to cram them into the elevator, through the lobby, and out onto the street, down the sidewalk, until I get to Timmy, a hundred or so yards away from the building.

"Got it?" he asks, sliding the mattresses off the cart with

surprising ease. He works fast, strapping them to the top of the vehicle with practiced efficiency, the ratchet straps whining under the tension. He's always good at this kind of thing—handling the physical stuff, solving problems when he's sober. And it's these moments that remind me why I love him, why I keep choosing him, despite all the chaos. When it's good, it's really good. That said, how much easier this whole move would have been if Timmy could have helped with the first part!

I go back upstairs to grab the remaining bags. The apartment feels hollow, stripped of my things and my plans. It was supposed to be a sanctuary, a place where I could write, thrive, and live the dream life I'd always imagined. But instead, it became just another failed attempt at stability. And it's not the apartment's fault.

The truth is, I knew what I was getting into with Timmy, even if I tried to convince myself otherwise. I could've stayed here, alone, in this overpriced little box. But that's not what I wanted, not really. I wanted love, companionship, adventure—and I've got all that with Timmy, even if it's wrapped in layers of complications.

I exhale deeply, letting the air fill my lungs before slowly releasing it. A wave of anxiety sweeps through me. What if moving doesn't change anything? What if the new apartment just becomes another trap, another place for him to spiral and for me to feel stuck?

But I ninja kick those thoughts down. We have a plan. We're getting out of Matty's cramped, chaotic apartment. We'll finally have our own space—just the two of us. No more third-wheel roommates blaring YouTube videos about excavating septic tanks. No more awkward mornings tiptoeing around cigarette smoke and greasy bacon.

Taking a final look around what was meant to be my dream apartment, I can't help but feel wistful. It definitely wasn't a big space, and was terribly overpriced, but it would have been nice to have enjoyed the amenities more. There definitely was some weird cultish obsession with regular human levels of noise, but Timmy contributed to the situation with his ridiculous behavior.

If I hadn't met him, I certainly would still be there, at least for now. But, I had a choice to make, and I've chosen Timmy. The one who loves and cares for me, who takes me on adventures, who believes in my dream of being a bestselling writer.

My chest is full of pressure and I take a giant breath and exhale as I close the door behind me one final time. It seems surreal, but at the same time, at least we're no longer going to be staying on the floor of Matty's cramped bedroom. We'll have our own place to focus on our work, side by side. Ride or die partners for life. And the apartment itself is nice, maybe a bit bigger than this one. And the amenities are nice, too. It feels like we're trading up in a few ways. The area is more than a bit sketchy, but as long as we stick together, we'll be fine.

The finality of leaving my apartment sinks in as I close the door one last time and hear the keypad beep, locking the door to what was supposed to be my fresh start. It's a bittersweet goodbye, a place I never got to fully enjoy—like a good meal abandoned halfway through. Sure, it had its quirks—the bizarre noise complaints, the overpriced rent, the neighbor wars. But it was mine, and now I'm walking away from it, dragging my life along on a cart, one heavy load at a time. And it's all because I chose Timmy. I chose love, with all its jagged edges and roller coaster loops, over my original dream.

I grip the cart handle harder, as if holding on tighter will keep my mind from wandering into places it shouldn't go.

Eventually, I get everything loaded into the elevator, sweat sticking to my skin, frustration bubbling under the surface. My mind races with a running list of everything that could have been easier if Timmy hadn't been banned from the building. If he hadn't dangled his dick off the balcony or screamed at strangers in the night. If he hadn't gone ballistic and turned my quiet retreat into a battleground, threatening to murder me, hurting me physically and scarring my mind.

But no use dwelling on what could have been. I push through the lobby, ignoring the curious glances from the doorman as I struggle with the load. When I finally make it to the curb, I feel a knot loosen in my chest as I see Timmy waiting for me. He's smiling, a cigarette dangling from his lips, already climbing into the back of the truck.

When the truck is loaded and secure, he flashes me a grin. "See? Told you I'd help."

I smile back, though the words I want to say get stuck in my throat.

I want to remind him that it would've been easier if he hadn't gotten us kicked out in the first place.

But I don't. What's the point? We're moving forward now, and I don't want to drag old fights into the next chapter.

I return the cart to the lobby, and with a final glance over my shoulder, I return to Timmy, who's waiting eagerly for us to leave town.

WHEN WE ARRIVE at the new place about an hour later, Timmy throws open the truck door and surveys the building like a conqueror inspecting his new domain. It's not fancy, but the upgrades really are nice, as well as the view, and it's a damn sight better than Matty's. I'll take any win I can get at this point.

"Not bad, is it?" Timmy says, giving me a playful nudge as he surveys the beach outside. "It's got potential."

I laugh, the sound surprising me. For the first time in weeks, I feel a sliver of excitement for what's ahead. Maybe this really is the reset we need. A place where we can focus on each other, on our work, on building something real together. I choose to believe in that possibility, at least for now. Because, honestly, what else can I do?

We unload the truck, working together in a surprisingly smooth rhythm. He's in a good mood, cracking jokes, making me laugh. And while we unload everything, I see the version of Timmy I fell in love with—the one who makes everything feel like an adventure, even moving a couple of mattresses.

Once the last of the bags are inside, we flop down on the mattresses, exhausted but content. Timmy wraps me in his arms, kissing my forehead.

"We did it, baby," he murmurs, his voice soft and full of promise.

"It's just us now. And everything's going to work out just how we planned."

I tilt my head up and kiss him back. And then, exhausted, I close my eyes, letting myself believe, for just a little while, that everything will be okay. That this new apartment really will be the fresh start we've been waiting for.

97

THE SURFER WHO DOESN'T SURF

Dex

I hack into her search history.

She seems to have been spending a lot of time on housing websites.

Oh no, she's picked the other side of the coastal range. It's gorgeous out there, but it's really remote. They have a real small-town vibe there, and if you're not part of the greater community through family, they're not going to accept you. She's really going to struggle with that.

It's as clear as day. He's trying to isolate her.

She has no idea what she's getting into.

She'll need a vehicle to get everywhere, and won't just be able to walk around without Timmy. It's a known drug haven, a place people go when they have no hope left. Lots of encampments, lots of meth.

This is going to be a fucking nightmare.

But I can't exactly call her and say 'hey, I was stalking you online and see that you're looking to move to the sketchiest part of Sunset Cay. And no, you can't live on the beachfront because that guy you're crazy for, and think is your soulmate, is trying to isolate you.'

That would not be well-received, and she'd never want to speak with me again.

I need more concrete evidence. I mean, I don't want him to hurt her anymore. But I need him to dig his own grave in a way, just by being himself.

I've been researching stats on scumbags like hum, and the worst part of it is they're just not likely to change. They can go through workshops and programs and to meetings every day for the rest of their lives, but they have to really want to commit. They need professional psychotherapy and multiple sessions a week.

And guys like this Timmy trash pile also tend to escalate in their behavior. Given he tried to kill her so soon after meeting, I'm really concerned.

But she seems so happy, and it seems like their communications have settled down a bit now they're working on a shared project— finding a new apartment so he can physically isolate her. God damn it! Circular logic.

She thinks he's the one. She thinks he's really improved. She complimented him via text and he seemed appreciative. Lots of GIFs flying back and forth which go from cute to gradually more suggestive.

Gross. I look away.

I mean, if she was sending them to me, it would be one thing. My cock twitches at the thought as I watch their conversation grow more sexual in nature.

I really need to focus on fixing the situation with this Temu Timmy, the surfer who doesn't surf. I'll be monitoring his every move like a hawk. Logging every keystroke. Tracking him via his camera. He'll have no idea, but I have a feeling that in addition to everything else, he's being duplicitous to Margaux, and we can't have that.

She deserves someone she can trust, the way she trusts me.

Someone just like me, in fact.

The fact her brother would never speak to me again is starting to wane in its impact. We've drifted apart so far now that I already speak with her way more than him. Besides, she's way cuter. So you could say I 'won in the divorce' of it all, if you will.

I check my watch. Fuck, I've been reading their back and forth for way longer than I thought, and I need to pack up and get to work.

Not sit here all day being a voyeur, spying on a girl who will never be mine.

But who, regardless, I'm committed to protect.

98

WHY TAKE CHANCES WHEN I CAN PANIC INSTEAD

I'm excited to be moving in, but it's bittersweet. Our time here already has a complication—Timmy had agreed a while ago to help Steve paint his barn over on Solvana, where his house is located. And Steve inconveniently booked his PTO for a few days after our move, and says he can't change the timing.

So we begin unpacking the essentials, arranging things just enough to make it livable, though it still feels temporary. The walls are bare, the furniture sparse, and the whole apartment feels more like a pit stop than a home. It's hard to invest fully when, in a few short days, I know we'll just have to leave everything behind for a bit. I want to nest, to make it feel like home, but we don't have time.

There's a nagging voice in the back of my mind telling me that maybe it's jumping the gun to get the apartment set up properly yet, anyway. Timmy's been quite volatile lately. But I know he's just stressed about the move. God knows I am, too. What if this place is just another temporary mirage of stability—we've only been together a few months, but how many 'reset moments' have we had already? What if I'm just wasting money investing in something that he'll find a way to ruin?

It's exhausting trying to stay positive. The weight of all the upheaval—moving out of my original apartment, crashing at Matty's and all that entailed, and now setting up this new space—is taking its toll.

I tell myself that being here is better than Matty's chaos, though resentment still simmers beneath the surface. It's hard not to think about what I gave up—my original apartment, with all its promise of peace and space for writing. But I know that's something I just need to get over, and that's a chapter I have to close. If I keep carrying that resentment, Timmy and I will never work. I know that much.

It's frustrating not being able to talk about any of this with anyone. I want to vent, to cry on a friend's shoulder, but I feel, in a weird way, like I have to protect Timmy's reputation. It feels wrong to expose all the messy details, even though they're eating me alive. He's not just some villain—he's the person I chose to stand by. So, instead, I carry it all inside, waiting for the moment we get back from Steve's to start therapy.

Then, as if the moving stress isn't enough, Timmy starts obsessing over the air conditioner. It becomes an entire thing that he can't stop talking about. "This air is making me sick," he insists, pacing the room, his hands rubbing his chest. "I swear, it's blowing some weird chemical or powder. My chest feels so tight. Like I'm going to have a heart attack."

At first, I try to reason with him. "It's just a dusty filter. We'll clean it. It's probably all it is."

But he shakes his head. "No, this isn't just dust. There's something wrong with the air. I can feel it. Like it's poisoning me. This is an older building, and there might be asbestos or lead paint or something."

I glance at the bed, noticing a faint residue on the sheets. It's barely there, but enough to make me wonder. The air conditioning unit could definitely use a cleaning, but Timmy's insistence that it's some kind of silent killer feels over the top. Still, the way he talks about his symptoms—how his chest aches, how he can't breathe properly—it starts to creep into my own mind. I find myself waking up with a tightness in my chest, questioning if I'm feeling something real or if I'm just absorbing his anxiety.

The next day, the air conditioning paranoia morphs into the perfect excuse.

"I don't think I can go to Steve's," Timmy says, sounding half-apologetic. "My chest feels fucked. If I go, I'll just be in agony the whole time. It's probably safer if we stay here and figure out the air conditioning situation first."

I sigh, torn between relief and guilt. I don't want to go either, but the trip is booked.

"Timmy, we kind of have to go." I'm surprised to hear myself say it, but Timmy's been adamant that he needs to be there for his friend, so I try to support him to do what he's been saying is the right thing, despite my own objections. "Steve's counting on you, and we need the money. You know how tight things are."

"I know," he groans, pressing a hand to his chest dramatically. "I'm just saying... I have a really bad feeling about this trip."

His words send a chill down my spine, stirring up my own doubts. I've felt uneasy about this trip from the beginning, and now it feels like Timmy's bad vibe is rubbing off on me. But backing out hasn't been an option until now, according to Timmy, despite me asking several times, so I try to take the higher road rather than putting my own selfish wants first.

Steve calls while we're mulling it over, and Timmy answers with a pained voice, like he's on the verge of collapse. "Hey man, I'm not doing so good. My chest is acting up, and I think it's the air conditioner in our apartment. I really don't know if I can make it."

On the other end, Steve's voice is calm but firm. "Look, Timmy. I need you, man. I'm counting on you to be here. The air over here is fresh, way better than whatever's going on with that air conditioning unit. You'll feel better the second you get here. Trust me."

Timmy looks at me, torn between guilt and self-pity. I see the wheels turning in his mind—he's balancing his discomfort with his loyalty to Steve. He groans again, rubbing his chest like the weight of the decision is too much to bear.

"I don't know, man," Timmy says. "I really don't."

"Come on, Timmy," Steve urges. "We've already booked and paid for the flights. I need you, and I'll cover your expenses while you're here, I promise. And I'll pay you well, like we've discussed."

Timmy hangs up the phone with a heavy sigh, his eyes narrowing. "We'll go, but like I said, I have a really bad feeling about this trip."

The words settle like a fog over the room, thick with the weight of unspoken fears.

I shift uncomfortably. "Well, you said it yourself—if we stay here, we're just going to spiral. We need the money Steve's offering. And the fresh air will do us good."

He looks at me, conflicted, before finally nodding. "You're right. We'll go. But the moment we get back, we're figuring out what's wrong with this apartment. I swear, I'm not living here if the air conditioning is blowing asbestos or something."

The way he says it sends a shiver down my spine. His fixation on the air conditioner seems irrational, but there's something in the way he clings to it that unsettles me. It's like a manifestation of something deeper—his fear of losing control, of spiraling back into chaos. Like he can't just stay still, that he always has to find the next drama.

"Okay," I whisper. "We'll figure it out when we get back. One thing at a time."

Later that evening, I lie in bed, listening to the hum of the air conditioner. My mind churns with thoughts I can't quite pin down. What if this trip is a mistake? What if the air conditioner *is* actually blowing in something dangerous, and we're slowly poisoning ourselves? What if this move, this relationship, this life I'm trying to build here, is all doomed to fall apart?

Beside me, Timmy's breath rises and falls in the rhythm of sleep. For now, he's calm. Peaceful, even. I reach out and trace the outline of one of his tattoos, feeling a strange mixture of love and fear. We're in this together, for better or worse. And maybe, just maybe, getting out of town for a bit will help us reset.

But the doubt gnaws at me, refusing to let go.

I close my eyes, whispering a silent prayer that the trip to Steve's will be uneventful, that the apartment isn't filled with invisible poisons, and that Timmy and I will figure out how to make this work. Because I'm in too deep now.

99

IF I CANNOT SMOKE IN HEAVEN
THEN I SHALL NOT GO

Timmy and I had talked long and hard about our move to this area of Sunset Cay, and he'd sworn that he'd stay close in the evenings, promising we'd settle into the neighborhood together.

But as soon as we move, I realize it's patently untrue. Maybe those were his intentions prior to our relocation, but as soon as we move in, Timmy keeps leaving the apartment for cigarettes. Ten o'clock. Eleven o'clock. Midnight. We're only days in, and he's already slipping out like it's a compulsion.

Each time, it's 'just for a quick smoke'—yet it never is. Fifteen minutes, thirty minutes. Much longer than it takes to smoke one cigarette. And that's part of the problem. He has no money to buy cigarettes, so he has to prowl the streets for someone willing to give him one or bum a drag from—gross, mixing with random people in a neighborhood that feels more dangerous with each passing night.

I don't want him walking around chatting with people in the middle of the night. I'm worried about him drifting toward something unsavory, unknowingly stumbling into the worst corners. This place hums with a strange energy after dark—a gathering of those who didn't find a way out or who never intended to. Right before we moved, a teenager was shot in the head at the beach park right beside our apartment building, and apparently, it wasn't a rare occurrence. It's a jarring new normal that I'd rather not get used to.

But I can see him warming to it, slipping into a new rhythm, discarding all the promises he made to me like they never meant a damn to him. I wish he'd feel the unease I feel, the sinking feeling I get every time the door swishes shut behind him, the keypad beeping like an eerie alarm reminding me everything's not okay. And I really wish that, to him, I was more important than a cigarette.

He doesn't seem to understand why it bothers me, why I'm so against him walking around this neighborhood at night. But I'd feel the same way in other parts of the Cay.

I'm not particularly worried that he's out looking for women—most of them out here are at least fifty or sixty years old and missing half their teeth—but this is a dangerous neighborhood surrounded by drug dealers and users, and, as the saying goes, nothing good happens after midnight.

In many ways, I wish we lived in a complex that wasn't smoke-free, and that he could just go out onto a balcony and smoke like he did back at Matty's place. I don't miss the stench of tobacco by any means, and I don't miss passively smoking by being around him, but I just don't like him going out to the street at night without me. From my standpoint, it's just not an appropriate thing to do.

For the next few days we argue. We argue about him going out for cigarettes, we argue about him not getting out of bed until the afternoon, we argue about the trip to the island to help his friend, we argue about arguing. He cries. I cry. I try to explain things to him over the next few days, but he seems to be oblivious, like he either doesn't understand, or he does and he pretends not to. Every argument boils over into more tears, and no progress is made.

My anxiety is peaking thinking about the upcoming trip to Solvana. I'm so sad that we can't just be here and figure out a healthier new normal and get everything in the apartment properly set up. The thought of traveling with a cat adds further stress.

I can barely bring up the upcoming trip without another fight. He knows I'm upset, and I can tell he is, too. But he feels this obligation to help his childhood friend. I kind of get it—Steve's PTO is scheduled for specific days when they can get it done—but the dates had moved around a few times, and I'd assume there would be more flexibility than there's proving to be.

It's just a really inconsiderate and inconvenient time to be traveling, but at least Timmy will make some money for us by doing it. That's the only consolation. I could really use some help with the rent and day-to-day living expenses.

Still, his behavior leaves me feeling lonelier than ever. This was meant to be *our* place. The location we were coming to work on our art, and our relationship. Instead, I'm left sitting alone at night while he gallivants around, smoking and doing goodness knows what else. I never would have moved there if I knew he'd act this way. And he knows that. We had extensive conversations about how this was a fear of mine, and each time, he reassured me I had nothing to worry about.

A FEW DAYS *later*

We drive to the opposite shore, hopeful for a refreshing change of scene.

As soon as we get over the hill, however, his personality changes again. His face shifts, and his energy grows tense and bristling. It's like a light switch every time we get to this part of the coast. I don't know if it's because it brings back difficult memories, or what it is, but Timmy just really seems to step into a different version of himself when we get over here, and it's one I don't particularly care for. His lightheartedness falls away, replaced by something else, an edge that feels almost dangerous. It's almost as if memories of the past haunt him here, ghosts that come alive when he sees these familiar places from his childhood. I should have known better and suggested something else. But he was insistent on visiting surf shops to check out their latest goods, and so I braced myself for it—there was a futile hope within me that, for once, we could just come here without arguing.

"Look!" Timmy exclaims. His sudden shout jolts me from my thoughts. He's in a chipper mood again, thank goodness, yesterday's arguments once again swept away by a comfortable sleep.

I glance up from my computer, my heart jumping, and there he is, shirtless, covered in black marker scribbles. He's drawn a giant face all over his torso, his nipples turned into makeshift eyes, and there's a giant tongue that extends down to his bellybutton.

It actually looks quite disgusting, like a crude, mischievous child has somehow got hold of a Sharpie and gone to town on him.

"Um, wow," I say. "That tongue looks a bit like a penis, by the way." He has a total dick on his torso. Like... why?

"Ahaha! I know!" Timmy cackles. He goes and looks at himself in the mirror, posing and continuing to crack up, as if he's both proud of, and delighted by, his masterpiece.

"Take a picture!" he demands. He poses while I snap a few shots and send them to him just to keep him happy.

He marches off to do laundry, still shirtless and covered in his 'artwork', and returns a short time later, looking shocked, "Oh shit! I forgot about this!" He chuckles, glancing down at his makeshift tattoos. "No wonder I was getting funny looks! People around here might be mad and think I was making fun of their tattoos."

I take a deep breath, feeling the irony of it. He's learning the new neighborhood quickly, but in ways that make me anxious, watching him take on its quirks and push its limits. It's the kind of behavior that might seem a bit odd but generally harmless in a different setting, but here it feels like he's courting attention from people who could be dangerous. He's spent so much time warning me about the people that live in this area that it feels quite hypocritical.

For the rest of the day, he carries the giant stuffed baby shark toy around the apartment complex, as if it's his badge of honor, Sharpie still smeared across his chest. People stare, some nod in amusement, while others glance at him with looks of concern and disdain. It's as though he's claiming his space here, doing whatever he can to make himself known. And even though he's in good spirits, there's something unsettling in the way he's acclimating, blending into the wrong rhythms.

It's strange behavior, but at least he's in a good mood, so I don't really question it. Clearly, he wants attention and so he's acting out. But it's not in a bad way, just a weird way, so I leave it alone.

There are worse things that he's done, and I have bigger fish to fry.

Inwardly, I'm a mess. The trip looms in my mind, full of what-ifs. This was supposed to be a time to settle, to start afresh. But everything seems to pull us in a different direction, scattering any hope for stability. He's adapting to the chaos, while I'm losing my footing, leaving me wondering whether this is a new normal I can even survive.

100

PENGUINS & PROMISES

he Day of the Trip

    I'm now beyond stressed that we need to go to help Steve to paint a barn before we're even properly moved in.

The one saving grace is that Sabre can at least come with us.

But I'd really like to stay here, set up our apartment and rest. I'm resentful that we don't get the opportunity to do that. It's delaying me from setting up my writing routine, and it's delaying Timmy from setting up his own routine, which he so desperately needs.

Everything feels out of sync, like wearing clothes that don't quite fit. I know it's just a temporary visit, but my mind keeps circling back to the apartment we haven't had time to properly set up. I crave structure, order, and a fresh start—something that seems impossible when everything is in flux. I can feel the weight of missed opportunities piling up. Every day we spend away from our new home feels like a step further from the life I imagined, the routine, the nest, I so desperately want to build with Timmy. And I know he needs that, too, even if he won't admit it.

Timmy's obsession with hunting takes over almost immediately, the moment we get to Solvana. Every other sentence is about shooting another deer or which rifle to use, and what a great hunter he is. His eyes light up at the idea of the hunt, and for a moment, I see the version of him that's full of life and excitement. But the shifts are quick, almost jarring. It's like he's clinging to these little moments of joy to avoid confronting the deeper chaos bubbling just beneath the surface.

Timmy and Steve spend hours out painting the structure, and I stay inside writing and watching TV. Timmy and I are staying in a small unit off to the side of the main house, with its own little kitchen, bathroom and living room. The bedroom is up a steep staircase, which is really more like a ladder.

The setting is beautiful, but it just feels off.

In the moments the guys come inside for a drink break or a meal, I can't handle some of the stupid comments that come out of Steve's mouth. He's so sexist, so misogynistic, little comments rolling off his tongue, making me more irritated with every encounter. He'd never dare make those types of comments in front of his wife, who is away for the next few days. But for some reason, he has no problem saying these things in front of me.

But I bite my tongue—it's not worth a fight. Instead, I focus on my writing and count the days until we can leave.

The store here on the island is super expensive, but I feel like I really need to eat healthy. My body isn't feeling great after all the greasy crap on offer at Matty's place. I need vegetables in my life.

So I spend hundreds of dollars on produce and other food items–there's really no other option. You can get things delivered by Amazon, but it takes a few days longer than usual. I fill up the fridge with produce and meats. Timmy's food stamp money for the month is already long gone, so, as usual, all the grocery costs come out of my savings. So does money for gas when we drive around the island, snacks, everything. It's all on me.

Steve invites us over to the main house for some dinners, which are nice. But I'm just feeling really off kilter. I need to be in my own space where I can feel comfortable, where I can set things up the way I want them.

This is clearly temporary, living at Matty's felt really temporary, and because of what happened at my first apartment here, that felt temporary, too. Like an extension of the purgatory I was feeling back in San Francisco. I'm slowly losing my mind, and I just need some sense of stability.

"I can't wait until we get back, babe," I say.

"I know, me too," says Timmy, kissing me on my head. "Soon enough. Just a few more days."

For some reason, he also barely wants to have sex while we're at Steve's. We're in a totally separate building, so it's not the noise factor. But his sex drive has almost disappeared, and I feel like a nuisance for initiating anything. I hate being rejected, and he's just not reciprocating my energy. Everything just feels... off.

A couple of days during our visit, while Steve is working, I get my hopes up because Timmy suggests we go on a few drives so he can show me around the island.

He takes me on a scenic drive along the coast, and the views are breathtaking. Waterfalls shimmer in the distance, and we stop at a secluded beach where a river winds into the sea. We snap photos, trying to capture the fleeting beauty of the moment, as well as some just of the two of us. For a little while, things feel okay again—almost normal. Almost good.

He takes us to another park, and we visit a monument.

We fuck against a tree, Timmy behind me, my arms and chest pressed into the bark. We're on a steep hill overlooking the ocean and a small island archipelago adjacent to Solvana.

He takes me to a few more beaches where we look for pretty shells.

It's all nice bonding time, and I feel closer to Timmy. Maybe this trip wasn't such a bad idea, after all.

"You are my penguin," he says randomly as we drive along a gorgeous, winding coastal road flanked by steep, emerald green hills to one side and sparkling turquoise water on the other.

"Your penguin?" I ask, quirking a brow.

"Penguins have one mate for life, and you're mine. I never want to be with anyone else. You're my person, and nothing can ever come between that. So you never have to worry about me even looking at another girl again. Because you're it for me."

I like his words, yet I have some reservations based on other stuff he's said and done. I weigh up the situation and decide to press a little further. "But what about when you said that you still get to look at other girls and say 'yeah, you!'? What about when you said you still wanted to be able to flirt? What about the times I've seen your head pivot like a ceiling fan when a girl walked past?"

His expression flickers with mild annoyance and some confusion. "Was I drunk all those times?"

I think back to each situation and nod. "Well, you'd definitely been drinking, but that's not really the point, Timmy."

He nods as well. "Listen, you really are my penguin. You don't have to worry about any of that. And I'm sorry for what happened in the past. That stuff didn't mean anything. You're it for me, I love you, and you never have to worry about me looking at anyone else ever again."

His words are comforting, soothing, and I feel myself exhale, releasing some of my tension. Sure, his actions might not have quite lined up with his words to date, but he has a way of explaining things that brings me comfort. It's like he's stepping our relationship up a notch. This is what I want to hear—his reassurances, his promises. I can feel the cracks in my resolve slowly sealing themselves up.

101

PSYCHOS & CHEAPSKATES

After a few days on Solvana, right before Steve's wife and child return home, things only get worse. Steve corners me, asking me to clean his house from top to bottom before his wife gets back. I'm exhausted and irritated—I find it quite rude of him to ask, but I do it anyway.

I vacuum and sweep, and worry that I'm doing a good enough job —he makes it very clear that his wife is a neat freak and strikes terror into him with her expectations which he has kindly passed onto me. It's a large house, and it takes a while. I hate how eager I am to be helpful, and how I feel like I need to earn the space I take up, even when I know I shouldn't have to.

Timmy starts drinking more, and so do I. It's the only way I can numb myself to the awkwardness and stress, and distract myself from how resentful I am that we had to make this trip. We bicker in quiet corners—nothing explosive, just those little jabs that come from being tired and on edge. I know we're both struggling, but his moods are becoming more unpredictable, and it's wearing me down.

Without warning, Timmy shaves his beard off for the first time since I've met him. He looks younger, and reminds me of a boy band member. He's cute either way, but I can't help but think this is a sign of him being more agitated, outwardly changing his appearance in a fairly drastic way to get attention, to soothe something simmering inside of him. Instead of adding bone necklaces or superman capes, he's removing facial hair.

Sabre's the only one who seems to be thriving, zooming up and down the steep loft stairs, his tail high in the air. He darts around the garden, chasing invisible creatures and sniffing plants. His happiness is the only thing that gives me a bit of peace—at least something in our little world is going right.

A few days in, Steve approaches us, an expectant look on his face. "Hey, so I need you to stay another week or so to look after the animals while we're away."

Timmy and I glance at each other. "Are you open to that?" Timmy asks me.

"Yeah, sure," I shrug. Not wanting to create a problem. I am getting some writing done from here, but it's just delaying setting up our apartment and establishing our new routine even further. I ordered supplies based on when we were originally meant to be back, but I figure they should be okay for a few days longer. At this point, I'm too tired to put up any kind of fight.

THE NEXT DAY, any remaining warmth from the moment Timmy called me his penguin well and truly dissolves. I have his phone in my hand, scrolling to find a song to play, when the bright pink and white Tinder icon jumps out at me from the screen like a flashing neon sign. My heart drops.

"What the fuck is this" I ask sharply, holding up the phone.

Timmy glances over and, for a moment, his face shifts—somewhere between annoyance and defensiveness. "What?" he says, his tone sharp enough to cut glass.

"Why is Tinder downloaded on your phone?"

He groans like I'm making a mountain out of a molehill. "I don't remember downloading that."

I scoff. "Tinder doesn't just download itself, Timmy."

He shrugs, irritated, but trying to play it cool. "Well, open it. I bet there's no profile set up."

I press on the icon. Sure enough, the login screen pops up. He's not logged in, and there's no active account. But that doesn't matter. The fact that the app is there at all makes my stomach churn. "Why would you download Tinder while we're engaged? That makes me feel sick."

His defense comes fast, as if rehearsed. "I was drunk and mad at you for hurting my feelings. I don't remember downloading it, but I guess I must have. But clearly, I didn't follow through with anything. I didn't message anyone. You're everything to me.:"

I stare at him, disbelieving. "So, what? It was a revenge download? You thought, 'Hey, I'll just download Tinder and see what happens?'"

He rolls his eyes. "Look, if I downloaded it, it wasn't serious. It's not like I'd actually talk to anyone. I'd only want to download something like that for sex, and I couldn't handle sex any more than what we already have. I can barely keep up with you."

The flippancy in his voice makes me want to scream. "That's not the point, Timmy. How would you feel if *I* downloaded Tinder when we were fighting?"

His eyes narrow. "You did, remember? When I was in jail."

"That was different," I argue. "You threatened to kill me. I was terrified and knew no one. It wasn't a Tinder download for fun—it was desperation."

He leans back in the seat, smug. "Well, I didn't give you shit for it, so you shouldn't be giving me shit now."

Apples and oranges, but he has a way of making me feel like we're looking at the same fruit. Wild.

I feel a dull throb in my temples. I want to believe him. I want to believe that it's all just a stupid mistake. But my gut twists with unease, and the cracks in my trust feel deeper than ever. This isn't just about a dating app—it's about the lies, the manipulation, the inconsistencies that keep cropping up like weeds. The way he lashes out with vindictive acts that compromise the trust in our relationship.

And the way that his actions constantly cause unnecessary angst and pain for me.

"You'd better not do it again, Timmy," I whisper, deflated that the day is somewhat fucked now. "I'm not joking. If you do, I'm gone. No questions asked."

He nods quickly. "I know. I get it. I'm sorry. It won't happen again."

THE NEXT NIGHT, Steve throws a little party, inviting over a few friends to admire the structure he and Timmy have been painting. I hear their voices drifting through the open window—lighthearted chatter, some good-natured ribbing about the project. But then the tone shifts.

I hear yelling, sharp and sudden. It's Timmy. My stomach tightens, and I know this isn't going to end well.

When Timmy storms back into the side house, his face is tight with fury. The tension radiates off him like a storm cloud. "They can all fuck off," he snarls.

"What happened?" I ask, trying to keep my voice calm.

"They were criticizing how we painted the fucking beams," he spits, his voice dripping with venom. He starts mimicking them in a cruel, sing-song tone, like a child mocking a playground bully. "I would have done it this way, I would have done it that way."

"Timmy," I say gently, trying to calm him. "Guys do that sometimes. They just can't help it when they see a home improvement project—they all have to throw their two cents in. It's annoying, but it's not personal."

His eyes darken. "They were making me look stupid. They wanted me to feel stupid."

I swallow hard. His face reminds me too much of *that* night. The night everything went so wrong. I try to defuse the situation, but his anger hangs heavy in the air, an uninvited guest neither of us knows how to get rid of.

I leave and head over to the main house where some people have gathered. It's mainly the female partners of their male counterparts who are still standing outside. A few kids. A few sober people. All oblivious to the tension brewing outside. I'm not proud of it, but I'm clutching a bottle of vodka. Partially because I feel like I need some for comfort, partially so that Timmy won't drink it all and get even crazier, or be a vindictive shit and pour it down the sink like he's done a few times before. All I know is that if he drinks more, things will only get worse.

When the rest of the guests are distracted, Steve turns to me and his wife.

"Timmy's really on one," he says.

"Yeah, he's being scary out there," I agree. "That's why I came in here."

"He threatened to kill everybody outside," Steve adds.

My heart skips a beat. "He did what?"

"Yeah." Steve sighs. "He's scaring the hell out of everyone, acting unhinged."

I press my fingers to my temples, trying to stave off the panic creeping in.

"You're welcome to stay in here as long as you like," Steve offers.

I nod, grateful for the offer, but knowing I'll have to go back eventually. This is my life now—cleaning up Timmy's messes, navigating his moods, and trying to keep us both afloat.

When I finally head back to the side house, Timmy is sulking on the couch, his anger simmering just beneath the surface. He looks at me with eyes that are wild, unreadable. I can't tell if he's sorry or just waiting for another excuse to explode.

I collapse onto the couch, my head spinning from the vodka and the stress. The weight of it all presses down on me, heavy and unrelenting. I close my eyes, hoping for sleep, for some kind of reprieve. Timmy stomps around, muttering crazed words under his breath.

An hour later, I'm jolted awake by the sound of the sliding door opening. Steve steps inside, his face grim. Without a word, he grabs the rifle Timmy had propped in the corner, the one meant for their hunting trip. He says nothing. Just takes the gun and leaves, sliding the door shut behind him. A quiet, deliberate act that speaks louder than any words.

Steve is saving us—from Timmy.

The next morning, Steve pulls us aside. "You guys have to leave," he says, his tone final. "I've booked you on an earlier flight."

"What about your animals?" I ask, even though I already know the answer.

"I've got a backup plan," he replies. "But you two can't stay here."

I feel a lump rise in my throat. We're being kicked out—banished, really. And while I understand why—Timmy's behavior has been unhinged—I can't help but feel humiliated. We've bent over backward to help, delayed our own lives, spent money on this trip when Steve promised to pay Timmy a decent amount for his labor, and this is how it ends?

Tears spill down my cheeks, a messy mix of anger, embarrassment, and exhaustion. It's always me cleaning up the messes, bearing the brunt of Timmy's chaos. And I get that Timmy's behavior has been completely insane. I understand Steve has a family to protect.

But I didn't threaten to kill anyone. I didn't hurt anyone. I feel like I'm constantly in a position where I'm being punished for Timmy's actions. And *worse*, sometimes.

Because I'm the one who has to replace all the items he breaks. So his actions are costing me financially, mentally. And spiritually, too. I'm under a constant state of stress. It's blocking me from being able to be creative, because I'm constantly worrying that he's going to be upset, and all my energy is focused on him.

I pay for everything, I soothe everyone, and now, I'm being cast aside once again because of him. It's not fair.

But fairness doesn't seem to matter anymore.

"I get it," I whisper. "We'll leave."

Timmy looks at me, his expression unreadable. I wonder if he understands what's happening—or if he even cares. He wraps an arm around me, as if that will make everything better.

"We'll be fine," he murmurs. "We always are."

I nod, but I'm not sure I believe him anymore. I feel like I'm sinking—drowning in the chaos of his life, and I don't know how much longer I can keep my head above water.

FOR OVER A WEEK'S WORK, Steve gives Timmy about two hundred dollars.

Timmy and I are both shocked, livid.

When we get back to our local airport, I pull the car up at the cashier's turnstile on the way out. The parking alone is more than what Timmy was paid by Steve for the entire week. Blood thumps in my temples and rings in my ears, my heart pounding in my chest, as I pay two hundred and forty dollars for the airport parking.

The trip ends up costing me personally around a thousand dollars.

This was meant to be a trip where Timmy helped his friend and made some money to help with our move-in costs. And it cost *me a grand*. Right when I can't afford it, and it's put me way behind on my work.

Are you fucking kidding me?

This is disgusting. Regardless of Timmy's behavior on the last night we were there, he worked for a week. We were both inconvenienced. The way Timmy is, there was no way I couldn't accompany him. And it's part of the fun of moving in together that you do it together.

Money I didn't have, all wasted on a trip that was supposed to help us, not set us back.

Fury builds inside me, hot and unforgiving. "You promised this trip would help with our move-in costs," I snap at Timmy. "Now we're worse off than before."

His face darkens, a storm brewing in his expression. "Steve screwed us over," he mutters.

I shake my head, exhausted. "Well, you need to talk to him. Because this trip was a disaster."

"He thinks he's better than me," snarls Timmy. "Better than both of us. Always has. He's always been a loser, though. Nobody liked him at school. I'm the reason he has any friends at all."

"Well, you need to speak with him, Timmy. You promised to help with move-in costs based on this trip, and you've cost me at least a thousand dollars across parking and unnecessary groceries and wastage at home, because you insisted we do a massive grocery shop before we go. I'm going to have to replace everything in the fridge, basically."

He frowns and sighs. "I'll see what I can do."

He calls Steve, and the conversation quickly goes south. "Sorry, that's all I'm prepared to pay," says Steve. "I've spoken with my wife, and we've decided that's what we're able to offer and what we think is appropriate."

"Well, it cost Margaux more than a thousand dollars."

"Well, she didn't have to come," he replies, his tone snide and self-righteous. "You should be grateful, you both basically got a free vacation."

"But it wasn't free," I say to Timmy, "and we didn't need a place to stay for a week. We have a perfectly great apartment here. One that I would have loved to have been moving into, instead of being stranded hours away while you argued with your friend."

Timmy reiterates my point to Steve, but he still won't budge.

I'm so furious. If I knew it was going to cost me a grand, I would never have agreed to go. I would have convinced Timmy to say fuck off to his friend taking advantage of him, and instead we could have used the money to go somewhere nice, just the two of us. I wouldn't have stayed in someone's shitty side house and had to listen to their misogynistic comments all week, and pay for the privilege. What a fucking tool.

Timmy slams the phone down, his face tight with rage. "I'm done with him," he growls. "Done with everyone. It's just us now."

Feeling tricked, and with the financial pressure mounting up even more unexpectedly, my resentment continues to build. Now it's not just Timmy taking advantage of my kind nature, because at least we have a relationship. But now it feels like his friend is doing the same, too.

"I'm so sorry he's doing this," says Timmy. "I never would have agreed to do this if I knew he was going to use me and waste your money. I should have known."

"This is why it should just be the two of us," he adds. "I'm never helping another user friend again. Fuck everyone else. Fuck everyone else, except for you and Sabre."

He pulls me close, wrapping his arms around me as Sabre weaves between our legs. "It's just us, babe. Our cute little family."

As we drive back to our barely set up new apartment, the weight of everything presses down on me—his lies and deception, the financial strain, the constant back-and-forth of highs and lows. I want to believe things will get better. I want to believe we'll find stability, that the move will give us a fresh start.

But a nagging voice in the back of my mind whispers that this cycle won't end. There will always be something. Timmy will always find some way to create chaos, and in the rare instance he doesn't, one of his friends will.

He reaches over and squeezes my hand. "We'll figure it out," he says softly. "We always do."

I nod, but I'm not so sure.

It really is starting to feel like Timmy and me against the world.

Except, minus Timmy, when he doesn't feel like it.

102

KNIGHT WITH A SHINING IMPACT GUN

Now that we're back in Sunset Cay, Timmy takes the lead on properly setting up the apartment, and it is *so* cute.

Like my last apartment, the configuration is way better than what I would have come up with.

He's once again thought about where is going to work best for me to write for the most inspiration.

The bed is in the corner, right by the window, so we can see the ocean at all times. The bed also serves as our couch and office. It faces the TV, which sits on a nice big stand with storage squares. We got cute little storage cubes to fit in each square.

He decorates the apartment with beautiful shells he's picked himself, and he ties some ti leaf leis to the curtain rod, so they can sway in the breeze when the sliding door is open.

Because the mattresses are different sizes, there's even a cute little ledge jutting out on the beach side that Sabre uses as his little cat bed.

He organizes a tackle box in the bathroom, placing my most frequently used cosmetics and toiletries so they're easy to access. He puts up the shower curtain.

As I survey the area, I realize things are shaping up really nicely.

This place is *finally* starting to feel like a home. Our home. Just Timmy, me, and sweet little Sabre.

My resentment toward having to go to Solvana starts to dissipate like a distant memory. This is our time now, to focus on each other and our work. To become a stronger couple, and to strengthen our ability to create and produce great books and clothing designs that people will love.

There are no more external stressors—no more court dates, no more mandatory trips to help friends, no bad influences, no extra worries weighing on our minds. Now, we just get to be us, and enjoy the life that we've both longed for.

I ask him to set up the kitchen cart, but he just doesn't seem to want to.

It's fine. He's done a lot already. And I pride myself on being able to put together furniture, even though it's not my strength.

So I kneel on the floor, the instruction booklet sprawled in front of me. Screws, hinges and wooden panels are scattered around me in relatively organized chaos. The kitchen cart idea seemed like a good one—a cute little addition to make our space more comfortable—but it's definitely one of the more complicated furniture assemblies I've done, and now, with the cracked wooden top and the drawer stubbornly refusing to align, I think I've met my match.

Timmy sits on the bed, sipping on his beer, arms crossed, watching me with a faint smirk curling the corners of his mouth. He's so handy, and probably could have done it much faster, but he's set up the rest of the apartment, so I figure I can do this part.

"You're really good at this, babe," he says, lazily. "Never knew you were built for furniture assembly. It's so hot watching you use my impact gun." His voice drips with amusement—not quite a compliment, not quite an insult—something in the middle, sharp and smug.

I shoot him a glance, my lips pressing together, but I say nothing. I have no desire to argue about a kitchen cart. I'm determined to finish this myself, my stubborn Taurus nature kicking in. I've already come this far, and I'd prefer not to ask for help—not now, and especially not from him. He made it clear he had no interest in helping for whatever reason, maybe believing he's already done enough around the apartment. The way he's watching me, it's as if he's enjoying watching me struggle with something he could probably do in his sleep.

I struggle to slot a hinge into place, biting my lip in frustration as it wobbles under my fingers, first in perfect alignment, and then way off kilter. "Stupid thing," I mutter under my breath, adjusting the screwdriver in my hand.

"What was that?" Timmy asks, smirking, even though I barely expressed any frustration. A strange expression flickers across his face. "You sure you don't want a hand? It's cute watching you try so hard."

My grip tightens on the drill, my knuckles whitening. "I've got it," I grit out, more to myself than him.

"Okay, okay," he puts his hands up in mock surrender. "I just figured, you know, two hands are better than one, and all that. Just trying to be helpful."

I'm starting to feel flustered now, like he's goading me. This is taking much longer to put together than I anticipated, partially because I expected his help from the start. I didn't think that was too much to ask. But it's like he's waiting, enjoying observing my frustration build, so he can swoop in at the last second and gloat about how he saved the day, and helpless little Margaux couldn't put the cart together.

I resist the very strong urge to scream 'then why didn't you offer to help in the first place?', and instead, I take a deep breath, forcing myself to focus on the task. The drawer clicks almost into place, and I groan as I realize I've put one of the panels on backwards. "For fuck's sake! Aaagh!" I say to myself, and he scoffs from the bed.

"Look at you getting all upset over a kitchen cart," he smirks. "What's that you say? Don't get upset over small things? What a hypocrite. But let me know if you want my help."

I turn around so my back is to him, mostly because it makes sense in terms of how I'm putting the cart together, but partially because I don't want to see his smug smirk any more as he watches me, his presence proving to be more an obstacle than a source of comfort.

Another screw rolls off the panel I'm working on, and I stifle a curse. I know I'm being stubborn, but I can't help it. Every time Timmy makes another backhanded compliment, it makes me more determined to finish it by myself.

"Margaux," his voice is soft now, teasing. "It really looks like you're about to cry over that thing."

I squeeze my eyes shut for a moment, inhaling deeply through my nostrils and exhaling slowly through my mouth. *Fine, just let him help. Just get it done.*

I place the drill on the floor with a quiet clink, and I sit back on my heels, my arms crossed.

"Alright," I say, hating how bitter the word tastes on my tongue. "You can help."

Timmy's smirk spreads into a wide grin, and he drops down beside me with an almost triumphant air, and gets to work.

He grabs the hinge and impact gun without hesitation, his movements quick and fluid, as if he's done this a thousand times. Within minutes, he has the drawer aligned, and the screws tightened in place.

"There," he says, his voice thick with satisfaction as he gives the drawer a little test pull. It slides smoothly, perfectly. He leans back on his heels, grinning at me. "Easy."

I bite the inside of my cheek, my frustration simmering just beneath the surface. I hate that it took him five minutes when I just spent over an hour working on the drawer. I mean, it's done, but he could have just helped me in the first place. It's like he loved watching me struggle, and then being so capable of fixing it, rather than looking at our respective strengths and offering to do it from the get-go.

"See?" he says, brushing his hands off like a job well done. "We make a great team." He punches me on the arm playfully, and I resist the urge to shrink away, even though both his punch and his words kind of hurt.

My stomach twists at the smugness in his tone, but I force a tight smile. "Thanks," I manage to say, even though the word comes out heavy and bitter.

Timmy stands, stretching his hands over his head as if he's just conquered Everest, not just partially helped to assemble a piece of DIY furniture from Amazon. "Told you I'd save the day. I'm your hero," he says, proudly.

I stay on the floor for a moment longer, my pride stinging, willing the situation not to get to me more than it already has. I know I'm being ridiculous—he helped, and because of him, now it's done. I have no reason to complain. Getting it finished is all that matters, right? But the lingering frustration gnaws at me.

Timmy leans down and gently kisses the top of my head. "Good teamwork," he says, clearly pleased with himself. "You did most of it yourself. You only needed my help right at the end."

I force a small, polite laugh, though it feels hollow. The cart is finished, but somehow that doesn't feel like it was achieved by team-work. Instead, it feels like a victory—his, not mine—and that leaves a bitter taste in my mouth.

103

MY FAVORITE FATHER FIGURE IS A DAD BOD

Timmy's decision to reconnect with his parents feels like a refreshing shift—a rare attempt to stabilize something in his life. He's been in intermittent contact with his dad, but hasn't called him since the day he proposed, and it's been months since he's spoken with his mom. It's nice to see this side of him, a version that's thoughtful and connected, and it makes me hopeful for us. Even though it's been messy between him and his mom for a while, he's making the effort, and that counts for something.

The conversations usually start with Timmy enthusiastically putting the call on speakerphone. I never feel like a passive bystander—his parents always make an effort to include me. "Hey, Margaux, how's the new book coming along?" or something as simple as, "What's the weather like over there today?" They seem genuinely interested, and the validation feels like a warm hug I didn't know I needed.

Timmy brags about me more than I'd ever expect. :She's incredible, Dad. You won't believe how good her books are. We're eating like royalty over here thanks to her cooking." I feel myself blushing as he lays on the praise, but it's sweet.

"We just went to the farmer's market and got dragon fruit and fresh pineapple and basil and kale," Timmy will share. "Margaux is making us an awesome salad for dinner. She's a phenomenal cook. Her books are going really well."

He spends a lot of time telling them about my accomplishments and my writing, and I'm flattered when his parents say they're interested in buying my books. Not that I want my in-laws reading my spicy books, but it's so kind of them to lean in and be supportive in this way.

"I love you, mommy," Timmy will say a lot. It sounds funny coming from a nearly forty-year-old.

"I love you too, son," she'll say back.

It's sweet, hearing them share affection back and forth, the way we do.

"I can't wait for you to meet Margaux in person," he says, beaming. "She's very beautiful. Actually, you two look kind of similar."

"Well, I guess you have the same name as my dad," I'll say. "So I won't be a hypocrite and say that's weird."

We both laugh.

His parents eat it up, too, encouraging him in that subtle, parental way to keep things steady.

"That's just wonderful to hear, son." His dad's voice is warm but matter-of-fact. "Now, when are you going to start working again?"

Every time they mention the job search, I feel a strange sense of relief. It's like there's finally someone other than me nudging Timmy toward responsibility, someone reinforcing the same things I've been saying all along.

"Yeah, yeah," Timmy says, brushing it off in the way he always does. "We're just getting settled in. You know, it takes time to get into a routine." He promises them that a job search is on the horizon, though he hasn't actually made any moves in that direction. But for now, hearing his parents push him to step up and act more like an adult, without it coming from me, feels like a small win.

And it's a relief that his parents sound... well, normal. They don't even show a hint of Timmy's chaotic energy, and instead just seem calm and friendly.

Not that I've seen him make much of an effort but, to be fair, we just got back from the disastrous trip to help Steve. He tells his dad what happened.

"That Steve has always been a bit of a wack job, hasn't he. He was weird back in the day, and it sounds like nothing's changed. I'm not surprised to hear any of this." It's a relief to hear his dad speak this way. Someone who has known Timmy for his entire life, and Steve most of his. At the same time, the level of disdain in his father's voice is startling. His words aren't just dismissive—they're laced with decades of judgment. It leaves me wondering if I've underestimated just how toxic some of these friendships in Timmy's life might be. How did I ever think Steve was a good guy?

These conversations alleviate my fears, making Timmy seem like he's part of a normal family background, not that my own is anything to brag about. They talk and laugh, and most of it is fairly superficial, but there is lots of affection exchanged, and they seem close.

In any case, the conversations feel easy, light. It's like I'm peeking into a version of life where Timmy is dependable, where we have a family network that supports us. In these moments, I feel hopeful.

I've enjoyed Timmy's parents' phone calls from the start, because I know he will be on his best behavior every single time. But the calls quickly begin to taper off. What started as daily conversations trickle down to a couple of times a week, and then less often, and I can't help but notice how Timmy's demeanor shifts along with them. His upbeat, motivated version seems to wither away the less he talks to his parents.

Sometimes his voice is slurred on the calls—a telltale sign that he's been drinking. But his energy is high, and his affection for me shines through during those conversations. "We're so in love," he'll say to them, and I can hear the pride in his voice. "She's it for me." And for a moment, I'll forget the stress, the rocky parts, the tension always bubbling just under the surface.

Between the dwindling calls and Timmy's lack of job search progress, I feel the pressure mounting. I try not to resent how easy things seem for Timmy. He talks about job hunting, but I'm the one stressing over money. He chats on the phone, upbeat and cheerful, but I'm the one keeping us afloat. It feels like I'm the only one aware of how close we are to the edge, and I wonder how long I can keep carrying the load.

Yet, when he's on those calls, everything feels like it's going to be okay. His parents believe in us, they're rooting for us, and Timmy sounds so damn convincing when he talks about our future. He can be so charming, so believable, that for a while, I forget the nagging doubts lurking in the back of my mind.

But then the calls end, and reality rushes back in. The air in our new apartment feels thick with unfinished business. There are still packed boxes, unestablished routines, jobs that haven't been searched for. And though Timmy's promises ring in my ears, I know deep down that it's going to take more than a few phone calls with his parents to build the life we've imagined.

104

———

DON'T MESS WITH MY PUSSY

The Past

First serious boyfriend: *I wish your ass looked like Britney Spears'.*

You should really work on that.

Two hours later:

First serious boyfriend: *Your ass looks like Britney Spears', but better*

∼

The Present

I'm sitting at my desk, typing, when I notice Timmy looking at me from across the room. His gaze feels heavy and cool, like a weight pressing down on me. His eyes narrow, and I can feel the tension radiating from him, though I've done nothing to prompt it.

"You're not very good with your cat," he says suddenly, his tone flat, matter-of-fact.

The comment slices through me, catching me completely off guard. I feel like he just backhanded me across the face—sharp and unexpected. He knows how much Sabre means to me. Sabre isn't just a pet—he's been my constant companion for over a decade. And now, Timmy is reducing my bond with him to nothing, attacking something sacred with cruel precision.

I sit here, trying to laugh it off, telling myself he's probably joking —or that I'm overreacting.

But he continues.

"You pretend to be this great cat mom. But he doesn't even like you."

I stare at him, stunned, my heart thudding painfully in my chest. Where did this even come from? The accusation feels so personal, like he's intentionally cutting me where it hurts most. I feel the sting behind my eyes, but I won't give him the satisfaction of seeing me cry.

"What are you talking about?" My voice is shaky, but I try to keep it steady. "That's not true and it's just... mean."

Timmy leans against the wall, his arms crossed, smirking like he's won some private victory. There's a mean gleam in his eye, almost gleeful. "I'm the one who he comes to," he continues, as if he's listing facts. "I'm the one that cleans his litter box."

His tone is condescending, his words like daggers, as if I'm a child being scolded for not doing my chores.

"Well, I appreciate you cleaning his litter box." I try to stay calm, although I feel like I'm on the edge of exploding. "He comes to me as well, Timmy. He just knows that you give him treats every time he comes into the kitchen. And he loves cuddling with you. That doesn't mean he doesn't love me. That has nothing to do with me being a good cat mom. And, as you may recall, I've looked after him since he was a kitten—through surgeries, vet visits, and everything else, and he's a teenage cat in wonderful health." I pause, my temper flaring. "So fuck you."

Timmy's smirk deepens, as though my anger amuses him, as if

I've just given him exactly what he wanted. "There you go, swearing at me again," he says, shaking his head in disappointment. "Margaux, you've really got to work on your temper. It's becoming a real issue."

The shift leaves me breathless, like I've missed a step on a staircase and I'm free-falling. A second ago, he was attacking me. Now, somehow I'm in the wrong for reacting to it. I feel trapped, caught between the need to defend myself and the desire to keep the peace.

A COUPLE OF DAYS LATER, we're in the apartment together as usual.

Sabre is lounging in his hammock, as sunlight streams in through the glass sliding door, casting warm patches across his sleek, black coat. He's purring softly, staring out at the ocean like a little king surveying his domain.

Timmy glances up at Saber and smiles. "You're so good with him," he says warmly. "He's so healthy—look at his coat. You've done a wonderful job of looking after him for nearly thirteen years."

I blink, stunned. It feels like my brain is breaking, short-circuiting. Did he really just say that? A few days ago, he was telling me Sabre didn't even like me. Now, I'm suddenly a wonderful cat mom?

"Um... thanks?" I say hesitantly, still trying to catch up with the emotional whiplash.

I mean, what he's saying is true. Sabre is a wonderful, mischievous, cheeky cat who purrs and snuggles and loves the sunshine streaming across his back. He likes naps and biting my ankles and chasing lasers around the apartment.

I've nursed him through intestinal surgery because he ate my hair, some earbuds and a piece of an eyelash curler. I've cuddled him and loved him and fed and watered him his entire life. Bought him all sorts of cat towers and treats and toys and cuddly blankets and scratching posts. I know all of this.

But none of this is what Timmy said a few days ago.

He rolls his eyes. "Jesus, Margaux. I was just trying to give you a compliment."

I swallow the lump in my throat. "Okay, thank you," I say, carefully. "It just threw me because of what you said the other day."

He tilts his head, frowning like he doesn't understand. "What did I say?"

"That I was the worst cat mom ever, basically."

He shrugs, as if it's nothing. "Oh. I was probably just being a jerk. You must have hurt my feelings."

The words land with a heavy thud in my chest. How am I supposed to feel? Grateful? Flattered? Hurt? His words are like an emotional riddle—each side canceling the other out, leaving me dizzy in the aftermath.

And I want to scream. *I* hurt *his* feelings? That's his excuse for deliberately saying something so cruel? And now, instead of an apology, I'm supposed to believe he was just lashing out because I somehow upset him?

It's like trying to navigate a maze where the walls keep shifting. One moment, I'm the villain with a temper problem. The next, I'm the hero of the story—the perfect cat mom who's done everything right. I feel like I'm constantly trying to catch my balance, only for him to yank the rug out from under me whenever he pleases.

It makes me question everything. Was he trying to punish me before? Test how much I can take before I snap? Or is this just his sick way of keeping me on edge, never quite sure where I stand with him? I feel like I'm chasing an impossible standard—constantly being pulled between approval and disapproval, praise and criticism, always trying to figure out what version of myself will make him happy.

I sigh, exhausted by the mental gymnastics. "You really confuse me sometimes, Timmy."

He grins, as if my confusion is a joke only he understands. "It's not that complicated," he says, as if I'm making things harder than they need to be.

But it *is* complicated. It's like he's wanting to keep me insecure, always guessing, always needing his approval. I want to accept his compliment, but it's as if something inside me cracked just a little hearing him criticize me the other day and compliment me now. It's like every compliment has a barbed wire edge, and every criticism comes with an afterthought of praise. And I'm left trying to make sense of it all—trying to understand if this is just how he is, or if there's something deeper behind the way he twists things around.

All I know is that it's exhausting. And even though I love the highs—those moments when he's sweet and affectionate, and like I'm the most important person in his world—the lows are starting to take their toll.

I want to believe the good moments represent the real Timmy, and that the bad moments are just an aberration that we can work through. But deep down, fear lingers—what if this is just another game? A way to keep me off-balance, always striving for his validation, always doubting myself when he shifts the narrative.

I'm seeing a vindictive side that I hadn't noticed as clearly before, even though a nagging part of me reminds me there have been hints of it all along. A side that's activated by any perceived little thing I do, say, don't say, a facial expression, a tone, or even just because he feels like it.

I glance at Sabre, still content in his hammock, and envy his simplicity. He doesn't have to navigate these emotional landmines—he just gets to exist, happy and whole, enjoying the sunshine and naps and snuggles and treats. I wish, just for a moment, I could be like him.

But instead, I'm here. Trying to love a man who changes the rules whenever it suits him, and trying to convince myself that I can keep up.

105

HEALING ON HOLD

The email confirming my health insurance deactivation sends me into immediate panic mode. I'm frantically clicking through endless loops of automated phone prompts. Press 1 for this, press 2 for that, only to be transferred, put on hold, or told to call another number entirely. My anxiety is building—the same kind that makes my heart race and my thoughts spiral into a tangle of worst-case scenarios.

I really need a therapist. I've been telling myself this for months, trying to hold it together through the ups and downs with Timmy. He's got a counselor already—and sure, he needs it—but I need one just as badly—maybe even more. And now, because of some stupid missed piece of mail during the move, I'm stuck without access to professional help.

I feel my hands shaking as I scroll through emails, looking for any shred of information I might have missed. I have to get this resolved —my mental health is slipping, my body is screaming at me for assistance, and I just don't have the bandwidth to keep managing everything by myself. I need to see a doctor, an OB/GYN. Something is really wrong with me.

The pain from my periods has become unbearable—nauseating, sharp, radiating through my entire body. Every month it's the same, but it's getting exponentially worse. I'm doubled over in agony, vomiting from the intensity, stuck in bed for two days each month while the rest of the world goes on without me. I'm convinced it's my endometriosis spreading, or something in addition to that. I just know this level of pain isn't normal. And yet, here I am, unable to get checked out, spinning in circles with the insurance company.

I file an appeal. It's straightforward enough—it turns out that all I need to do is submit the missing documentation. It feels like a minor victory when I finally get an email acknowledging receipt, but then— nothing. No updates. No confirmation that the appeal went through. The days stretch into weeks, and I can't muster the energy to follow up.

Every day continues to be a battle with Timmy—his unpredictable moods, his endless demands, his passive-aggressive jabs— and my brain is locked in a perpetual fog. I know I need to be persistent, but it's like all my mental resources are being drained, funneled into managing his emotional chaos.

Eventually, I manage to get the issue escalated. They officially accept the documentation I sent through, and I'm told my ID cards will arrive soon. When they finally do, I hold them in my hand and feel a strange mix of relief and exhaustion.

The first thing I do is log into the local health clinic's website to make appointments—doctor, OB/GYN, therapist. I feel frantic, like if I don't schedule everything right now, I'll lose my chance. I need to get checked out, physically and mentally, and I need it as soon as possible.

I feel like I'm having both a physical and mental breakdown. The stress is beginning to consume me. I feel it in every part of my body— the tightness in my chest, the tension in my shoulders, the exhaustion in my bones. I'm not okay. But I haven't been okay in a long time. I'm losing myself, piece by piece, and it's scaring me.

The worst part is the constant rumination. I replay every fight with Timmy, analyzing his words, the way his tone shifts, trying to figure out where things went wrong. It's like my mind is in a loop of all the things he's said to hurt me or confuse me, and I can't escape it.

I'm starting to sound like him in my own thoughts. I can hear myself thinking in the same patterns—second-guessing, doubting, accusing. And that makes me feel crazy, which only makes the anxiety worse.

I've basically stopped bringing things up with him altogether. Every time I try to advocate for myself, he gets defensive, turns it around on me, and I just end up feeling worse. So now, I stay quiet. But the quieter I become, the more he pushes, testing my limits, poking at my boundaries to see how much more I'll let slide.

I'm angry all the time. On edge, waiting for the next argument, the next blow-up. It doesn't even matter what sparks it anymore—the outcome is always the same. He'll snap at me, I'll react, and then somehow it's my fault. And every time, it chips away at me a little more.

I'm grinding my teeth in my sleep now more than ever, the stress leaking out of my body in ways I can't control. I feel trapped. I tell myself it'll get better once we're fully settled in, once he finds a job, once I get back into my writing routine. But I know, deep down, that the real issue isn't logistics.

The real issue is that I'm constantly managing his emotions, his behavior, his moods—and it feels like it's slowly killing me.

With my insurance reactivated, I cling to the hope that therapy might save me—that a professional might help me make sense of all of this, help me navigate the tangled mess of this relationship. Help me find myself again.

But the intake appointment isn't for a couple of months, and, for now, all I can do is wait.

106

———

ARE WE HAVING FUN YET

Few Days Later

Timmy's excitement is electric, almost contagious—but instead of exhilaration, it sends a sharp wave of dread through my entire body.

"Let's drive to the Point!" he announces, his eyes gleaming with reckless enthusiasm. "But this time, we'll go further. We'll go right to the end, get deep into the good spots!"

My heart sinks. The last time he took me there, we stuck to the main road—safely, predictably. This time, something feels different. There's an edge to his excitement, a hunger to push limits.

"Isn't there a gate?" I ask, uneasy.

He grins, wild and gleeful. "Don't worry about that. You'll see."

I know better than to argue. Any attempt to challenge him will be met with accusations of being controlling or no fun, and I don't have the energy for a fight today.

When we pull up to the end of the road, I think—hope—he's just going to stop, like we did last time. But instead, he cranks the wheel toward a narrow path to the left of the gate. It's clearly not meant for trucks like this—maybe for dirt bikes or zippy little 4WDs—but that doesn't stop Timmy.

"Are you seriously going to do this?" I ask, my heart hammering.

His grin widens. "Yup! Hold on tight!"

With a squeal of excitement, he slams his foot on the accelerator, sending the truck bouncing up the steep embankment, rocks clattering beneath us. The truck's undercarriage groans as we lurch over the terrain. Each jolt threatens to punch a hole through the oil pan or snap the axle.

We land hard on the other side of the gate with a metallic crunch, and my stomach twists in on itself.

"Woohoo! That was awesome!" he cheers at himself. "Man, I'm such a good driver."

I freeze, and just sit there, with a tight smile.

The path is uneven, lined with sharp rocks on one side and a sheer drop into the ocean on the other.

We bounce along the jagged path, the truck swaying dangerously from side to side. Hikers stop to stare, wide-eyed, as we rumble past. This isn't normal—this isn't a vehicle meant for these kinds of conditions. We look insane, and I can feel their judgment.

Timmy, though, doesn't care. He waves at the hikers like he's on a parade float, grinning from ear to ear. "Hi there!" he chirps out the window, acutely aware of both how ridiculous and dangerous this whole situation is.

We reach a precarious point where the narrow path barely fits the truck's tires. On one side is a rock wall, and on the other, a dizzying cliff that drops straight down into the swirling, frothy ocean below.

Timmy jumps out of the truck and snaps a picture, beaming with pride. "Look at this view! Isn't this awesome? I can't believe we're doing this!"

My pulse is in my throat, and my palms are slick with sweat. I can feel the cliff's pull—just one wrong move, and we could be tumbling into the sea. But I know better than to show fear—my fear just makes him more reckless. If I show any hesitation, he'll double down, and take it as a challenge to try and freak me out more, to elevate my discomfort.

He gets back in and turns to me, serious for once. "Hey. Get out of the truck."

"What?" I blink at him, confused.

"This part's dangerous," he says solemnly. "If something goes wrong... if I die, I want you to be safe."

The words hit me like a punch to the gut. Chivalrous and terrifying all at once.

"This is so unnecessary," I mutter, but I obey. I'd rather be out of the truck than in.

I slide out of the truck, my legs shaky beneath me. I watch as Timmy revs the engine, his face lit up with manic determination. This whole thing feels like some kind of test—a dare I didn't agree to but have to pass anyway.

He successfully makes the turning maneuver, and I breathe a sigh of relief as he motions for me to get back in the truck.

He grins. "You're so brave! I'm really impressed."

His words make my skin crawl. This isn't bravery—this is survival. But I force a smile and nod, trying to play along. He thrives on validation, and the last thing I need is to piss him off mid-stunt, when he really needs to be concentrating and believing in his driving ability more than ever.

We get back to the gate. My heart is in my stomach as I see the steep angle he's going to have to swing the truck around, a cliff just a foot or so away if he gets it wrong. Somehow—against all odds—he manages to wrench the truck over the bend without sending us careening into the ocean. I let out a breath I didn't realize I was holding as he steers us back toward the road. We survived.

He's giddy on the return trip, verbally patting himself on the back.

I sit, silently, as my heartbeat starts to slow back down, while Timmy chatters non-stop, buzzing with excitement. "I can't believe we did that! I can't believe I just did that!"

Neither can I. What the hell just happened? How did I let him put me in that situation? This isn't the life I imagined for myself. Sure, I wanted adventure—but not like this. Not reckless, dangerous, could-have-died-today adventure.

Honestly, while I feel young at heart, I also think we're both way too old for this kind of stupid, reckless shit. We're not in our twenties anymore.

"I'm so impressed with you," Timmy gushes. "Most people would've freaked out. But not you. You're the bravest woman I've ever met."

His words don't comfort me—they make me feel like a fool. A fool for pretending to stay calm while my heart hammered in my chest, blood pounding in my temples, a fool for letting him drag me into this.

What kind of person doesn't say no to something like that?

But I know the answer. A person who's scared of being called boring, controlling, a buzzkill. Mocked for being responsible in any manner. A person who's afraid of rocking the boat. A person who's trying too hard to hold onto a relationship that feels like it's slipping through her fingers.

When we finally return to the apartment, I'm trembling inside, but I mask it. Timmy is too high on adrenaline to notice. He's grinning like a child who just won a dare.

"That was *insane!*" he exclaims. "We should do it again sometime!"

I shake my head firmly. "No. Absolutely not. Never again."

He pouts for half a second, but then sighs. "Okay, okay. You're right. That was kinda crazy."

He looks at me again with boyish delight, like he's waiting for praise. "But, come on, admit it. That was *awesome*, wasn't it?"

I force a tight smile—the gritted-teeth emoji plastered across my face. It wasn't awesome. It was terrifying. And reckless. And completely unnecessary.

And the worst part is, I know this isn't the last time. He'll push the limits again. Maybe not next week, maybe not next month, and not in the exact same way. But I have no doubt he'll find a new way to test boundaries, to see how far I'll go. And the stakes will keep getting higher.

107

THE WEIGHT OF AN ALBATROSS

Writing is becoming increasingly difficult. Every time I carve out even a small amount of time to focus, it feels like Timmy senses it in the air, notices my focus sharpening—and pounces.

Every time I have a deadline with my editor, Timmy will invent some sort of crisis.

"This is ridiculous. Is every fucking book going to be like this?" he snaps from across the room, pacing dramatically as if my concentration is somehow a personal attack on him. "You're impossible to be around when you're writing," he sneers, his tone sharp enough to cut through whatever creative flow I've managed to muster.

It feels like he's flipped the switch on me. How many times have I told him the same thing, but in reverse? That it's impossible to write when he's lurking nearby, demanding constant attention and affirmation. If I don't respond immediately to whatever mundane thought pops into his head, he acts insulted. As though my silence, and not wanting to constantly be pulled out of my work, is some grand betrayal.

"It's so unfair," he pouts, his arms crossed like a petulant child. "I don't think I can be around you when you're like this."

This from the person who used to tell me how proud he was of my writing career. Who used to boast about my writing to others. Now, it feels like my work has become a battleground—a constant reminder that I have responsibilities he refuses to acknowledge.

Every time I say I'm busy, that I just need an hour or so, the passive-aggressive remarks begin, diminishing the value of whatever I'm working on.

"Oh, I'm so sorry I interrupted you from sending an email."

"Oh, so doing a TikTok is more important than me, now?"

"Oh, you can't write if I talk? That sounds like a fucking excuse to me."

The message is clear: nothing should matter more than Timmy.

"Timmy," I say, my voice strained, barely holding onto civility. "If I don't work, I can't make any money, and if I can't make money, then I can't pay our rent." I dig my fingernails into the palms of my hands, my knuckles turning white. "All I'm asking is for you to be quiet while I get this done. That's all."

He scoffs, dismissive as usual. "Wow, you're so fucking extra, Margaux. I wish you would just go and work in the back room, if this is such a big deal."

His words make my blood pound in my ears, hot and relentless. I fight to keep my voice calm, but my frustration bubbles dangerously close to the surface. "There's no way I'm going to pay all the rent and go hide in the fucking back room while you sit out here doing nothing, Timmy!"

I'm starting to think that if he had his way, I'd be locked in the back room all the time, churning out content like a machine—spitting out anything that could make enough money to keep a roof over our heads. Meanwhile, he'd stay out here, enjoying the beachfront view, sprawled out across the bed watching movies, living off the lifestyle I'm paying for.

The back room is a nightmare, stifling and cramped with little air flow and the noise of people constantly walking past, surrounded by uninspiring cinder block walls. It feels like a prison cell. It's a stark contrast to the front room, with its wide-open windows facing the ocean, where I can see swaying palm trees, and waves spraying up over the reef. With access to the kitchen, air conditioning, and natural sunlight. The only place in the apartment where I can breathe. Where I feel creative. He has to be joking. It would be more inspiring to write while sitting on the toilet. *There's no way in hell I'm writing from the back room.*

But any time I push back, which is increasingly often, he automatically goes on the defensive, twisting the narrative. "All you care about is money," he hisses, as if I'm the greedy one here.

"I contribute food stamps," he snaps, as though that's a sustainable solution that somehow levels the scales. "And don't forget the value of the truck. You have to include the value of the truck."

I bite my tongue, but my resentment festers. He's made it abundantly clear that his contribution—those food stamps that he does literally nothing to earn—mean that I should carry the rest without complaint. As if keeping a roof over our heads, paying all our bills, and providing emotional labor aren't monumental tasks I shoulder every single day.

Then I see it. A text exchange between him and his father, sitting open on his phone, carelessly left on the kitchen counter. They're talking about the truck. The truck Timmy gave me—that's in my name—as though it's still his. They're scheming about how to maintain Timmy's ownership of the truck, even though the title is mine, even though I've paid for registration and safety checks and maintenance and everything else.

They're scheming behind my back, planning how to pull the rug out from under me. My heart sinks, twisting in my chest like a vise. It's not just Timmy—it's him and his father, plotting together.

After everything I've done for Timmy.

I feel so betrayed, and quite frankly shocked by his dad's involvement.

I've been shouldering the load for months—paying the rent, bills, *and* food over and above what the food stamps are able to provide, entertainment, vehicle costs, things we need to keep the house running... making sure that Timmy's okay. And now, behind closed doors, they're over there conspiring how to fuck me over further, discussing how to take even more from me. It's a betrayal I can't quite wrap my head around.

A hollow ache settles deep inside me. It's not just about the truck, or the rent, or the endless excuses. I know that part of my resentment is because I don't have this type of support on my side. No family scheming to help *me*, although I have a feeling if I did they'd be telling me to run. No safety net waiting to catch me. I've been shouldering everything alone.

And it hurts.

It's not Timmy's fault that I don't have family to fall back on and he does. It's not his fault I've never had anyone looking out for me the way his father looks out for him.

But the pain lingers, gnawing at the edges of my mind. It's hard not to feel bitter when you realize you're the only one fighting for your survival, while others conspire against you—even the ones who claim to love you.

I shake off the guilt creeping in. *This isn't my fault.* I know that. But knowing it doesn't make it any easier to bear.

~

AS THE DAYS GO ON, the tension builds every time I sit down to write.

I'm running out of money, deadlines are looming like dark clouds, and my brain is screaming for me to focus. But the constant interruptions, the dismissive comments, the subtle digs—it's like trying to write with a ticking time bomb under the desk.

I catch glimpses of Timmy messaging his dad late at night, their conversations quiet and secretive. I know they're planning something. And every time I confront him about it, he brushes me off.

"Relax," he'll say, with that infuriating grin. "We're just talking. Dad thinks you're great. You're overthinking everything."

But I know what I saw. And the pit in my stomach tells me it's only a matter of time before the other shoe drops. I just don't know what the shoe is—what style, what size, anything. Just that there is one, and it won't benefit me in any way.

I can feel myself unraveling, piece by piece. My writing—once a refuge—feels like a burden. Every word I manage to get on the page is a battle, every chapter a war fought against the chaos of my own life.

And all the while, Timmy looms in the background, sabotaging my efforts with a smile.

I'm drowning, and the people closest to me are the ones pulling me under.

108

VIOLATED

A few days later

Timmy's voice is light and playful, as if he just shared a funny secret instead of something deeply disturbing.

"I had sex with you while you were asleep!" His grin stretches wide, his eyes bright and proud, like he expects me to find this hilarious or cute. The satisfaction in his tone is unmistakable.

I freeze, my heart skipping a beat. "Excuse me, you did *what* now?" My stomach flips and my brow knits, hoping—*praying*—that I misheard him.

"Yeah," he repeats as if it's the most natural thing in the world. "I've done it before, too! I have sex with you while you're sleeping." There's a giddy excitement in his voice, as if he's expecting me to join in on the joke.

I feel the blood drain from my face, my skin cold and clammy. My brain struggles to keep up with what he's just said.

I feel numb. Well, my *mind* feels numb... and I definitely don't share his enthusiasm.

My pussy doesn't feel numb. It feels like it's been battered by a twelve-foot dildo. But that's nothing new. We have sex a lot, now that we're in a place of our own. I wouldn't expect it to feel any other way, even if he did what he just told me he did.

Surely he means when he wakes me up, right? That has to be what he means.

"You mean when you wake me up in the middle of the night and we have sex?" I damn sure hope that's what he means. I'm grasping for clarity, desperate for a reasonable explanation.

"Nope," he shakes his head, still grinning. "Like I bang you when you're *fully* asleep." His smile widens, and what he said next makes my stomach churn. "I love having sex with you that way... because you don't talk." Then, as if he's just cracked the funniest joke, he laughs—a short, sharp laugh with a disturbing edge to it.

Oh my fucking god.

The air feels thick, suffocating, as the weight of his words sinks in. I sit here, numb—mentally paralyzed. My mind is reeling, trying to process what he just admitted to. My body feels cold, disconnected, as if this isn't really happening. But the dull ache between my legs suddenly feels sharper, more intrusive. It's a reminder of all the times I've woken up sore, thinking it was just the result of the marathon sex we have while I'm awake.

But now, knowing this... *Jesus.*

I understand snuggling against somebody and then they wake up... like I've been poked awake by plenty of dicks before. But like... against my leg or back. Not inside of me. I get waking up in the middle of the night for some spontaneous sex. And the people attached to said dicks have never just tried to ram it in there while I'm knocked out cold.

He doesn't even seem to notice my silence. He's too busy flicking through TV channels, completely nonchalant, like what he just admitted to was no more scandalous than stealing a sip of my drink when I'm not looking. Which he does a lot too.

I know somnophilia is something people are into, and I know it can be enjoyable—exciting, even, where both partners are on the same page and have consented to it in advance. Even free use situations where partners will agree their body is accessible at their partner's will. *But that's not what this is.* There's no consent in what he's doing. No agreement. No opportunity for me to say yes or no.

And that's what makes this so deeply wrong. He decided—on his own—that it was okay to have sex with me while I was unconscious. That it was okay to bypass my ability to consent, the implication being that, to him, my body is available to him at any time. *His to use.*

It's unsettling in a way that makes my skin crawl. The act isn't even what terrifies me the most, although that feels incredibly violating—it's the way he said it. Like he's entitled to my body. Like my silence isn't just expected—*it's preferred.* His words drip with entitlement, with the implicit belief that he can do whatever he wants to me, even when I'm unconscious.

And the worst part? He knows I've been drugged and assaulted in my sleep before. He knows how haunted I've been by that experience, how deeply it's scarred me. And still, he thought this was okay.

I feel sick. My gut twists painfully as memories resurface— memories I've spent years trying to work through in therapy, to move past. And now, here I am, reliving it. Only this time, it's the person I'm meant to be able to trust most. Someone who is supposed to love me.

Does he think I should be flattered? Is that what this is? Am I supposed to be grateful that he wants me so much that he can't even wait for me to be conscious? Or that he graced me with the presence of his massive cock as some kind of sleep treat?

I shift uncomfortably in my seat, trying to make sense of the confusion swirling inside me. I don't want to overreact. I've been through trauma, and I know it can skew my perspective. Maybe... maybe I'm overthinking this? Maybe he thought I'd be okay with it. Maybe he thought it was just another way to show me he loves me, that he's still attracted to me, even while I'm asleep.

I think about all the times he's gently woken me up to initiate sex, with kisses or playful touches. I was aware then, able to say yes or no. Those moments were intimate, consensual, enjoyable. But this is not that.

My gut churns again, and I remember the time he made me feel guilty at the start of our relationship when I asked him to wear a condom. How he pushed back, subtly manipulating the situation until it felt like I was unable to maintain that boundary. And now this?

I glance at him, sitting there so casually, flicking through channels like it's just another day. I feel a mixture of anger and sadness, confusion and betrayal. He isn't angry or defensive. He's... pleased. Like he's proud of what he's done.

I open my mouth to say something—to confront him, to tell him how what he's just shared has made me feel—but no words come out. I feel strangled, trapped by the weight of my emotions.

My mind flashes back to stories of 1950s marriages where some husbands felt that they could take what they want from their wives sexually, whether they wanted them to or not, no questions asked. Is that what this is? Some twisted version of that?

I feel like I'm standing on a ledge, teetering, trying to decide if I'm overreacting or if this is the massive red flag that, deep down, I know it is. I want to believe that he loves me. That he wouldn't knowingly hurt me. But the way he's acting now—like my discomfort isn't even on his radar—it scares me.

And the scariest part? A tiny voice in the back of my head whispers, *what if this is just the start of it? What if there are other things he's doing that I'm not aware of? What if this is just another crack in the foundation of something that's meant to be solid?*

I exhale slowly, trying to steady myself, trying to figure out what to do next.

He flips the channel again, oblivious, laughing obnoxiously at some silly show.

And I sit here, numb, with the weight of his words pressing down on me like a stone.

109

CUZ CAN

A *few days later*

The first crack of the plastic startles me, my pulse quickening as he holds the remote control in front of me, staring unblinking into my eyes. His fingers dig into the sides of the small rectangular device, pressing it until it begins to give way, bending under the relentless force of his grip. His knuckles whiten, and the remote disintegrates in his hand. I can't quite believe what I'm seeing. He just *crushed* it. Crumpled it almost as easily as if it was a piece of paper.

He's strong, and the remote is no match for him.

It feels like this isn't about the remote, though. It's like he's reminding me of how strong he is, how much more powerful he is than me.

My jaw drops, and I'm unable to hide the flicker of fear in my expression. My voice comes out distant, thin. "Why did you do that?"

He smirks, his eyes glinting with cruel satisfaction. "Because you're a fucking bitch...and because I can." The words land heavy, sharp-edged, accompanied by a look of twisted amusement that tells me he *enjoys* this.

"Why am I a bitch this time?" I quirk a brow, glad the remote wasn't me or my cat.

His face contorts with disgust, transforming him from a cute but angry surfer boy into something more sinister. Definitely not cute. Definitely not a surfer. Definitely not a boy. Angry, rageful, aging man. "Because you insisted on watching this fucking stupid show."

The smirk lingers as he stands there with the broken remote in his hand, knowing he's left me to deal with the inconvenience, the cost. The fact that I'll have to replace something else that he chose to destroy on a whim, all because I wanted to watch something he didn't. Just because he chose to have a mini tantrum, because he could. His tantrum has now become my problem, just the way he likes it.

I've never been around someone who just... breaks other people's things all the time. And who seems to get some pure, vindictive joy over seeing something belonging to their supposed soulmate being destroyed. Of wasting the money they worked so hard to make.

And when he gets mad and destructive, he never damages his own stuff. He *loses* his own things with regularity. He's gone through countless pairs of flip-flops and shoes and phones that he leaves behind here or there, usually while he's drinking.

But in his fits of rage, he doesn't seem to break his own possessions. No, it's *my* things he targets. The items I've saved for, the things that mean something to me. Or just trivial things that still need to be replaced for day-to-day convenience—remotes, chef's knives, chopping boards. They're his chosen victims when he's in a mood, like they're tokens he can obliterate just so show he can.

It's curious that his lack of self-control, his violent impulses that he's unable to harness, are... quite selective.

LATER, I go to text Paulo just to say hey, and I notice nearly all the contacts in my phone are missing.

"Babe? Did you do something to my phone?" I call out to him in the bathroom.

"What do you mean?" he asks, trying to act casual, but I hear a note of guilt in his voice.

"All my contacts are gone."

"Oh, yeah. I deleted them all," he says, nonchalantly, returning to the living room, scrolling through something on his own phone, a smirk on his face.

I furrow my brow. "Why the hell would you do that?" I ask.

He shrugs. "You hurt my feelings and I was mad at you."

I scrunch up my face, squeezing my eyes shut. How the hell does he so casually use the same excuse over and over again to justify the most bizarre behavior? "Timmy, you can't just go into my phone and delete things. That's really fucked up."

"Well, you also made me get a new phone number, so I thought it was only fair for you to have all your contacts deleted." His gaze meets mine, a curious gleam in his eye.

I'm furious. "Timmy, how could you? I didn't make you do anything. Getting a new phone number was completely your idea, your suggestion. I never asked you to do that. You said yourself that you wanted to break contact with bad influences—sure, I appreciate that you did it, which I've told you already, numerous times. But now you've gone into my phone and deleted information on all my friends, so I can't just text them. That's just..." I can't find the words.

"Oh well, you'll survive," he shrugs. "Besides, you don't need them, anyway. You have me now."

A FEW HOURS LATER, I jolt awake, a scream caught in my throat. My heart is pounding, my skin damp with sweat, the terror of the nightmare still clinging to me.

Because in that dream, which felt incredibly real, it wasn't our sleek black remote that he crushed with his rage. It was my sleek black cat, Sabre. I see him there, his eyes wide with fear, pinned in the grip of those same cruel hands.

And in my subconscious, I can see the same cruel smirk twist his mouth, the same eyes glinting with the pleasure of hurting me, of stripping me of something I love.

And I realize it's within him to do that to Sabre.

To me.

And I am terrified.

The thought paralyzes me. My heart races, and I lie in bed, staring into the dark, haunted by the realization.

These small displays of destruction, these casual demonstrations of power keep accumulating, each one chipping away at my sense of safety. He's building a world of tension, an invisible fence around me. And I don't know if I have the strength—or maybe the courage—to push back.

I glance at the TV, feeling sick. Even the shows I once found mindlessly enjoyable aren't safe from his judgment. Just mentioning *60 Days In* and *Life After Lockup* brings on a tirade. "I refuse to watch that depressing prison shit," he snaps, his face scrunched in disgust. "My biggest fear is going to jail or prison. I just can't do it. It's too real. It gives me flashbacks."

Okay, well, those are two more shows I can check off the list. I'm starting to run out of shows that he will allow me to watch without making me regret it. My choices are shrinking, the simple comforts I once enjoyed being removed one by one. Any reality TV, anything too sad, too dramatic, too fluffy, too Margaux chose it.

And then there's his driving. When he's calm, he drives with this easy confidence. But when he's angry, he transforms into this other person entirely, someone who treats the road like his personal territory. He takes his aggression out on the wheel, swerving and weaving, tailgating with terrifying precision, jumping lanes when it's risky to do so. And I feel like saying anything only makes it worse, makes him more reckless. When I glance over as he's doing this, he just sets his jaw more firmly, his hands tightening on the steering wheel, his anger infusing every sudden swerve and acceleration. If I so much as suggest he slow down, I know he'll only push it further, veering dangerously just to prove he's in control.

Like he's entitled to do that, even when it makes others feel unsafe.

Especially when it makes *me* feel unsafe.

More and more, it feels like he's not in control of just the car.

He's in control of me, how safe I feel. Whether I make it to our next destination.

And somehow, I'm the only one terrified of where this could all lead.

110

ON NIGHTMARES AND DAY DREAMS

I'm starting to be so closely attuned to his moods, moreso than I am to my own.

If he's having a good day, we'll both have a good day. If he's having a bad day, we'll both have a terrible time. And it can change with the wind.

He's found a new way to torture me.

His foot is getting wigglier and wigglier.

Whenever he's anxious about something he says I did, he will shake his foot more aggressively until the entire bed is rattling so hard I think it would probably show up as a reading on the Richter scale.

"It's anxiety," he says when I mention it. "I can't help it. Stop making me feel bad for something that's part of my mental illness, something I'm unable to control. That's just mean. You, of all people, should know better. Imagine if I said that to you. You would go crazy."

I feel sympathetic—after all, I suffer from anxiety too—but there's a point at which Timmy's behavior gets a bit much, that it feels like it's more of an intentional act than a real symptom of an underlying anxiety issue."Well can you please try not to shake it so hard, baby?" I keep my voice soft and low, careful as possible not to set him off. "Let me know how I can help you. But shaking the bed is pulling me out of what I'm doing."

"Fuck you, Margaux. Talking to me like that."

The foot shaking intensifies.

I've never experienced someone else's mental health issues be so destructive to my day-to-day life.

He seems angry when I ask him to work.

He seems angry when I work.

He promises repeatedly to help me with my work, but rarely seems to follow through.

I look up the mood disorder he says he has, and I don't see any symptoms of that. No visual or auditory hallucinations. If anything, he's more controlling, more rageful, more vindictive.

I try to understand it, so much so that I join a group online for sufferers and allies of people who have his supposed mood disorder. It's a highly active group, and I seek to understand where he's coming from. But these aren't the same symptoms he's describing at all.

Sure, he has periods where he seems more excitable—possibly manic—and others where he seems more down. The people in this group, however, primarily describe voices in their head.

He says he has none of the typical symptoms, just seems to use 'I have a mood disorder' as a blanket excuse to behave however he wants, and to never take any constructive feedback, no matter how carefully I time it, how precisely I word it, how much I emphasize that we're in this together and I'm not judging him, just trying to help make us a stronger couple.

I'm not a psychiatrist though, so what do I know?

And the foot situation just gets worse. To the point that every time he gets even slightly upset, he shakes his foot more.

The entire bed will bounce, and it feels a little bit being on a trampoline.

And then he'll let out these little moans, grunting noises like an animal in pain.

It's torture, sitting here listening. Being bounced up and down while I'm trying to sleep, and then even more when I try to work. He's depriving me of sleep, depriving me of being able to concentrate on writing.

And I go through this cycle of feeling like a bitch for asking him to stop.

But it's like he knows it annoys me, so he does it more. He puts it on, in addition to whatever might be real.

Sometimes he starts off the day shaking his foot and moaning, and the moans are actually traumatizing to listen to, like a wounded animal crying in the night. I almost expect Sarah McClachlan to start singing with a voice-over asking us to donate to animals in need.

Those are generally the days where he describes having had a bad nightmare that will typically impact his mood for the rest of the day. He'll be short, irritable, take everything extremely personally, start fights for no reason, find excuses to storm off.

And when he's in the apartment, resentfully sitting on the bed next to me, he will shake that foot harder than a blender on the highest speed setting.

And I get it. I have nightmares too, and mornings where I wake up screaming because something terrifying happened while I was asleep. But, after a moment of disorientation, I'll realize it was just a bad dream and I'll move on with my day.

But with Timmy, he wakes up in a mood and he lets it pervade every aspect of both of our days. Like he's wearing his nightmare like a badge, and justification for bad behavior. It's almost like he's saying 'because I had a bad dream, you have to endure me dragging it into our day and making you have a real, living nightmare'.

And then other days, it feels like I'm able to catch him at just the right time.

"Timmy, let's watch the movie you mentioned. We can hire it." Or, "Yes, we can add that extra streaming service I can't afford." Or, "Let's go to the store and you can pick out what you want."

Many days, when I give into his never-ending list of wants or needs, usually resulting in financial cost to me, he's nice for a spell. And the foot shaking stops. But it never lasts. The good periods seem to be getting shorter and shorter. His wants and demands seem to be bottomless, ever-expanding, illogical, greedy.

I feel like he's training me in some ways. Giving me positive reinforcement whenever I give into his spontaneous whims. Punishing me when I don't.

Sabre can be like that, sometimes. If I give him a treat—especially if it's a Churu—he'll purr and rub himself up against my leg, cuddling me as a thank you for the treat. When I don't give him a treat, however, he's prone to biting my ankle.

And Timmy is starting to act a lot like Sabre. Sleeping all day, being selfish. The reward and the punishment.

But the difference is that Sabre is a cat.

And Timmy is a nearly 40-year-old man.

111

BROKEN THERMOSTAT

A *Week Later*

Timmy's voice is calm, his eyes soft when he speaks, and for the first time in what feels like forever, I feel like maybe—just maybe—things are finally changing.

"I've been thinking," he begins, his eyes locked on mine. "I've been taking for granted all the amazing ways you contribute to our life."

There's a subtle tremor in his jaw, and then I see it—a single tear slipping down his cheek. It catches in the light, magnifying the brilliant blue of his eyes. He frowns slightly, a look of worry etched on his face, and I feel my heart clench in response.

It's like he's finally cracked open, finally seeing what I've been trying to say all along. His words are cautious, deliberate, and they carry a weight I haven't heard from him before. It's not just the content—it's the delivery, the vulnerability.

"Margaux," he continues, his voice trembling slightly. "I guess I just took for granted that you'd be paying rent and bills anyway, with or without me."

The words land like a punch to the gut, and for a second, my hope falters. *Really? That's how he's been seeing things this whole time? My* brain can't help but flag the entitlement dripping from his words—this casual assumption that because I'd already be supporting myself, he can simply slide into the arrangement, rent-free. Like my effort and financial burden are somehow expected when it's *our* life.

I mentally file it away—another, not insubstantial, red flag—another ick.

But then, before I can dwell on it, he keeps going, his expression softening, as if he senses he's on thin ice.

"But I see it now," he says earnestly. "You make sure we have such a nice life, and I just want to say thank you." His voice catches slightly, and I watch him closely, trying to gauge whether he really means it. "I know I haven't been doing my part. But I promise you, I'm going to work harder, try harder. I'm going to do better by you—for us."

His words, for all their flaws, carry the weight of sincerity. His eyes are still locked on mine, desperate and full of emotion. I *want* to believe him.

"You really mean that?" I ask, still cautious, but with a flicker of hope in my voice. "Because it's going to take work on both of our parts. It's not just about words—we need to be consistent with our actions."

He nods, his gaze unwavering. "I'm ready, Margaux. I want to be with you for the rest of my life. And if that means working harder to make things right, I'll do it."

A relief so deep I can feel it in my bones washes over me. He pulls me into his arms, and for the first time in weeks, I let myself sink into his embrace. It's as if he's had some kind of revelation—a lightbulb moment where he realizes how much I've been carrying. To his credit, he has been keeping up with his therapy appointments, and he's shared they've been discussing our issues. Maybe the therapy is starting to work.

He strokes my hair and presses a kiss to my temple. "I know I've been an idiot," he murmurs. "And I know I've come so close to losing you. More than once. I get it now—if I screw this up, I'm going to lose the best thing that's ever happened to me. And I can't let that happen."

His words are everything I've been waiting to hear.

But still, a tiny part of me hesitates. "What makes it different from the other times?" I want to believe him, but he's promised me real change before, and he's backslid every time.

"I'm willing to change... for you."

"Timmy," I whisper. "You need to change for yourself. Not because of me. You need to want to change for yourself in order for it to be sustainable—otherwise it won't last. And I'm here to support you. But it has to be for you."

He grins, a spark of the playful Timmy I fell for glimmering in his expression. "See? That's why I appreciate you. Holding me accountable already." He tousles my hair, and for the first time in a long time I feel us slipping back into something familiar, something good.

He gently cups my jaw, tilting my chin up in a kiss that feels deliberate and deep. "Let me show you how much I appreciate you," he growls softly, his voice dropping an octave.

I feel a surge of warmth spread through me, my pussy clenching in anticipation as he yanks off his board shorts, revealing his massive cock.

And for the rest of the day, I let all my troubles melt away, letting myself float in this new bubble of him—of us.

Timmy rubs my back, his hands slow and steady, working out the tension that's been building for weeks. He kneels to soak and rub my feet, giving me a pedicure, laughing softly as he tries his hand at applying nail polish. "I love being able to do this for you," he smiles, his voice kind, his eyes gazing at me with a tender adoration that reminds me of how he looked at me when we first met.

"Me too," I smile back at him, the knot in my chest loosening. "Thank you so much, baby."

It's a small thing, but it feels monumental. Symbolic. And like maybe I've just never dated a guy whose love language was physical touch. I think the longest massage I'd received from a partner before Timmy was about thirty seconds.

"I'm going to rub your feet all the time, because you deserve it, my love," he promises, his voice low and sweet. "And your back, and your shoulders. And give you scratches and tickles. And I'm going to eat your pussy every day like I promised when I proposed." He gives me a wicked grin. "I should have been doing it all along, because I gave you my word. And because you deserve it, too."

And for the first time in what feels like forever, his words are soothing, his touch grounding me.

And we fuck, and he's gentle—so tender it almost makes me cry. He goes down on me twice, his hands steady on my thighs, and uses my vibrator to bring me to a shuddering, toe-curling climax for a third time. When I squirt, he grins and groans with pleasure, kissing my inner thighs as my body pulses with an insane release.

In the shower, he soaps me up slowly, massaging my skin as the hot water cascades around us. His hands move with care, and every kiss he presses to my forehead feels like a promise—a silent vow that this time will really be different. When we're done, he wraps me in a fluffy towel, his eyes shining brightly with something that looks a lot like love.

I sink into the warmth of it, allowing myself—for at least a little while—to believe that things can be good again. That this Timmy, the one standing before me now, is the real Timmy. The one I fell in love with. I feel adored, cherished, just like I did in the first few weeks of our relationship.

And for once, my mind is calm.

I don't know if this change will last, but right now, I want to believe that it will.

And for tonight, I let myself believe.

112

HIERARCHY OF WEIRD SHIT

I begin to see a pattern that I can't believe I haven't noticed before—a direct and unmistakable correlation between what Timmy chooses to wear on any given day, and how he's likely to behave.

I begin to dread all of it, like an internal weather system predicting the storm before it begins.

At the lowest level of this strange hierarchy is the claw necklace. When he wears it, he wants to stand out, but not too much—just a bit of flair to fish for compliments. The claw necklace means he's feeling a little restless, maybe seeking validation, but still manageable. I can handle him on claw necklace days.

I'm glad he doesn't have that hideous fucking bone necklace anymore, or I'm sure it would be next.

But god help me when the Superman cape comes out. Nothing good happens when Timmy wears the cape. It's like slipping on that ridiculous piece of red fabric, made for a child, gives him permission to abandon all self-restraint, as if the flimsy costume allows him to become the version of himself that only exists at the height of his mania. The chaotic supervillain that nobody wants or needs.

And I'm grateful—so grateful—that the giant coconut hat is gone, destroyed after the day he exploded on me in the first apartment. It was a harbinger of chaos, its appearance always preceding an outburst, like an omen. Timmy himself admitted that wearing that hat made him feel mischievous and invincible, reckless.

Without it, we're down to the cape, the claw necklace, and occasionally my sunglasses. That little accessory feels like a warning, too—like some part of him enjoys stepping into my world and twisting it into his playground.

There are other red flags, too. The days he asks me to braid his hair, for example, aren't as innocent and cute as they first seemed. Sometimes, it's just vanity—he likes the way the soft lilac hair ties I got him look against his finer hair. And I agree—he looks cute with his hair done like that. But if the braids appear alongside the Superman cape? That's a double warning. A sure sign that his playful energy is spiraling toward something more dangerous. It's like he's slowly assembling armor—becoming a caricature of himself, gearing up for behavior even he struggles to contain.

By now, the sight of him putting on the cape alone is enough to give me instant heartburn. I get that sick, anxious feeling, like my body knows what's coming before my mind can fully process it. It's almost like, by slipping into these costumes, Timmy gives himself permission to unleash the parts of him that he usually hides. The parts that frighten me. It's like he believes the clothes transform him into something untouchable, someone wild and untethered and accountable to no one. He's waving a red cloth at a terrifying, raging bull, but he's both the bull and the matador.

He starts off mildly excited, practically bouncing on his toes, but I can always sense the tension bubbling just underneath the surface. Excitement turns into hyperactivity, and then, inevitably, agitation creeps in. His energy feels combustible, like a powder keg ready to explode at any moment.

He thrives on the attention these costumes bring him. It doesn't matter that people are staring at him because he looks absurd—he revels in all of it. Positive attention, negative attention—it's all the same to Timmy. All publicity is good publicity in his mind. And if someone offers him even the smallest compliment, he clings to it, repeating it over and over, embellishing it each time. The five people who said something nice become ten, then twelve, then more. It's as if every kind word becomes a trophy he hoards, a shield against the reality of his spiraling behavior.

Meanwhile, I'm left in the background, desperate for even a fraction of the affection and praise he once lavished on me. When we first met, his compliments came in waves—almost too much—making me feel beautiful, talented, special. But now that well has dried up, and all I get are the odd scraps.

Instead of praise, I get picked apart. Constant little jabs that chip away at my confidence—comments about what I'm eating—even though I've asked him not to, how I'm cooking, how I'm cleaning. It feels relentless, like there's no aspect of my life too small to be criticized.

The only thing he doesn't seem to criticize is what I wear, and I don't know if that's a relief or just another way he's checked out.

These days, I don't feel so pretty looking in the mirror. I don't feel so confident in my ability to get things done. My brain is in a constant fog. I can count on one finger the amount of nice things he'll say to me in a day. Sometimes no fingers. But the jabs are becoming exponential.

I start to keep a mental catalogue of the things I do that upset him that might set him off, no doubt inviting more jabs—putting on a show he doesn't like, putting on a song he doesn't feel like listening to, saying no when he wants me to buy him something, saying no when he wants to smoke cigarettes out on the street in a dangerous neighborhood late at night, saying no when he wants to jump off a bridge—that one really seems to set him off, asking him to get out of bed before midday, asking him to contribute financially, bringing up his promises to do the dishes—which he inevitably ignores, letting them pile up until he's furious about their gross state—and I end up cleaning them at that point, anyway.

It's not that my requests are unreasonable. In a healthy relationship, none of these things would be issues. They'd be quick conversations, followed by compromise and mutual respect. But with Timmy, setting even the tiniest boundary feels like poking a bear.

Any resistance on my part unleashes an avalanche of hostility. It's like he expects me to adjust to his shifting moods, no matter how chaotic or contradictory they become. If he changes his mind about something from one day to the next, I'm just expected to know and go along with it—even if it hurts me.

But when Timmy gets what he wants? He's euphoric. He's happiest when he's in control of what we watch, what we do, how we spend our time, when he's receiving compliments and admiration—especially from strangers, when I buy him things without complaint, when he remembers prior praise and compliments, and when he garners new praise from people on the street or on the beach—wherever he can find it.

His need for external validation has grown insatiable. He seems far less interested in my opinions now, as though my praise has lost its value. But if a stranger says something nice, he's over the moon—grinning for hours, replaying the moment in exaggerated detail.

It's like dealing with a toddler: do what Timmy wants, receive love—set a boundary with Timmy, all hell breaks loose.

The exhausting whiplash between his fleeting joy and explosive anger is taking its toll. I feel like I'm constantly walking on eggshells, trying to navigate his moods without triggering an outburst. But it's impossible—no matter how careful I am, something always sets him off.

I used to believe that all adults, even the most complicated ones, could be reasoned with. That love and communication could solve most problems. But Timmy's emotional landscape feels less like the nuanced complexity of adulthood, and more like the volatile whims of a child.

I know he's hurting. I know that there's a part of him that's lost and desperate for love and validation. But his need for control, for attention, for things to go his way at all times—those things are swallowing him.

And I'm starting to wonder if there's any version of this relationship where I don't get eaten alive too.

113

GUESS I DIDN'T NEED ANY OF THEM, ANYWAY?

ANONYMOUS:

Hey. You okay?

ME:

Who's this?

ANONYMOUS:

You know who this is. You've had my number
for years.

ME:

Sorry. All my numbers in my phone got
deleted.

ANONYMOUS:

Oh, weird. It's Dex.

ME:

Dex!! So good to hear from you.

DEX:

Glad you remember me, haha.

How could I forget?

Now I feel guilty for having that immediate thought.

DEX:

> How'd all your contacts get deleted?

I have the urge to write back 'because my fiancé is a sociopath and thought it would be a good idea to go into my phone and delete all my contacts,' but instead I reply:

ME:

> Long story. Let's just call it a technical glitch.

DEX:

> Right. Anyway, I just wanted to check in on you. It's been a while.

I feel butterflies...well, not so much butterflies as a comfortable warmth in my chest. It's been so long since I've spoken to him, but he's always made me feel... I don't know. Special, cared for.

ME:

> I'm good! Enjoying life on the Cay.

DEX:

> Good to hear.

Timmy walks out of the bathroom and back into the living room, and immediately leans over to look at my phone.

"Who are you talking to?"

I put my phone down.

"No one. Just my brother's friend. He checks in from time to time."

"Weird. What did you tell him?"

"Oh, barely anything. Just that I'm enjoying island life here with you."

He nods. "Good. Let's watch the rest of this movie and then fuck."

He jumps onto the bed and pulls me close. I snuggle into his arms, and I feel safe and secure.

Thoughts of Dex melt away.

Dex

The moment she says all her contacts had been deleted, I know exactly who had done it and why. It's that Timmy creep. Trying to control her by moving her all the way to the other side of the island they're living on. And then deleting contacts for everyone she's ever known.

What a petty, controlling little fuck he is. It's dangerous, removing contacts that someone might rely on, whether it's for work or social reasons. Who would do that to a woman? Especially a woman like Margaux. It's depraved, idiotic. And it shows who he really is at his core. I just wish she could see it.

But she played it all off casually, and it wouldn't have been right for me to jump in and tell her what I really think. Not yet. Even though I'd really like to have a conversation with this Timmy fellow. Me and him, alone in a room. Oh, I know exactly what I'd do. And it wouldn't be my mouth that would be doing the talking.

I clench one of my fists and roll it around, examining the land-scape of scars that have developed over similar conversations with people. All of those have been for work.

But with Timmy, it would be personal—for fun.

To avenge Margaux and all the shit he's put her through, that he's continuing to put her through. What I'd give to see the look on his face when it's just me and him. When he doesn't have a vulnerable, trusting woman falling for his bullshit.

When he only has me to answer to.

114

GUSHING

For a couple of weeks, things feel almost normal—as normal as life with Timmy can be, anyway. He's relaxed, funny, affectionate. He keeps his word on the little things—cooking meals we both enjoy, cleaning without being asked, remembering my preferences in small but meaningful ways. He brings me a beautiful shell from the beach one day, holding it up with pride like he's found buried treasure just for me.

We swim together most afternoons, splashing around like carefree kids. His laughter is infectious, and it's hard not to feel charmed when he pulls me close, kisses me with genuine affection, and tells me how lucky he feels to have me. It feels like a balm to my frayed nerves, soothing the chaos that's been swirling around us for so long.

Our sex life is back to being incredible. Every day, without fail, he goes down on me with enthusiasm, as if it's his new favorite hobby.

There's a spark of playfulness between us that had been missing for a while, and I find myself relaxing just a little bit more each day.

I start thinking that maybe this move really was the right thing for us, and we're finally turning that corner that always seemed just slightly out of reach.

Of course, I'm still careful around him. I have to be mindful of how I speak, how I ask for things. I've learned to monitor my tone and delivery, softening my edges so I don't trigger one of his moods. It's something I've become hyper-aware of—like walking a tightrope without a safety net.

But part of me wonders if this is just something I need to work on, my own growth edge. Maybe I've always been a bit too blunt, too demanding, and perhaps this is what compromise looks like in a healthy relationship. Maybe this is growth for both of us. After all, Timmy has admitted many times that he's sensitive, that words can hurt him deeply, and he seems to genuinely want me to adjust for his sake as he appears to be doing for mine. It feels like a fair ask.

When Timmy calls his parents, he still always makes sure to sing my praises.

"Margaux has changed my life, Mom and Dad. She got me to quit smoking, which I honestly thought I'd never do. She's literally extended my life by years." He beams at me as he speaks. "And she's been planning all these hikes and outdoor activities to keep us healthy. I'm so lucky to have her. I love her so much." He leans over to kiss me sweetly on the cheek, smiling at me with those soft, sparkling blue eyes I fell in love with.

"That's wonderful, son," his father replies warmly, but then comes the question that always lingers in the air like a storm cloud. "So... do you have a job yet?"

Timmy grimaces, but his voice stays upbeat. "I'm working on my graphic design stuff, Dad. You know these things take time."

His father doesn't miss a beat. "Well, you should probably find a job in the meantime. It's important to contribute."

"Yes, Dad, I know. I will. Thanks for reminding me," Timmy replies, his tone light and agreeable, though there's an edge of impatience lurking beneath it.

I sit quietly through the exchange, feeling both validated and unsettled. It's a relief to know his father is nudging him toward responsibility, but there's also something about the conversation that doesn't sit right with me. It feels... juvenile. Like a grown man being coaxed out of bed by his parents—it reminds me of a boss I once had who had to call his mid-twenties son every morning just to make sure he got to work on time. It's unsettling. Why does Timmy need this much pushing to do what's expected of any adult?

But still, things have been good between us, and I want to hold on to that. I want to believe that this is the new normal—that we're finally—*finally*—settled into the kind of relationship I'd been hoping for.

And yet...there's another growing knot in my stomach.

It's subtle at first—just a nagging, creeping sensation. But now that I'm hyper-attuned to Timmy's patterns, I can sense something shifting beneath the surface. The manic energy is starting to bubble again. It's not quite here yet, but, somehow, I can tell that it's coming.

I've seen this play out before. We've been through this cycle too many times for me to ignore it. First, Timmy realizes he's been a bit of an ass. He drops his defenses, apologizes profusely, and treats me with kindness and affection. There's a honeymoon phase—a week or two where things are great, and I think maybe, just maybe, things are changing.

And then... something sets him off.

It's often something seemingly harmless—his own decision to deep-clean the apartment or reorganize the kitchen. He'll throw himself into it with manic energy, insisting it's for both of us, a way to make our space more functional and inviting. But somewhere along the way, things twist.

He becomes irritable, snapping over small things. Suddenly, the goodwill he'd built evaporates, and it's as if those one to two good weeks give him permission to behave badly for the next however long. It's a pendulum, swinging back and forth. And right now, I can feel the shift beginning, like the moment before a storm breaks.

Timmy is still sweet and affectionate most of the time. He makes me laugh, cooks me dinner, and cuddles me until I fall asleep. But there's an edge to his energy again now—a restlessness that makes my skin prickle.

It's in the way he taps his fingers against the table, a little too fast.

The way he starts projects and abandons them halfway through. The way he paces the apartment, muttering to himself.

I try to push the unease aside, telling myself that I'm overthinking it. But the bile rises in my throat every time I catch a glimpse of that manic gleam in his eyes. Something is brewing. And this time, I'm scared it's going to be worse than before.

I hate that I feel this way, that I'm always bracing for impact, waiting for the moment when the switch flips and everything falls apart again.

It's exhausting, constantly analyzing his moods, walking on eggshells to avoid triggering an outburst. And yet, I keep doing it. Because the good moments—the laughter, the affection, the way he holds me like I'm the most precious thing in the world—those moments make it feel worth it.

But how long can I keep riding this roller coaster? How many more times can I convince myself that the good will eventually outweigh the bad?

Because I know the pattern now. I can see it coming, like dark clouds on the horizon. And this time, it feels bigger, heavier—like a storm that's going to break harder than ever before.

The scariest part is, at this point, I know I'll stay. At least for now. And he seems to know it too. Because I love him, and I want to believe in him.

But deep down, I'm not sure how much longer I can keep convincing myself that love is enough.

115

VINDICTIVE

he Next Day

I get up and start working, sitting on the bed like usual, while Timmy continues to sleep. At one point, he turns over and faces me, his eyes open, and he mutters something unintelligible. I ignore him at first, but he speaks again, and I realize he's talking to me.

"Good morning, babe," I smile at him. "How did you sleep?"

He suddenly startles, his eyes flying wide open, filled with rage, his arms flailing around so wildly it makes me jump. "What the fuck? Margaux! You fucking woke me up! Fuck you!" His mouth forms a tight scowl.

"Oh no, Timmy. I'm sorry I woke you," I whisper softly. I really thought he was awake. "Your eyes were open, and you were talking to me."

"Bullshit." Timmy's response is immediate and sharp, like a whip crack. "Fuck you for waking me up."

My stomach twists at the venom in his words. I haven't even had a coffee yet and I've already managed to get him so upset he's swearing at me. Great.

I stay quiet for a moment, willing myself to stay calm, not quite trusting myself to navigate my way through this unexpected conflict. "I said sorry," I say evenly, keeping my voice soft. But the truth is, I'm scared.

With Timmy, apologies seem to play on repeat. They're a trap, a twisted game with no winning move. Not by me, at least. I try to tread carefully, to be the bigger person, to say sorry when the offense was trivial and even sometimes when I didn't do anything at all, just to smooth things over.

But somehow, every apology I give gets swallowed into some invisible abyss between us, as if I never uttered the words at all. He simply seems to forget every time I've taken accountability, saying I never uttered the words I know in my heart and memory that I did so many times.

Today appears to be no exception, and his glare lingers, heavy with resentment at my early morning faux pas.

Later, when he's fully awake and watching a movie, his expression grows sullen. "I still can't believe you woke me up and didn't even apologize," he scoffs. His eyes scan me with barely concealed irritation.

I straighten, looking up from my work on my laptop, feeling the familiar knot of disbelief coil in my chest. "I *did* apologize," I say carefully. "More than once."

"No," Timmy snaps, his jaw clenching as if I just insulted him. "You never said sorry."

My breath catches. It's like talking to a wall—or actually, worse than a wall. It's like talking to a version of him that flips reality on its head, twisting everything upside down so I'm always in the wrong, and then accusing me of doing that very same thing.

"Timmy, this is the *third* time now that I'm saying I'm sorry. I'm truly sorry I woke you up, and I know you hate that. But it was a mistake, and I genuinely thought you were awake. I hope we can move past this." My voice shakes slightly. I want so desperately to be heard, to get through to him.

"No, you didn't," he replies, shaking his head. "Stop lying." His tone turns sharp and final, as if I'm being dismissed, as if his version of events is an unshakeable truth. "You *never* apologize," he adds. "You always blame me for everything, and nothing is ever your fault."

His words hit me with the force of a wave, leaving me reeling. He can't be serious. I feel like I'm suffocating, trapped in an argument that bears no resemblance to the actual truth, and where logic simply doesn't apply. It's as if there are two versions of reality—his and mine—and no amount of reasoning will bridge the gap between us.

My head throbs as I fight back tears. I want to scream, to grab him and shake him until he admits I'm not crazy, that I *did* apologize, and that I'm not the monster he's painting me out to be. But instead, I press my lips together, locking the frustration inside. I know where this is going, and I can't bear it.

I've thought so hard about recording our conversations—I've even joked to myself about wearing a bodycam. That's how crazy this situation is making me feel. Just to force him to confront reality and prove I'm not losing my mind. But even then, deep down, I know even that might not be enough for Timmy.

It isn't just about the apologies. It's about how Timmy's entire version of reality twists, depending on his mood, and depending on who he's telling about it, a constant distortion that leaves me feeling disoriented and unsure of myself. He has this way of flipping things back on me, making me feel like a villain for things he's done or said. As if he's projecting his worst qualities onto me, punishing me for crimes I didn't commit.

And the worst part? If he really believes what he's saying—if he really thinks I'm this unkind, unapologetic, selfish, dishonest, manipulative, unloving person—what does that mean for what he's capable of, and for my safety?

He's already joked multiple times that he's going to kill me. I shiver involuntarily as I'm reminded of the cold, matter-of-fact way it's rolled off his tongue. It's generally followed up by an apology and a rescinding of it, saying he'd never hurt me. But in the moment, it feels like he means every word.

He always plays those comments off as throwaway lines, almost offhand, but his words are lodged in my brain as if there's a siren ringing in the back of my head, warning me to be careful. That he just might follow through one day. Because it's not just the words he uses, but the ease with which he says them, as if such a dark thought doesn't trouble him in the slightest.

And when it comes down to it, that's really what troubles me the most... that the man who claims to love me, to truly believe I'm his soulmate, to be the greatest and only true love of his life, is also someone who holds the potential—and apparently the occasional intent—to destroy me.

His devotion feels suffocating, like being trapped under glass sometimes—something fragile, breakable, with jagged pieces threatening to tear me apart just below the surface. After all, what does it mean to be someone's 'everything' when that same person is capable of imagining your end?

I feel myself unraveling bit by bit. I'm starting to see through more than a few minor cracks in his facade—his charming grin, smooth words, affectionate gestures. It's all starting to feel like an elaborate ruse, a flimsy cover for something far darker lurking underneath.

From a distance, with Timmy, everything looks normal. Perfect, even. But when you get close enough to touch it, you realize how flimsy it all is. How it's only a hair away from completely falling apart. Like he himself is a human comb-over, one gust away from causing it to slip out of place, revealing the truth behind it. And now that I've seen it, I can't unsee it.

The cracks are spreading, a seismic rift deep at the core of our relationship, and I don't know how much longer I can pretend they aren't there.

116

THE ONLY BLOCKING I APPROVE OF
IS IN ROLLER DERBY

If there was a soundtrack to my life right now, it would be aching, bittersweet, tinged with regret.

Timmy's silence stretches, heavy and sharp, as I wait for his response, amplifying the growing tension between us. I can feel it—the way he's building up, gathering his words like stones, ready to hurl them.

"Timmy, that's not what happened and you know it," I say, my voice trembling despite my effort to keep calm. My heart races as the knot in my stomach coils, twisting tighter with each passing second. I know I'm right, but calling him out always makes me feel like I'm stepping onto thin ice.

His face shifts, his eyes narrowing, his mouth curling into a thin, tight line.

He doesn't respond right away. Instead, he just stares, his silence deliberate and punishing, growing heavier by the moment.

"Are you seriously accusing me of lying about something so stupid?" he asks, his tone calm in a way that makes my skin crawl. The softness in his tone is unsettling—it's not kindness, but a quiet, controlled rage. He crosses his arms tightly across his chest as if he's pulling back from me, protecting himself from my 'attack', retreating behind a wall of self-righteousness. "After everything I've done for you? After all the times we've had together? This is how you treat me?" His face twists into a wounded expression, like a hurt puppy dog, his eyes downcast, his lips trembling ever so slightly.

He plays the victim so convincingly that I almost believe I hurt him.

It's hard to believe that we're arguing, once again, about him going out at night to smoke cigarettes. He told me he'd smoked alone, and then he later admitted he'd smoked with a woman in her seventies. I'm not at all worried about her, obviously—just annoyed he lied about it.

I can feel the weight of the guilt he's trying to push on me, almost suffocating, but I hold my ground. "Timmy, I don't want to fight with you. I can see you're upset, and I am, too. All I want is for you to admit that you lied. You weren't honest, and I know it. I just want to talk about why you did and we can move on."

My words hang in the air, but instead of acknowledgment, I see his expression change to something darker. "You're fucking unbelievable, you know that?" he spits, his voice low and sulky, tinged with bitterness. "You always do this. You're just like my ex. Always trying to make me the bad guy. I guess that's what I get for being so kind and generous and patient with you? Fucking bullshit," he mutters.

His words are like little jabs, making me second-guess myself, even though I know what he said first, and then what he said second, and the two don't align. My mind races. Maybe he's right. *Maybe I'm overreacting. Maybe I am too demanding.*

Without waiting for a response, he turns on his heel.

"Timmy—."

"You're pathetic," he spits over his shoulder, venom lacing his words.

Before I can even reply, he swishes the door open and I hear the familiar beep as he locks it behind him. The door slamming shakes the walls of the apartment, and I flinch, then sit in disbelief, stunned, the sudden silence suffocating.

My chest tightens, and all I can feel is the hollow, sinking feeling like I'm drowning in quicksand.

I know it was right for me to bring this up—I had to for my own sanity—but he's left me feeling like I'm the one who's being punished. My mind races as I replay the conversation in my head over and over again. How could I have got it so wrong? I just wanted the truth, but now all I feel is a deep, churning emptiness, like the ground has been ripped out from underneath me. Somehow, as usual, I've become the villain in his story.

I try to replay the conversation in my mind, but it's just a jumbled mess of accusations and guilt. I was only asking for honesty, but now all I feel is a hollow ache, like I've been punished for daring to question him.

TIMMY INSISTED early on that we share our phone passwords.

"I have nothing to hide," he'd said, "I want you to know you can trust me. I'll do anything to make you feel comfortable and secure in this relationship, because I love you so much. I'd do anything to make you happy."

I'd agreed, because I'm not doing anything behind his back. For the most part, with obvious exceptions, what I found in his phone put me at ease.

There were things from the past—messages and contacts that made me feel uncomfortable—but I convinced myself that these don't matter anymore, and, when he got his new phone number, that took many of those concerns away. He's not reaching out to new people, just keeping in touch with a limited circle.

I checked his Facebook messenger, just to be sure, and it was the same.

I felt relieved.

Then, shortly after, he insisted that we share locations.

"Especially living out here," he says. "If we get separated for any reason, it could be really dangerous. So we should know where the other person is at all times. Plus, I want you to know that you can trust me."

At the time, it felt like an extra layer of trust. Practical, even thoughtful.

I've never been in a relationship where I've felt the need to really check my partner's phone or share location. I've laughed about couples that share Facebook accounts.

And everything he said made sense at the time. Made it sound like it was coming from a place of love, so I went with it.

But now I see how easily he's used these promises against me.

The location-sharing promise soon turned into another manipulation. Now, every time we argue—no matter how minor—he switches off his location. Sometimes for hours, sometimes longer.

"Timmy, why bother sharing locations if you just block it every time you're mad, which is often?" I ask him, exasperated.

"I'm sorry," he says, his expression solemn. "I promise I won't block you ever again."

"Seriously? You keep saying that, but the moment your feelings are hurt, you do."

"Yeah, I know. I'm really sorry. I understand."

But the promises mean nothing anymore. Each time, it happens again. And again.

He knows it bothers me, and so it's become another cruel form of punishment.

IT FEELS like his behavior is escalating, and he's going back on every promise he's made to me. He seems to get a sick, perverse enjoyment out of my constant misery. And he creates conflict over literally nothing.

Anything can set him off. He's getting mad because I'm not doing dishes to his liking now. Because I move around on the bed while I'm working when he wants to be asleep, even though it's the middle of the day.

He's a rageful powder keg, and he's acting more and more unhinged. I don't know what's driving it, and I try to be sympathetic to his mental health issues. But it seems like he's trying to destroy this, to destroy us, and I don't know how much longer I can keep doing this.

I'm sick of crying.

I'm tired of becoming someone I'm not.

I need some reprieve from this constant madness.

But he seems to thrive on drama, and look for it in places it doesn't exist.

The happier, the more successful I am, the more he seems to want to punish me.

But then he's the one who comes back to comfort me, to give me the notion he's remorseful, and that he's truly going to change.

Yet his words and actions are getting further and further apart, like they're magnetically repelling each other. And he's seeming more and more justified in his actions.

I can't do this anymore.

117

___

SLASH & BURN

Every day the bitterness inside me grows, like rotting fruit in my chest—festering, sour and heavy. At night, it seeps into my dreams, distorting them until even sleep offers no refuge from the frustration I feel toward Timmy.

Sunset Cay was supposed to be paradise, but instead, it feels like I've been trapped in an endless cycle of disappointment—caught between the consequences of his past actions and the relentless toll of his present behavior.

I try to tell myself that 'things' shouldn't matter, but the list of damaged items keeps growing, each one a small but meaningful loss.

While Timmy is very mindful and protective of his own possessions, he handles my belongings like they're disposable, smashing them in tantrums triggered by things I don't even remember saying. The slamming of dishes into the sink feels like gunshots to my nerves, sharp and sudden.

"I've always done that," he says casually, driving a knife straight into my favorite cutting board as I watch in disbelief. His careless excuse grates against me. He knows I've asked him to stop doing that specific thing before. He knows. But it's like asking water not to be wet.

Then came the irreplaceable mug, the one I carried with me across cities and continents, through fifteen years and multiple life chapters. One of the only possessions I carried around for that long. "I didn't know it was important to you," Timmy says when he notices my expression, his voice dismissive, as if the loss is trivial. The worst part? He didn't even break it by accident. "You hurt my feelings, so I threw things into the sink to break them."

Who does that? Timmy, apparently.

Then there's the custom-made tiki carving of Sabre as a kitten. It was special to me, but meant nothing to him. He intentionally scratched it, gouging lines into it when he got upset. And when I confronted him, he couldn't even recall why he was angry in the first place. "I just remember you hurt my feelings somehow," he shrugged, as if that justified destroying something so precious to me.

Every time I try to move past these things, to let the resentment go, it pulls me down further. I can't unsee the way he sleeps until at least noon, and then insists on binge-watching TV for the rest of the day, all while my savings dwindle away under the weight of his endless list of wants. It feels like living with a human CVS receipt—his desires just keep adding up, into a longer and longer list, multiplying every time he watches something new or takes another nap.

I try to force a smile each time, try to pretend like it doesn't bother me. But I'm not a good actress, and Timmy is too attuned to my emotions to miss the growing distance between us. The more he senses my resentment, the more erratic his behavior becomes. The apartment feels darker, colder, suffused with an unsettling energy that makes my skin crawl.

I start noticing things I hadn't before, new aspects to this recurring cycle that have crept in—the way he watches me, peeking around doors when he thinks I don't notice. He's always lingering on the edges of my vision, just out of reach, as though keeping tabs on me has become his new obsession. He continues to invade my space constantly, continually stepping into the bathroom when I'm showering or even when I'm just peeing.

And every time I catch him spying on me in the shower, he laughs it off like a joke, insisting he's being playful. But it doesn't feel cute anymore, like it did at the very start of our relationship. Now, it feels invasive, like a game with invisible rules that only he understands.

Even the smallest conversations have become more charged, more intense. Every word is a potential trigger, and he's more easily irritated than ever before. I find myself shrinking, calculating every word and action more than ever in a futile attempt to avoid setting him off.

My body responds in ways I can't control. My throat feels tight, as if it's being squeezed shut. A strange buzzing floods my hands and feet most days, like my blood is rushing to prepare for flight, even though it feels like there's nowhere to run. The cortisol spikes leave me feeling swollen and out of sync, like a bloated sausage in a freckled casing stretched too thin.

And knowing I look and feel this way just amplifies the anxiety further—anxiety that clouds my mind, giving me brain fog so thick it makes every decision feel impossible. Even something as simple as choosing what to eat has become overwhelming.

Timmy notices everything. He always does. I can't tell if he's feeding off my emotions or responding to them in real-time, but it's unsettling either way. It's like he's anticipating my next move, waiting for the exact moment when my defenses are down, or when I do something he can pounce on.

And all the while, he keeps watching, waiting, lurking—until I feel like I'm suffocating inside, smothered in my own skin, trapped in a life that's no longer mine.

And he notices all of this..

Hell, he might even be more aware of how I'm feeling than I am.

118

I'M THE PROBLEM

"You are *so* abusive," Timmy sneers, his voice sharp and cutting. His eyes narrow, his face twisting with disdain. "You pretend to be all sweet and cute, but you're just a fucking bitch. It's all an act. You're a real piece of work. I see who you really are. I see you, Margaux."

The words hit me like yet another slap. My heart stings with the venom in his tone, and a tight knot forms in my chest. I frown, my voice wavering, but rising. "I am who I say I am, Timmy. No more, no less."

His gaze darkens, his eyes turning into sinister slits, malice swimming almost visibly beneath the surface. There's a hatred there that's become disturbingly familiar. "You call me names," he snaps. "You make me feel bad about myself. You're the problem in this relationship, not me."

The absurdity of it is so blatant that, for a brief second, a twisted laugh bubbles up in my throat. But there's no humor in any of this. My stomach churns with frustration and disbelief, and the anger inside me flares.

I've heard this script too many times now—the constant role reversal, the way he twists reality to suit his narrative. It's always my fault, even though I've basically stopped giving him any constructive feedback, or asking him to have any accountability. My words, my actions, my existence, somehow warped into the root of every conflict we have. It's a sick game he plays. He prods and pokes me all day with passive-aggressive remarks, dragging his feet when it comes to helping with the simplest of tasks, making snide digs when I cook or go about other aspects of my routine.

And when I finally do snap from time to time—because no one can take endless poking without breaking—he smirks. He points at me with gleeful satisfaction, like a child finally triggering a sibling into reacting.

"See?" he'll say, his voice smug and triumphant. "Look at you. Here she is. The *real* Margaux."

My heart sinks every time he says it. That phrase. It's not just the words themselves, but the way he says them, like he's caught me in a trap I didn't know I was walking into.

He used to say, 'there she is' when I laughed or smiled, looking at me with adoration. But now, the words have been twisted into something horrible. He acts like each time I react to his inappropriate behavior, this outburst defines who I really am, and everything I do outside of it—the patience, the care, the love—is just an elaborate performance.

I feel the frustration bubbling under my skin, burning to scream, to fight back, to explain. Because the 'real' Margaux he's so proud of revealing isn't real at all—it's a product of his relentless needling, his constant erosion of my boundaries, his slow poisoning of my peace.

But then a darker thought creeps in—isn't this what abusers say? They justify their actions—'I wouldn't have hit her if she didn't push me.' 'I only snapped because she drove me to it.' It's a slippery, terrifying slope, and I wonder if I'm slipping down it, too.

He's projecting. I know that. I see it clearly, the way he twists everything about me into a reflection of his own behavior. 'You're not a nice person.' 'You can't be trusted.' 'No wonder your friends don't like you.' Every accusation he hurls at me feels like a confession in disguise, the things he knows are true about himself but can't face.

It's like a hall of mirrors where his worst qualities are forced onto me.

And still, I doubt myself. Every word, every argument, every step feels like walking on a tightrope stretched too thin, ready to snap at any moment. I feel unhinged, like maybe he's right and I really am the one with the problem.

In moments of clarity, I realize the truth—I don't wake up and pick fights with him. I don't make it my mission to ruin his day. It's not in my nature. And, in fact, I tiptoe around his moods so carefully that I sometimes feel like I've disappeared entirely.

But no matter how cautious I am, it's never enough. He picks, and picks, and picks—until I can't take it anymore, and the frustration spills over. Then it's my fault. Always.

And slowly, he's been closing me off from the world and continues to do so. It wasn't so obvious at first, but now I feel it happening with increased velocity—the isolation creeping in like a thick fog. I came to Sunset Cay with dreams of community, of finding friends, of building a life. Now, I barely talk to anyone. I'm too embarrassed to reach out. What would I say? That my fiancé, the person who promised me the world, is the reason I feel trapped and alone? That I don't feel safe in my own relationship?

More and more of the promises he made feel like lies now. Every time I try to make a friend, he pulls away, takes issue with something, or deserts me emotionally. It's like he thrives on watching me flounder—like he gets off on tearing down every boundary I've tried to build, every bit of happiness I try to create.

I try to convince myself that we're just going through a rough patch, that he's stressed and it'll pass. But his life seems to be a rough patch, finding thing after thing to have a problem with, whether legitimate or invented, and the agitation within him continues to build. His moods are darker, more volatile, than I've ever seen them. He's no longer just poking for a reaction—he's playing whack-a-mole with every bit of good we have.

One day, he's cooking dinner and cuddling me on the couch, planning our next adventure. The next, he's smashing dishes, screaming, or stressing over imaginary problems. He creates storms where there are none, inventing conflict out of thin air. And no matter how hard I try to anchor us, we're caught in a riptide of his making.

And the scariest part? I'm starting to feel increasingly unsafe. Really unsafe.

It's subtle, creeping in the way he watches me out of the corner of his eye, like he's waiting for something. The way he looms over me when he's agitated, how his words turn from sharp to sinister without warning. And those throwaway jokes—the ones where he casually talks about hurting me, about killing me. They linger.

He says them like they're nothing. Like it's funny. And then he apologizes, brushing it off as just a bad joke. But I can't unhear them. They rattle around in my mind, filling the space where trust used to live.

Every day, I feel myself slipping further away from who I was. I wake up anxious, and go to bed exhausted. I have no energy to write, so I don't even try most of the time. The good moments—the laughter, the cuddles, the plans—feel like little islands in an ocean of uncertainty, gradually getting flooded with more and more bad until each one is fully submerged.

And I don't know how much longer I can tread water until I sink, too.

I know I likely need to leave. I know that. But then, where would I go? He's isolated me so well that I don't even know if I have anywhere to run.

And yet, staying feels like slowly drowning in quicksand, each day pulling me a little deeper, each fight taking another piece of me until there's nothing left.

I sit there, my heart pounding, my hands clammy with fear. And, not for the first time, I wonder if love is supposed to feel this way.

And if it's not, how the hell did I let it get this far?

119

—————

KIDNAPPED

he Next Day

T   We go for a drive down to the Point—the legal road part —and Timmy seems upbeat, almost hyper. It's one of those days where he's just happy to be alive. He's joking, telling me stories about his childhood, sharing memories that make him seem so innocent and carefree—as if all the darkness is gone. For a while, it's easy to forget the other side of him.

We pull over at a beach. The sky stretches wide and cloudless, the water sparkling beneath the sunlight. I breathe in the salty air, trying to anchor myself to the present moment, to hold on to the parts of this relationship that still feel good.

"I love you," he whispers, wrapping his arms around me from behind. His chin rests on my shoulder as we both stare out at the horizon. "I want us to be like this forever."

My heart softens, and I lean into him. This is the version of Timmy I love. The one who's sweet and present, who wants to build a future with me. This is the man I moved here for.

We've been bickering a bit, but there haven't been any severe incidents since his most recent outburst. More just day-to-day, me spending all my energy trying to get him out of bed to be productive while also trying to keep my author business going.

It's exhausting, and I feel like a hopeless hamster on a very unsatisfying wheel. It feels a bit like living inside a snow globe—everything looks picturesque from the outside until it's suddenly shaken up, chaotic, fragile. Timmy alternates between apologies and excuses, leaving me grasping at every thread of normalcy, trying to pull us back to where we were before things fell apart. And, for a moment, I let myself believe we'll get there.

Every day feels like walking on a tightrope, balancing between fleeting peace and the inevitable crash. His apologies now feel more like band-aids on a broken bone—temporary, flimsy. I want to believe he means them. I need to believe it. But there's this persistent throb in my gut, a warning that the worst is yet to come.

It's a pleasant surprise when I get a message from one of my childhood friends, Charlie, saying she's in town. It's been years since we've seen each other, and she'd love to catch up. We quickly make plans, and as far as I know, it's just going to be her, her kids, and Timmy and me, meeting for lunch. It sounds like a nice way to break us out of our routine and see some new faces. And a nice opportunity for Timmy to meet another of my friends.

Right before we're supposed to meet, Charlie casually mentions there will actually be a larger group joining us. I don't think too much of it—just a bigger table, right? But when we arrive at the restaurant, my heart sinks a little at the sight of the large party waiting to be seated.

The staff has to join a couple of smaller tables together to accommodate the entire group. Charlie greets me warmly, giving me a tight hug, and I try to relax as I take in the sheer number of people—her husband, her kids, some stepchildren, and a handful of family friends and their families. It's overwhelming, but everyone seems friendly and laid-back, which helps me exhale a little.

"It's so nice to see you again after all these years!" I tell Charlie, holding onto the nostalgia of our shared past.

"Likewise!" she beams. "And here, of all places! What are the chances?"

As we settle in at the long table, conversation flows easily. Memories of childhood adventures resurface and, for a while, it feels like no time has passed at all.

At our end of the table, Timmy hits it off immediately with Charlie's fourteen-year-old son, Jackson. They're deep in conversation, discussing the nuances between rugby and football, their voices animated and full of excitement. I watch the two of them with a small smile. Timmy's good with kids when he's in the right mood—his playful energy and love for storytelling make him a natural magnet.

"They're getting along really well," Charlie observes, glancing toward them with a smile.

"Yeah, like a house on fire," I agree. It feels nice—wholesome, even. For once, things seem to be going smoothly.

As lunch wraps up, Charlie mentions they're planning to head to a nearby beach for the afternoon. Timmy and I offer to show them to one of our favorite hidden spots—a quiet, secluded stretch of sand just up the road.

"We have extra beach chairs and towels if you need them," I tell her.

"That'd be amazing! Thank you," Charlie replies.

After lunch, we swing by our apartment to grab the beach gear. Jackson tags along in the truck with us—he and Timmy are getting along so well that it feels natural.

Once we drop off the chairs and towels at the beach, Timmy turns to me with a grin. "Hey, why don't we take Jackson for a little drive around the neighborhood?"

I hesitate for a second, but it seems harmless enough. Timmy is in a good mood, and Jackson is clearly enjoying himself. I don't see the harm in giving the kid a little tour before they hit the beach.

"Sure," I agree, shrugging off the small flicker of hesitation.

Jackson settles into the back seat, and Timmy shifts the truck into gear with a little more force than necessary. The engine hums, and I notice Timmy's foot lingering on the accelerator a little longer than usual, but I tell myself it's just his excitement spilling over.

At first, the drive is easy and relaxed. Timmy launches into his usual stories—self-aggrandizing tales of wild adventures, always casting himself as the star. I've heard most of them before, but they're relatively harmless. Jackson listens politely, occasionally throwing in a comment or two.

He even plays a few Kiwi songs for us, which Timmy seems to get a real kick out of.

But gradually, the stories begin to shift. Timmy's words become louder, more boastful, as if he's trying to impress Jackson by pushing the boundaries of what's appropriate.

"Once, I threw a beach party that got so wild the cops had to shut it down," he says with a laugh, glancing in the rearview mirror to see Jackson's reaction. "There were so many people there we blocked the whole street. They couldn't even get the squad car through."

Jackson chuckles politely, but his body language shifts—he leans away slightly, as if sensing that things are about to take a weird turn.

Timmy speeds up, the truck weaving slightly as he accelerates around a corner. I glance at him nervously. "Timmy, slow down a little."

"We're fine," he says, brushing off my concern with a grin.

Then, without warning, he dives into a new story—one far darker than the harmless party tales.

Timmy grips the steering wheel, one hand loosely draped over it while he weaves down the road. His other hand gestures wildly as he launches into the story, as if it's the most entertaining thing in the world.

"So, these two chicks were in my car," he says with a grin that makes my stomach churn. "Both of them were hot, and I knew they wanted me. I was trying to decide which one to fuck."

I stare at him, horrified. "Timmy, stop."

But he's lost in his own narrative, ignoring me. "And one of them —man—one of their pussies smelled *so* bad. So I kept pretending I needed to mess with the stereo, leaning down to figure out which one it was." He laughs, his voice high-pitched with amusement. "But I couldn't tell, so I aborted the mission."

The words hit me like a slap, leaving me stunned.

"That's fucking disgusting, Timmy!" I snap. "Why would you say that in front of me? Or Jackson?"

He shrugs, utterly unbothered by my reaction. "What? It's just a story. It's what happened." His grin widens, full of boyish glee.

"Telling that to *me*—your *partner*—that's gross. And to a *14-year-old kid*?" I glance at Jackson, who's shifted uncomfortably in the backseat, staring out the window like he wishes he were anywhere but here.

Timmy howls with laughter, practically gasping for air. "Ahahaha! You're so uptight, Margaux." His eyes sparkle, delighted by the way I'm squirming. He's enjoying this—feeding off my discomfort, knowing he has an audience.

I swat his arm, a light tap meant to signal that he needs to cut it out. "Stop! That's not funny."

Timmy's reaction is instantaneous and dramatic. His eyes widen, and he gasps as if I've physically assaulted him. "Oh my god! You hit me!" He turns to Jackson, outrage smeared across his face. "Did you see that? She *hit* me!"

"You know I didn't hit you," I say through gritted teeth, my patience evaporating.

"Un-fucking-believable." He shakes his head, scowling at me, condescension dripping from his words. "That's not okay, Margaux."

"Timmy, cut it out," I say through gritted teeth, feeling my patience wear thin.

He laughs again, and I notice his foot pressing harder on the gas. We're speeding now, and the road is narrowing.

"Timmy, seriously, slow down," I plead, my heart racing.

He ignores me, lost in his own manic energy.

The truck swerves around a corner, the tires skimming the edge of the road. My pulse quickens as the landscape blurs past us.

I glance out the window, trying to steady my breathing, and my stomach drops. We're miles from home. The familiar streets and landmarks are gone, replaced by endless stretches of highway heading toward the city. I've been so focused on Timmy's vile commentary, I didn't notice how far we'd driven.

"Timmy, we're way out of the neighborhood. We need to go back."

He shrugs, nonchalant. "I'm showing Jackson the island. It's a special tour."

"His mom didn't say you could take him this far," I say, my voice sharp with warning.

"She'll be fine." He waves me off, as if the rules don't apply to him.

Timmy's words blur into another inappropriate story—something about an old hookup—and I feel like my brain is starting to short-circuit. He just won't stop.

"Timmy, enough!" I snap, my voice cracking with frustration.

"You're so fucking uptight," he hisses, his grin twisting into something uglier. "Always pinching and hitting me, nagging me. Jesus."

"Stop saying disgusting things!" My voice rises, teetering on the edge of panic.

Jackson leans forward from the backseat, trying to play mediator. "Dude, what you said wasn't cool. And she barely tapped you. You're overreacting."

For a moment, Timmy's face darkens, his playful grin vanishing like a switch has been flipped. His expression contorts into something feral—his features tightening with rage.

"Please, Timmy," I plead, my voice softening in desperation. "Just stop. You're not okay right now, and you shouldn't be driving."

My words seem to ignite something inside him—a fire that burns too hot. With a sudden growl, Timmy slams his foot on the accelerator, and the car surges forward.

I grip the seat as Timmy speeds through another turn, barely missing an oncoming car. My heart slams against my ribcage, and I glance back at Jackson, who looks equally alarmed.

"Timmy, stop!" I yell. "You're driving too fast!"

His grin twists into something darker, and he slams his foot on the accelerator even harder.

He's too far gone, his jaw clenched, his knuckles white as he grips the steering wheel. He's driving like a madman, swerving between cars, tailgating so close I can practically see the fear on the drivers' faces ahead of us.

"Timmy, please!" I beg, panic swelling in my chest. "You're going to kill us!"

His only response is to laugh—a manic, high-pitched cackle that sends chills down my spine.

The car barrels down the road, veering dangerously close to the edge of the lane. My fingers dig into the seat, my entire body tensing as I brace for impact.

"Fuck you!" he explodes suddenly, his voice thick with venom. "You two are trying to sleep together! I knew it all along!"

Jackson and I exchange horrified glances.

"Um, no. That's disgusting," I say, incredulous. "I'm an adult, Timmy, and he is a 14-year-old boy. And I'm engaged to *you*. What the hell are you even talking about?"

"Timmy, chill," Jackson says, trying to keep his voice calm. "Nobody's trying to do anything. You're being weird, man."

But Timmy's rage only escalates. He swerves dangerously close to the edge of the road, the truck lurching as he jerks the wheel.

"Timmy, pull over!" I scream, panic rising in my chest.

When we finally reach the city, Timmy's rage hasn't abated. If anything, it's intensified. He screeches into the parking lot of a gas station, the tires screaming as the car jerks to a violent stop, throwing us forward in our seats.

We all scramble out of the car, and I slam my door behind me as if that alone could shield us from Timmy's madness.

"You're a fucking stupid bitch and I fucking can't stand you, you abusive cunt!" Timmy screams at me. "I fucking hate you, you ugly bitch!"

Shocked, Jackson snaps into action. "Leave her alone! Stop talking to her like that!" he roars.

I run between them, horrified at what Timmy might try to do. It looks like they're about to have a fist-fight.

Clenching his fists, his jaw tight, Timmy gets into the truck and slams the door.

"Get the fuck away from me!" Timmy roars, his voice hoarse with fury. "Leave me alone, you fucking cunts!"

Without another word, Timmy peels out of the parking lot, the tires screeching as he disappears into the dusk, screaming something unintelligible out the window.

120

THE OTHER SIDE OF FEAR

Jackson and I stand there, shell-shocked, as the sound of Timmy's truck fades into the distance. My heart pounds in my chest, my hands trembling as I try to process what just happened.

"What the actual fuck?" Jackson mutters, his face pale. "Is he always like that?"

"No," I whisper, my hands trembling, my voice shaky. "I mean... he gets upset sometimes, but never like this."

Jackson shakes his head in disbelief. "Probably too many drugs."

I pull out my phone and dial Charlie, my hands shaking as I explain what happened, and I give her our location.

As we walk toward a nearby café, my mind races, trying to make sense of Timmy's spiral. The enormity of the drive crashes over me. His manic energy, his vile stories, the reckless driving, his wild accusations—it's like I've just seen a side of him I never knew existed, like I've been dropped into a nightmare I can't wake up from.

Jackson and I sit at the café, and he tries to reassure me. "You did nothing wrong. He was acting crazy as hell." My brain feels scrambled, trying to reconcile the Timmy I love with the person I just witnessed—a man unhinged, spiraling out of control.

I glance at my phone, half-expecting a message from Timmy. Apologies, excuses, promises—it's always the same. But this time, I feel different. This time, the fear won't go away.

Because deep down, I know this isn't just a one-time thing. It's part of a pattern—one that's getting impossible to ignore.

~

THE REST of the group meets us at the café. Before we get a chance to share what happened, my phone rings, and Timmy's name lights up the screen like a flare in the night, signaling disaster. Everyone in the room reacts instantly, tension thick in the air.

"Speakerphone!" they all yell in unison, their voices tinged with urgency.

I hesitate for a moment, knowing deep down that whatever Timmy has to say won't be good. But part of me hopes—maybe—it'll just be him venting, angry but manageable. I press the speaker icon, my heart pounding, and set the phone on the table.

What comes through is far worse than anything I could have imagined.

"I'm going to throw your cat in the ocean, you stupid cunt," Timmy's voice snarls, the words crackling through the phone like venom. "You're fucking awful, and I'm going to do to you and your cat what should have been done long ago!"

The room falls into stunned silence, the words hanging in the air like a toxic cloud. Several people gasp, hands flying to their mouths, their eyes wide with disbelief. The weight of his words hits us all at once, like a gut punch, knocking the breath out of everyone at the table.

My heart clenches, my breath catching painfully in my chest. *Sabre.* My sweet, innocent baby, alone with him. Timmy must have somehow made it all the way back to the other side of the Cay. And now he's threatening to take Sabre—my child, my constant companion—and throw him into the ocean.

Who does that?

Who threatens to hurt a helpless animal just to punish someone?

"Please," I whisper into the phone, my voice barely audible, raw with fear. "Please don't hurt Sabre."

Timmy's reply is laced with venom, dripping with spite. "You're a fucking dumb slut. Fucking a fourteen-year-old."

My mind reels, trying to process his words. "What are you talking about? That's disgusting!"

But Timmy isn't done. His voice rises, lashing out with unhinged rage. "You're fucking gross. I should call the cops and tell them what you're doing."

My hands tremble as I try to calm him down, feeling helpless. "Timmy, please," I beg, tears threatening to spill over. "Please don't do this. Just be calm."

But my plea only seems to fuel his anger.

"Fuck you, slut. You're going to pay the consequences for what you did. I hope you have a nice life with your fourteen-year-old boyfriend."

And with that, the line goes dead.

The silence that follows is deafening. Everyone at the table is frozen, their expressions a mixture of shock, horror, and disbelief. I sit, stunned, as the tears I've been holding back begin to spill over, hot and relentless.

Charlie's friend, a woman I've only just met, shifts her chair closer to me without hesitation. She places a supportive hand on my forearm, offering quiet comfort. The warmth of her touch is the only thing grounding me in the moment.

"Oh my god," someone mutters under their breath. "Did that just happen?"

Another person, pale with disbelief, shakes their head slowly. "He really said he was going to—throw your cat in the ocean?"

I can feel their eyes on me, but it all feels distant, like I'm watching the scene from outside my body.

"He's threatening your cat," Charlie whispers, horrified. "That's... that's insane."

I press the heels of my hands to my eyes, trying to stem the flow of tears. But it's no use. The emotions flood in too fast—fear for Sabre, shame for being in this situation, disbelief that the man I love could say something so monstrous.

The woman beside me gently takes one of my hands in hers, clasping it tightly. She leans in, her expression earnest and full of empathy. "Margaux, you're in an abusive relationship," she says softly, her words cutting through the fog of my mind. "I've been there. I know how hard it is. But it's going to take a lot of strength to break away. Trust me, though—it will be worth it."

Her words hang in the air, heavy and clear, but they don't fully sink in. It's like I'm hearing them through a thick layer of denial, as if they're meant for someone else—not me.

Timmy's just upset, I tell myself. *This isn't who he really is.*

He hasn't hurt me physically since the deer antler incident—that was a one-time thing, an aberration. This must be the same. A fluke. An anomaly. The second-worst thing he's done, if I had to rank them —but somehow, this feels worse. Maybe because it involves someone else, or because he's threatening the thing I love most.

I cling to the idea that this isn't the real Timmy—that he's just having a bad day, and that once he cools down, he'll see how wrong he was and apologize. That he didn't mean it.

But even as I try to convince myself, I feel the creeping weight of doubt pressing in on me.

The woman squeezes my hand again, her gaze steady. "It doesn't matter if he's just upset," she says, as if reading my thoughts. "What he said—what he threatened—is not normal. It's not okay."

I nod numbly, but my mind is spinning, tangled in the cycle of justifications I've built to protect myself from the truth.

He'll calm down. He always does.

He didn't mean it. He couldn't have meant it.

I'll call him later, and we'll sort this out. It'll all blow over.

But deep down, I know I'm lying to myself. *She's right. This isn't normal. This isn't okay.*

And the scariest part is that I don't know how much longer I can keep pretending it is.

I hug my arms around myself, trying to hold everything in—trying not to shatter completely in front of these people.

"You don't deserve this," the woman whispers, her voice soft but firm. "No one deserves this."

I nod again, more out of politeness than agreement. The words don't feel real yet. I feel like I'm floating, untethered, unable to process what just happened.

But one thought cuts through the fog, sharp and clear—I need to get home. I need to get Sabre. Whatever happens next, I have to make sure my baby is safe.

The others exchange concerned glances, and I can feel the weight of their worry pressing down on me. But for now, all I can focus on is getting through the next hour, the next minute, the next breath.

Because right now, that's all I can do.

My phone buzzes violently in my hand. The screen fills with messages from Timmy—one after another, each one more twisted and hateful than the last. It's like watching a dam break, and I can't stop the flood.

TIMMY:

> You're so fucking dumb. This truck's not gonna go much further, and you're... it's going to get fucking ripped.

> You're just... you're just dumb and... collect your baby 14-year-old. You're so fucking retarded.

> You're still the dumbest fucking retarded person I've ever fucking known.

> The most abusive, punching, pinching, fucking twisted, fucking a 14-year-old.

> You're just a fucking retarded cunt.

> You're a stupid fucking whore thank you bye.

> I can only imagine you're happy bc you're fucking around with your 14-year-old.

I stare at the screen, my heart pounding so loudly I can barely hear myself think. The words don't even make sense—they're jumbled, manic, incoherent—but the anger behind them is unmistakable.

The accusation about Jackson sends a shiver down my spine. Why is he fixated on this disgusting idea? I've been nothing but clear, and the accusation is beyond repulsive. The fact that he's hurling such vile things at me... it's more than just an insult. It's cruelty for cruelty's sake. Or he's just so sick and twisted he actually believes his own story.

My fingers tremble as I respond.

ME:

That's gross. I'm actually with his mum.

His reply comes instantly, the rage boiling over in his words.

TIMMY:

Fuck you, fuck you, and fuck you.

I hope you make it back in time.

I'd like to see all three of us alive together.

The air leaves my lungs in a sharp gasp. *What the hell does that mean?* And then it hits me—like ice plunging into my chest. He's not just raging. *He's threatening to kill me. To kill Sabre.*

I clutch my stomach as nausea twists through me. I try to retch, but nothing comes out, just dry heaving sobs. My poor Sabre. Alone, defenseless, with a man whose mind is unraveling.

The next texts arrive, relentless.

TIMMY:

I'm the one just trying to ask people for help with gas money to get home... like I'm not going to make it there, but I really hope... I don't even know why I'm talking to you.

Still, you're such a fucking cunt. Like, why the fuck am I even talking to you?

I'm going to get your truck and drive it up your ass at some point, you fucking piece of shit.

I slap a hand over my mouth, stifling a cry. *He's threatening to drive the truck into me.* The very thought of it—a steel frame and screeching tires, aimed at me in rage—makes me shiver uncontrollably. My hands ache from gripping the phone too hard, but I can't loosen my grip. I have to keep reading.

TIMMY:

Fuck yourself.

Hanging on some kid, walking off hanging out with some child.

You're a fucking dumb cunt.

You're the dumbest fuck. Most apologetic. Fucking opposite cunt I've ever seen in my fucking life.

Go fuck yourself and I hope your cat fucking dies.

I gasp aloud, the words slamming into me with the force of a punch. *Sabre.*

TIMMY:

I meant you, sorry.

Another gasp. My heart falters for a beat—relief mixed with horror. At least for now, Sabre's not his target. But what happens when his rage shifts again?

TIMMY:

I watch you and your stupid choice.

When someone doesn't have a single second to talk to someone, it's because...

> You're a fucking cheater and I fucking hate you.
>
> And you're also very fucking gross.
>
> So fucking gross.

I burst into tears, the dam inside me finally giving way. I can't stop the sobs from wracking my body. *None of this is true.* It's all lies—hateful, hurtful lies. The accusation is literally insane. But the venom in his words makes it feel real, even though I know it's not.

The only person I want is him. And yet, here I am—being accused of the most disgusting, repugnant things. I can't even wrap my mind around the fact that he thinks I'd be interested in a child. How could he say that? How could he even *think* that?

But then there's the other layer—the more immediate fear clawing at the back of my mind. *The death threats. He said he hopes we don't all make it.*

That thought alone makes my blood run cold. If I don't get back soon—if I don't intervene—what will happen to Sabre?

I wipe my face with the back of my hand, but the tears keep coming. *I have to get home. I have to protect my baby.*

The pit in my stomach grows heavier as another realization creeps in—Timmy has shown me, time and time again, that when he gets like this, he doesn't just stop at words. He damages things. He breaks things, destroys what he can't control. And right now, he's alone with everything I own—everything I've built and cared for. *It's only stuff*, I tell myself, trying to be rational.

But it's *my* stuff. And he's already cost me so much. If I don't get back in time, what else will he take from me?

My phone buzzes again, but I can't bring myself to look at it right away. Instead, I clutch it in my hand, rocking slightly in place, trying to steady my breathing. What if he follows through on these threats? What if I lose Sabre? What if I lose everything?

I shake my head, trying to force the spiral of fear to stop. But it's relentless, wrapping itself tighter and tighter around my mind. *I need to get back.*

I wipe my face again, trying to collect myself, but it's useless. I'm unraveling.

The thought of walking back into that apartment terrifies me—facing Timmy, his rage, the unpredictable storm that he's become. But I know I don't have a choice.

I have to go.

For Sabre.

For me.

121

A LONG NIGHT

"Margaux, dear, he seems like he's on gear or something." Charlie squeezes my arm, her voice gentle but weighted with concern. Her expression is serious, her brows knitted, as if she's carefully choosing her words.

"Gear?" I echo, a nervous laugh escaping me. "What do you mean? Like... drugs?"

She nods. "Yeah. He just doesn't stop talking. His speech is so fast, and he keeps repeating himself. I don't know—it's just weird. Even earlier, his behavior seemed really off, like he's not all there."

Her words hit me like a cold slap to the face. It's the first time someone from the outside has mirrored back the things I've started to notice but haven't dared to say out loud. Timmy's chaotic energy—something I've grown used to, even when it's exhausting—suddenly feels like a glaring problem. Through her eyes, I can see what she means.

It makes me feel a little defensive, though, a little embarrassed. Nobody wants to hear their partner described like that, especially from someone they trust. "I mean... that's just kind of how he is," I say weakly, feeling the need to explain him. "He gets really excited sometimes."

She tilts her head sympathetically but doesn't back down. "Excited is one thing, Margaux, but this—" she gestures vaguely in a random direction, seeing she wasn't there when he peeled off in the truck—"this is something else. He doesn't seem right in the head."

I want to argue, but the truth is lodged in my throat, uncomfortable and undeniable. I know exactly what she's talking about. Timmy's frenetic energy can feel exhilarating when it's directed the right way—like a spark of inspiration that lights up everything around him. But when it spirals, it's suffocating. Like trying to hold on to a tornado. And tonight, it wasn't just suffocating—it was terrifying.

"I get it," I say, my voice low. "He was... off today. I don't know what that was."

Her son, Jackson, flashes through my mind—the awkward tension in the car, Timmy's reckless driving, the sickening stories he kept telling. My stomach churns with guilt. I feel terrible for putting them in that position. I never would've introduced them if I'd known Timmy was going to act like that.

I sigh heavily, the weight of everything pressing down on me. "I'm really sorry this happened, Charlie. I didn't mean for things to get like that."

Charlie gives me a warm but worried smile, wrapping me in a hug. "Don't apologize. I'm just glad we're all okay. But are *you* okay?"

"I'll be fine," I say, though the words feel empty.

"Are you sure? Because, Margaux... he's acting fucking nuts."

I force a smile, though my heart feels heavy with doubt. "He'll calm down eventually. He always does. I'll be okay."

Charlie pulls back and searches my face with concern. "I really hope so. If you ever need anything—just call me, okay?"

I nod, feeling the sting of tears threatening to surface. She gives me another squeeze before I climb into the Uber that finally arrives. As the car pulls away, I watch her standing there, her worried expression lingering in my mind long after she's out of sight.

The Uber ride back takes nearly an hour, giving me more than enough time to think—but my thoughts are jumbled, spinning in frantic circles.

I stare out the window, watching the night slip past in a blur of streetlights and shadows. My mind replays the events of the day, over and over, like a broken record. Timmy's manic energy, the way he kept pushing boundaries, laughing at things that weren't funny, driving like a man possessed. And then the switch—how quickly he turned cruel, throwing out wild accusations like grenades, leaving me stunned and scrambling to make sense of what just happened.

I can't shake the feeling of wrongness that settled over me during that ride in the truck. It was like watching someone I thought I knew unravel right in front of me, piece by piece, until I couldn't recognize him anymore.

He went from friendly and sociable to cruel and vindictive in the span of minutes. One second, he was charming Jackson, and the next, he was hurling accusations that made no sense. It wasn't just upsetting—it was scary.

And now, with every passing mile, I find myself dreading what I'll walk into when I get back to him. Will he be calm and contrite, apologizing the way he always does? Or will he still be riding the high of whatever manic wave he's caught on?

I try to convince myself that he'll have calmed down by the time I get home. He has to. He'll realize how out of line he was and feel guilty—like he always does after a blow-up. That's the cycle, right? He explodes, then apologizes, and we move on.

But tonight feels different. The anger in his eyes, the reckless way he drove, the way he kept escalating even when I begged him to stop —it wasn't just a bad mood. It was something darker, something I don't know how to handle.

What if he's still angry when I get home? What if he hasn't calmed down?

The thought makes my chest tighten with anxiety.

I press my forehead against the cool glass of the car window, trying to steady my breathing. The Uber driver hums along quietly to the radio, oblivious to the storm raging inside my head.

I keep checking my phone, half-hoping for a message from Timmy—some sign that he's come to his senses, that he realizes how badly he messed up. But there's nothing. Just silence.

My mind keeps racing, trying to piece together how things went so wrong so quickly.

Was it the alcohol? Drugs? Stress? Or is this just... who he really is? A part of him I hadn't wanted to see until now?

The Uber driver glances at me in the rearview mirror, his brow furrowing slightly. "You okay back there?"

I nod quickly, forcing a smile. "Yeah, I'm fine. Just... a long day."

He nods, seeming satisfied with that answer, and turns his attention back to the road.

But I'm not fine. Not even close.

122

WHIPLASH

Twenty minutes pass before my phone buzzes again. Timmy's name flashes across the screen.

TIMMY:

I'm almost home where you should be and I hope you have a good time.

Good night love of my life.

I don't know what to make of his text. I don't respond, and then more start flooding in.

TIMMY:

I'm so sorry, do whatever you have to do.

I love you. I love you so much.

I'm at home now.

I would've grabbed you but I had zero gas, and I was lucky enough for someone to help me.

> I just wanna to go to bed and cuddle with Sabre.

> You do what you've gotta do.

> I wish you would've just come home with me.

> I wish I never took him.

> I took you that way, and now I hope you guys have fun.

> I really wish the best for you.

> I love you. Bye.

The tone of his messages shifts so abruptly from rage to regret that I can hardly make sense of it. Has he really calmed down? Or is this just the eye of the storm?

Something feels off. His words are laced with blame disguised as an apology. It's like he's painting himself as the calm, reasonable one while I'm the villain running off to 'hang out with a fourteen-year-old.' A twisted narrative that makes him the victim of some imagined betrayal, and me the monster. It's manipulative. But worse, it's dangerous. I've seen how quickly his mood swings can shift, and I know this fragile peace won't last long.

I feel the knot of anxiety tighten in my chest. I need to get home—now. I need to make sure Sabre is safe before Timmy spirals again, or worse, lashes out in ways I won't be able to control. I repeat it in my head like a mantra: *Just stay calm. Be rational. Hopefully, he'll go to sleep and wake up in the morning as himself—whatever version of 'normal' that may be.*

When I finally reach the apartment, my heart races. I fumble with the keypad, swing the door open—and with relief, I see he's not here.

"Sabre!" I call out, panic seizing my chest.

A soft meow answers from the corner of the room, and relief floods me so intensely I nearly collapse. I rush over and scoop him into my arms, burying my face in his fur. He purrs, his warmth grounding me, momentarily cutting through the storm in my mind.

"I'll never let anybody hurt you," I whisper into his fur, my voice trembling. "I promise."

I hold him close, savoring the comfort of having him safe, until the sound of the front door beeping makes my heart stutter. The door swishes open, and Timmy steps inside.

Timmy's face is a strange mix of sheepishness and sorrow, his eyes downcast as he trudges toward me. He looks almost like a child caught doing something wrong.

"I'm so sorry," he murmurs, hurrying over to wrap his arms around me. I flinch instinctively, but he holds on, his voice soft and full of regret. "I just got really overwhelmed. I can't handle big groups of people. I get so agitated in situations like that, and I wasn't expecting it today."

His words seem reasonable, almost understandable. I know people who need mental preparation before being around crowds—even I sometimes feel that way. But something about his explanation doesn't sit right. Timmy seeks out attention from strangers all the time. He's the kind of person who thrives in chaotic environments—bars, clubs, spontaneous encounters.

And his behavior wasn't in line with the actions of someone who was having an anxious moment—he was literally insane.

"I should've been more careful," I say, as guilt prickles uncomfortably at my skin. "I didn't know the group would be so big until the last minute. I'll try to make sure you know what to expect next time."

The words feel hollow, but I mean them. Maybe I could've handled the situation better. Maybe I do need to do more to help him cope.

Timmy nods and wipes his face. "I wasn't trying to upset you. And I shouldn't have driven Jackson so far. I was just trying to show him a good time."

"You told him some really disgusting stories, Timmy," I say softly, the memory of his words still making my skin crawl. "It was disrespectful to me—and to him."

His frown deepens, and he looks down at the floor. "I know," he whispers. "I don't know what got into me. I was just trying to impress him."

Suddenly, tears well up in his eyes, and before I can react, they spill over. "Margaux, I need you to help me. I want to be better. I *need* to be better. I can't do it without you. I don't want to be this way anymore. I'm so sorry. I'll make it up to you, I swear."

Despite the anger simmering in my chest, and the fear scratching at my skin, my heart twists painfully.

He looks so genuine, so broken. And for a moment, all I want is to believe him. To believe that this version of Timmy—the remorseful one—can stick around.

"You threatened to kill Sabre." My voice breaks as I say it aloud, the weight of those words too much to bear. "And you threatened to kill *me*."

Tears pour freely down my face as I think about how close I came to losing everything I love.

"I would *never* hurt you or Sabre," Timmy insists, his voice cracking with emotion. He sobs openly now, his shoulders shaking. "I was just really upset. I swear, I love Sabre—I could never hurt him. And I love you, Margaux. You're the love of my life. I don't know why I said those things. I thought... I thought you were cheating on me with the kid." He shakes his head violently. "I'm so fucking sorry."

The exhaustion weighs down on me like a lead blanket. *I'm so tired.* Tired of the rage, the apologies, the fear, the endless cycle of highs and lows. But this time... this time, he's owning it. For once, he's not deflecting or denying what happened. And I just don't have the energy to fight anymore.

This whole situation feels surreal—like something from a nightmare that I keep waiting to wake up from. It would be easier to believe it isn't real. Easier to let his apology wash over me and move on. I can't afford another fight. Not tonight.

"I'm sorry," Timmy says again, his voice soft and pleading.

I swallow hard, forcing down the lump in my throat. I could keep questioning, keep pressing, keep trying to hold him accountable—

but right now, I just want peace. I want to pretend, for a little while, that everything will be okay.

So I let the emotions drift away, floating like debris in a river, and I just nod.

"It's okay," I whisper, the words slipping from my mouth like a release valve. "Let's just... move on."

Timmy pulls me into a tight embrace, burying his face in my neck. His tears dampen my skin, and I feel his body relax against mine as if my forgiveness has given him permission to let go of his guilt.

I stand here, numb, letting him hold me.

Maybe tomorrow I'll have the strength to unpack what happened. But not tonight.

For now, I'll take the peace, however fleeting it may be.

123

PIT OF RAGE

D^{EX}

I CHECK HER PHONE RECORDS.

This guy has lost the fucking plot. I read with rage.

He's threatening to kill her. Her cat.

His behavior is escalating.

I feel like I need to book that ticket. Because this shit is getting crazy. And if there's one thing I've learned, it's that when people like Timmy tell you what they're going to do, you should take note. Because there are little signs along the way where they'll expose themselves if you look hard enough. Hidden in jokes and quiet little comments, as if they're teasing you with the truth.

In the meantime, I shoot her a text:

ME:

Hey, Margaux. Just checking in to see how you're doing.

She takes a while to reply, and my scalp crawls with anxiety as I wait for her response. I can't stop squeezing my hands into tight fists as I think about slamming Timmy into the ground and pummeling him until he's a pulpy mess. Because that's what he deserves, and no more.

MARGAUX:

Good thanks. You?

Fuck. Maybe I shouldn't have done that. Maybe he'll check her phone and think she's cheating on him with me. He's so controlling and suspicious. And he's texting people behind her back.

Can't she see that? The hypocrisy of this vile 'man' she thinks she loves, that she trusts to love her the way she should be.

I feel stupid for texting her. What did I think? That she was going to open up like a book and tell me everything and beg me to come and rescue her?

It looks like she just had a lucky escape from him.

It's not normal to threaten to kill people. To routinely accuse people of cheating.

But that's what he does.

Never mind his own shitty behavior.

I've known many guys like him. Because he's the type my mom used to go for.

The charming bad boy. Until he isn't.

Until he reveals his control and aggression and blames you for everything bad in his life.

A pit of male rage.

I'm just hoping he's back in his well-behaved phase. The one where he is on his best behavior to suck her back in. That should give her a brief period of respite.

It is, after all, why people go back time and time again to their abusers.

I just hope she sees the light and gets the fuck out before it's too late.

124

I LIKE BREWING COFFEE, NOT STORMS

The next morning, Timmy is eerily calm. Too calm. The type of calm that makes the hair on the back of my neck stand on end. His words are measured, his tone soft—almost soothing—but the tension beneath his quiet demeanor hums like a live wire.

I've seen this kind of stillness before, and it's never just stillness. It's the deceptive quiet, the invisibly brewing agitation that occurs right before a storm. He may seem peaceful on the surface, but underneath, I can sense something volatile waiting to break through, like a pot about to boil over.

He's outwardly doing and saying all the right things, but I can tell that something's up. He moves around the apartment with a strange kind of precision, almost like he's on autopilot, his pace a touch too fast, his gestures just a hair too sharp. I notice little things—a foot tapping a bit too eagerly against the tile, the gleam in his eye catching the light wrong, making his gaze feel both manic and cold. His smiles are fleeting, mechanical, as if he's trying to convince us both that everything's okay.

But it's not okay. Not even close.

I feel it in my gut, the way animals sense a predator lurking nearby. I don't know what's coming, but I know it's not good. And that makes me hyper-aware of everything I do, as if I'm walking barefoot across shards of glass.

I tiptoe around him, desperate not to set him off. I've seen the places his mind can go—what he can say when he feels cornered or wronged. I can't afford to step wrong again. Not after yesterday.

The memories play on a loop, haunting me. His accusations, each one more unhinged than the last, echoing in my mind. The way his voice twisted with venom as he said I couldn't be trusted. And then, the moment his anger boiled over—the threats, wild and surreal, like they came from a stranger's mouth.

He threatened to hurt Sabre.

He threatened to hurt *me*.

He was out of control, his rage escalating to a place so dark that I barely recognized him. But now, standing here in the deceptive calm of a new day, he's told me it wasn't really him. That he was over-whelmed, that his mood disorder was flaring up. That he didn't mean it.

I want to believe him—*need* to believe him. Because, if I don't, what does that say about me?

What does it say about the fact that I'm still here, in this apart-ment, breathing the same air, sharing the same bed?

I need to believe that it's a one-off. A mistake. That it will *never* happen again.

It can't happen again.

But the fear lingers, coiled tight in the pit of my stomach. I don't hang out with people who behave like this. I've drawn boundaries in my life, especially in my career—held people accountable when they crossed the line. But now? Here I am, in the thick of it, pretending everything is fine. Tiptoeing. Apologizing with smiles and kind gestures, as if I'm smoothing over cracks in a fragile vase, hoping it doesn't shatter in my hands.

I play the part of the perfect fiancée as best as I can. I laugh at his jokes, offer him snacks when I grab something from the fridge, compliment him on things I know he likes to hear. I mirror his mood, carefully watching him for any signs that he might be slipping. I want to keep him happy—*calm*—just long enough to survive the day.

I let him pick what we watch on TV for the entire day, even though the thought of sitting through more mind-numbing action flicks and slasher movies makes my skin crawl. But, if it keeps him stable, it's worth it. Anything is worth it.

Every now and then, his eyes flash with irritation—over a misplaced tone in my voice, or when I hesitate too long before answering a question. It's subtle, but it's there. I have a feeling he's observing me as closely as I'm watching him. Little pinpricks of agitation, bubbling just beneath the surface, waiting for an excuse to erupt.

I glance over at him, out of the corner of my eye, trying to gauge where he's at. He's still too quiet, too still. It's like he's recharging, saving up his energy for something.

The memory of yesterday twists in my gut again. It could have gone so badly. If I hadn't managed to defuse things, if I hadn't said the right things to calm him down… I shudder to think of how it might have ended.

He *has* to stop, or he has to be out of my life.

It's that simple.

Because, while I care about him, I know I'd survive without him. I know it would hurt—God, it would hurt so badly—but I'd be okay, eventually. And, most importantly, I'd be alive.

He shifts on the bed beside me, pulling me closer like nothing happened. His arm around my shoulders feels both protective and possessive, and the contrast unsettles me. There's a part of him that loves me, I know that much. But there's another part—dark, angry, and unpredictable—that terrifies me.

"I'm glad we're good now," he murmurs into my hair. His voice is soft, almost too soft, the kind that makes you aware of just how easily things could tip the other way. I attempt to relax. He's so attuned to my emotions that I don't want an argument to start because my shoulders are too stiff, or that I'm not reciprocating his affection in my normal way.

"Me too," I whisper, forcing a smile. My heart is hammering against my ribcage, but I keep my voice steady. "Everything's going to be okay."

He tilts my chin up with one finger and kisses me gently, like he's sealing a promise between us. But it doesn't feel like a promise I can trust. It feels more like a warning, wrapped up in affection—a silent reminder that I'm his. That everything is fine, as long as I stay in line.

The air between us hums with tension, and I feel like I'm holding my breath, waiting for the other shoe to drop. Because it will. I know it will. It always does with Timmy.

But for now, I tell myself to hold on.

To ride this wave of calm for as long as it lasts.

Because the storm is always waiting, right around the corner, ready to strike the moment I let my guard down.

125

A NIGHT FULL OF STARS

T*he Past*

Uncle: He harmed you physically and everybody believes you, regardless of what he says. Please know that. Anybody who says otherwise is lying to themselves and you.

Me: But... but it could have been so much worse. I feel for all those girls who walk down the street and get dragged into a dark alley by a complete stranger.

Uncle: How is this any less bad? Because you knew him?

Me: I feel partially responsible.

Uncle: Why?

Me: Because I agreed to go on the date. Two of them, in fact.

And I let him into my apartment.

Uncle: So, because you knew the guy, because he wasn't some completely random person... you think you're partially responsible for him sexually assaulting you? For putting something in your drink and then messing with your body while you were unconscious? Man, girl. You are very hard on yourself.

Me: Sure.

Uncle: Well, what I was trying to say is that there's no question he harmed you physically, Margaux.

But the mental... the psychological trauma is there, too.

Please remember that. Bruises on your body fade, but the less visible damage is what's going on in your mind. You need to get some help. It's too much for anybody to deal with by themselves, no matter how strong they are.

A tear betrays me by escaping from my eye and rolling down my cheek. My lips also tremble as his words sink in.

Me: Okay... I'll think about it.

Uncle: That's good enough for me.

~

The Present

Things have been calmer for the past few days. Timmy has been fairly quiet, and has made an effort to do things around the apartment. Cooking, some cleaning. Insisting on soaking my feet and rubbing them. Being extra cute with Sabre. He's even rearranged some parts of the apartment to make them less cluttered, and the atmosphere feels much nicer.

There hasn't been much bickering, although I've noticed he's starting to get a little agitated again about which movies we're watching and what music we're listening to.

"Why don't you watch that sci-fi movie you've been wanting to watch, and I'll listen to music on my headphones for a while?" I suggest. I'm not in the mood to fight over movies for the millionth time, so he can have his way and watch whatever he likes. And it will be nice to have a bit of quiet time, even though we'll still be in the same room together. It's my attempt at de-escalation, and keeping things chill. I'm done with the fighting and the stress and I'm terrified of any further erratic behavior.

I just want peace. I need peace so badly.

"Fine," says Timmy. "If you want." He sounds almost insulted, offended that I don't want to watch exactly what he wants to at all times. That our eyes and ears need to be consuming exactly the same material in order for me to prove my love to him or something. But I take his words at face value, that he's okay with my suggested plan,

and I put my headphones on.

AN HOUR OR SO LATER, we're both sitting on the bed and I'm listening to a Machine Gun Kelly song while Timmy is watching something or other on TV. We've had a couple of drinks, and so far the evening has been pretty chill. I'm enjoying having the headphones on and having a break away from his constant commentary. Which is fine, because partners don't need to be joined at the hip and doing the same thing at every waking moment.

And then I giggle, because the song has a funny part where a cartoon of Lil Wayne dances around singing about how people smell like Guns N' Roses. It's ridiculous, and my favorite part of the song.

Without warning, Timmy suddenly flings his arm back, and there's a blur of motion as he backhands me in the face. Hard. The crack of his hand against my skin echoes in my ears, and my head snaps to the side, the sting spreading like a wildfire across my face. The headphones are knocked partially off my head, my eyes well up with tears, and I taste the metallic tang of blood where my lip split against my teeth.

My jaw drops, my eyes widen in disbelief, as if I'm frozen in place by the force of his fury.

What the actual fuck? I didn't see that coming for a second.

"What the hell, Timmy? You hit me!" I touch my lip and it's bleeding. "You made me bleed!"

"You were laughing at me." His eyes are no longer kind and blue. They're dark and wild, that same reptilian look I remember from the first time he attacked me, gleaming with a dangerous intensity. It's come out of nowhere.

He doesn't look like the kind, cute and funny man I fell in love with.

His features have hardened into a mask of fury, his lips pressed thin, caught between a sneer and a snarl.

He looks demonic, murderous, like another entity has taken over his body, transforming his laid-back persona into something terrifying and unrecognizable.

Even his posture has changed from relaxed surfer dude to taut, hulking monster.

His entire personality has become rage, and I'm his target.

I recoil instinctively, my body tensing. The shock of his backhand has left me frozen, blinking, as if my brain can't quite keep up with what just happened. The sting lingers, throbbing hotly beneath my skin, my face pulsing with every beat of my heart.

"No, I wasn't!" I plead, my voice squeaking. "I was laughing at the song. Why would I laugh at you? What the fuck? You just hit me in the face!"

"You were making fun of me!" he yells. "Stop lying, you fucking cunt!"

A sharp intake of breath escapes my lips, my hands trembling as I stare at him, wide-eyed at his unexpected outburst. My mind struggles to process this sudden eruption of rage.

"Oh my god," I touch my lip again and wince at the stinging sensation. My brain races to try to figure out what to do. How to get out of this situation. "You can't hit me like that, Timmy. I'm calling the police!"

His face drops further, contorting into a mask of pure rage. "No you're not!" he yells.

I flinch, and my eyes dart in search of an escape. *Leave. I have to leave.* My subconscious wills me forward, to get out of this and get to a place of safety.

I start to head for the door, when suddenly he roars and lurches toward me.

He lifts me in the air and slams me downward.

My body crashes into the concrete tile floor with a sickening thud, recoiling and bouncing slightly before coming to a halt, as if the floor itself is violently rejecting me.

My head bounces against the hard surface, and I see bright lights shattering and exploding in my peripheral vision, as if a million little stars are bursting around me. I land like a rag doll, limp and defenseless, and everything goes gray.

And then he's kneeling over me, and his hands are squeezing around my throat.

He's choking me, strangling me.

Pressure builds inside my head, as if it's about to explode.

I gasp for breath, but can't take in any air.

My chest heaves and my head bobs as he continues to constrict my airway.

The tunnel of gray gradually becomes darker, the world around me shrinking as my lungs scream for air. Sounds become muffled as everything closes in, replaced by a ringing in my ears.

Black spots dance around my vision, growing, swallowing everything.

I try to resist, to thrash around, but my body feels sluggish and weak. It's no use.

There's something deep in my instincts telling me to play dead so he'll just stop squeezing.

Because this man is trying to kill me.

I still my body.

And then he's checking my pulse, leaning over me with his fingers against my carotid.

And he's whispering, "I'm sorry. I'm so fucking sorry."

And then everything fades to black...

Her pulse is fading. Her body isn't moving. You felt it, didn't you? That moment when everything shattered. When Timmy struck, and she didn't get up. You can scream, you can beg, but the pages won't answer you. Is this how it ends for her? Or is there still a chance? Find out in Beautiful Terror.

Enjoyed Pretty Red Flags? Sign up here to get early announcements about new releases, giveaways, bonus scenes, opportunities to join my ARC team for future releases, and more!

ALSO BY HEIDI STARK

Blood and Sand (Dark Why Choose Mafia Romance)

- Sea of Snakes(Book 1)

- Sea of Sinners(Book 2)

- Sea of Rage (Book 3)

- Sea of Pain(Book 4)

- Sinners, Rage & Pain: The Brixton Trilogy(Books 2, 3 and 4)

- Sea of Demons(Book 5)

- Sea of Redemption(Book 6)

C(r)ouch Bind Set Series (rugby why choose sports romance)

- Rucked

Standalones

- Pretty Lovely Lies (FBI/mafia romance, single parent, international)

- Ruthless Choices(romantic horror)

- F*CKBOYS(dark revenge romance, second chance, enemies to lovers)

Billionaire's Takeover Collection

- Irreversible Decision

- Compelling Proposal

- Love Merger

- The Billionaire's Takeover Collection (all 3 of the above)

Novellas

- Love in a Seedy Motel Room

Sign up for my newsletter here for the latest on new releases, promos, giveaways and events!

Join me on social media:

Facebook: @heidistarkauthor

Instagram: @heidistarkauthor

TikTok: @heidistark_author

Bluesky: @heidistarkauthor

Website: https://heidistarkauthor.com

ABOUT THE AUTHOR

Heidi Stark writes contemporary dark romance with a twist of danger, desire, and the occasional sports scandal.

Known for her badass heroines and irresistibly morally grey men, Heidi has captivated readers with 20+ titles, including the gripping *Blood and Sand* series, the fiery *Pretty Red Flags*, and her highly anticipated new release, *Beautiful Terror*.

Originally hailing from the lush landscapes of New Zealand, Heidi now calls the U.S. home, where she shares her creative chaos with her feline sidekick, Fang.

When she's not crafting heart-pounding stories, Heidi is a whirlwind of energy—hitting up barre classes, devouring true crime podcasts, dabbling in roller derby, people-watching, or indulging in her guilty pleasure: reality TV binges. Always on the hunt for inspiration, she's probably plotting her next book—or her next travel adventure.

Dark, daring, and deliciously addictive—Heidi's world is one you'll never want to leave.

ACKNOWLEDGMENTS

There's a little truth in everything I write, but never so much as with this one. Thank you for reading Margaux's story, and if you can relate to it in any way, I'm sorry and I stand with you.

There are so many people to thank for this book existing, and I'm grateful to all of you. I know I'm going to forget to include some people so I'm going to keep it short.

Alexia, Dani, Anne, Jess, Orlando, Mel, Melissa, Belinda, JB, Joel, Sarah, Brian, Raylene,and my sister, Donna. You know why you're here. You're why I'm here.

My editor, Trish. You are the best.

My person, Ed. I'm so glad we finally figured it out.

And, as always, Fang.

RESOURCES

If you have experienced, or are experiencing, a relationship like the one outlined in this book, here are some resources you may find helpful. I do not have personal connection to the creators of these resources, so use them at your own risk. But they're all publicly available, and I'd rather share than not in case they may be helpful to you.

Books:

Lundy Bancroft: Why Does He Do That: Inside the Minds of Angry & Controlling Men

Kay Douglas: Invisible Wounds: Help, Hope & Healing for Women in Abusive Relationships or Recovery

Podcasts:

Why She Stays - Grace Stuart

Dimming the Gaslight - Mac & Phil

Navigating Narcissism - Dr. Ramani

Dr. Nadine Macaluso/Dr. Nae

TikTok:

Synthia (@synful_)
Lee Hammock (@mentalhealness)
Or just look up narctok - there are a ton of helpful resources

www.ingramcontent.com/pod-product-compliance
Lightning Source LLC
Chambersburg PA
CBHW061028310726
48969CB00004B/881